SICK DICE

David Mathew

David Mathew's collection mixes slipstream with crime fiction to great effect. Sharply written and full of surprises.

> Gary Couzens, author of *Out Stack and Other*
>
> *Places*

Mathew leads the reader into stories of calm and controlled prose, which contrasts with the unsettling way in which he turns our world slant and hallucinatory.

> Iain Rowan, author of *One of Us*

Take a glass. Pour two shots of the gritty British workaday angst of the Angry Young Men. Pour a shot of the deep surrealism of China Miéville, add a soupçon of William S. Burroughs – then you have *Sick Dice*. No matter how you roll them, you come up with a grim world spangled with multi-chromatic psychedelic stars. Like the fate of one of David's characters, after you read this collection, strange thoughts will ride you like a *pony*. Remember to take your amphetamines so you won't commit any *dreamcrimes*. Highly recommended.

> Don Webb, author of *Through Dark Angles*

Mathew is a master of subtle unease. His characters, inhabiting a world that is always an inch off-kilter, walk the margins of moral ambiguity in a selection of stories infused with sadness, surrealism and slow-burning mystery.

Neil Williamson, author of *The Moon King*

David Mathew has always had a talent for getting inside the heads of damaged criminal minds . . . you'll be taken to some very disturbing places, in the borderland between the strange and the terrifyingly insane. It might just make you doubt the world around you. It might just make you doubt yourself. . .

Keith Brooke, author of *The Accord*

Dysfunctional characters whose lives may have been shattered by childhood abuse, identity confusion and submerged memories inhabit the boundaries between reality and fantasy in these psychological tales: not for the faint-hearted.

Lawrence Dyer, author of *A Cottage on the Moss*

Dedicated to Lucas and Ava Kent
and to Rosie and William Baker

CONTENTS

Residua

Some days he drew a good crowd. He could hear them chanting – 'Bilty's not guilty!' – if the Wing was quiet and the wind blew in the right direction. The last time he'd spoken to Hammish, he had asked him to thank them for their support, but had also requested that they gave up the protest. After all, Bilty had added, there was snow on the ground, and he wouldn't want anyone catching a chill on his conscience. Although the comment had not been intended as a joke, it was taken as one, and it made it onto the evening news. The truth was, he found the public support embarrassing.

Orwenson unlocked the door and entered the cell. 'Got a something for you,' he said. 'Didn't get it from me, though, okay?'

'Sure. What is it, sir?' Bilty asked.

Orwenson handed over a small brown tatty paper bag. Inside it was a cola bottle.

'You shouldn't have, sir.'

'I confiscated it off some lads on C. Brewing it behind the radiator, for Christmas Day.'

'I don't drink, sir, never have, but thanks anyway.'

''Tis the season to be jolly, Steve, and all that. I can't resist the festive spirit. Even here.'

'Why, sir?' Bilty asked, unscrewing the top.

'Why what?'

Bilty winced; he jerked his head away from the bottle.

'Yeah, an interesting aroma, I agree,' Orwenson said. 'Have one for me. That's an order.'

'Why take the risk, I meant.'

Orwenson shrugged. 'Because I know you didn't do it, and I feel sorry for you.'

'Well I'd be glad if *that* didn't get around, sir. The feeling sorry for me bit.'

'It won't. It would be as bad news for me as it would be for you.'

Bilty drank a sip. As soon as he'd swallowed he gasped for air; his stomach was hot from the poison. Orwenson laughed, to see such fun. 'Your *face*, Steve!'

'The fuck *is* it?'

'Shouldn't you've asked that before? A mango preparation, I believe. They do tend to vary in quality. On the old palate…'

'Well that's one way of putting it, I suppose, sir.'

'Put hairs on your chest, that will.'

'Put nails in me coffin,' Bilty returned. 'But thanks for the thought, sir.'

'Sloppy work on our part,' Orwenson admitted. 'We're supposed to count the rinds back in.' Good deed executed for the day, Orwenson turned to exit.

'Sir?'

'What, do you fancy some peanuts to nibble on while we're at it?'

'No, sir. It was something you said. About knowing I'm not guilty.'

'What of it?'

'…How come you're so sure?'

Orwenson flicked Bilty a brief smile. 'You get a nose for it, Steve, been doing it long as I have.' He had removed his keyring. 'And besides, I know the wanker who *did* do it.'

*

The next morning Bilty had Sociology. As soon as he'd arrived he had signed up for Education, and his Sociology class was every Wednesday morning at 9:15. Lovingly and at such length as was permitted, he showered and shaved; he slapped on cologne. He even performed his morning press-ups in a reasonable frame of mind (he detested exercise).

Along with a handful of other lags he was led from the Wing and across the yard. The supervising screw was Board. 'Would it be possible to speak to Officer Orwenson at some point today, sir?' Bilty asked him.

'Why? You run out of hooch already?' Board asked with a sadistic note in his voice.

Bilty kept walking: they were midway between the Wing and Education – just abreast of Recycling. The day's activities in the workroom had yet to begin: there was not enough noise in the air to mask his questions, but he could not afford to wait.

'I have no idea what that comment refers to, sir,' said Bilty.

'No, of course you haven't,' Board told him. 'No. No it would not be possible to speak to Officer Orwenson at some point today, Bilty. Or tomorrow, more's likely. Officer Orwenson is off sick for the foreseeable.'

'He was all right –' Bilty stopped himself.

'Tell me about it. Not so much as a sniff yesterday. Today's at death's door with man flu!'

Bilty found the information bracing. 'I'm not sure what you're implying, sir.'

'I'm not implying nothing. Have a good class,' Board concluded, for the party had reached the doors to Education, where they were met by different officers for the exchange.

'Is that you with the aftershave, Bilty?' one of the new leg on this relay enquired.

'Yes, Mr Adamson.'

'Well you might want to tone it down a wee bit, mate. You're giving Garridge the horn.'

'Oh fuck off, sir!' said Brian Garridge, with a smile on his lightly-bearded face... Garridge was in for eleven counts of rape. He was also Bilty's Study Buddy. They sat together.

Once they had been locked into the classroom, while their teacher, Clive, doled out the biros and their cardboard work folders, Bilty whispered to Garridge: 'I want to ask you something, Brian. About Orwenson. There were rumours about him. Couple months ago.'

'Were there now.'

'Specifically, Brian,' Bilty went on, 'there were rumours about him and you. Which you denied strongly. And which are none of my business, even if they're true.'

Garridge turned to his left to address Bilty. 'Then why bring it up?' he hissed. 'I'm here to reform my character if you haven't noticed. It don't do me much good to have *that* kind of nonsense thrown in my face! As if I would!'

'I'm not talking about you,' said Bilty, speaking fast and keeping voice low. 'I'm talking about the screw. All I want to know is if he made you the proposition...'

Clive had moved in front of their desk. 'What are you guys yakking about?' he asked, handing Garridge his folder and a pen.

'Nothing, guv. Jibberjab,' Garridge answered.

'Well let's get started, shall we?' Clive adjusted the position of his spectacles on his face. At some point Clive had suffered a Bell's palsy which had left some of the muscles on the left side frozen; as a result, his glasses often slipped and needed frequent readjustment. Now addressing all eight members of his class, he said: 'Last week we were talking about the Chicago School of the 1960s – what Matza referred to as *appreciative sociology* in *Becoming Deviant*...'

The lesson had begun, and Bilty was no further forward. What he'd hoped to do was confirm that there was at least a *smouldering*, if not an actual fire, that had started the smoke of the rumour, back in August. The rumour was that Garridge had offered Orwenson sexual favours in return for a certain type of pornographic DVD to be smuggled in. But what if it had been the other way around? What if *Orwenson* had suggested the proposition?

What is that hooch going to cost me?

'I need the toilet, sir. Sorry,' said Bilty. Still talking to the rest of the class, Clive met Bilty by the door and fished for the right key in the pouch strapped to the belt of his jeans.

One of the corridor officers accompanied Bilty from the classroom to the toilet stall. While Bilty waited to conduct his business, thoughts tumbled through his head.

Orwenson was selling Bilty a glimpse of freedom; a peek at hope. The bottle of rancid (but effective) booze might have been little more than a sweetener. The fact that Orwenson knew – or *claimed* to know – the identity of the miscreant was the real goods on offer. At what price?

A voice from outside called: 'Have you got lost in there, Bilty?'

'No, sir,' Bilty called back. 'Bit of gutrot, sir.'

'That'll teach you not to drink shit, won't it?'

Did *everybody* know? What did Orwenson do? Put a memo on the staff noticeboard?

Bilty said nothing. Taking his time about it, he finished and flushed; he gave his hands a good scrub in tepid water, using the detergent slime that smelled of autumn ponds.

He had not been back in the classroom long when the Redband from the library pressed the laminated A4 pass on to the wiremesh-strengthened window.

Clive saw the sign and said, 'Our turn, guys. Library.' The nine of them bustled along the corridor for their weekly visit. Four of the classmates queued at the desk where they could order

TV Guides and softcore magazines. Garridge entered Non-Fiction and browsed among the encyclopaedias. But Bilty headed straight for Horror: he knew that his greatest chance of happiness – of avoiding the reality of this pit, however temporarily – lay in fiction that was close to reality, but with a ghoulish twist thrown in for the ride.

Generally he chose at random…whatever looked good. He didn't bother to read blurbs. Within half a minute this morning he had settled on *Ghostly Gallery,* edited by Alfred Hitchcock. Merely holding it again – and *here* of all places! – raised a smile on Bilty's face. He almost chuckled, but that wouldn't do; he suppressed it, thinking back to when he'd first seen this book – indeed, *received* this book – when he was ten years old, at school. The children had ordered from a Puffin Books catalogue. And how easily it returned to him now: that delicious spark of expectation he'd experienced on opening the book and reading the list of titles and authors' names. 'The Waxwork' was the first story, Bilty recalled, opening the volume before him.

'Have you chosen, Stephen?' asked Mrs Lyon, the arthritic prison librarian who had moved into his orbit. 'Mr Courts is waiting for you by the door.'

'Sorry, Miss… I used to have this book when I was a nipper. Wonder what happened to it.'

'Ah nostalgia, Stephen,' Miss Lyon answered. 'It's not what it used to be, you know.'

'I suppose not. Sorry to be slow…' Bilty had taken a few steps away from Mrs Lyon when he stopped in his tracks. 'Yeah, I got it,' he told her.

'Slow in more ways than one this morning.'

'Didn't sleep well.'

'No. No, I heard about your… your lifestyle choice with the fermented mango. I must say I might have expected better of you, Mr Bilty.'

Why? Bilty wondered. *Why* would she have expected better of him? Because he had yet to raise his voice or attempt to stab her with a pencil? He would have to be careful: if he didn't watch his back, he was likely to get a reputation for being a good guy.

*

By Saturday morning Bilty no longer wished to quiz Orwenson. Quite the opposite. He didn't even want to *see* Orwenson, though he knew that he would have little choice in the matter when the other man returned to work. Not only was he frightened of Orwenson's 'gift', he was frightened of the vestigial interest that he was accruing by not having paid Orwenson's debt up to now.

He stayed in his cell. He declined the offer of morning exercise in the yard, preferring to do his push-ups against the side of his bed, with his body at a shallow angle to the floor. Nor did he shower: he washed in the basin, from scalp to toenails, using what remained of a sliver of blue soap. He only spoke when spoken to. Watched TV. Read his book in the evening. Refused his food.

Needless to say, the change in Bilty's behaviour did not go unnoticed – or unchallenged. Time after time landing officers asked him what his problem was; Bilty's identical response on each occasion was a surly 'Nothing, sir,' which did nothing to help the general mood. He had gone from a talkative, upbeat prisoner to something like a starving mute, and the authorities wanted a reason why. One officer – Board – even offered to paint him a picture of his future. 'There's talk of putting you on suicide watch,' the screw informed him; 'unless you buck your ideas up.'

But Bilty didn't *know* what the issue was. All he knew was that ever since Orwenson had entered his cell, he had started to feel lethargic in mind and body. Perhaps he was coming down with something. After all, Orwenson himself had called in sick the following day: the officer might have shared some of his germs. However, if this was the case, Bilty wished the contagion would simmer up into something real, something noticeable; something that could be treated after a visit to the prison nurse.

Just before noon, with Bilty getting ready to refuse his lunch when it arrived, he was surprised when his door was unlocked. From his supine position he shot a beam at the TV and killed *The Rockford Files*. The door opened. It was Orwenson.

Trying to disguise his terror, Bilty sat up quickly on his bed.

'You've got a visitor,' Orwenson told him.

'It's Saturday, sir.'

'I know what *day* it is, Steve! Jesus! You'll need your top: parky out there.'

Visits on a Saturday were rarer than hen's teeth. The circumstances had to be dire.

'Are my family all right, sir?' Bilty asked, reaching for his trainers.

'How the hell should *I* know?'

'Sorry, sir. Do you know who it is at least?'

'Not sure; but a Mr Hammish, I believe, was mentioned.'

'My solicitor.'

'Yes, Steve, I read the papers – I know who Mr Hammish is. And so do your loving admirers at the gate, by the way. Thought I'd be asked for an autograph this morning. Bloody ghouls.'

Bilty pulled on his sweater. 'Are you feeling any better, sir? Heard you been tom and dick.'

'Shitting ribbons and razorblades. And you haven't been the full shilling yourself.'

'…It was something you said on the night you gave me the – the present.'

Orwenson frowned. 'I don't know nothing about a present. You ready?'

'Yes, sir. But you do recall saying something about knowing who did it. My offence, sir.'

Orwenson sniffed. 'It's not my place to speculate on such matters, Steve,' he answered primly. 'You were tried by a jury. You were found guilty. End *of*, mate.'

They exited onto the corridor. The Wing was noisy with music, and believing that there was no fear they'd be overheard, Bilty risked pushing the matter.

'I'm not going mad, sir,' he protested.

'That's not for me to judge either. Or *you* to judge, for that matter.'

'Sir, please. You said you knew who did it. The *wanker* who did it, was your precise words.'

'Oh, you're Mr Memory now, are you? Jog on, son.'

Wordlessly they approached the gates at the end of the corridor. In a baffled huff, Bilty stared down at his trainers, unable to fathom it. Had Orwenson been bluffing after all?

The wind was as cold as frost. 'Bilty's not guilty!' was chanted from the direction of the main gate. 'Don't they ever *shut up?*' Orwenson asked. 'How much do you pay em?'

Pay them: that was good. The thought that Hammish might be using some of his retainer as a way of keeping the story of injustice alive and fresh in the public imagination made Bilty grin. Bilty wouldn't put it past the sly bugger... And it was certainly a better thought than the one he'd nursed for the last two days: the possibility that the crowd *was not there at all*. In his current condition, Bilty had almost convinced himself that the voices were recorded; that the images shown on the news were library footage. That it was all a sham for the scandal-munchers.

They approached the gate to the Main Block, and Orwenson said, 'I'll deny I ever told you this, all right? It was a Frenchman. A doctor. His name's Bourdette.' He unlocked the gate. 'And that's all you're getting from me on the subject, Steve.'

'Someone's yanking your chain, sir. It's a joke.' Bilty stepped in the Main Block and stamped slush off his trainers.

Orwenson followed him into the warmth. He closed and locked the gate; then he closed and locked the door. 'How so?'

'Dr Bourdette is a murderer, sir...'

'I should cocoa! Lead the way, Bilty.'

'He's in a story, sir – a ghost story called 'The Waxwork'. He's a man who collects throats.'

Orwenson huffed. 'In a story? Try telling *that* to his victims!'

'But I can't tell that to his victims, sir –'

'No, because they're dead!'

'No, sir. Because they're characters! It's a *story*,' he repeated. 'From the 20s.'

'Have it your way, Bilty. *I'm* not the one doing eighteen years for a crime I didn't commit.'

'Nor am I, sir,' Bilty answered quietly.

'Why, what are you planning to do? Fly over the walls?'

'I'll be out on appeal, sir. My solicitor says I've got a good case.'

'So did Adolf Eichmann. In you go.'

The Visits Room consisted of twenty tables of hardened plastic in strident rainbow colours; all of them were bolted to the floor. Only one was occupied... but it wasn't occupied by Marcus Hammish. A smartly-dressed woman in her mid-forties had chosen a table in the middle of the room. On seeing Bilty and Orwenson she stood up and extended her right hand.

Bilty strolled over and shook it: an almost forgotten formality.

'Mr Hammish sent me,' the woman explained. 'I'm Emmeline Valiant.'

'....Oh I get it,' said Bilty, taking his seat. 'So where's your broomstick then?'

'Excuse me?'

'What are you talking about, Bilty?' Orwenson demanded.

'First it's Dr Bourdette, sir, and now it's Miss Emmeline from 'Miss Emmeline Takes Off' – it's the second story in the book. She finds a broomstick and she can fly on it.'

'What *book?*' Orwenson continued.

The visitor sat down opposite the prisoner. 'It's *Mrs* Valiant actually,' she said, flashing Bilty a glimpse of her ring finger. The rock was the size of a pork scratching.

'Wouldn't do that around here if I were you,' Bilty advised her. 'Place is full of criminals.'

'I'll bear that in mind, thank you. Now –'

Bilty laughed. 'That was intended as a joke, *Mrs* Valiant.'

'You won't be surprised if I tell you I've heard that one before. And mostly people call me Emma or Em. I'll invite you to do the same if my surname is proving problematic. Now to business –'

'This is *all* proving problematic,' Bilty told her.

'What's got into you, Steve?' Orwenson wanted to know: it was less a genuine enquiry than a veiled threat. 'I'll ask you to show due respect. Unless you'd rather go back to the Wing.'

Bilty sighed. 'Sorry, Em. What's brought you out on a Saturday morning?'

'My job. Marcus is ill with a stomach upset, so he asked if I would call on you instead.'

'And ask me out to play.'

'Bilty...'

'Not exactly; but it *is* encouraging news, Steve. There's been a breakthrough. A confession.'

'To what?'

'To the Great Train Robbery... What do you think I'd be talking about?'

'Sorry. Tell me all about it.'

'Well, there's a media embargo until Monday at six a.m. Which is why I thought I'd see you today – before you hear all about it with your morning cornflakes.' Mrs Valiant appeared content with her own earthiness – her own *panache*. 'You could look pleased, you know, Steve...'

'But I don't know what it means,' Bilty complained. 'He could be a crank!'

'Who said it was a man?' Emmeline's eyes twinkled, as if with mischief.

'Are you serious?'

The solicitor nodded and consulted some notes in front of her on the table. 'Her name is Lesley Bourdette.'

Bilty frowned. 'And she's French, I would guess.'

'She is indeed.'

'A doctor?'

'Yes; apparently she's got a PhD in something computery. Hardly the profile of a crank confessor, I would venture. Though I'm no expert on such matters yet.'

Bilty looked up at Orwenson, who said, almost-but-not-quite apologetically, 'I heard Dr Bourdette. I assumed a man. Sue me.' Then he shrugged. 'Anyway, Lesley's a unisex name.'

'So it is. Sir, I think I'm...' Bilty reconsidered. 'I think we're all being taken for a ride.'

'On a broomstick?' asked Mrs Valiant.

Bilty did not think much of the interruption. 'I would like to go back to my cell, please, Mr Orwenson. I don't feel well.' As he stood up and slid out of the booth, he added to Mrs Valiant: 'Please pass on my best wishes for a speedy recovery to Marcus.'

*

Ghostly Gallery was on his desk, next to a half-empty pouch of tobacco that he intended to sell; and Bilty picked up the volume with fresh reverence, his heart speeding, his palms damp. Before he opened the cover again he felt obliged to take a deep breath: he had decided that the Contents page would look different – the stories would be in a new order, perhaps. And this would prove that he needed an urgent appointment with the Psych Nurse. It did not occur to Bilty that his self-diagnosis was rather a rational call for a man flirting with insanity. Bilty *wanted* to be a fraction unhinged; as long as the prognosis for an eventual recovery was hopeful, where was the damage in admitting the oddball fancies that had crawled through his unconscious? They would blame it on stress.

However, when Bilty turned the pages to the Contents there was nothing amiss; the anthology was exactly as he'd left it. More puzzled by this particular betrayal than by anything else, he abandoned the idea of earning some money from the tobacco and he rolled himself a matchstick-thin cigarette. Having had the book from the library since Wednesday, this evening's story was due to have been the fourth in the book: 'The Haunted Trailer' by Robert Arthur. Lying back against the cold wall, his roll-up smouldering between his lips, Bilty cast his mind back and tried to remember the story from when he was a boy. He could not deny a desperate truth: that he was seriously considering not reading the story after all. Not in the wake of today's fun.

Don't be a wet all your life, son, his father admonished him. And this inner voice had a point: regardless of the coincidences of names in the anthology's first two tales ending up in the real world, there'd been nothing from the third tale, had there? Nothing from Algernon Blackwood's 'The Valley of the Beasts'. Nothing had forced its way into Bilty's existence.

The cell was opened; Orwenson stood in the doorframe. 'Are you decent?'

'Bit late if I'm not, sir.'

Orwenson closed the door partway, and Bilty didn't like this. The only time doors were closed with the screws inside was when a punishment was about to be doled out; or when the con was about to be searched for contraband in his anal cavity – the old squat and scratch.

'It's about that book,' the officer said, pouching his ring of keys. 'And don't pretend you don't know which one. I have dinners to look after soon.'

'...What about it?'

'Oh I almost forgot.' Orwenson slipped his left hand into his trouser pocket; pulled out a packet of Benson & Hedges cigarettes. 'Some Benny Hedgehogs for you. Not quite full.' He tossed the packet towards the bed; Bilty caught it. 'About fifteen, though – fifteen, sixteen...'

Bilty said, 'Thank you, sir; but forgive me if this sounds blunt, but why, sir? Why the gifts? First the hooch, now the fags...' His voice toughened. 'I would like to know, sir, why you are favouring me – and at what cost to myself in the long run.'

Orwenson sat down at Bilty's desk. 'At what cost to myself in the long run,' he repeated. 'You've been rehearsing that, haven't you, Steve?'

'Yes. At what cost, please, sir?'

The officer sighed. 'The cost of your freedom,' he answered presently.

*

Bilty woke from a bad dream in which he stood on the outside of the crime for which he had been imprisoned. He was urging his younger self not to do it – the precise nature of the offence remained undefined. His younger self looked over his shoulder, imploring the dreamer for omnipotent wisdom with calfy eyes. A darkened road, itself breathing with snore-like pulses, lay ahead, directed downwards into an urban valley. *We mustn't go there;* and yet, despite the dreamer's exhortations, the subject continued walking towards his doomed fate. Through the smoky air flew Emmeline; swift as a trigger, she cut advice into the darkness with her broomstick. The word read NO.

'No...' Bilty read, opening his eyes. At the sight of the cell he experienced a sense of relief so enriched, so profound, that it was close to being dreamlike in its essence.

Bilty washed. He felt agitated. He exercised (push-ups and sit-ups) before thumping on his cell door and requesting a razor when the nightscrew finally attended. Although the water and the soap provided a familiar sting to his chops, it was a pleasure to shave. It felt normal to do so; it helped calm him down a jot. He washed again. He was ready for the day.

The cigarettes lay on his windowsill. He didn't want them. But if Orwenson was to be believed, he couldn't afford not to have them.

*

'Ever feel like your life's sprung a leak, Steve?' Orwenson asked.

Bilty assumed that the screw was slinging banter. 'All the time, sir.'

The answer did not meet with Orwenson's full approval. Sitting on Bilty's chair he shook his head briskly. 'No, don't rush, Steve. Really think about it. I can wait. Or come back.'

Bilty regarded the flimsy smile on Orwenson's face — and didn't like it one bit. He reminded Bilty — in a flash — of a man who'd taught Maths at Mill Vale Middle School... where Stephen had first taken *Ghostly Gallery* into his hands. But what was the name of that teacher?

'It was Malcolm,' Orwenson answered.

'Mr Malcolm! I haven't thought of him for thirty years!'

'Yes you have.'

Bilty waited: he waited for some tide of logic — failing a tide, a wave would do — to roll in. He had not asked a question as to the Maths teacher's identity, and yet...

'Are you reading my mind, sir?' Bilty asked.

'Why not ask me with your mind?'

'You know the question now.'

'Ask me another. Meanwhile I'll take one of them Benny Hedgehogs off you.'

Passing the officer a smoke, Bilty frowned and thought carefully: *Are you Mr Malcolm? Are you the same person?*

'Cheers, Steve.' Not missing a beat, Orwenson replied, 'Of course I'm not! How old do I look, you cheeky bastard!'

By this point Bilty was sitting hunched on the edge of his bed, his hands adroop over the cliffs of his knees. He sighed a quart of air out; he gasped a quart of air in: the same stale air. Returning to Orwenson's initial question he thought: It would be *good* to spring a leak.

'That's right. You think of springing a leak as a *bad* thing. Quite the contrary, Steve. We *need* leaks: as a species, as a world even... What's the earliest thing you can remember?'

Bilty's answer was immediate: he had been asked this question numerous times. 'I don't believe in memories, sir.'

'Even your own?'

'Especially my own.'

'All right then. What's the earliest thing you *think* you remember?'

'Darkness. A confined space.'

'The womb?'

'Possibly.'

'Or a cupboard, Steve. Cupboard under the stairs.'

Bilty frowned again. 'I don't know...'

'And you thought there'd be spiders, didn't you, Steve? Maybe rats. Who told you there'd be spiders and rats?'

Bilty hesitated. He knew the answer.

'Who told you that, Steve?' Orwenson pressed.

'I don't wish to discuss it.'

'I'm sure you don't. But if you haven't already noticed, you're not a resident of a five-star hotel in the Bahamas, where the customer calls the shots. You're in the nick and on my watch. So I'll ask you again, Steve, and this time I'll expect an answer, okay? Who warned you about the cupboard under the stairs?'

'My parents.'

'It was a punishment, wasn't it, Steve. For when you were a naughty boy.'

'...I don't remember telling anyone this.'

Orwenson smiled. 'What did you say about trusting your memories? It goes both ways. There are things we remember that never happened, and there are things that did happen we *can't* remember.' He shot a hand out in the direction of the book. 'Don't you ever ask yourself how the people in those stories remember what's happened to them? After they've had their imaginations scrambled by ghosts, does it make sense to you?'

'It's fiction.'

'But how do you know that?' Orwenson rose to his feet, the lecture or psychotherapeutic session evidently drawing to a close. He slapped his thighs as he got up. He ashtrayed the half-smoked B&H.

'Wait!'

At the door Orwenson turned, an expression of disgust on his face. 'I beg your pardon.'

'Please, sir.' Bilty also stood up. 'You're trying to teach me something, or I think you are; and I'm trying to learn.'

'Get on with it.'

'If the people in the stories,' Bilty began, 'can remember what they've been through then it's not as *bad* a thing to have gone through as the thing people go through when they *can't* remember it. Because we hide the *really* bad stuff from ourselves — we lose it. Deliberately.'

Orwenson sniffed. 'It's a theory, Steve.'

*

All I can think of is the cupboard under the stairs, Bilty wrote unsteadily, the biro an unfamiliar tool, the paper thin, the table surface hard and slightly pockmarked. *There wasn't much room to move. But there weren't no*

Bilty made the *tsch* sound: a recognition of his own fallibility. He crossed out *no* and wrote *any*, but this infinitesimal edit had cost him his train of thought. There weren't any what?

any rats or spiders either. Or none that I saw any rate.

Filled with a sense of dissatisfaction, Bilty reread the gob-
bet memoir. It wasn't what he'd hoped to capture. So what had
he intended to bring back to life on the page? The memory had
ferreted away.

Bilty stood up, his autobiography dead at the grand old size
of four sentences. He judged against the decision to break the
biro; instead he placed it neatly next to the paper. Who could tell
when inspiration might come knocking?

The book lay on the bed, unwanted. On Wednesday he
would return it to the library: he had formed the opinion – if not
the dread – that he didn't need to know how it ended.

Tonight he was all of a dither, and his cell was noisy. Music
of a dozen varieties was washing up on the shore of his cell door.
Trying to pluck one tune out of the cacophony, and hold on to it,
became his task; but the selection process proved nigh-on impossible. He sat down. He smoked with desensitised languor, trying
to blot out some of the din in which he'd become enveloped. It
was futile: there was nowhere to go. Nowhere *quiet*.

When darkness came, at first he was frightened. The Wing
took a while to settle – golden rule – but tonight the main silence
was eerily swift. Bilty rolled on to one side after the other, seeking
a way somewhere – he wasn't sure where exactly.

Why hadn't the comparison occurred to him before? The
similarity between his cell and where he'd waited for forgiveness
in the cupboard under the stairs. Now that Orwenson had helped
him stir up this grain, the similarity was obvious: the silence, the
darkness… and Bilty tried to remember his way back there.

It was not a trouble-free voyage. It was as if Bilty were warning himself not to travel – the seas were too rocky this evening –
and for seconds, for minutes, the journeyman had no choice but to
return to the prison bunk. Slowly but surely, however, he was able
to send himself further away from his point of origin; and before

much longer Bilty was aware of two darks clashing. And although much might have happened among the years that separated the apogee between the two darks, they were also linked by a piece of mental space no wider than a neurone.

Bilty chose which of the two darknesses he would rather sleep in tonight.

*

The first thing he noticed was the cold... but it was not the lived-in chill of a space that has lost temperature gradually. It was the cold of shock – and it was Bilty's own to nurse.

The second thing was that it wasn't as dark as he had imagined; there was more space than predicted, too. Actually, as recent dreams went, this one was not so bad. The triangle of light surrounding the oddly-shaped door was enough to convince Bilty that he had tripped and slipped into no void. Outside this door was the hall.

I could climb out.

What stopped him doing so immediately was the murmur of voices, somewhere above him, up the stairs. From his parents' room, most likely. Arguing or foreplay? Safer here, he realised.

The cupboard wasn't a *punishment*, he remembered suddenly; it was a *hiding place*. It was where I went to take refuge – from the arguments. It was where... it was where I felt safe.

And they had tried to dissuade him from coming in here. Conversations from long ago – they rippled in Bilty's mind, like shredded banners in a gale. That talk of spiders and rats – that had not been to scare him into not being naughty; it had been a lie to discourage the boy from entering the cupboard willingly. So what was to stop him exiting it?

He didn't want to see the house, that was what. Didn't want to see who lived there either. Didn't want anything but to stay in the dark, along with the box of second-choice older shoes; the upright vacuum cleaner; the rolls of leftover wallpaper...

It was where I came to read. The memory was like water on a dry tongue: how his bedroom, next to his parents', had seemed too close, too familiar. There was a wind-up torch on his homework table, pride of place adjacent to a tape-to-tape recorder, a pile of cassettes labelled neatly in a childish hand with the date their contents had been recorded off the Radio 1 chart countdown, and a Tottenham Hotspur hat and scarf that he'd received as a birthday present the year before... Stephen would take the torch and a book, and descend the stairs while his parents made noise in one room or another in the small house... and he would close himself into the cupboard.

It was where he'd read *Ghostly Gallery*... and how he'd struggled with some of the prose, some of the constructions! It must have taken him months! There were happy days.

Experimentally, Bilty felt around in the darkness. His fingertips counted shoes in the big box, leather and plastic footholes like the throats of dead animals; and then both hands continued the inventory. The vacuum cleaner, as ever, was chilled to the touch...

Ah! The wind-up torch leapt into Bilty's hands; it felt smaller than he recalled it being, but that was of no consequence. The handle to crank up the battery was in place, and slowly at first – carefully, almost with reverence – Bilty turned it, holding the base in his other hand. It whirred like his mother's sewing machine. He span the handle faster; a tangerine glow seeped out, pale and flickering close to extinction; so Bilty revved harder and the glow strengthened, pulsing with every turn of the handle, gaining power. Within seconds the inside of the cupboard had been coated in a golden glowing vigour. And it was then that Bilty could see that he wasn't alone.

*

He tried to keep his eyelids closed. He didn't want to see. He heard his name.

Orwenson was at his bedside. 'Who was it?' the screw demanded.

Sitting up (and reflexively squashing himself closer against the corner where the walls met), Bilty rubbed his eyes. 'Mr Malcolm. My Maths teacher.'

'What had happened?'

'He was dead.'

'I guessed *that* much, Steve. *What had happened to him?*'

Bilty did not need to close his eyes to refresh the image. 'His head was bashed open.'

'Good. What else?'

'...Did you say *good*, sir?'

'*What else?*'

Bilty shook his head; he sprayed smoke in a semicircle, from a cigarette that he had lit while on autopilot. 'What's *good* about finding my teacher with his brain caved in?'

'It means you're leaking,' Orwenson replied matter-of-factly. 'Remember what I said about lives and leaks?'

'...Well, yes; but I didn't really understand.'

'Neither do I. What else happened, Steve? Do you mind if I sit down? I've been on since six.' He perched on the end of Bilty's bed. 'We thought you were leaving us, mate,' he said. 'It was my idea to give you the hooch and the fags – to keep you offguard a little bit. You were getting too comfortable – we had to keep you awake.'

'Sir? I don't have the first idea what you're talking about.'

'Are you sure?'

'Of course I'm fucking sure!'

'Well forgive me,' Orwenson bit back, 'there was I thinking you're getting closer.'

'To what?' Bilty shouted.

'To your freedom, you silly cunt!' Orwenson answered, leaning forwards. 'Or do you *want* to stay in here for the rest of your life?'

Bilty shook his head again. 'What choice have I got? The appeal won't be –'

'*Fuck* the appeal, Steve!' Orwenson pointed a finger. 'That's baby talk.' Now he placed his forefinger against his own right temple. '*This* is where your appeal is – it's in *here*. It's got nothing to do with a month from now or a year from now. There's no such thing – not in here.'

'...In my *head*, sir?'

'Well, who else's? What's my name, Steve?' He clicked his fingers. 'Quick answer!'

'Mr Orwenson.'

'And what's your dad's name?'

'What?'

'What's your dad's name, Steve? Quick snap!'

'Owen.'

'Right. So you're Owen's son. Orwenson, Owen's son. Close, yeah?'

'What...?'

'And he came to your house, didn't he, Steve: Mr Malcolm.'

'He was my Maths teacher.'

'But why was he at your *house*?'

'I had private lessons. I was crap at Maths.'

'You still have nightmares, don't you? About not being able to do your Maths homework.'

'Yes. When I'm anxious. Your point being?'

By way of response Orwenson touched his temple again. And although the gesture solved nothing directly, it did at least provide momentum to Bilty's further questioning.

'You mean I'm *imagining* this?' he asked. 'I'm not... I'm not *here*?'

'You're as here as much as you want to be... You didn't like your private lessons, did you?'

'No, not much.'

'You resented them, in fact.'

Bilty saw the man in the understairs cupboard; the vision quickened his pulse, and absentmindedly he sprinkled ash in a random fashion with a waist-high sweep of his arm.

'...and I hope you're going to clean that up, an' all.'

'Clean what up?'

Orwenson pointed again, this time at the cell floor; but Bilty's defiant mood had yet to desert him. Shrugging his shoulders, the latter argued, 'Why, sir? Why bother – if this is all in my head, as you say?'

Orwenson grinned. 'You never heard the one about tidy house, tidy mind.'

Bilty snorted. 'Seems rather redundant in this case, sir, if you'll forgive me saying so... So where am I – where am I really?' he asked.

'Where *are* you?'

'Yes, sir. If I'm not here, where am I?'

'I didn't say you weren't here. You're not listening – to yourself, I mean.'

Bilty squashed the cigarette against a bar across his window; he left the butt on the narrow windowsill. He was breathless with it all; his head rumbled.

'Let me ask another one,' Orwenson continued, 'and then I really must be off. There's breakfast to supervise. I got the booby prize.'

Bilty stood with his shoulderblades touching the cold wall, his buttocks clenched on the radiator. He did not invite Orwenson to speak further; resigned and abashed, he merely nodded.

'Why do *you* think you're here, Steve?'

'I committed an offence.'

'Did you? What was it?'

The prisoner laughed: this one was simply too absurd. *Are you kid* – he thought of saying. *Are you hav – What do you –*

'Your crime, Bilty. What was it?'

The chill that Bilty had experienced in the understairs cupboard – that of shock, raw shock – returned now; he was obliged to sit down on the edge of his bed. His neck muscles weakened; his head dropped, the lips moving but producing no sound. There was nothing to say. Whatever misdemeanour had landed him in this prison had completely abandoned his memory.

*

He dreamed of the haunted trailer.

In his dream the book flapped open on the desk in his bedroom. No seasonal breeze through a window provided the impetus: the windows were shut tight against the cold and against the night. From the pub behind the house came the bassline thumps of a band playing live; some loud conversation rendered muffled...

...The boy isn't interested in sound: it is the visual that claims his senses. *The book is leaking*. Sitting on the bed, crosslegged in his pyjamas, the boy watches dust rise from the pages of 'The Haunted Trailer'. The dust climbs the air in his bedroom, the column threadbare at first but swiftly solidifying, the motes themselves growing in size into iron filings. When the column has become dense – a filthy pole of grey and brown – it whips from the bedroom and onto the landing, the boy left unsure as to whether or not to follow the vanguard or remain where he is. He stays put.

The flow continues. At the sound of glass breaking the boy starts but does not rise from his lotus position: there is no need to move to decipher the sound. The will-o'-the-wisp has forced its way either through the window in his parents' bedroom or that of the spare.

Now that the dam has been breached – some rubicon between the world inside the book and the world of the boy's room – the pieces emerge larger: warped metal hinges, rusted nuts and bolts, flotsam giving off a fierce heat, burning off its afterbirth.

The boy shivers at the increase in temperature. He decides to move.

The river of junk flowing across the landing makes it hard for the boy to step into the spare bedroom: he is scared that should he fall into the flow he will be swept away – either that or mangled by the fragments whizzing past. He kneels on the single bed. Frosted air reaches in through the broken glass, chilling sweat on the boy's neck; still the junk piles through the gap, but it doesn't land randomly on the small lawn below. There is a pattern forming: the pieces of metal and shards of other matter are *knitting themselves together*, there in the front garden.

Something is being constructed for the boy's solitary appreciation. It's the caravan, Bilty tells his younger self in the second before both versions of the same person wake.

*

'Where am I?' the prisoner croaked.

'Health Care. You were taken bad in the night,' a female voice answered... and for a second Bilty was hopeful: the lone voice, the antiseptic smell – this could be anywhere! A health care unit outside the prison! It was only when he sat up (his stomach twanged with pain, as if he'd been sick a number of times) that he saw the screw statuesque by the door, observing the proceedings and keeping guard. He lay back down with a sigh.

'What's wrong with me?'

'You were complaining of chest pains.' His interlocutor moved closer; she was middle-aged, puffy about the face – it came as a pleasant surprise to Bilty that he hadn't conjured up anyone too unrealistic, too desirable.

'What's that for?' Bilty asked, referring to the syringe she carried.

'A mild sedative. You're suffering from anxiety, Bilty... You can refuse it if you wish.'

Bilty closed his eyes. 'No, go on, stick it in – it can't hurt me.' He felt a sting of tears; he felt unwell…but there was no trace of a chest pain. This in itself was startling considering the way his heart continued to pound – as if it was trying to drill free. With his eyes still closed he asked: 'Miss? Can I talk to you about my mental health, please?'

The silence that ensued stretched for so long that Bilty invented a fresh fear with which to taunt himself: the fear that when he opened his eyes she would be gone – or she would wear someone else's face… or there would only be more darkness.

He felt the needle prick the crook of his left arm. Her voice lower than before, she answered, 'That's not my field, Bilty. I'm a prison nurse acting on medical orders to calm you down.'

'Whose orders, Miss?'

'Dr Higgins. He works at the –'

'Let me guess!' Bilty interrupted. 'It's *Spike* Higgins, isn't it? As Spike as the spike in my arm.'

'Bilty…' the screw warned from the door, but it was almost as if the prisoner hadn't heard him. Sitting up quickly (his stomach pinched again) obliged the nurse to take a step back from the bed: he had surprised her. And so wild-eyed was Bilty that he was unaware of his surroundings: of the syringe drooping impotently from his arm; of the officer getting ready with his baton.

'Spike Higgins is a tramp!' the prisoner ranted.

'*Bilty*,' the screw repeated.

'He's in a story called 'The Haunted Trailer', Miss! He's a ghost! He haunts the bloke who buys the trailer…'

The officer was no further away from the bed than two metres. His weapon was drawn. 'I don't want to use this, mate,' he stated flatly.

Bilty acknowledged both his presence and his threat. He held up his hands. 'I'm calm, sir; all I'm asking is for you to listen. Spike Higgins is a *character* –'

'It's Mike,' the nurse interjected. 'Dr *Mike* Higgins.'

Bilty smiled. 'Close enough... Is your name Monica, by the way?'

The nurse fluffed up. 'It is. How did you –'

'It's the name of the woman in the story – the narrator's fiancée – the one he's trying not to let know about the ghost.'

The officer's voice sounded disgusted. 'Have you been on the hooch, Bilty?'

'No, sir. It doesn't matter.'

'It bloody well *does* matter.'

'The *names* don't matter, sir. It was the caravan we had in the front garden: it's where Mr Malcolm gave me private lessons, when I was a boy... Can I speak to Mr Orwenson, please?'

'He's not on shift.' The screw and the nurse swapped glances. 'Why don't you take that thing out of your arm, Bilty, before you hurt yourself?'

'Before I hurt *you*, you mean,' Bilty replied, plucking the needle free.

'Is that a threat, mate?'

'No, sir. You're not listening –'

'I've heard enough. Give it to the nurse handle first and then we'll continue to discuss things. All right? I'm in no mood.'

The prisoner counted his options. This didn't take long: there were only three. Fight and rant. Subserve and rant. Turn mute... Bilty handed the hypodermic to Monica the Nurse and gummed his lips down hard on his protruding tongue. There was nothing useful he could say, unless it was to Orwenson; but this didn't mean that his mind would keep quiet.

*

I didn't want the lessons, his pen scratched into the thin paper. *I felt like I was being singled out for unfair treatment. So I played the system – I invited my parent's*

He crossed out *parent's* and wrote *parents*. Then he studied it with his head at an angle and through squeezed eyes: it looked wrong.

'Do you need some help?' Clive asked him cheerfully, looming close. Bilty blinked and smiled up from his classroom desk. His motion the answer to nothing but unrefined instinct, he folded his arms over the paper and said, 'I don't understand apostrophes, sir.'

'It's never bothered you before, Steve.' Clive frowned gently and adjusted his spectacles – they had slipped from position.

'Well it's bothering me now,' Bilty replied, tickled by minor annoyance.

'What have they to do with Skinner's views of operant learning?'

Though Bilty was of a mind to tell Clive where he could stick Skinner's views of operant learning, he instead unfolded his arms to reveal his handwriting. 'Piece of reflexive composition, sir.'

From his expression, stance and demeanour, the teacher gave the impression that he believed he could smell a rat. 'Who for?' he asked in the tone he used to imply canniness.

'Dr Higgins the Psych Doc. Wants me to write stuff down when my brain is going on safari.'

'Even in my lesson?' Clive demanded.

'Especially in your lesson, perhaps, sir.' This opinion belonged to Brian Garridge, today seated a couple of desks away, alongside the row of narrow windows, one of which was open to allow in some air that was, if not exactly fresh (it carried aromas from Recycling), then at least moving. Garridge had complained of a gestating nausea: his repositioning near the window had been regarded as a sensible precaution. Up till now this session he had been as quiet as a mollusc, apart from the occasional self-indulgent (ignored) groan.

Heads turned to Garridge now, Bilty's included.

'I don't follow you, Brian,' Clive added after a beat of time.

Visibly under the weather, Garridge lifted his chin. 'This is all about operant learning, yeah? The rats and that?'

'In a manner of speaking,' Clive conceded.

'My man's an operant for his own learning by writing self-important wank. Is it important to *me*? Is it fuck, sir. Is it important to *you* –'

'Yes, I think I grasp the point, Brian, thank you.'

'But *do* you, sir? Do you really?'

'Guys. We do happen to have an *exam* rolling closer, in case you've forgotten. The summer's not as far away as it seems, you know.'

'It is to us,' Garridge said. 'And you should know that.'

Clive redid his spectacles once again. 'And why's that?'

'Because of the subject you teach.'

While Bilty was not sure what exactly had come about in this room, he was convinced of one thing: that Brian Garridge, his Study Buddy – no doubt for reasons of his own – had tried at least to be of assistance. It was true that this constituted a future debt, but Bilty was happy that a seed of doubt had been sown. He said, 'Would you have any violent objection, sir, if I continued?' 'I'm not certain I have any choice in the matter,' Clive answered. 'So what is it exactly? The apostrophes, I mean. I might as well be *some* bloody use.'

Bilty took the opportunity, saying: 'Where does the diddle go? If it's *both* violent parents…'

*

A few hours later, when Bilty had returned to his cell, he completed the prose… but the going was not easy. What wriggled in his mind was the thought that he had forgotten to thank Garridge (these things meant something here), and what also bothered Bilty was Orwenson's unwanted presence. The officer had sat on Bilty's bed and said, 'Finish what you're doing. I'll read your ghost book.'

'I took it back, sir.'

With Orwenson's role resembling nothing more than that of a stern but silent invigilator, the composition felt like sitting an exam. It produced just the right amount of sweat for it to qualify as work. When he finally closed the paragraph that he'd been drowning in, he shut it down with a triumphant grunt and a dirty full stop that drilled into his desk. The biro broke. This felt symbolic. It was all that Bilty could do not to grin at having penned his new confessional.

Orwenson stood up. 'About time.' He pinched the sheet of paper and flapped it as though the ink had yet to dry properly. He said nothing about the broken pen and prison property. For Bilty, this omission alone was telling.

'We had a caravan on the front lawn...'

'Shut up, Steve, you'll spoil the end.'

But Bilty was not of a humour to shut up. 'Abandoned half the year – God alone knows what the neighbours thought – it just sat there, getting rusty. And that's where Mr Malcolm came to give me statistics and arithmetic and whatnot. And I hated it.'

'So you told lies about him.'

'I waited until I heard Dad's footsteps on the gravel in the drive. Then I ripped off my T-shirt and sat on Malcolm's lap. With my arms around him.'

Orwenson sat up straight. 'And he found the two of you together like that,' he said quietly. Bilty nodded. 'And then your old man clobbered him one.' Bilty nodded.

'With an iron in the cupboard by the stove.' Bilty had closed his eyes: he was as good as there, back in the caravan, bare-chested... and there was Dad giving the lie to Mum's recriminatory jibes about him not even knowing where the bloody iron lived because he never used it. In that caravan he had known precisely where the bloody iron lived.

'You never forget the *noise*, do you, Steve?'

'Well I *thought* I had, sir.'

'Metal on bone: nothing ever sounds quite the same… Did he die immediately?'

Bilty opened his eyes and shook his head. 'I thought he was going to get up, I really did. It didn't even look that bad.'

'Ah! If I've heard that once, I've heard it a thousand times.' Orwenson clapped his knees and rose to his full height. 'I only hit him once, guv. Banged his head on the way down, guv. What's missing from these accounts is any sense of…*sobriety* that you shouldn't have been hitting him in the first place. Or her, I suppose.'

'They tried to wake him.'

'Your Mum as well?'

'She knew a bit of first aid, but there was nothing to be done. That was when I got…'

'Your word here is *hysterical*. And I can't say I blame you.'

'But I only remember *them* as calm. I'm probably forgetting things again.'

'Not necessarily… So they decided to hide him in the cupboard under the stairs.'

'Probably Dad did. And don't ask me why they imagined this might be a good idea: I'd been sent off to my room to put some bloody clothes on, in my mother's words. I don't think the idea was to leave him there *long*… in my memory it was an age. And I was told never to go in there. Order.'

'Which you ignored.'

'Which I ignored, obviously. The charge was reduced to manslaughter, on account of the evidence – and my lies.' Bilty spoke monotonously now. 'He only did two years. For murdering an innocent man who was moonlighting for extra cash. I've lived with that for nearly thirty years… I'm feeling weepy, sir.'

'Go ahead, Steve: let it out. If anyone asks, say I smacked you for insubordination.'

'I won't cry in front of you, sir.'

Orwenson shrugged and handed back the piece of paper. 'Suit yourself. Now I've got one for you. Are you sitting comfortably? Then I'll begin. This won't take long.'

*

'I used to work at a Young Offenders Institute, right; and there was a little gobshite there, fancied himself rotten. A regular fucking diva; and me, I drew the short straw, didn't I, and I had to be in a classroom with the prick, keeping an eye. Well, what happens is, this boy calls the teacher a wanker. Just like that. So I tell him to mind his manners and he starts calling *me* a wanker. Winding me up. Over and over again, trying to get me to react. But I wouldn't. I *wanted* to but I wouldn't – and he was getting frustrated. So I waited – and I waited – and then, when the timing was perfect, I called him a cunt. In a calm voice. And not once: again and again.

'Well, you can imagine: he's on his feet bleating about civil liberties, and I tell him: *Sit down, cunt. Lower your voice, cunt. Don't make me give you an embolism, cunt.* Relaxed as you like. And he didn't know what to do with the information. So every time I saw him after that I used the same word. He says *Good morning, sir*; I say, *Good morning, cunt.* Deliberately grinding him down.'

Bilty let a respectful pause pass. 'This is all very interesting, sir,' he finally said (quietly amazed at the confession), 'but unless I'm missing the point...'

'The gobshite's name was Bilty. It was you, Steve.'

*

During Association Time after dinner, Bilty took his phonecard and slipped into the booth near the pool table. He knew Hammish's number by heart, but he hadn't trusted himself in his current frame of mind so he'd jotted it down on a cigarette paper, having had to fish the broken biro from his bin. It still worked... He dialled, expecting at this hour to reach the solicitor's answering service. He was surprised when Hammish himself picked up and spoke.

'I'm fine, Steve. Working late, but fine. Why do you ask?'

'Emmeline Valiant said you were rough as houses. That's why she came in your place.'

'*Who* said? What do you mean, *in my place*?'

'...You didn't send her, did you?'

'Steve, I don't know what – Someone's been to see you saying I sent them?'

'...Massive wedding ring.'

'I've sent no one, Steve. This is worrying.'

'A computer scientist called Bourdette has confessed. You were working on my release.'

'Well, the last part's true,' said Hammish, 'but I don't know about any confession.'

'So I made it up.'

'I'm not accusing you of *lying*, Steve. I'm merely stating –'

'No, I know – it's not about lying, Marcus. Some strange thoughts have been riding me like a *pony*. I'm lying to myself if anything. And do you know something else? There are people outside the walls every day chanting *Bilty's not guilty*. But they're not, are they?'

'I have no idea.'

'They were outside my *dad's* prison: the people who thought even two years was too long a sentence for a father who's caught his underage son in the arms of his private tutor. They're not for me – they never were – they were *his* fans.'

'I don't know what you're talking about.'

'Was I ever in a YOI?'

'Young Offenders? No of course you weren't. What's got into –'

'My credit's running down, Marcus. Tell me one thing before you go, okay? What offence did I commit? What crime did I get caught for?'

'Well, you know what offence?'

'Tell me, Marcus.'

The line died. A credit total of forty pence was displayed, so Hammish must have put down the receiver. His blood ringing with rage, Bilty did exactly the same thing. To the prisoner next in line to use the phone he handed the phonecard, as a gift. He played and lost a game of pool. He found Garridge and thanked him for his intervention in Sociology (leaving the younger man with a warm glow but thoroughly perplexed). Then Bilty returned to his cell to have a think about killing himself.

*

Troubled by dreams, Bilty woke in the early hours. His sleeping mind had convinced him that someone was scratching at his window; upon checking, however, he found this not to be true. All was well: silent and serene. What better conditions were there under which to plan suicide?

It had all become clear. If Bilty was living a lie conjured up by his much younger self, surely all it would take to return to that younger self was the death of the older. The hard part was conceiving a suitable strategy. Sheets, presumably, could be fashioned into a workable noose…

The story that Orwenson had told about the young offender – it was this story that had provided Bilty with the answers. How many other versions of himself existed – at different ages and different stages of their lives – all strangers to one another? And all of them born of a boy's guilt – guilt that he had caused the death of an innocent man, and had gone on to lie under oath that the man had always told him what a nice handsome boy he was.

Orwenson had watched him sink under the weight of failed appeals and had tasked himself with shocking Bilty back into his own suppressed memories. He had seen a different Bilty – a YO – and had done nothing with the material before him.

In his own way, Orwenson was every bit as guilty a man as Steve had become.

So, to death! Bilty would commit suicide, or die trying: just to get back to that scared little boy under the stairs, with the corpse of Mr Malcolm taking up more than his fair share of space. In the morning he would cry wolf about a headache, and as soon as he was alone again he would throw up the paracetamols that they gave him. Store them. Get some more in the afternoon... When he had enough pills, he would grind them down (make a morning of it; these matters shouldn't be rushed) and he'd soon be back home. And this time the boy would say: *He never touched me.*

Time consuming, though. Hanging was at least swift – provided it went well and he wasn't left as a brain-damaged nil-by-mouth as a result – but perhaps there was another alternative. He could *get* himself killed. Chat some nonsense about some of the cons; demote their crimes to sex offences, and ire was certain to be stoked. A matter of days.

Failing this, he could get Orwenson to do it.

*

When Bilty woke, his face and body wet, he was aware of someone else with him, standing in the darkness by the door.

'Mr Orwenson?'

'No,' the male voice answered.

'Mr *Malcolm*?'

'No. Malcolm's dead because of you.'

'I *know*. I'm trying to do the decent thing, aren't I?' said Bilty.

'Are you? How?'

'By killing myself!'

'It won't give *Malcolm* his life back,' the visitor argued.

'Tell me what then! *Marcus*? How did you get –'

'Shut up, Steve. There's no Marcus, there never was. He's a figment of your guilt, telling you you'll be out on appeal. You won't be out on *anything*. You're doing eighteen years for a crime you can't even remember.'

'I committed no crime,' Bilty answered in protest. 'This is a projection from my childhood.'

'How convenient. Realistic, ain't it?'

Bilty paused. He had never heard Hammish use the word *ain't* – it didn't fit – but there was a man that he had once known who had used it often.

'*Dad?*'

'About time, son. Where were we?'

The prisoner sat up, urging this dream away.

'Your heart was bad, Stephen – it's not your mother's fault for once, and it's not mine either: it's just the way things are. You need help. Medical help. You're on oxygen a lot of the time… There wouldn't be any *point* going back. You don't even live to see your eighteenth. It's a life sentence.'

'You're only *saying* this,' Bilty replied.

'Well go on then. I have a razor if you want it. Test me out!'

'…I have to *die*? In the real world, I mean.'

'You're already dead, more or less. It's better here. Stay here. Stay safe.'

'I don't *feel* safe.'

'What can harm you?'

'*You!*'

'What did *I* ever do to you?'

'…I can't remember.'

'Exactly. So go to sleep. In the morning I'll be gone and you'll've forgotten about wanting to top yourself. Coz if you did you wouldn't be going back to your younger self; you'd be going back to the crime scene. Because nothing else matters. And I'm sorry about that, I really am.'

'Dad? Before you go…'

'What is it, son?'

'How's Mum?'

'Your mother killed herself when I went away. Don't go back, I beg you. Can you imagine the *nagging* if your return brought her back to life as well?' The visitor laughed. 'This is better. This is *safe*, Steve. This is safe – as safe as houses.'

Mia and Zoe

1.

The taste of sleep brought Mia to full attention. Her contacts twitched against her eye-skin; she sneezed. Across the aisle, a fat woman tutted; she was wielding a baby on her lap, and she tugged the child closer, giving Mia a look of reproof. Mia didn't see her accuser. She had begun a brisk climb into panic, and she sat up straight on the uncomfortable chair, her small hands pressed together, writhing over one another, like toads at play. She blinked away moisture in her eyes and her legs felt cold. The taste in her mouth made her angry. She looked out of the window.

Calm down, she told herself. Chewing gently on her tongue, the better to free saliva that might quench the alkaline flavour, she took her own advice. She was sitting on the right side of the third storey of the bus; there was enough space between the seat in front and the vehicle's wall for her right hand. She clenched as hard as she could. Her left hand she put on top of the seat in front. The boy in his school uniform, with his hair slicked back and a tuba sitting next to him, turned slightly. Thefts were common on public transport; perhaps he imagined Mia intended to steal his instrument. Nothing was further from her mind. It was all she could do just to concentrate on staying awake.

'Zoe, it's me. Call me. It's urgent.' Mia's words stirred the taste of sleep around her mouth and the late lunch she'd consumed showed signs of upward creep. Breathe she told herself. She killed the call; went back to holding on to the seat. It was then she noticed how many people around her were clinging to her private disquiet. Must be some show, she thought and then set about shooting down the stares with mad looks of her own. The young mother across the aisle proved to be a particularly tenacious observer, one on whose face a greedy form of disgust was perfectly tuned. The two women stared at each other trying to burn each other down. Only after the parent had turned away did Mia decide to let the woman off: after all, she had a baby to protect.

By now the upper half of Mia's body was flushed, greasy with perspiration; the lower half chilled to the sinews. Despite her unwillingness to get caught in the rain, Mia decided she would disembark early and walk the remaining distance home. She moved to the stairwell and took her mind off some of her panic by considering, albeit briefly, a parting shot: By the way, everyone: I have breath-herpes, perhaps. Or: I've just wet the seat; you'll be smelling that all your way home. She didn't smile at her thoughts but she couldn't deny feeling better. Why not go the whole hog and aim lower? You might want to know I'll be detonating an explosive on this bus in precisely nine minutes. She descended instead.

The first thing she noted as the coach drove on was a group of young men, five or six strong. She pretended that they weren't there. They were sitting on a bench outside The Netherfield pub and passing around a parcel of chips. Groups like this always made her nervous, but tonight she was already rattled enough as it was. She felt trapped; telling herself to stop panicking only drove her on to further panic. One of the youths called her 'Gorgeous' at the top of his voice; others cackled, one whistled. Gulping damp air, Mia surveyed the row of shops in the shabby arcade. Most were already closing. This served somewhat to improve the state of Mia's brain: if she intended to buy anything she would need to do so quickly; it made her concentrate. Shoes. She had the interview in a fortnight's time and she always bought new footwear for such an occasion.

The light inside Kirsty Heels was too bright but at least the person in charge had had the good sense to leave the heating off. The door closed slowly. Mia had never been here before. Mia and the woman behind the counter – tall, red-haired – exchanged smiles. 'You're not about to shut, are you?' The woman told her to take her time. There were no other customers present, and the saleswoman returned her attention to some reading matter. Mia browsed. She thought about what to wear. Black flats, she decided.

She couldn't choose. She had traded feeling frightened, ill and furious for confused. She plucked down three left-footed flats at random, and sat on the chaise longue, where the saleswoman joined her. 'Can I help you with those?' She was dressed in a navy blue shirt and a sky-blue blouse; pinned to the latter was a decal that read EMMY. This was pleasing: Mia liked knowing the names of people who served her in shops. Furthermore she liked Emmy's look: her twenty-something face, the wiry rivers of hair pulled down from a fringe that was otherwise wrenched back and secured as part of a ponytail.

'I need posh shoes.'

'Occasion?'

'An interview.'

'Fine. They didn't give you grief, by the way, did they? Outside?'

Mia shook her head. 'Bit of banter,' she answered.

'They act like kids. Wannabe gamesters…What's the job?'

'It's not a job.' Mia never had a problem with revealing her secrets to strangers. She believed that being lied to was a privilege you only earned through knowing someone well. 'My right-to-remain interview. It's annual.'

Emmy nodded. 'Where you from?'

'Somalia.'

'Been here long?'

'Five years.'

Emmy grinned. 'Let's make it six then, shall we? Size?'

'Ahh… I need a three for my left and a four for my right. I hope that won't be a problem.'

'Not at all.' Emmy walked away.

Fear returned. She couldn't go back there. But the bitter taste of sleep was scratching at Mia's tonsils, scouring the insides of her cheeks. When she regarded her appearance in a full-length mirror, she was obliged to blink hard, her contacts itching. Mia closed her eyes. Don't sleep she told herself. She used her left hand like a claw; she reached up her beige skirt and through the fabric of her panties and pinched her labia together with force. This jolted her awake.

Mia stood up. In turn she shook either leg at the mirror, determined to increase the blood flow and retain all sensation in the lower half of her body.

'There's good news and bad news,' said Emmy, reappearing from the wings with four white boxes and the three original shoes in her arms. 'I've got threes and fours in two out of the three of the ones you like.'

Mia shrugged. 'Decent odds,' she said.

'Take a seat. Let's see what they look like on you.' Still encumbered by her stock, Emmy knelt at Mia's toes. She laid out the boxes. Before Mia could kick off her own scuffed footwear, Emmy had laid a light grip on Mia's right calf and was removing the shoe. Her touch was warm. Heat climbed up from Mia's right ankle. The sensation charmed and scared her. Mia fought an urge to touch Emmy's head – to gauge the temperature and texture of her hair – but did not fight the urge to glance down the other woman's blouse. The brassiere was black and plain. 'Which foot first?' Emmy asked. She lifted the lids off the paper boxes. 'This is a four.' Once more Emmy took hold of Mia's calf, and the touch was no less precise than before; it was like a massage. Emmy helped Mia on with the new shoe, making Mia wonder if she performed such a service for all of her customers. 'How's that?'

'Comfy.'

Emmy repeated the operation on Mia's left: the removal of the existing shoe, the gentle replacement. So tired was she that Mia didn't even worry about what Emmy would think when she saw the wounds. 'And that?' the other woman asked, but her face didn't look up to catch the answer: Emmy was staring at Mia's knees. Mia felt weak. Uncertainty had blanketed every other emotion, but there was only one way to test a moment, an instinct. Leaning back slightly, Mia went up on tiptoes and opened her knees to allow Emmy a blinkered view down the tunnel of her thighs. Emmy's face moved closer. Softly she kissed Mia on the left knee and then licked at the inside of her upper left leg, her nose primly perched on the fringe of Mia's skirt.

'Not here.'

'You've been sweating,' said Emmy.

Mia took hold of Emmy's shoulders. 'Someone might come in.'

Emmy looked up. It was as if she'd awoken from a lush, fruity dream; she blinked, owlish concentration on her face. 'I saw you,' she said in a tone that was meant to imply explanation. 'Touching yourself. I was watching.'

'You don't understand,' said Mia.

'Is it the mirrors or the shoes?'

'The shoes?'

'Lot of people have a thing for shoes.'

'Well I don't. Sorry.' The taste in the back of her throat again. 'Have I spoilt it?' she asked, not knowing for sure how events had come to this poor excuse for an apology. Or even what 'it' was meant to be.

'Yes. Do you want the shoes?' She started to get up.

'Sorry. I've not been feeling well. I'm tired.'

'You can have them. Mum'll never notice.'

'Mum?'

'Kirsty. She owns this horrible little box and gives me a few bob to manage it when she's getting herself tarted up at the salon.' Emmy was exuding an air of strained professionalism. 'Still, it's better than Crew,' she added.

'Crew?'

'What those posers outside call 'emselves. So-called gang. 'Join Crew' this, 'Fear Crew' that. Load of nonsense. You'd be amazed how many fall for it.'

'They made me fear them,' Mia said.

'Well all right. But you don't have to live with 'em every day,' remarked Emmy. 'Gang's only use if there's another one to fight against, surely?'

'I suppose so. Anyway… it's a nice shop,' Mia continued.

'The lights are too bright,' said Emmy.

2.

'Zoe, it's me. Call me. It's urgent.'

Zoe sighed. Mia had used these words before, more than once; and very often the matter at hand was important, but urgent? Rarely. Being unable to choose which movie to rent wasn't urgent. Nor was realising she'd left the house keys in the bread-bin. That said, there was something in the tone that lent an uncomfortable weight to the words. The plum-coloured nail of her thumb pinched down on REPLY.

'What's up?' Zoe asked.

'I've got the fear. I'm going into one.' Mia sounded breathless.

'Calm.' This wasn't what Zoe had been expecting. 'I'm nearly home. Where are you?'

'Silbury Boulevard. Near the statue of the black horse.'

'Wait there. I'll pick you up.'

'I've got to keep moving.'

'Five minutes,' Zoe told her.

'It's raining!'

'It'll keep you awake. Jog on the spot.'

Five minutes turned out to be an exaggeration, but Zoe completed the journey from Wolverton, where she worked, in thirteen. The brakes were squeaky: they sounded like a harpooned seal. 'Climb in.'

Mia's face was awash with tears and raindrops; her makeup sat in doughy blotches from where she had rubbed her chin and cheeks too hard. At the sight of her, a memory stabbed through Zoe's concern: Mia, when they were both aged twenty-one. Mia had taken the wrong pills. To this day, if the subject were ever raised, she would insist it had been a mistake.

Mia was shaking in the same way as she had on that day. She floated into Zoe's body; they shared her spasms for nearly two minutes. Mia donated a speech mark of snot to Zoe's lapel. 'Now now...'

'It's coming,' said Mia. 'I'm falling asleep again.' It was the first clear utterance she'd made, and the clarity frightened Zoe.

'No you're not. I'm here.'

'I can taste it. The sleep.'

'I'm here. Let's go home, eh?'

Mia nodded. 'Home,' she replied, as though stunned, as though she had never again expected to hear the word, to engage in the concept, or to recognise the beast of that name. 'We'll eat early,' she declared.

They did just that. Mia roasted thumb-thick steaks in foil parcels of butter, peppers, onions and mushrooms. Zoe opened the wine and let it breathe for nearly two minutes while she watched the headlines. A cricketer had been murdered. His body slumped over the steering wheel of his car. Mia scrubbed two large potatoes. Another earthquake had raped Istanbul. Mia lacerated a lettuce. More fighting had erupted in Somalia. Mia spun around to watch the television.

Zoe moved up behind her. She hoped Mia would be able to sense the smile on her face: sense it through the hug she now provided. 'It doesn't mean you're needed,' she said.

'It's too much of a coincidence.' This said as if Mia's interlocutor was someone selling insurance, a credit card promotion, or a burial plot: the voice was dispassionate. Realism stank.

'You can't be certain.'

They ate in silence. Or rather, they ate wordlessly; Dorothy Anthony's Stable of Bongo and Brass was playing. The women pretended to listen to the rhythms while concentrating on the earlobes of sliced mushrooms, on the lagoons of meaty juices.

'I want to gaze,' said Mia. 'Leave the plates; I'll do 'em tomorrow. I'm not going to work.' She stood up. Paxo, their pet, a four year-old budgerigar, squawked 'Nuisance' and then beaked his bell.

'Let's have a smoke,' Zoe suggested.

'No. I want to see what's going on.'

At the top of the house was Mia's laboratory. Zoe was discouraged from entering, which was rich since it was a house in Zoe's name, and Zoe had no area of her own. Nevertheless, Mia knew she didn't need to lock the door. Mia drank some grape juice from the small fridge next to the printer. Then she sat at the telescope and tore a nail getting the focus sharp. Focus was weird: it changed regularly. Same sky, she thought, same stars; so why did some nights they look like diamonds and some nights like boils of pus? On different nights altogether, the sky seemed clean; on some – shadowed, filthy and dull. The sky has a character, thought Mia, and a series of dark grey overcoats. She twisted her nose-stud.

She had popped seven pills that would keep her awake through the night. Mia hadn't slept in fifty-three months, almost four and half years. Still her stomach was full. She felt happy, the bitter taste of sleep had receded. Using the mirror on the telescope, Mia removed her contacts. She kept a pair of glasses in every room, and at the end of the day she ensured she returned them. Then she read the sky.

Downstairs, Zoe was watching a quiz show called The Twitching Curtain. It was designed to assess your knowledge of your neighbours. While watching, she alternated between burning matches and then sucking them when they'd cooled, and thrashing out a kilometre on the stationary bike. She had programmed the machine to berate her if she failed to clock nine kilometres a day. It was doing so now. 'You're a disgusting herpes-carrier,' it informed her in the voice of Johnny Rotten.

'Get fucked,' Zoe told it.

The system, the premium version at the time she bought it, recognized the pre-programmed insult. 'I won't. Get busy, you lardy minge,' it said.

'Get fucked.'

'I won't. Get busy, you lardy minge.'

Zoe had inherited a pessimistic streak from her mother; it was spliced in among the other, more positive, impulses. She didn't approve of this pessimistic streak; however, she knew it defined her. Daily she knelt at its throne, and genuflected with a sigh. Nothing lasted. Even love failed the final exam. It always had, and because of this Zoe jumped at every shadow in the early stages, sensing portents of doom everywhere. The effects were magnified even further for a week every month, during which her hormones tried new dances on her. Becoming clumsy as she invariably did at this time, she would read a question mark or a death's head into the shape of a spilt lake of milk; discern something worse from a shard of crockery when she accidentally dropped a mug... Was failure looming, or would they endure? With the aid of tablets, did they even have enough left, would they endure?

There was also the intercultural angle to contend with. Mixed-race set-ups seem to have a built-in bomb, a dormant leprosy. A cancer, even; and for Zoe, fighting the affliction was a full-time occupation... Zoe struck another match. She watched it burn; she viewed the television screen through the flame and wondered what it would feel like to set fire to the whole house with her in it. Hell with it, she thought and took a cigarette from Mia's pack, on the coffee table. While inhaling she made a decision. Paxo called 'Nuisance' from the kitchen, and Zoe whispered to herself 'Come what may.' She was sticking with Mia. If need be, she would fight. Fight for the woman's long eyelashes; for the fizz of owner-hated hair around her nipples; for the deconstructed left foot. Smiling broadly, Zoe toasted her dedication to her love with a sip of wine and a further drag. She would talk to her all through the night if she had to; she would tease her, keep her waiting, keep her taut. Zoe stood.

The bike had timed ten minutes. Jamesny Rotten said, 'What are you drinking, fatso? Wine? Million calories a glass. No wonder you're so obese...a real human burger.'

'Get fucked.'

'I won't. Get busy, you lardy minge.'

With a flick of the wrist Zoe sent the remaining contents of the glass in the bike's direction. 'Now you get fat too.'

Outside Mia's laboratory Zoe paused. She listened for sounds of typing; for humming or whistling (Mia was contradictory in that she didn't wish to return to her mother country but could not break the link altogether: most of the tunes she summoned up were patriotic songs with titles that translated into 'New Dawn' or 'The Rose With No Thorns'). Nothing. Zoe knocked. Nothing. When she entered the room there was fear in her head, rattling from temple to temple like a squash ball on a court.

The window was open. Zoe crossed to where the curtains were struggling against their hooks; she peered out. Mia was sitting on what had become known as the sunroof: a small, nine metre squared terrace that served no purpose, Zoe had opined, other than to make burglars' lives easier. It was there for a storm of pigeons to congregate every lunchtime, like old men around park-square chess-tables. Mia fed them. Before they left for work in the morning, when Zoe drove her partner as far as the bus stop, Mia left breadcrumbs and bacon rind on the terrace. She cut the rind into pieces as small as ants: she was frightened of being responsible for choking one to death. Mia had a way with birds. Here she was, right now, at nine in the evening, with the moon sharply focused, with a rook in her arms. A rook. Zoe smiled, but the bird had sensed an unfamiliar presence; it called, it flapped.

Mia released the bird. Its wings churned the air as it made good its escape. 'Are you coming in or am I coming out?' asked Zoe.

'You're coming out.' Mia waited until Zoe was halfway through the aperture before adding: 'I've got something to tell you.'

3.

Children were ordered to stand near the tank: their parents wanted photographs. Defiance was in the smiles of the people – the people from each generation. On televised news reports, brown eyes twinkled proudly. Two neighbouring farmers, business enemies for their entire adult lives, had been moved to reconciliation in a story that was syndicated worldwide, and offered as a message of hope. They both agreed to siphon the petrol from their tractors; the yield was poured down the tank's deathtube – the cylinder from which so much destruction had been caused – and a burning rag was thrust into the same nozzle. For a few minutes the tank resembled a dragon, fallen and wounded, filthily snorting out its final gusts of flame. Then the smoke emerged, black and rich. The soldiers who had brought the vehicle to the village were shredded in the teeth of an ancient combine harvester, and abandoned. The slurry they became nourished weevils, crops and wild dogs.

Halima watched it all. She was twelve years old and elec-
trified by curiosity. This, it appeared after a few years of possibilities, was deemed, had been declared, no less, though by which
higher power she did not know, the year in which wild things
would happen. Nor was she solely referring to the newest violence. She had been wearing a headscarf for seven months. Her
brother had been taken. The village – the entire village – had
had an operation performed upon it: an unwanted operation, and
one conducted without the courtesy of a general anaesthetic. The
joy had been removed. As if a cyst, their joy had been extracted.
Until today, nobody had laughed for eighteen months; Halima
could not recall the last time she had watched anyone smile. She
sat in the dirty field and photographed two dogs fighting over a
soldier's spine.

Her ambition was to find Osman, her brother, who was older by two years, and in doing so to refute every scrap of sandpa-
per logic that whispered that by now he must be dead. Halima
wouldn't accept this until she had smelt his skin, or at the very
least engaged with his eyes. Halima placed the camera in her bag.
She walked home, dreaming of the city.

Dinner was ready. Her plate had cooled somewhat and her
parents had already begun to eat, their faces close to the food.
Halima's father preferred not to use a knife and fork. Between
mouthfuls scooped up by his pinched-together fingers, he reminded his remaining family there'd be ragged times before there
were smooth ones, but that this day marked a significant development. They weren't to lose hope.

Halima consulted her books. She completed her mathematics homework, sang a song, and smelt her father's pipe smoke
from the lounge. She had often viewed this smell – signifying as
it undoubtedly did the close of the working day – as her cue to
turn in for bed. She removed her clothes. But she could not rid
her nasal passages of the smell of sorghum and blood, no matter

how many times she blew her nose while lying on her side. And sleep dilly-dallied as a result; it took its own sweet time to arrive.

Eventually she dreamed of an apocalypse. The land and the sky were green. Horses had wheels instead of legs. Rice grains were black, and the stars up above were rice grains themselves. Halima – tiny Halima, childlike Halima – she had a gap in her face where her nose should be, and she squatted, whipping a dog, intending it to convey her faster to her destination, wherever that lay. She was yelling…

Suddenly she knew her purpose: she was travelling to the city, to New Trozenxus, in order to sell her photographs. But on the back of a dog? As small as she was in real life (and even in the clasp of the dream she knew this) she was not small enough to use a dog as a means of transport. It was good, she understood, to have this sort of perspective, this grade of cunning. Of sorts, it was a get-out clause. It meant whatever happened next was not her fault and could be sloughed off like an unexpected skin. It wasn't real.

'Whoah!' called Halima.

…And Halima was in an office. The temperature would have been pleasing, surely, only to gadflies and koalas. The blades of a fan moved exhausted overhead. A gold polo trophy had melted across the desk – a desk that now faced Halima. There was no one sitting in the buxom, muscular chair of dark green leather. Halima noted her eyesight was sharper than it was when she was awake. A bee settled softly into the molten gold, its buzzing effervescing as it panicked in the shiny morass. Leaving the desktop again wrenched off its legs and one wing, the bee screamed.

The door behind Halima opened. Although the girl didn't turn, she knew instinctively that what was entering was far from human. She could smell its backside.

There were two heavy footfalls, a grunt of effort… As it landed on the desk, the thick glue of gold was splashed in a score of different directions. An eruption of gold landed just below

Halima's left eye; she started. It was hot; it cooled quickly. Halima gasped. The animal – naked but for a waistcoat – turned. Apparently it did not wish to present the rucksack of its posterior; instead, still standing, it gripped the edge of the desk, leaning forward. The teeth were rank with bad diet; the ape smelled worse than exertion – worse than sweat. Its penis was twitching, growing slowly, and its mouth wrapped itself round her name.

'Halima...'

A gorilla. She was facing a gorilla.

'You need us more than we need you,' it said slowly.

4.

'You slut.'

'Zoe...'

'How could you? Haven't I put up with enough?' Zoe asked.

'Haven't I?' Mia answered.

'God. I was going to stay up all night,' said Zoe, 'with you.'

'You still could.'

'Right. Yeah right,' said Zoe, 'that sounds logical. Stay up with the woman who sticks a syringe in your heart. Think about it, Mia.'

Mia thought about something else entirely. Mia thought about the time the soldiers had entered her home.

Chocolate night. Distant smudge of watered-down yellow, hanging above the city... This time it was not a routine enquiry; there was more in the soldiers' veins, on this occasion. They did not knock. Their dirty-cream jeep came ploughing into the side of the house; the soldiers, spiked on amphetamines, had wedged the accelerator to the floor with a golf club. The impact set off, not an explosive, but the radio, which was tuned to a station from Cairo. Carrying machine guns, the soldiers followed the vehicle inside; they barked their orders, with barely suppressed terror in their eyes. She could see it through the pools of dust that followed them. The jeep had landed the men in the kitchen. The table had been shoved against the wall and had lost its two front legs.

There were three of them. And there were three people present in the house, although the soldiers had expected to find four. Mia was collected in an ad hoc fireman's lift, against which she did not bother to resist. She was plonked on her parents' bed; her father drew her close with an arm that smelt of diesel, and it was this unfamiliarly protective gesture that shocked her fully to a wakeful state.

'Where is he? Where is he?' the soldiers kept screaming.

'Not here!' Mia's father protested.

'You have him already!' said her mother. 'Leave us in peace!'

One of the soldiers found this latest complaint hilarious. The drug made him speak quickly. 'In peace? Have you been asleep for the last two years?'

'I don't want to go back,' said Mia quietly, though not to the soldiers.

'Well, you should have thought of that, shouldn't you,' Zoe told her, 'before you started whoring around on me.'

Mia closed her eyes. 'Please,' she didn't quite begged. 'I didn't whore around. It was a moment of madness. I can't believe it even happened.'

'You're telling me!' Zoe got up, as carefully as usual, she was frightened of falling to the crazy paving below, and hooked her left leg onto the windowsill. 'We'll continue this inside,' she declared. 'I'm getting cold.'

'I want to be cold.'

'Stay out all night then. See if I care. I'll lock the window.'

When Mia failed to respond to the threat, Zoe accepted a rich pang of envy to the stomach. She did care. She was slightly drunk but that didn't change the fact she had spent a fair chunk of the evening in convincing herself that Mia was a cause worth fighting for. Zoe left Mia's laboratory. She entered the bathroom and sat on the edge of the bath, shivering; when she began to cry she reached for the toilet paper and tugged. The paper gutted forward in arcs.

Mia remained in Somalia. One of the soldiers – the one who spoke too quickly – was using a strength and an endurance beyond that of most men. He was holding Mia upside-down by the left ankle. 'What if I bite off her toes?' he asked. 'Then will you tell us where he is?'

'You have him!' said Mia's father. At gunpoint he and his wife remained in their marital bed. They were watching their daughter not struggling; they were listening to her not complaining. The soldier moved Mia's foot closer to his open mouth; his teeth were as yellow as the bedroom light.

Mia felt dizzy. More than the discomfort of being gripped so hard by the ankle, she was experiencing – and trying to combat – a sensation of acute embarrassment. When the soldier had inverted her, the hem of her nightdress had fallen down around her head; she was now inside a thin tent that smelt of her own skin – on display, a piece of meat.

She'd heard the stories, of course: girls of any age, was what they said. This was why she now struggled, not to escape (futile) but to resist her other leg's tendency, as it was not supported in the same way, to drift aimlessly. She had to keep her legs together. Her right upper thigh was stretched; it was unfamiliar for Mia to use the muscle in this way. But she was determined to keep contact with the soldiers' knuckles – keep contact with her right ankle.

'Please let her go,' Mia heard, inside her cotton cocoon.

I'm a small girl, she thought. Everyone told her how small she was, as if that might be something she longed to have confirmed; as if being small was desirable. I could hurt him from here.

Hurt him before he hurts me, she thought. She could feel his breath on the sole of her left foot. Before he bites my toes.

'Please, no!' Mia's father said – but there was a swelling in his voice; a richer pulse of panic. Mia sensed movement in the room; it ruffled the nightdress in front of her nose. One of the soldiers had moved close – and Mia's mother now screamed. What was happening? Mia's heart rate increased. Something cold was placed on her big toe.

Father said, 'Don't shoot her! Please!'

Shoot me? A salty taste flooded her mouth. Mia's fear got the better of her, and without really knowing what she was doing she writhed. She lashed out with her fist, aiming for the groin of the man who held her.

On the terrace, Mia shivered. The night was doing its frosty work against her skin, but so was the memory. A few doors away, the lid of a bin slammed: someone had deposited their rubbish for tomorrow's collection. The nose had a fraction of the decibels of that gunshot. Reflexively Mia touched her mangled left foot: the foot with no toes, the foot whose end now resembled a ploughed field.

'Why don't you come in?' Zoe said through the open window. The tear-tracks in the moonlight were icy paths. 'Mia? Mia? Halima?'

Mia nodded. 'Sorry. Miles away… Looks like rain,' she said. She stood up and rubbed her palms together. 'They couldn't find him.'

Zoe waited for a second, sifting. 'Your brother? I know, Mia.'

'They couldn't find him. He'd already gone.'

'I know, Mia,' repeated Zoe. 'But we will. I'll keep you awake.'

5.

Easiest thing would be to forgive and forget. This was why Zoe, come lunchtime, was sitting in her lounge-sized car, looking for a parking space. She always chose the path of highest resistance; this was what made her good at her job. But this wasn't work. This was love. Zoe was doing this for the love. She parked on Farthing Grove and climbed out into the grizzling autumn air. She removed chewing gum from her mouth and wrapped it carefully, cleanly, in its original foil, depositing the parcel in a fire-ravaged bin outside Kirsty Heels.

Inside it was bright and cool. A child was having his right foot measured. Zoe walked to the counter and waited for the young woman to finish her call.

'Can I help?'

This wasn't the one. Her tag said Kelyeena, which Zoe thought a very pretty name (with uncertain etymology) – so appropriate for such a pretty face.

'I was looking for Emmy.'

'She's called in sick today, I'm afraid. Are you a friend?'

Zoe bit down on the irony, and forced its tone away from her answer. 'Friend of a friend,' she replied. 'Is it possible you could get a message to her?'

'Sure.'

'Better still, could you give her my mobile number. Say it's about the Somalian lady.' Zoe returned to her car. Having made the break to get out of the studio for an hour (she never stopped for lunch, for reasons of her own, and how suspicious the team had been!), she was now reluctant to go back so soon. She decided to get a drink. She felt the lure. She felt the pulse that constituted the reason why she did not take lunch breaks. There was a pub a few doors down from Kirsty Heels: The Netherfield. She liked it that the establishment seemed rough; she relished the impact her business suit might make.

Although it was scarcely past noon, the place was full of drinkers, tabloids, bald pates and empty crisp packets as shrivelled as used condoms. Near a gambling machine a group of youths in their late teens or early twenties were talking at volume about the previous evening's TV offerings. If things didn't calm down quickly, Zoe thought, there was going to be a fight.

'A large glass of your finest chardonnay, please.'

The barman was wearing a white vest. His left eye was made of glass. Every millimetre of his skin had been decorated with scenes from the Bible. 'We've got red and we've got white,' he told her.

'White, please.'

The barman turned to fetch down a suitable glass. Zoe saw his name – Dave – tattooed on the back of his neck in purple ink. She wondered why anyone would feel the need to let everybody know his identity. She accepted her drink with a thank you that sounded false to her own ears. She sat.

The first sip of the day was a relief. Her cells responded with gratitude. As she moved down her glass, she watched the patrons of The Netherfield at rest. Or perhaps this was work – for them, perhaps, this attendance, this dedication, it was work. Perhaps. She could certainly recall a time when drinking had been a full-time job for her.

Alcohol was to thank for Zoe's introduction to Mia. The scene was the South of France. Having finished her A-Levels, Zoe was beating her wings on a two-week holiday in the sun, with a friend from school. She had completed her final exam (the Metaphysical Poets, and as it happened she'd been drunk through that as well), and after taking a drink with her classmates, she went home to throw clothing and cosmetics into a bag. In the morning she would set off, with Greta, for the sea. On the third night the girls attended a beach party. Mia was also present. She had made it that far, on her exodus from Africa.

The phone in Zoe's handbag rang: 'Wouldn't It Be Nice?' by the Beach Boys. UNFAMILIAR NUMBER, said the display above an electronic rendition of the Mona Lisa. Zoe accepted the call and said her full name.

'It's Emmy.' But before Zoe was given a chance to respond, the caller went on. 'She's given it to me, you bitch. I've got it bad. I'm dissolving.' Something brittle and static-like in her voice.

'She's given you what?' Zoe asked, a second or two later, when words seemed to mean something again.

'I don't know. I'm frightened.'

Tell her straight; tell her not to touch Mia. Tell her to back away. Tell her life won't be worth living. Use the phone as your weapon and the distance as your shield... But this was the easiest thing to do: to summon anger in the face of your lover's adultery; to scream into the ear of your challenger. And Zoe shied from the obvious as oil does from water.

'Where are you?'

'At home,' Emmy whispered. 'In bed.'

'I'll come and see you. Come and help. Do you live in Netherfield?'

'Beanhill.'

It was nothing more than a word on a road sign to Zoe, but she would find it: she would find the address Emmy now provided in a voice that sounded, word by word, increasingly clogged. What burned in her breast was more than curiosity, although that was there too. What burned in Zoe's breast was a desire, a need, to punish. She returned to the bar and ordered another glass of white wine, which she intended to drink slowly, the better to make the cow wait.

6.

Twelve flies on a body means it's dead, her grandmother had taught her early on. Grandmother had been dead herself for five years, but Halima took her out walking from time to time. She needed the exercise, or so the twelve year-old believed. Grandmother was with her now, beside the river. And beside the horse: the roan that was entertaining a party of flies a good deal larger than twelve strong. What was more, Halima had only been down to the riverbank's 45-degree angle for twenty minutes.

'I told you not to go,' said Grandmother.

'No you didn't!' Halima said with such ugly vehemence that the older woman was obliged to take a step back.

'Well I thought it,' she offered sulkily, then remained silent for some time.

In the interim Halima knelt. There was space enough in her grief for her to wonder: why do flies always gather around the eyes? What's so attractive about them? Poor old Osman, she pined. What have I done to you?

The horse was as dead as its own brown apples, which were lying trussed-up in the hairs of its tail. Lying, also, like punctuation marks or mathematical symbols in the road behind its rump. It had shat itself upon expiration, it appeared. The sight made Halima feel sadder. Poor beast. She was crying. She hugged Osman's neck. Horse-smell had always comforted the girl, but now it punched pimples onto her scalp. 'I'm sorry.'

She was four days away from the village. With insects in her hair, she was heading towards New Trozenxus. Some people eat horses, she thought. She couldn't do that, but what could she do? Can't leave him here, she thought feverishly. Her mind scratched around for a solution. One image proved more obdurate than others: the image of a role-reversal, with Halima carrying the horse on her back. Halima giggled. Then she started to count the flies on Osman's lips: one, two, miss a few, ninety-nine, one hundred – that was the joke when they were little. One of the children of the village would cover his eyes and the rest had to run and hide. But the counter would cheat, the children would laugh. Usually. There had been that time, of course, when Muna had been counting – she'd only been six and she'd wanted to play funny, like the other kids. But they'd been angry with Muna; they had knocked her to the ground and kicked her until her right hipbone speared through her cotton dress… Halima was laughing now. It wasn't the memory that caused such mirth: it was the flies, they seemed to be multiplying before the girl's eyes. In her head she recited the powers of two. Two squared was four; two cubed was eight; two to the fourth power was sixteen, thirty-two, sixty-four, one-two-eight.

She was hungry; this didn't help her state of mind. Four days from the village and she had already eaten her week's worth of food. Boredom and trepidation had conspired to make her greedy. Now that Halima's laughter was dying down (she couldn't double the value of 8192), horror and loneliness was starting to weigh down on the top of her head. Cast adrift; and for the first time since setting off before the birds had started singing, Halima was scared. Guilty, too. If she hadn't eaten so much, perhaps she wouldn't have needed to take that break in the shallows of the river. Maybe Osman would still be alive.

Stupid! Why had she come? Why had she spent a fortnight on the collection and storage of food? Why risk public outrage by sneaking into the headmaster's office at dawn, to break open the filing cabinet containing his weapons? Why had she stolen that pistol? Because of dreams? It was too late to do so – too late by four long days – but Halima told herself to grow up. The bushes were whispery with insect life and snakes; the sun was a blazing semi-colon in a cloak of clouds... and Halima was miles from anywhere, friendless, foodless and quietly desperate.

The road had once been handsome. Before the soldiers came, when the only thing to fear had been rumours, the country had been proud of its thriving economy. Money had gone into the Department for Roads, and battered trade routes had been improved with toupees of tarmac. Now, after months of mortar bombardment and tank deployment, even minor roads looked pocked and mottled, with pieces of bone as decorations. Two days ago, Halima had seen a brain – just a brain – on top of a fencepost, resembling a wet loaf of bread, and of uncertain origin. A rook perched on the brain: a king on his throne. Silently the rook had watched Halima pass by on her horse. Halima had seen the indentations the rook's feet had made on the surface of the brain, and she'd wondered how, in the heat, the organ had remained so efficiently preserved. Halima told herself, and possibly Osman, too, and even her grandmother, that this was going to be the year the wild things happened.

The road stretched out. Continue towards the city, or sit down, mourn Osman, and wait while her brain fried for some adults to find her, she wondered. Even if they happened to be soldiers? Third option was to turn around and commence the long trek home. A worm of nausea crawled in Halima's breastbone. She thought of her parents; she thought, surprisingly, of her schoolbooks. And the thought of what she was doing – or intended to do – the promise she'd made to herself and to them in a farewell letter – to find their son – this made her cough twice and start walking. Walking in the direction she'd been headed.

She was not alone.

The decrepit old road dipped and climbed. When Halima was down in the dip she thought back to Osman; of how she might, strength willing, have shoved the horse down the riverbank and into the water. This achieved, she might even have had something to look forward to on the off chance she reached the city: something other than hunger and fear. Osman's sweat would be in the water; his dead eyes would see her down the long watery path.

Her regret felt as strong as nostalgia. Halima could taste it, too: coppery and vile. Feeling weak, she crested the hill, a suspicion niggling her brain – a suspicion that the forced breaths she could hear might not be coming only from her own mouth. She stopped on the crest. The sight before her made a clutch for her breastbone, and suddenly Halima felt weak at the knees.

Two dogs were standing in her path. One was grey, a mutt, a mongrel; it had an old wound stamped to its left flank. When Halima was able to think again, she thought: Bullet hole. Someone had used this animal for target practice. The dog to Halima's right, on the other hand, was a handsome beast, with a full coat of lavishly-attended-to brown fur. Both dogs were considerably larger than adult elephants.

'You're late,' said the dog with the brown fur.

7.

Mia was shaking. It happened from time to time: a reaction to amphetamines and to the exertion of staying awake. And to the fear, of course: to the fear whose shawl she wore; the fear she was being hounded by the past, being shadowed, always shadowed, leaned-upon, eavesdropped and analysed. During panic attacks, Mia doubted her own contention that she was living proof human beings didn't need sleep. She doubted sleep was nothing more than a conspiracy. She questioned her beliefs, sank into a trance of depression.

She made some coffee. Soaked her face in the boiling steam glutting from the kettle. Shit, I fell asleep. The realisation hit her in the gut. Her hands were shaking so badly that the teaspoon rattled in the mug, and it did so with the urgency of a bellringer informing the city the enemy is on its way. Lifting the mug to her mouth, she spilled coffee onto her breasts and lap. She tried to imagine when it could have happened.

Last night she had slept with Zoe, but only (she had believed until a second ago) in the euphemistic sense. Not that Zoe's tongue or fingers meant that Mia had been forgiven. Far from it, if precedence had anything to say for itself. No; Zoe used sex as a sign of temporary appeasement. There would – and how Mia loved this phrase in English – be hell to pay. Wasn't that great? Mia continued shaking. Every time she slept she made herself vulnerable. She risked the cancellation of all the bodily effort she had endured: that wasn't fair. A simple snooze, and she might as well not have bothered to escape from Somalia. The trek – the trucks, the hitchhikes, not to mention the permitted fumbles of feigned appreciation – would all have been to waste. She'd go back. In-deed, on a dozen or so occasions over the last sixty months, she had contemplated giving in. Just surrender; it's not worth it. But she had always managed to convince herself otherwise. She would picture a colossal astral vacuum cleaner, playing down upon Mil-ton Keynes, her home: sucking back the years as if they were tumbleweeds of fluff. This image made the hard work worth the effort: this image, and the thought of her life slipping back five twelve-month-long chapters. The appropriation of a new identity; the tongue-twisters of a new language; the journey across Europe; meeting Zoe. The ghosts of a wiped out existence would stumble across the skies, from star to star.

Never again would Mia kill a human. If she refused to let the gorillas into her dreamscapes, they couldn't force or train her to commit more dreamcrimes. Never again would she wolf on unprotected skin.

So reiterating, Mia took her place on the exercise bike. She pedalled slowly, cigarette in her mouth. The bike admonished her for her filthy habit (Zoe's programming), but after all she'd survived Mia was less receptive to bullying and insults than Zoe was. Mia told the machine to show some respect. If it didn't, she would starve it of electricity. The machine shut up. The threat of deprivation was a beautiful one, thought Mia, laughing out loud. Considering her own predicament, she was sure that the state-ment qualified as irony.

She was in a good mood, then, when the phone rang. It hadn't lasted long, and it was about to be stabbed dead, but it couldn't be denied: Mia was in a good mood. This meant, unfor-tunately, that she wasn't ready for the call. Not moving from the bike, she said 'Hello?' and the mike picked up her voice.

'Mia Abdi,' said an officious voice. For a second Mia imag-ined this was going to be about her interview. 'My name is Ser-geant Haines.' Your name is Sergeant? thought Mia. 'I'm calling from the police station,' he said, padding out the inevitable. 'I'm afraid I have some bad news. It's about Zoe Field...'

'Yes?' Mia stopped pedalling. The motor whirred on for a few more seconds. That was more than could be said for Mia's optimism.

'I'm afraid there's been an accident,' said Haines. 'A road accident.'

'No.'

'I'm sorry to tell you this, Miss Abdi.'

'Please don't,' begged Mia. 'Just don't. Don't say it.'

8.

It wasn't on the drive to Emmy's house, but rather on her swift drive away from it, that Zoe crashed the car. Nor did she have time to regret the alcohol she had so passionately consumed; there were other matters very much on her mind. The universe folded in on itself in a riot of pain and din.

Zoe shouted once for her mother.

Less than two hours earlier, she had arrived at Emmy's place: a thin, three-storey affair and an authentic slice of history. When the builders had created this hellhole, back in the twentieth century, they had needed somewhere to live for the duration of the construction. These homes had since been the subjects of concerted, genuine-spirited makeover, but the original ghosts – the poor quality materials, the burglarable facades – had endured.

Girding herself for the task in hand took Zoe next to no time. She was drunk. All she had to do was ensure her limbs were moving satisfactorily and this sorry incident would soon be no more than a footnote. She held her breath for ten seconds (she was hiccupping) and rang the bell, which rattled like a pea in a matchbox.

Long wait. The door was opened cautiously. With the possibility of further action (a slamming, for example) remaining visible. 'Zoe?'

The woman wasn't even pretty. This damaged Zoe's ego – with a swift salvo of pins – far worse than would have been the case if a supermodel had arrived to greet the afternoon drafts in her underwear. 'Yes.'

Emmy nodded. 'Come in,' she said, and abruptly turned away from the door. She followed the passageway for three short strides and turned right. Zoe entered; she closed the door and acknowledged the music of the Bee Gees: 'Staying Alive'. The house smelt of sickness and citron.

'Take a seat. Drink?'

'I haven't come here to be your friend,' said Zoe.

'I haven't invited you here for that either,' Emmy replied. 'Drink?'

'White wine?' said Zoe through a sigh.

'I've got vodka or gin.'

'Vodka.' Remembering her manners, Zoe added 'Please. Ice and lemon, if you've got them.'

'Two secs.'

It was brought to her: a quadruple or even quintuple measure, in an Empire State glass; there was an Antarctica of ice therein. It was positioned on the right-hand side of Zoe's armchair.

'Thanks.'

'Don't mention it.' The tone was pure salad dressing: necessary, but tart. 'I'd give the fucking Ripper a drink if he came here. Doesn't mean-'

'-we love each other,' said Zoe. 'Understood. Thanks anyway.' Weren't they reiterating their earlier points? Business loomed. There were words that Zoe had to utter before the wall clock's ticking drove her mad. 'What did you mean, dissolving?' she asked. 'You look pretty formed to me.'

Emmy nodded. 'It's mainly on my chest and arse at the mo,' she answered, sitting down in the opposite chair. She established her position like a hen. 'And you're expecting me to say: wanna see? Well I won't.'

'What are we doing here?' Zoe asked. She took a good pull on her drink. In pleasure she gasped and licked her lips. The vodka was chilled and strong, just as she enjoyed it.

'Okay, you want the floor show? Here goes. Be warned.' With which Emmy lifted her top to clavicle height.

A moment of stunned silence ensued.

'Jesus Christ...'

'... won't help me now. But exactly.'

Emmy wasn't dissolving. But beneath the ramparts of green brassiere the skin was in a state that was far from healthy. There was mottling; there was blood-show. At a couple of points – and here logic took a bow to the senses – it appeared as though the skin disguised nothing. It was transparent. Above Emmy's left hip was a narrow but crystal-clear path of visibility to one of the woman's pulsing organs.

Not knowing what to say, Zoe sipped her drink. The Bee Gees moved into 'You Win Again'. 'I know what you're thinking,' said Emmy. 'You intended to be all butch and territorial...'

'Butch?'

'... and tell me never go near your girlfriend again. Thought you had the upper hand. It's amazing what a disfiguring skin condition can do to change things, isn't it?'

Ice burned on Zoe's upper lip. Only when it had become clear that Emmy requested an answer to what ordinarily would have been a rhetorical question did Zoe say: 'You seem to know a lot about human behaviour.'

Emmy shrugged. 'I'm doing Psychology at the college.'

Bully for you, thought Zoe. 'I suggest you get yourself to the doctor. I don't know what else to say. Yes I do. What makes you think this has anything to do with Mia?'

Emmy smiled. 'Did you think this couldn't get any weirder?'

'Not really.'

'It's about to. She came to me in a dream.'

'Mia did?'

Emmy nodded. 'Now I know her name, Mia did. She visited me last night. Told me my soul had no chance. Prophetically enough.'

'You seem to find this amusing,' Zoe told her.

'Yeah. And you haven't seen the really funny bit.' For a fraction of a second Emmy paused. Zoe inferred from the silence that the other woman was making a decision – doing the calculations, the tallies, the pluses and minuses – of whether or not to allow someone into a secret. 'Come on,' said Emmy, standing up. 'It's in the kitchen.'

Zoe followed her through, even sharing (although she hated to admit it) Emmy's unquestionable pleasure at knowing what was about to be revealed. It was like Christmas Day, Zoe thought. As a child she'd always been delighted by her parents' excited expressions as she'd torn open her presents.

An odd aroma in the kitchen: medicinal. This scent had been buried under a layer of cleaning product breezes. Here was a woman who really loved to keep things spotless. She looked about the small room. 'Where?'

'In the sink. But you'll have to look hard,' Emmy warned.

Zoe put one hand on the draining board and the other on the fridge; she leaned forward, squinting into an inch of pistol-grey water, where a lone teaspoon was anchored. She'd expected that medicinal smell to be stronger, with her face nearer the surface. This wasn't the case.

Aware of movement behind her back, Zoe was halfway to her full posture when she felt the force and dampness of a piece of cloth being applied to her face. That smell: closer now, as close as it could get – sense-blurringly close. Zoe struggled. But Emmy was strong and determined. She held the chloroform-moistened cloth over Zoe's mouth while maintaining a hold on the woman's upper body with her other arm around Zoe's neck. Darkness was pooling in the corners of Zoe's eyes. Not that she had given up her thrashings. Quite the reverse: desperation had made her powerful; but the wrestle was short lived.

9.

The brown-furred dog was called James Carbon.

'Pleased to meet you, Halima,' he had said before offering her his back as a means of transport. What Halima had taken for imperial impatience soon thawed; within minutes, she was defending the dog. Perhaps he had sounded tense as the result of mastering a foreign dialect. Nothing else was real about the situation, after all, so why not direct some more dream logic its way?

Frank Mice. The other dog, the mangy dog, went by the name of Frank Mice. This one couldn't speak. Halima regarded the inability with amusement.

They were heading for New Trozenxus. A rare but welcome rain was falling – falling as gently as feathers, as though upset by the prospect of causing offence or irritation. Gratefully Halima looked up. She smiled. She'd been staring at James Carbon's back for the duration of some miles. Enough. She sent a heartfelt blessing to the sky. As a result, 'You're a lovely girl,' said a voice at the back of Halima's head. The sound of her grandmother's tones made Halima smile wider. Silently they trudged on. Halima's hips were wriggling to the dog's walking rhythm: so different from that of Osman! And the girl was comfortable; not once was she tempted to leap from the tower. It all seemed perfectly prepared; it seemed apt.

The circumference was marked by its hamburger shacks and an oily accrual of motorised traffic. Halima felt both horrified and appeased, like a May Queen on a float. To observe the procession thin children kicking balls stopped doing so, grinning; their parents, or at any rate adults, ceased their roadside bartering, their arguments. They didn't smile. There were vehicle spare parts establishments; cafes too. There were shops selling foam rubber, hats and pets. Embarrassed, Halima was not sure how to respond to the children waving. She didn't know if she felt better or worse with the understanding that sitting astride a giant dog was still a novelty. Even here: here in the cultured city.

Still they followed the river, more or less. Occasionally James Carbon would take a detour through a suburb of canvas, where the air smelled of burning beans on a camp stove. But they always returned to the river's green yawn. And its scent: ancient and yet alive. Grinning bandidos logged her progress towards the heart; Halima even witnessed the aftermath to a violent crime: using a penknife, a man was spooning out a dead man's eyes. His moustache twitched and writhed in no more then minor irritation. The air thickened with the stench of petrol; it shimmered with the risky pulse of commerce and economic agility.

'We're nearly at the Tower of Crumbs,' said James Carbon. Then he sneezed. Halima sneezed too. You could taste the germs in the air. 'This fuckin' city always makes me feverish,' he muttered on.

Halima knew all the answers she required were on their way. Why query the Tower of Crumbs? With the shoe shops, the fruit stands, the juice bars, the restaurants, there was plenty more to squabble for her attention; there was always that acute sense of embarrassment to cultivate as she became more and more of a viewpoint, an item — for lorry driver and bus driver (and passengers) alike. Even the city's insects were circling for a gozz. Traffic made its way through the city's polluted fibres, through its chambers.

The two dogs — James Carbon and Frank Mice — stopped outside a narrow grey building and briefly glanced up toward the zenith. Mice barked — the first sound Halima had heard him make.

'Here's here,' said James Carbon, settling gently onto his belly.

'Thanks,' said Halima, suddenly nervous. What next? 'Do I get down?'

'Unless you want to stay up there all day,' he answered curtly.

After swinging her leg over, Halima slid down James Carbon's left flank in a brisk abseil. For the first time she noticed the dogs had not been wagging their tails. This worried her.

The tall doors opened as Halima climbed the short flight of stone steps. Her approach triggered off a puff of flowery scent, which helped to calm her for a few seconds. Inside it was cool. The lobby was made of glass. It was the cleanest building Halima had ever entered. She walked towards the desk, behind which a beige woman wearing a headscarf looked up from her screen. She said: 'Hello and good morning.'

Halima tried to copy the older woman's smile, and to embark on an adult construction – an adult sentence. 'I'm told I've been expected,' she said. 'James Carbon brought me here.'

If she had expected any recognition of the name, the receptionist's response disappointed her – it squashed that instinct as flat as a pillowcase. 'Twelve floor. Room 96B. You'll have to sign in.' Then she repeated the direction as if Halima had failed to comprehend.

'Who am I here to see?' Halima asked.

'Mort Fega,' said the receptionist. 'Thank you.'

Halima still wished to challenge the dream that had waved the starting flag for this entire adventure. 'And what does he look like?' she asked.

'Miss?'

'What does Mr Fega look like? Please.'

The receptionist took a second to adjust her headscarf. 'He is a gorilla, madam. So he looks like a gorilla. I'm not sure I understand your question.'

Halima walked towards the elevators. She felt she had aged a year for every day she'd spent on her travels, and then a year for every second she'd spent inside the building. A rock song from the west was playing inside the car. Over the guitars, the elevator's voice asked her where she wanted to go. She arrived five seconds later. She stepped out.

Children's voices reached her ears: not words exactly, but shrieks and laughs. It was playtime in the crèche.

Halima knocked on the door. The glass was warm from the temperature inside the room. A fly approached the glass from the opposite direction, as if to see who had come calling, or to escape the monstrous heat. But Halima didn't pay it any mind. Her attention had been totally claimed by the primate in the green leather chair. It waved her in.

Mort Fega waved her in. The temperature caused Halima to disappear into a momentary shock, far worse than a dousing of ice-cold water would have been. She snapped out of it as Mort said 'Good morning.' She thought about asking if they could leave the door open.

As if he had read her mind, Mort added, 'You get used to it. Take a seat.'

Halima's fear returned with all the urgency of a repressed memory. It was like something blooming inside her chest.

'Five years ago,' said Mort Fega, 'we didn't even know it could be girls. We thought it had to be boys.'

'What couldn't?' Halima asked.

And he told her.

10.

Mia had stopped loving English buses. The five-year honeymoon had finished. As a worker she had always enjoyed their boredom – their predictability, their usefulness, their sense of communion as she learned to recognise the faces of her fellow passengers – but this was no longer the case. Now she hated English buses. They had cheated on her; Mia now associated buses with bad times. Panic attacks, weighty news. Their cumbersome burden through the estates.

She was on her way to Netherfield. Fuck it, she thought, a wormish wriggling appearing in her womb, I'm not getting off.

I'll ride till the end of the line and get shouted at by some scab of a driver for not disembarking. Coffee Hall, Beanhill, Leadenhall was it? Or the other way around? Although she had made the journey from home to work and work to home on countless occasions, Mia remained unsure of the geography of her adoptive city. It was one of the things she most liked about herself.

Matters couldn't be postponed. Mia stepped off at the hospital and sold her soul to the devil for a safe passage across the V-Road. As fast as she could she walked to the shopping precinct. Spittle was in the air.

There was no ambulance. There were no spectators. The air was as grey as glass at gloaming. The properties were steadfast and defiant. What did you expect? they seemed to say. Bass from a rap record thudded – from the chicken express joint at the toe-end of the parade. The clouds were muscular.

What's going on? thought Mia, feeling hot. She looked around.

A man dressed for the rain finished his phone call at the line of booths and approached her. He had a scarecrow's face. 'You must be Mia.'

'Yes.'

'Do you remember the Tower of Crumbs?'

The words were an efficient vehicle – every bit as efficient as the buses on which she depended. The words took her back to New Trozenxus. Back to her recruitment...

A world of blood. Mia remembered the feel of the spear she'd pushed through the breastplate of the wailing mechanic. The knife she'd used to remove a baby's fingers; she could hear the girl's parents as they whistled their pain and outrage.

'You've led us quite a dance, Mia,' said the man, reaching into his glistening raincoat. 'Cigarette?'

'Who are you?' Mia asked.

'Sergeant Haines, if you like.' He pinched a smoke free of its box. 'Or maybe you'd prefer James Carbon.' He sparked up.

'You're coming back, Mia.'

'I'm not. Where's Zoe?'

'No idea. I wanted to get you away from the house.'

Mia felt a bright flare of hope. 'So the bit about the road accident…'

'Fabrication.' Carbon exhaled. 'I owe you an apology for that: thought it best to catch you weak. Now I see I needn't have bothered.'

Sensing no immediate threat, Mia even risked a smile. 'Your English is very good,' she said.

'Thank you. Just an implant. Are you hungry?'

'No,' Mia lied. Absurdly, briefly, she felt superior to Carbon: she had learned from books, and from experience. Like a drought-ravaged flower the sensation withered and died. There had only been one reason to eschew a language implant: she couldn't afford one. Books and headphones had been her only option. She was sick of only having one choice.

'There's a chicken place down the parade. We could have some wings.'

There was also the shoe shop: Kirsty Heels. From this angle Mia could only just see the door, thin as a side of card. Nevertheless, Emmy's face entered her consciousness. 'No,' said Mia. 'Do you like Indian food?'

'I'm a dog, Mia. I like all food.'

'Okay then. You drive.'

James Carbon smirked. 'How far?'

'Ten minutes. Westcroft.' Such was Mia's relief at learning the news of Zoe's death had been a hoax that she had yet to feel angry about the lie – or even nervous. Determination was one thing (she wasn't going back) but that had been there all along. Only while eating did Mia understand that she'd experienced less emotion on meeting James Carbon again than she would have done on a blind date.

They ordered pappadums. 'So how you been, Mia?' asked Carbon as he spooned sweet chilli onto a broken-off piece the shape of a door key.

Mia realised she hated the way he used her name in nearly every question. Had always hated it, in fact. 'Fine.'

Carbon swallowed his mouthful. His eyes were as bright as newly minted coins. 'You're not going monosyllabic on me, are you, Mia? Relax! Nice meal…'

'I've been fine. So I said fine.'

'Fine.' Carbon rammed a huge piece of pappadum into his mouth and crunched earnestly, his brow furrowed, for a few seconds. 'Well,' he said, his breath spicy, 'if you'll forgive me, Mia, you don't look fine. You look tired.'

'Surprise surprise.' Mia applied chutney, unable to resist the food any longer. Something yawned inside her belly: it was gratitude.

'You've done well,' Carbon told her. He could even munch appreciatively, Mia decided at this moment. 'You were a devil to find. No pun intended.'

'None received.'

Carbon frowned. 'What was it I ordered again?'

'Lamb tandoori,' said Mia.

'Ah yeah… You were saying.'

'Nothing.'

'No, I was saying: you were a slippery fish, Mia.' He pointed an arrow of starters at her. 'I'm not the first to try looking.'

'What happened to the others?'

Carbon shrugged. 'Missing in action.' Like a prizewinner he grinned. 'Hey, what do you think they'd do if I took a piss in their fish tank?'

'Serve it up in a sauce. You can't find him?'

'Her. And no, Halima, you're not the only one to work out your masking techniques. But you've had the most stamina, I'll give you that.'

Mia pouted. 'Who's Halima?'

'Sorry?'

'You just called me Halima. Who is she? My pursuer?'

'Yes,' said James Carbon. 'Slip of the tongue, I apologise.' It appeared as though he was about to say more, when the main courses arrived, sizzling. The volume in the restaurant dipped: the other diners treated the moment of delivery as reverently as those who were about to consume the food.

After the volume had risen again, James Carbon said: 'Mia. A question.'

'Okay. Why don't you leave me alone?' Deliberately misunderstanding his request. 'I've got someone who loves me here.'

'You amuse me. So what was all that in the shoe shop yesterday?'

The knowledge terrified Mia. 'How would you know about that?' she demanded. 'How, James?'

'Seriously: do you think I arrived yesterday? I've been watching you for quite a while, Mia. You've got a nice home, by the way.'

'...Where's Zoe?'

'Where did you leave her? At work I'd imagine. How's your food?'

'Fuck the food...'

'An interesting idea.'

'Where is she?'

'How would I know?' For the first time since their reunion James Carbon seemed annoyed. Mia glimpsed, through the parcel of new human features he'd adopted, a muzzle and a long pink tongue, sharper teeth. 'Who you choose to share your bed with, Mia, is none of my business, okay? Rely on that. I don't care.' With which he ducked his head to the lamb. Although he continued to use his knife and fork, there was now less caution and fewer manners employed.

Mia remembered how to hate him. She remembered the night the drugged-up soldiers had driven into her home; she remembered the darkness, after they'd blown away half of her left foot. That darkness had lasted for days. When she'd felt the prick of the needle in her arm, she'd opened her eyes…

'My pursuer: Halima. Was that her real name?'

'No. This is good. Try your food, Mia. We changed her mind. We had to. I lost a lot of face when you escaped – no pun intended. I passed her off as you.'

'Why?'

James Carbon looked up. 'Why? Because you escaped. No one had managed before. And I wanted to see how far you would get. I followed you.'

Mia swallowed several mouthfuls of her jalfreezi. Although the taste was good, and she was hungry, she did not enjoy what she was eating.

'You know what I've done, James,' she said.

'I do indeed.'

'And yet you're not scared of me. Why not?'

James Carbon shrugged his shoulders. 'It's obvious, isn't it?' he asked. 'Because you're going to have to sleep sometime. Sleep properly, that is. And when you do, I'm close enough to get you. You're going home, like it or not.'

11.

A square of light was getting bigger – getting longer. This was how Zoe was measuring time. It seemed like a civilised thing to do: measuring time. And there was nothing else to do anyway. In spite of the fact that her brain and senses seemed close to an area known as frantic, her body was not up to the transition. Her limbs remained deadened. There was nowhere for her limbs to go.

The light was entering through a spotted window. Beyond the glass grew a few green weeds. I'm underground, thought Zoe with a confident nod. *I'm in a basement...* She traced the path of light from the glass to the floor and back again; in this path swam a thousand motes of dust. She tried to move.

Upright on a chair, Zoe had been tied into place, using a rope or a cable that pinched at her wrists. Her ankles were shackled to the chair-legs. Outside the lengthening rectangle of light on the floor, there was nothing to see: the basement had been left unilluminated. *Did the varying shape of the rectangle mean the sun was sinking or rising? How long have I been here?*

Full consciousness was returning. One by one little spots of darkness lit up, and the effect had nothing to do with her eyes becoming accustomed to the gloom. She could smell the rag that had been forced onto her face; a trace of the scent had been placed on her upper lip. A jumbled set of memories slowly shuffled itself into the correct order...

Mia.

Emmy, thought Zoe. *I'm in Emmy's basement.* She didn't shout. Her throat made a click and a whine, as it sometimes would if she had smoked too many of Mia's cigarette, but Zoe did not shout. Apart from anything else, she wanted more time to think... When she next opened her eyes, Emmy was in the room with her. Emmy had turned on the light. The rectangle had been dissolved in this artificial illumination, and Emmy said: 'Sleepybones.'

'I'm awake.' But Zoe's voice was groggy and there was a time-lapse: a beat between Emmy's utterance and a full computation of the delivery. 'What do you want?' she asked quietly. She looked around the basement.

'You were saying some interesting things in your sleep.'

'Was I now?' *A bench. Tools. Drums of engine oil. An old racing bicycle, one flat tyre.* 'Like what?' Zoe asked. *A washing machine. Red plastic tub full of black socks and underwear: boxer shorts and knickers... A man and a woman lived here,* Zoe reasoned. *Where was Emmy's partner? Was he in on this too?*

'Like stuff about New Trozenxus,' said Emmy. 'About Mia.'

There was no point denying what was plain to be inferred. 'You're here to take Mia back, aren't you?'

'No. I just want to understand.'

Understand what? thought Zoe sorrowfully. She made sure she could feel all ten fingers and toes wriggle. Then she moved her head about until her neck cracked with a satisfactory volume. She was just about to speak. Indignation made her stop in her tracks. Was she wrong or did she have a bargaining point here? 'I'll tell you anything if you untie me.'

Emmy smiled. 'Or what about this?' she counter-offered. 'I'll agree to feed and water you if you give me what I want. How's that?'

'I don't know what you want!' Zoe protested. The dry air in the basement tasted of dust. 'How about: Please? Please untie me. Okay? If you're involved in Mia's life, then I'll cooperate. For her sake...'

But something was wrong: the logic was wrong. In Mia's account, she had been looking for shoes; the shop she had chosen had been entirely a random decision. How could Emmy be part of the tapestry?

Zoe couldn't answer that. Nor was she certain an alternative was more comforting. If Emmy wasn't interested in Mia, what did that make her?

Emmy moved back towards the stairs. Zoe followed her with her eyes. The same bottle they'd drunk from earlier was on the fifth wooden step. Emmy picked it up and carried it over to Zoe's chair.

'Why not?' Zoe said.

'Hold your head still.' Carefully Emmy decanted some of the vodka into Zoe's mouth. And again. Again. 'Enough?' she wanted to know.

'Maybe you could just leave the bottle and a straw.'

'I'll tell you what. Are you left or right-handed?'

'Right.'

'I'll untie your left. You can hold the bottle. If you look like you're about to do something stupid, I've got any number of weapons on that bench. Deal?'

Zoe nodded. 'Deal.'

Getting drunker wasn't the answer, Zoe knew, but it made the truth more palatable. The thought of her station at work sprang to mind. Surely people would be wondering where she'd got to. With regret she acknowledged she hadn't told anyone where she was going. Perhaps her manager, Carl, would call the house; perhaps Mia would answer. Maybe Mia would intuit how to put two and two together. God knows how, Zoe reasoned, but maybe...

'Thanks.'

'Don't mention it,' said Emmy, sounding as though she meant it. 'You were saying.'

Zoe swigged. The vodka blazed a trail. 'She's from Somalia,' she said as soon as her throat had stopped throbbing.

'She told me that much.'

This sentence struck Zoe as something to meet with indignance. 'Well did she tell you she's killed people?' she asked.

'No. My dreams told me that much.'

Zoe wondered if she'd heard the other woman correctly. 'Excuse me?'

'My dreams. Last night. I followed her to Netherfield. You wouldn't believe what we got up to.' Emmy's eyes were shining like pins. 'She called me something I didn't understand: Halima. Does that mean anything to you?'

Zoe shook her head. What her loved one might have doled out on the streets of Netherfield last night seemed more important. 'What did you do?'

'Forget that. I want to know how we did it.' Emmy frowned. As though she had never seen the basement before she looked around. 'It was like I wasn't there – but I know it happened.'

'What did?'

'Come on. You're not meeting me halfway,' said Emmy. 'Have a drink and tell me about New Trozenxus.'

Zoe had a drink. 'There was a counter-intelligence force in Somalia. Still is. They called themselves soldiers but they were nothing to do with the government.'

'Counter to what?' asked Emmy.

Zoe shrugged. 'The government. The peace-keeping forces. You name it. Their only aim, as far as I know, was anarchy. And they had a novel way of perpetrating this. Have you ever heard of somnambular energy?'

'No.'

Zoe recalled the explorative lectures she'd heard from Mia, and wondered how best to summarise the facts. To this day she wasn't certain she had it all straight herself.

'Someone worked out how to harness what you burn in your dreams,' Zoe said. 'His name was Mort Fega. So what does anyone do when he finds a new form of power? – forms a cult; establishes a fresh way of abusing people.'

Emmy was frowning. 'But what did he do?'

Zoe drank deeply; there was not much vodka remaining in the bottle and she wanted to ensure she completed the task before Emmy asked for another taste. 'He found a middle ground: between sleeping and being awake.'

'Like being hypnotised?'

'Much bigger.'

12.

'Imagine this.'

Halima had become distracted by the same fly that had tried to batter its way out through the glass door a half-hour earlier. It was now attempting to read, Braille-like, the words on a wall-mounted medical certificate.

'Girl?' said Fega loudly. The certificate rattled against the wall.

'I'm listening,' said Halima, scared. Roasting, as well. Despite what Fega had promised, the heat in the office had not become any more tolerable.

'Imagine this: the human existence – a life, Halima – with the shape of evolution corresponding with it.'

'I don't understand.'

'Not yet, perhaps; you will. You're a smart girl. You've studied your sciences, haven't you, Halima?'

'Yes!' Halima's tone was proud.

'You know we started with a one-celled organism. And then the amoeba… and then the hydra… Evolution, my dear. The fish, the amphibian, the reptile, and so on. The mammal. You know all this.'

Uncertainly Halima said, 'Yes…'

'Well, we all take after one creature or another. Look at Chinese astrology. Or rather, don't.' Mort Fega grinned: on his gorilla face the effect was monstrous. 'Even you, little Halima.'

'Even me…'

'Don't let it bother you; it's nothing you can control. And it's nothing you'll want to, anyway. It's in your blood.'

'What is?' said Halima, exasperatedly.

'The animal instinct, darling. And I can help you with anything you want help with.' Again, the gorilla smiled.

'I want to find my brother. My brother Osman.'

Mort Fega nodded. 'We can help with that. For a price.'

'I haven't got any money.'

'We don't want any. See, we thought we could only use boys, until we encountered Mia. It was quite a revelation. Our early experiments showed only boys responded to the training. Until Mia…'

Halima was lost. The fly had settled down on Fega's polo trophy; Halima was waiting for the gold to melt, as it had in her dream. 'Who is Mia?'

Mort Fega answered, 'An assassin for the Cause.'

Feeling quite adult about it, Halima made a protest. 'I'm just a child! I don't want to know about an assassin.' But her thoughts returned to the village; the pictures were jerky, amalgamated, distorted, but she saw, heard and smelled the past. The dead winking at her as minuscule muscles spasmed; bodies slow to catch fire, smouldering and stinking on makeshift pyres. It was too late to be an innocent; it was too late to go back to her parents. She sat still.

'Mia ran away from us, Halima, when she was your age. One month she was with us, with the Cause, and the next she had fled. The embarrassing thing about it is, we didn't even know she'd gone – not at first. She was sneaky; didn't go as herself. She borrowed someone else's energy. We couldn't track her.'

'I'm hot,' said Halima. 'Please could you open the window?'

'No, sorry; it's too risky. The glass is bulletproof. Snipers, you see.'

We are still in my dreams, thought Halima, now using the back of her hand to rid her brow of a caul of perspiration. Her clothes felt heavy with damp. Her outlook brightened. Any moment now she would wake...

'Halima? It was your energies Mia stole,' said Mort Fega.

Was it worth it for Halima to repudiate the notion? To say she knew no one by the name of Mia? She was breathing noisily – and hard. Of a sudden, in her mind was the face of her brother – Osman was beaming from ear to ear. Mouthing something, his lips at first pursed, then opened a crack, then opened fully as the chin ducked down. He was mouthing Mia. Mia... What are you trying to tell me, Osman? thought Halima. She had closed her eyes for the message. The picture showed her Osman the young man, stroking Osman the horse. But there was something wrong with the film: man and beast kept blurring together, their solidities overlapping, as Brother Osman repeated Mia... until the message reached some sort of conclusion. At this point it began to roll backwards. What Osman mouthed now (the horse meanwhile was inhaling its own snorts) was the sound of the word 'Mia' in reverse: ah-yeem. It sounded like the result of one who'd sampled too much fermented rice. Ah-yeem. Dream talk: gibberish. Ah-yeem, ah-yeem… A few seconds passed before Halima heard Osman get one out that was clearer to her ear. The ah-yeem morphed into I am.. I am…

You are what, Osman? Halima was desperate to know.

Eyeballing his audience of one, Mort Fega was still talking. 'She did it with the help of your brother, Halima. Osman helped her make her escape.'

Mention of the name made Halima sit up straighter. 'He's with you?' she demanded, scarcely willing to believe her quest had borne fruit after all.

'Always was. Hiding in the one place we didn't think to look,' said Fega. 'Right under our noses. He'd learned to alter his scent.'

Halima was angry. 'You came to our home for him. I lost my toes.'

'Yes, Halima.' Mort Fega glanced away – he looked at his medical certificate. 'And I'm sorry about that. Truly I am.'

'Sorry?' She was panting now. 'You're sorry? They were barbarians!'

Fega slammed a fist on to the desk. 'This is war, young lady. And those who serve in a war are never barbarians. Do not insult me. They are soldiers!'

Halima's voice was quiet. It hurt her in the gut to say it. 'They are pigs.'

'Young lady,' said Fega, 'please do not assume you are immune to anything. What you have in here…' He touched his left temple with a forefinger as black, bent and large as a rotten banana. '…is priceless. But that doesn't make you exempt from anything. Any more than it did your brother.'

'I want to see him.' For the moment Halima ignored the implication in what Fega had just said. Then it struck her. Had they tortured her brother?

'Impossible for now. But soon, I promise. First you have a job to do.'

Halima shook her head. 'I'm too young to have a job.'

'What do you call searching for Osman, if not a job?'

She had nothing to use against that; but Fega appeared eager to have her respond. Voice-free seconds stretched and twisted; Halima had no idea how much time passed. Every second was an hour, but perhaps she had been in the office for over a day already. She wondered what had happened to James Carbon and Frank Mice. Their duties executed, where might they have gone? Were they, in fact, anything more than creations of her own devising? As realistic as the journey here had been, perhaps she had made it all up. Perhaps she remained in bed, safe and warm, thinking about waking up.

Halima considered the construction of her next sentence; it emerged as a well-built conditional sentence. She said: 'If it means I can make Osman safe, I will do your job for you.'

'Why do you assume he's not safe, Halima?'

'Because he's fighting for you. You said so yourself.'

'You sound like you disapprove,' said Fega, seemingly amused.

'Do I have to repeat why? I lost half my foot...'

'We thought you were hiding him. We're going round in circles.'

He had a point. The past was a lake of dirty water; it would serve her no purpose anymore. Better by far was to follow the river, as she had the way here. Soldiers had done what soldiers do. Osman, she gathered, was alive and well.

'What's the job?' Halima asked, once more wiping her face clean of sweat. She thought of numbers; taking little more than two seconds, she recited the magic number of pi to twenty-five decimal spaces. Homework, back in the village, had been a chore but she had thrown herself into the job. No difference.

'To find Mia,' Fega told her.

'I already told you, I'm a child,' Halima complained. 'What can I do?'

Fega raised himself to full height. Presenting his young visitor with an unimprovable view of his rump, he turned to the window; his eyes and whole head slowly followed the paths of pedestrians and vehicles alike.

'Who knows her better, young lady?' he said softly.

'I don't know her at all... I've got to stand up, Mr Fega. I'm melting.'

Fega turned her way. He lifted his hands, palms up, a few inches – as though giving Mia permission to do what she was doing anyway. 'The thing is, Halima, we have sensors; we know when people are ready. We know when they've moved along their animal-line as far as they can go. We know. It's there for anyone to see, but no one dares to look. But we know. If that person has got inside him – and now her – the right instinct, the right... pulse, we know when the dreamlife is ready... Halima. Ask yourself this. Could you kill someone?'

'No! You want me to kill her when I've found her?'

'Not necessarily. That depends what you find. You'll be trained,' said Fega. 'But for what it's worth? I think you could. That's why you're here.'

Halima felt like crying. So near and so far, she thought as she clenched her small fists together. 'I'm here to find my brother!' she squealed.

Once more Fega was annoyed. 'Mia stole your thoughts, young lady! You will know her when you find her. Even with the years between your ages, you know her better than anyone else does. Her given name, before she took on Mia, was Halima, after all. You are her younger version. And you can be a better version of her when you get to be her age. No mistakes. Simply part of the Cause.'

I can't do anything he wants, thought Halima. Can I fool him into believing I can? No: fool him into believing that I believe I can.

'Why else would I desire a little girl? Think about it.'

Halima smiled falsely; she didn't feel it – she didn't feel in the slightest in a cheery old mood. But she did, as Fega commanded, think about it. The series of crackling insights resulting ushered nothing forth but more questions. Such as: 'Why are James Carbon and Frank Mice dogs?'

'Because that's as far as their evolutionary line has taken them.'

Halima frowned. 'So are they human or not?' she wanted to know.

'As you or I. That's a joke.' Mort Fega sat down again and adjusted himself in the green leather chair. 'Halima, listen. The animal status means next to nothing, other than the fact that some animals are better at fighting than others. What matters, really, is you can open your eyes to the world between waking and dreaming; it's a whole new parallel, and one in which we get to know our compatriots' true identities. Accessing the state is the important bit.'

'Accessing the state,' Halima repeated. She chewed the words around her mouth, like a toffee; they tasted good, she was surprised to note.

'That's right.'

Halima wanted her family, her maths class, her horse. Above all, she wanted her brother. 'So tell me exactly what do you want me to do.'

'To listen.' Mort Fega picked something from his teeth, examined it, and then pressed it to his tongue. 'I want you...'

Halima interrupted him. 'Can I take a photograph of you?'

The gorilla looked puzzled. 'Why would you want to do that?'

'To prove to myself we were here.'

Fega laughed. 'And by 'myself' I take it you mean just about anyone! But fire away! It'll just show a man to anyone else. To most people anyway. Not everyone has the gift.'

Halima was old enough to understand false flattery; when Miss Esma, her Mathematics tutor, red-penned a smiling face onto her work, despite the fact that she had got half of her imaginary numbers and simultaneous equations wrong, Halima was always disappointed. She would have preferred a pencilled frown and an unambiguous: SHIT. True, she knew Miss Esma was attempting to rally the troops (a bad comparison, thought Halima) and to encourage the girls on the back of sound achievement. Even so...

But Halima could taste sincerity when it was portioned onto a plate in front of her. It made something crawl and shrink for cover behind her breastbone. It made her strong. 'What gift?'

Again the gorilla stood up; this time his knees clicking, a pronounced hunch revealed itself as he flicked himself behind his left ear... Halima found Fega more threatening when he was standing. More so as he loped around the desk. 'The gift,' he said – 'The gift of violence.'

Halima was as surprised by the statement as she was by the anal stench being hissed through Fega's teeth as he leaned closer mouthing the words. She jumped as he made a sudden move. Fega lashed out with his left arm. His fist closed quickly and tightly. As part of the same manoeuvre, Fega shoved the fist into his own mouth. Halima heard a muffled complaint. Fega had caught and eaten the fly.

He winced. 'I hate the taste of insects from his country,' he said.

Halima felt closer than ever to tears. 'I'm not violent,' she whispered.

'You have to.' Fega leaned closer. 'We've examined your dreams, and you're powerful, Halima. You're a tiger. You're an asset to us. All we ask is that you try to swell our numbers. Somehow, we have to suppress the oppression that's smothering this country. We're the good, Halima.'

She could feel that only a few seconds were left. Halima spent them exploring her memory: especially the soldiers that her village-folk had murdered and diced into pieces in the fields. If Fega was right, was her family wrong?

'I need to be somewhere cool, somewhere to lie down,' was the first of her requests.

13.

Halima, I need to talk to you, Mia said.

She was standing on the toilet seat, one knee against the top lip of the cistern; she was opening as wide as it would go the tiny window.

The Halima she wanted to reach was not her pursuer – lost in action, if Carbon had been preaching gospel – because of that young lady Mia knew nothing. No; the person she wanted to reach was her own younger self. Halima had become Mia, but who had Halima been? Names meant nothing. Who had Mia herself been? The younger Mia would have known how to get out of this.

I won't fit through that, she thought, referring to the window. The yawn of the window from its sturdy frame wasn't wide enough, irrespective of her slim, petite size. Answering this negative thought automatically, Mia went on, inside her head: You won't know until you try, will you?

So she tried. While Carbon was waiting in the restaurant, Mia hiked herself up onto the cistern – Don't break! – and squeezed her head through the gap. Impossible, surely! She had seconds. She had left him bombastically clicking his fingers for the bill. Let's hope the staff take umbrage, Mia had said to herself as she'd excused herself to visit the lavatory. Maybe he'd get beaten up – the living daylights kicked out of him – and this bedroom farce could be over. With a disgruntled sigh, Mia climbed back down. Her shoulders, too wide.

Frustration made her kick the door jamb of the toilet stall. A tall woman applying a refresher layer of make-up looked her way. 'Lousy date?' she asked.

It was enough to make Mia chuckle, despite everything. 'Aren't they all?'

'Well…' She slipped her compact into her handbag. 'If he does everything else the same way he eats I'd say stay away.'

'The way he eats?'

The woman nodded her head. 'Half the restaurant was watching him, darling, and probably feeling sorry for you as I was. You looked trapped.'

'I am.' Always tell the truth to strangers, thought Mia. 'I was looking for a way out so I wouldn't have to see him again.' She laughed. 'I sized up the window in there but I'm too big.'

Mia's interlocutor picked up her bag from beside the basin. She took a step towards Mia, saying 'My poor girl, that bad?'

'Worse.'

'Your first date? Somewhere safe for lunch? Somewhere bright?'

'Um…' The truth would tax the credulity of any stranger; because of this, Mia decided to dilute the measure somewhat. 'I've known him quite a while.' That was vague enough, and not in-criminating. 'But what worries me is I know he's going to try to kiss me, and I think he's got breath-herpes.'

'Ugh. Maximum gross-out. If I were you? I'd go out the back way.'

'I was thinking of that,' Mia continued, returning to the full truth.

'Through the kitchen, darling.' A wicked, conspiratorial grin appeared on her Samaritan features. 'I'll try talking to him, how's that? At least until he tries to kiss me instead. That should give you a few minutes at least. Did you both drive yourselves here?' Mia shook her head. 'He drove, didn't he?'

'I can't drive,' Mia admitted. 'I catch a bus everywhere.'

'Then you're rather in the stew, my darling,' the woman added, distracted and deep in thought. 'You won't get a cab around here unless you call for one.'

'I've got a phone!' Mia's voice sounded elated.

The Good Samaritan shrugged. 'They'd have to come out from the centre or the sticks,' she said. 'Could be ten, fifteen minutes. If I were you?'

'Yes?' Mia raised her eyebrows.

'You're young and you look fit. Run till your boobs ache, darling! Run into the housing estate behind this place.' She smacked her lips. 'At least if you get lost you can admire how the other half live. Those piles cost an absolute bomb!'

For all the attention Mia got as she slipped through the restaurant's kitchen, it might have been because it was regularly employed for emergency egress. Carving knife in hand, before a detonation of pink chicken pieces on a large wooden board, one assistant chef even went as far as to nod sideways in the direction of the door. Mia bid him thanks with her own quick nod. The area outside was no advertisement for the high stakes of culinary hygiene – a hundred cardboard boxes had been crushed flat and abandoned in a pile, an odds-on near-future demolition if a strong wind had anything to do with it; a few flies grumbled around oil dripping from a dented, rusty drum – but Mia was in no mind to be concerned about the slivers of unrecognisable meat and portions of hard congealed rice that had been torn away from a high dune of reeking black plastic bags. She made her way through weeds and unmown grass. Lifted the gate's latch, and stepped out on to Woughton-on-the-Green.

Halima, I need to talk to you now, she thought to herself again.

The Good Samaritan's advice seemed sound, so Mia made a run across the part of the restaurant's car park that she presumed was only used during diwali festival seasons or very large wedding bookings, for the automotive overspill. Beyond the fringe of concrete was a wide stretch of grass and a few freshly-planted saplings. Not that Mia had banked much on there being a good deal of foliage to cover her running away. In her mind it had been only grass between her and the restaurant the whole way. While she knew she had a matter of minutes remaining before Carbon grew suspicious, she was at least at the back of the restaurant – perhaps where her tormentor would not think to look first.

Still running, her breath hot and stinging, Mia saw the fence looming but moved towards it anyway, as if expecting it to dissolve like a mirage. It did not. This far from the building, from where the outside tables were bolted down for diners on warmer days, from where the same diners' children could play on a set of swings, a slide or a see-saw, the fence had the ugly, unpainted appearance that brayed NO ADMISSION. And it was a full head taller than Mia's. Maybe…if she stopped herself from giving up. She jumped up and gripped the rough wood running along the top; her feet dangled six inches from the grass. Mia tried to pull her own dead weight up the sheer surface of the grey-brown plate, kicking her toes at it for purchase. The effort was futile; a forlorn exasperation made Mia feel dizzy and enervated. It was time – for pity's sake wasn't it time, already? – to give up. Carbon should win.

Self-pity and self-disgust were brewing in equal portions in this realization. As a result of this recipe, Mia kicked out at the fence with her damaged foot in despair. To her utter astonishment, two profound reactions were experienced.

The first was like a shard of glass. Shaped sharp and forged hard, the arrow stabbed into her plump round ball of memories – some of them the truth and some stolen from a different female's identity – as the pain registered up her foot, to her shin, and into her thigh. A flash, nothing more, this piece of glass; but the memory it carried on its gleam was this: a vision of herself, lying supine on a dirty bed, back in the old country. She is feverish. She is high on medication, adrenaline and uppers; she is holding in her two-gripped palm the very pistol with which she has ended more lives for the sake of the Cause than she has had taken bedroom partners. That in itself was no easy feat. She is aiming the barrel at her left foot...

Although it was no time for reverie, the picture struck Mia powerfully. I did it to myself, she thought for the first time in years; to copy the Halima girl...

The second result of the kick was the instantaneous appearance of a roadmap of cracks in the wood. The fence was not as strong as it looked.

Using the other foot this time, and now not in agreement with her frustration (her mind was focused on the project), Mia kicked at the fence again. There was noise. Not enough, she hoped, to draw attention, but enough to mean something; she kicked and kicked. From the other side of the restaurant's building came a loud 'MIA!', bellowed widely,– at which point Mia knew that James Carbon had seen through the smokescreen and had ventured outside to see if she'd already stolen his car somehow, now knowing that she hadn't.

The fifth of Mia's kicks broke a hole in the fence. It was nothing more than a small hole – an image of a handful of sand crossed Mia's mind along with the knowledge that she needed to dig a well – but it was a beginning. Her assault on the wood became more frantic. At one point, after a particularly savage strike, her foot went right through to the other side, up to the calf. Pulling it back scratched grooves in her skin; she started bleeding. Only seconds had elapsed but Mia knew she was running out of time when she heard her name for a second and third time. Carbon was bound to be lured by the sounds.

With the gap as large but no larger than the toilet stall window had been, useless in other words, Mia readdressed her options and removed the mobile phone from her skirt pocket. Expertly she thumbed for TONES – her menu of choices for possible tunes to hear when someone called – and she settled indiscriminately on the first one, labelled 'Foxtrot'. It started to bleep its melody, with the volume setting as ever on its top rung. Mia placed the phone through the hole in the fence, on to the grass on the other side. Then without further thought she ran back in the direction of the restaurant's back entrance. Either the noise of her footfalls, her exhalations, or the simple distance she was putting between herself and her phone was killing the volume of the ringtone. Mia begged silently for a gust of wind to carry the noise Carbon's way...

Back inside the restaurant's rear courtyard, Mia searched for a place to hide. Somewhere in among the black bags of rubbish, was an option – albeit a putridly smelling option. But she didn't want to go inside the building. If Carbon went in there he was liable to do things to people in order to get what he wanted: information. As Mia selected one of the less full bags of refuse, she had time to hope that the Good Samaritan had emerged unscathed; it wounded her slightly to think that she hadn't considered the woman's risk one iota. No time! Bag in hand Mia climbed into the oil drum as quietly as she could, hearing first the faintest whisper of an electronic foxtrot, and then the thud of heavy footsteps beyond the closed-in courtyard. Squashing herself down into the few inches of acrid cooking oil at the bottom of the drum, Mia placed the rubbish bag on her head. It would look, she assumed with a prayer, like a drum stuffed with crap.

She waited, heartbeat heavy. Long seconds dragged and Mia listened for signs of life beyond the courtyard. All she could hear were sounds from the kitchen – pans jousting, the scrape of metal objects, the deep-throated rinsing noise of an industrial dishwasher – until it came to her ears: one of any number of possible alternatives that would have satisfied her as beautifully.

Carbon had found the phone that he would presume Mia had dropped while she'd crawled through the gap in the fence. He screamed: 'BITCH!'

14.

'That's some pretty decent muscles,' the man said, 'that story, like.'

'Oh good,' replied Zoe, the sarcasm sluiced dead by the slurring of her voice; 'I do like my stories to have a bit of muscle.'

A beat. Then the man laughed. 'You're all right, Zoe.'

'Excellent. So perhaps you can let me go.'

'Not yet. Crew ain't seen you yet and ting.'

Zoe had taken it as a sign that she was being at least partly trusted when her environment of incarceration had shifted up the house, from the basement to a small back room that held a bank of turntables, two-foot-high speakers, trailing wires, and box upon box of vinyl twelve-inch records. She was in the home of a DJ, a 'spitter'; she was handcuffed to the feed-pipe of a painted green radiator, the warmth against her skin being welcome as the alcohol in her system went about its duty of thinning her blood.

'Who's Crew?'

The man, who'd arrived thirty minutes earlier, stared down at where she sat slumped on the floor, her arms pulled to her right. On his face was an expression of the purest incredulity. 'Who's Crew?' his voice climbed. 'Crew's not a person, Zo; Crew's Crew.'

'Okay. What is Crew then?'

His face went soppy with pride. 'My boys,' the man said. 'My massive. My selective. Crew is family and ting.'

The old resilience in Zoe was at the surface. 'And does Crew know that Crew's going to be facing five years in prison for hostage taking and ting?'

'Crew don't care. You're fighting a cause. You look for enemies if needs.'

'I see.' Where have I heard something like that before? Zoe wondered to herself. Still brave from the booze, she added: 'And what time does Crew intend to arrive? Is Crew punctual?'

He couldn't be as old as twenty, reasoned Zoe. Wasn't it a given that she could out-talk the young man and make him see the error of his ways?

'Crew'll be here when the moment's brewing.'

'Jesus. Do you parents know you've learned this new language?'

'Do yours?'

What was that supposed to mean? 'I haven't got any parents,' Zoe said.

'Well then, neither have I.'

'I think I preferred arguing with Emmy.'

'Emmy's passed her test,' the young man replied. 'She's resting.'

'What test?'

The young man took up position behind his turntables. 'The clue is,' he instructed Zoe as though she hadn't spoken, 'to leave 'em on all the time. When you're out. They collect the energy in the silence. This'll sound fresh as a daisy.'

Zoe very nearly didn't want to know, but she asked anyway. 'What will?'

'The answer to your question. In spit-form.'

'Christ...'

A button was depressed, a knob was gently twisted: a bass drum, snare drum, two bass, snare drum – BOM-dee-BOMBOM-dee – blasted from the speakers and the young man, who now in the form of rhyme finally revealed his own name, picked up the microphone dangling by its cord over the U-shaped stalk of a wall-mounted upturned lamp. He spat.

'My name is Rick V and I'm talking to you...'

No, you're not, you're shouting at me. Pump down the volume, thought Zoe, fidgeting without much hope against the handcuffs. They were made of pink plastic, these handcuffs; they had soft pink fur around the shackles. Bedroom bondage; most likely breakable, given enough time.

The pretentious tosh of the rap eventually subsided. Clearly pleased with his performance, Rick V was grinning like a window-licker.

'That one's called 'The Initiation',' he announced.

'Other spitters beware,' Zoe nodded, thinking quickly. 'Rick V, could you do me a favour if I'm going to be kept here. Could you turn up the heating? I'm freezing on the floor here.'

'Oh, okay. You really liked it?'

'I loved it,' she told him though she'd scarcely been able to discern a word. One chimed. It chimed again. Initiation. 'You're trying to join the Crew.'

'Not the Crew. Just Crew. I'm trying to join Crew.'

Zoe fidgeted again. 'And I'm your ticket in, aren't I? You have to do something to earn your place. Am I right?'

Rick V performed an unnecessary dance on the spot. 'Gotta prove your place and ting,' he answered. 'It's not a sports club, Zo.'

'Suppose not. Yes. Ten years for hostage taking and Section 18 will make them take notice. Congratulations. I'm sure you're in. Apart from one ting.'

Rick V's expression spoke more of suspicion than anything else. 'What's Section 18?' he asked with his eyes squinted together.

'Uncalled-for violence. Piercing the skin.'

The young man held up his hands. 'I ain't touched you!' protested Rick V.

'Not me you haven't. But what about Emmy? I saw the marks, Rick. Trying to tell me you haven't knocked her around from time to time?' Zoe attempted to smile but it wouldn't come. 'Between us? I don't think she wants to be Crew at all; I think you had to convince her hard to knock me out. And that's where we come to the real problem with your initiation, Rick...'

'What?'

'Apart from bellowing at me through a microphone, pal, you haven't done anything to justify your place in Crew. And I'll tell 'em so. Let me go.'

Rick V paused for a few seconds before making for the door. 'You're not going anywhere, Zo,' he muttered. 'I'll get the heating up.' He turned on the threshold. 'How come you know about the law anyway?'

I don't remember, Zoe thought. 'Common knowledge, Rick,' she answered. Something Mia told me at some point? Must have been.

Evidently Rick V adopted a hands-off approach to domestic arrangements. At the top of his voice he roared for Emmy to increase the temperature in the house... Zoe had no choice but to jump at the barked order. Soon, she thought, soon. The radiator would heat up and yes, it would be uncomfortable – but with the rise in degrees the plastic handcuffs would have to weaken. Wouldn't they? Rick V returned to the room. He was pointing a finger.

'All I have to do is repeat what you told me and Emmy. You get me?'

'Right. As if I'd say that lot again.'

'You will if we convince you hard enough,' Rick V said.

Zoe put on a front; she laughed out once. 'You didn't buy that, did you?'

'Don't play it and ting. You were telling the truth, and I think Crew'll be very interested in using what you got to its advantage, Zo.'

Zoe frowned. 'Who exactly are you fighting, Rick?'

'We're taking control of the streets.'

'From who, though?'

'From anyone who gets in our way!' Rick V replied.

The accusation of partner-beating had been at best a wild poke in the dark; though there hadn't been a denial there were times when a silence could hit as hard as a stone. Yet... hadn't

Zoe seen something on Emmy's skin – hadn't she thought – yes, thought – she'd seen organs inside Emmy's body?

'I need to have something to drink,' Zoe told her captor.

'We're out of vodka. Thanks for that, by the way.' Rick V re-established his position behind the decks. This time he did not rely on a pre-recorded drum and bass; there was already a record on one of the turntables. 'That's a big chunk of my Income Support, you know!' He dropped the needle in the groove.

'I meant like a glass of water.' Zoe's words were drowned by the noise. Cupped hand behind the right ear, Rick V gave the 'pardon-I-can't-hear-you' mime, mouthing What? Zoe shouted, 'Take some money from my purse!'

That's not a bad idea, she could see him contemplating. Bless his heart but his thought patterns were so simple to read and follow. If indeed he was expecting members – maybe founders – of Crew, it wouldn't do for them to arrive and have nothing awaiting them on the social niceties front.

Rick V nodded his head and left the back room. Zoe chanced an attempt at escape. Moving as swiftly as she was able, she shuffled on her bum, inching her legs under the bridge formed by her wrists secured to the radiator. In this way, curled up though she was, she had her feet against the wallpaper. She pushed back as hard as she could. It was like using the rowing machine: the muscles at the top of her legs stretched and strained.

The noise in the room was outrageous: more rap music. In spite of that, however, Zoe imagined she heard something else sewn into the din: a collection of sounds from beyond the open door of her prison. It wasn't only the high-pitched complaints of the pipe against which the chain of her bracelets was pulling, though that was loud enough. Was he beating on her again? Zoe wondered; she went on to the belief that ten years would be too good for scum like Rick V, regardless of how immature, misguided and even innocent he was.

That was pain. No doubt about it in Zoe's mind – none whatever – that yelp was riddled with agony. Except... it had sounded like male pain. Go girl! thought the captive, her legs now all but straight; as a consequence her back was bent in a curve, her hands still secured. But the pipe was groaning. Could it be, in such a short time she had managed to distort the pipe by a fraction? If so, it wasn't what Zoe had expected. She'd imagined the cuffs giving way first – giving way quite easily. Sex toys were made of sterner stuff these days, obviously. The next effort squeezed a low moan of dismay from her throat.

Finished; it was over. Zoe could feel him – sense his presence behind her back, although how close she wasn't certain. Musty smell; something different, she wasn't sure what. He had caught her fighting her bounds. Not for the first time, but for the first time in at least half an hour, Zoe panicked.

Instinctively moving closer to the wall, she bundled herself up into as tight a ball as her frame would permit. She screwed her eyes tight. She felt him approach; she couldn't hear his footfalls, deadened as they were by thin carpet and the roar of a rapper spitting urban angst from the turntable. When she opened her eyes again she could smell his odour stronger, as proximate to her skin as her own perfume. He was leaning over her body – and a knife came into view to the right side of her head. Its blade was murky and red. She couldn't scream. No was the only word she had. But she couldn't scream. She was dead, and she knew it.

The blade reached past her, as if to prick the wall. The hand that held it was red as well, spotted on the top joint of its thumb and on its fingernails. Zoe was shaking her head – as the blade balanced on the chain between the handcuffs. Pressure. Snick! went the chain. The knife blade cut straight through.

'You're free.' The voice was not Rick V's. It certainly wasn't Emmy's. Trembling madly, Zoe twisted on her backside and did her best to move to one side, knowing that the motion was pointless. She looked up – into a face frozen free of emotion. The dark eyes, if anything, gave away a scintilla of sadness, and even that only for a second. 'You're free.'

The man pulled Zoe up from the floor. 'We have to go, Halima,' he said.

Too stunned to correct the identification, Zoe accepted the hand and was dragged up, her legs shaking from the fright, the cold floor and from sitting in one position for too long. Wordlessly she followed her saviour into the hallway. Her own hand went to her mouth at what she saw there.

Rick V was lying half in and half out the doorway to the front room. If the gash in his belly didn't kill him, the slice across his throat, gurgling with popping red bubbles as he attempted to speak, most surely would. He was using what remained of his strength to writhe. Emmy, on the other hand, had already given up the battle. She was lying on the stairs, the slit down her back as straight and perfect as the zip of a dress.

'He told you his boys were coming. Crew right? I want them to find him alive.'

Together they left the house. There were no thoughts – no successive, sensible thoughts at any rate – in Zoe's mind and so she didn't think too much as she stumbled, numb-thighed, with hot shins, in the direction of her car down the curb. Then a thought struck her. 'I can't drive. They took my handbag.'

'So?'

'The keys are in it!' Zoe shouted.

'I've got your keys,' the man replied. 'Which ones are they?' Saying this, he pulled from his left trouser pocket two bunches of keys. 'I picked up whatever they had on the rack by the door.'

'Neither of them! We have to go back!'

'We can't, Halima! His Crew will be there any sec…'

But Zoe was already retracing her steps; the dissipating effects of the alcohol she'd taken in were still potent enough to give her sufficient nous to comprehend that she couldn't be leaving her handbag at the scene of two murders. Containing as it did her passport, driving licence and security fob for work, it wouldn't take a great detective to place her in the house of horrors.

'We can take their car!' she faintly heard as she re-entered.

She saw the bag near the chair in which she'd originally been sitting, in the front room. She saw it from the threshold, and now tensing the muscles of her stomach, she stretched her legs to bound over Rick V's motionless body. She had all but cleared the gatekeeper's physical bulk when Rick decided on one last act of insurrection against logic. His left hand reached out for a grip...

It caught Zoe's ankle. The woman in her screamed – the noise finally emerged – and the contact was enough to knock her off balance, mid-flight. Zoe fell to her knees, her left ankle remaining in Rick V's grasp. Grunting and puffing like a steam train, Zoe kicked at Rick's head with her other foot, blood smearing all over her work shoes and tights. She clasped hold of her bag. It might not have been as heavy as she'd have appreciated, but when she thumped it down onto her assailant's face the shock was ample to force the man to let go.

What was it – the impending sense of release? the mashed terror? – that formed the words in Zoe's mouth? She said coldly, 'And your lyrics are shit too.' To the din of a drum and bass track whose equal Rick V would now never compose, Zoe exited the house for the second time, not truly anticipating seeing her rescuer waiting for her – admittedly agitatedly.

'Come on, Halima!' he called.

'I thought...' She'd thought he would have taken one of the other cars, that's what she'd thought, but he'd waited for her. Why? Who was he?

'Who are you?' Zoe asked, skittering a key into the ignition with shaking fingers, missing twice before securing the slot. She turned it. Fired the revs.

The new man in her life chuckled sweetly. The bubbling-brook sound of humour chilled Zoe's marrow. She'd heard it before. She raced to the end of the road and pulled out without checking in either direction. Her fingers were vibrating on the steering wheel, and with shock Zoe realised she'd wet herself.

'Don't you recognise your own brother, Halima. I'm Osman.'

There was stillness and silence. The car moved quickly – away from Netherfield – if she never saw that damn fucking place again in her life it would be too soon – towards the centre... or where? Home? She thought of Paxo, in his cage, calling 'Nuisance' at their arrival but secretly pleased to see one of his owners home early from work. The streets were blurry. I shouldn't be driving, Zoe thought.

'You were trying to find me but I found you, Halima. Always the contrary!' And the man name of Osman chuckled harder, louder, his body quaking.

Zoe cast a glance over at him. 'Will you please, for God's sake, put that knife away?' she asked him, her tone exasperated and aerated. Knife? Pictures of Rick and Emmy... but also earlier pictures, forcefed to her at this instant. A ride along a long road – much longer than this one, and unpaved. Human detritus as markings and milestones. A rook perching on a brain. Two big dogs, one could talk, a gorilla in a stifling office – Mort Fega; the Cause...

She did it with the help of your brother, Halima. Osman helped her make her escape... 'He's with you?' Zoe whispered... Always was. Hiding in the one place we didn't think to look. Right under our noses. He'd learned to alter his scent. 'You altered your scent,' Zoe carried on whispering.

'Pardon?' said Osman.

'But I didn't lose my toes!' she shouted. 'It can't be me!'

'Drive safely, please Halima!'

'It can't be me! It was Mia who lost her toes!' Erratically, suicidally even, Zoe jockeyed between other cars, past the college, and turned left on to the faster moving H8. The gas station whipped and curled behind Zoe, to her left; she all but ignored it, the station was nothing but a tumbleweed. Zoe's eyes appeared wild and bloodshot in the rearview mirror; the sight unnerved her. She thought back to another mirror: the full-length version in the bedroom she shared with Mia. Peeling off each other's sports clothes; sweaty skin tight leggings, the session on the automated bike over. They are laughing. They are lovers. They are comfortable together. Their sizes and shapes are compared: their bellies, bottoms and breasts. And their similarly disfigured left feet.

Halima was angry. 'They came to our home for you. I lost my toes,' she accused, 'and all the time you were fighting for their Cause. Did you understand what you were fighting for?' She turned to face him. 'I feel sick. You make me.'

'They gave me no choice, Halima. Watch the road!'

'You helped her escape, didn't you?' Zoe was raving on. 'That's what Mort Fega told me. Then they sent me after her. I was supposed to bring her back...' A car horn beeped at her, its driver unimpressed with her skills on the road. 'Fuck you back,' she yelled at him. 'Did I really meet Mia in France?'

'Yes. Yes, I swear... You have to slow down.'

'She changed my dreams,' Zoe muttered – or Halima did – or maybe no one did. The meaning of the sentence was rich with possibilities, granted; but the words themselves meant nothing. 'Where's Mia now?'

'In danger. John Carbon got tired of waiting for you, Halima.'

The very mention of the name was enough to petrify the woman steering the motor. A knee-jerk reaction made her stamp on the accelerator. There was too much traffic, she told herself, and it was all too near.

So it wasn't on the drive to Emmy's house, but rather on her swift drive away from it, that Zoe crashed the car. Nor did she have time to regret the alcohol she had so passionately consumed;

there were other matters very much on her mind. The universe folded in on itself in a riot of pain and din.

Zoe shouted once for her mother.

15.

The heat inside the oil drum was overbearing. Mia had failed in her attempts to zone out, to disconnect her mind from the present reality. But she was tugged, in the head, between two addictive focuses. If she didn't want to think about now – about the threat of James Carbon – her masochistic self tugged her back to Somalia – back to the Tower of Crumbs. The heat was similar: the oil drum and the office. But those aren't my memories; I stole them… It didn't matter; as deeply rooted in her conscience were the memories as cancer in an organ.

How long had passed? Mia moved the rubbish bag on her head a few inches so that a chink of light illuminated her womb-like world. Her left wrist was naked; somewhere she had lost her watch – or hadn't she put it on in the first place. Once more, it didn't matter; she had no idea when she'd left the house anyway, or how long she had spent arguing with James Carbon.

For her Lazurus-like rise from the stinking drum Mia had an audience of three. Two were young men, dressed in the black, sharp-creased trousers and immaculate white shirt of waiters everywhere. The third was the Good Samaritan. Her eyes and Mia's eyes met and held. Something was needed to break the silence. One of the waiters did the honours. 'He gone,' the boy said.

Mia was helped out of the drum by the other waiter. Because of the way she'd crouched in the remains of the oil, her shoes, ankles and upper back thighs were wet with grease; she stank to high heaven. Her left foot throbbed from her initial kick at the fence; her right foot, despite the more heartfelt attack on the same with which she'd used it, did not complain – it was right at home, executing that kind of assault. She had done it so many times in her history, and not on inert planks of wood. All for the sake of the Cause she didn't get... All for demands in code and in explicit language both. She'd been a soldier – and she had done what soldiers do. But not once had she truly comprehended it.

'Nice boyfriend you've got there,' said the Good Samaritan. Mia didn't know how to respond. Should she run? She could run: that was it.

'I'm so tired,' she thought aloud.

'Not surprised. Did you see that he hit me?'

Mia shook her head. 'I'm sorry about that,' she said.

'But I kept him busy as long as I could,' the woman continued, the ghost of a smile at her lips suggesting that she had in fact enjoyed the contest.

'I owe you something.'

'No you don't, unless it's a change of clothes, darling. Forgive my brusqueness, dear, but you are rather whiffy right now...'

Mia laughed. 'I'll change my clothes with pleasure.'

The other woman made a snap decision. 'Come on, I'll give you a lift,' she said. 'Where do you live?'

'Conniburrow.' Although the offer was sorely tempting, there might be another issue that should be under discussion. 'Aren't you here with anyone?'

'Just the team. It's a working lunch, once a month: helps to keep up morale.' She took hold of Mia's right arm. 'Come on. They've all gone back to the office.'

'I don't want to get you into trouble...'

'I'm the manager, darling; I don't do trouble.'

Again, Mia laughed. 'You're doing trouble now.'

'Thank you, boys!' The Samaritan waved to the nonplussed waiters over her shoulder. Remembering her manners, Mia copied the words if not the action. There were tears in her eyes; her body felt heavy and weak. The older woman took the lead, her heels clicking on the path, and the two women walked around the building in the direction of the main car park. 'It's the husband's car, I'm afraid, mine's in for a service. The Testostocar.'

'I'm very grateful,' said Mia. 'I only hope I don't get the seat dirty.'

'You can sit on Bertie's blanket. He's our dog.'

'I'm very grateful,' repeated Mia. She could find no better words to say.

'Give it a good slam,' said the other woman from the driver's seat. 'Thirty grand for a jam jar and the bloody doors are faulty. My name's Kim, by the way.'

'Mia. Nice to meet you.'

Belated an introduction as it was, the women shook hands. Kim told Mia her hands were shaking and that she wasn't surprised either; what a baboon the poor girl had ended up with for a date. (Gorilla, thought Mia; evolution, thought Mia; the Tower of Crumbs, Mort Fega...) Mia agreed with a quiet yes.

Where is Zoe? Mia oozed backwards into the seat. 'Have you got a phone?' she asked. 'I have to call my friend.' Mia was looking straight ahead.

'Right there. Hands free.'

It had been a long time since Mia had needed to prod in the number, but the pattern her fingers made was confident and speedy. In the car the dialling tone was comfortingly loud.

'Hello?' a voice said eventually, just as Mia was expecting the slide into voicemail. It was a man's voice. Frank Mice has found her, thought Mia.

'Where's Zoe?' Mia demanded angrily.

'There's been an accident. Are you Mia? The phone says Mia.'

Mia's body was cold. She sensed Kim's worried glance. She said, 'Where?' and the voice answered, 'H8, A5, at the roundabout.'

'We're five minutes away,' Kim remarked, immediately indicating right to perform an illegal U-turn in a bus lane. 'I'll get you there.'

An ambulance was already at the scene of the carnage – it had been sent from the nearby hospital, at Netherfield. As Kim pulled her car over to the grass verge by the side of the road, bumping up the curb with little regard to the Testostocar's suspension and alignment, Mia heard another siren – a fire engine, perhaps – in the distance, but getting closer. Mia had her seatbelt unfastened before the car had come fully to a halt. 'Be careful of the traffic!' she heard Kim call behind her. Mindful of earlier instructions, Mia slammed the passenger side door.

There was indeed a good deal of traffic. Mia's eyebrows slotted together as she frowned her worry and fright; she could see Zoe's car. Along with another vehicle, it was mangled and crumpled on the roundabout itself. Mia swore under her breath, and waited for a break in the line of cars streaming slowly from the right to trace round the island; though her legs ached she made a good break for her destination, already picturing the collision in her head from the positions of the cars. Evidently Zoe's vehicle had struck a car that was also coming from the right. The impact had pushed them both up onto the roundabout.

Mia climbed onto it herself. She was hoping for an official of some sort – a paramedic, anyone! – to stop her: in truth she didn't want to have a good view. No one did. The car that Zoe's had struck was the shape, more or less, of a boomerang, its left side entirely caved in. A man Mia guessed to be in his fifties – the driver, presumably – was sitting by one of the many bushes that had been planted on the roundabout, visibly quaking but apparently unhurt. A paramedic in a bright yellow coat was leaning over him, offering palliative care in the form of words. Zoe's car, similarly, was a wreck.

The two people inside (two?) were not moving. Disregarding the feelings of the passenger for a moment, Mia strode over to the driver's side, where the other paramedic was holding her hand through the shattered side window. For some reason Mia pictured a man in a kiosk, doling out a ticket.

'Get her out of there!' Mia screamed.

The paramedic was as old as the other driver in the accident; wisdom scored in the lines of his face told Mia he had seen it all before – he was used to hysteria. Very calmly he informed her: 'The door's buckled. We're waiting for the fire service.' The siren, Mia realised, was almost upon them. She felt impotent; her tiny fists were shaking at the air around her waist.

'What about him?' Now she looked into the car properly, past Zoe (breathing in gulps, mouthing words in another language), to the passenger: a man with close-cropped rook-black hair, his midriff coated with a patina of blood, a sense of enchantment on his face. 'My God,' whispered Mia. 'Osman.'

The name brought a fluttering of eyelids to Zoe; she was waking up in fits and starts. 'We found him, Mia,' she managed to say.

At the same time the paramedic was also speaking. 'The passenger was carrying a knife, we don't know why. The collision drove it into his leg. I'm sorry.'

'Osman,' Mia repeated. All this time... Her face was pure query mark and indignation as she looked up at the paramedic while remaining bent at the waist and not needing to speak a single word.

The paramedic said, 'He bled very quickly if that's any consolation.'

Tears had been pent up for too long. Mia released them. Through the following squall she said to her partner, 'You'll be all right, Zoe...'

'It's Halima, Mia. Halima, not Zoe. I'm not angry. I love you.'

'I love you too. Please hold on.'

'We found him.'

'I did nothing. You found him. Keep awake!' Mia squeezed Zoe's hand – unless she squeezed Halima's. She wasn't clear on the point. It struck her very briefly as ironic, the fact that for once the roles were reversed: it was Mia doing her best not to let Zoe close her eyes, rather than the other way round.

'He found me. I couldn't find you, but he found me. It's funny.'

Mia smiled. Keep her talking, she thought. 'It is funny, Zoe.'

'Halima. I'm Halima. Zoe's dead. She died in a car crash.'

Was it Mia's imagination or did the woman with whom she had shared five good years appear slightly younger in this light? Maybe the aroma of spilt blood was jabbing her senses; she wasn't sure. No, she was sure; something was drifting away from the woman's features. She was looking slightly... girlish. Mia rifled through her stolen thoughts and dreams; she closed her eyes, breathing in Halima's scent –the scent of chocolate. The smell of pollution in New Trozenxus had made the girl think about chocolate.

'We're going back there, Mia,' Halima breathed. 'You and I.'

It was not the time to speak of James Carbon, so the best Mia could offer was a simple platitude. 'They'll never take us back, Halima,' she said – and the name sounded smooth and clicked into place in her mouth, in her head. For the first time she could smell the alcohol on Zoe's breath.

The fire engine had arrived. 'You'll have to move aside,' the paramedic to her left informed Mia, a light hand on her elbow. 'They're here to release your friend.'

'We'll go,' Halima told her, squeezing Mia's hand, 'by choice. We'll go to the Tower of Crumbs. We'll go...' She breathed deeply; a dribble of blood left her mouth and rolled down her chin. 'We'll go as soldiers, Mia.'

'Don't speak...'

'And we'll do as soldiers do. Not for the Cause: but to kill the Cause.'

'I love you...' said Mia again.

'I know.'

'And I did it because I love you.'

'I know that too,' Halima told her. 'Hush now; my rescuer's coming. Where's Osman? Osman saved me. Where's he gone?' She was babbling.

'I'll be here when you wake up.'

To kill the Cause, thought Mia, though not in response to Halima's question – or perhaps it had been Zoe's final question. They would live in the same skin; die there, too. Don't think like that. Instead Mia thought of Halima's thoughts of Osman... Mia straightened up – her back clicked – and she accepted the paramedic's professional embrace. The words were like an ointment; the words burned and then salved the itch and distress. To kill the Cause. Who would be first? Through her mind's eye Mia viewed the simian bulk of Mort Fega, falling storey after storey from his sweatbox in the Tower of Crumbs. At the window, Mia and Halima – the former a younger woman, the latter the child whose only future had been pilfered and warped.

But there was one enemy so very much closer. Mia gritted her teeth. After watching the fireman don a pair of wide goggles, Mia chose not to view anymore of the here and now. She closed her eyes. Perhaps she'd sleep. Only with her subconscious could she be sure once again to summon James Carbon. The difference was, this time she would be ready.

The Slope

When Martin heard the *click* of the phone being put down at the other end, he was certain the call had been for Robbie. Martin should have been at work.

'Who is it?'

Martin walked back through the hall and joined his wife in the ripe radio noise and the breakfast-heat of the kitchen. 'The caller put the phone down. I *hate* that,' he said.

'Daddy?'

Robbie turned her back on Martin to monitor the bread's deepening tan under the grill. More aggressively than was needed, she shuffled the pan back under the glowing strips.

'Yes, darling,' said Martin to his daughter.

Noelle pushed her spectacles up the slope, to the bridge of her nose. 'What does this say, H-E-I-R?' She was reading a comic at the bar.

'Heir. The person who's going to be the king or queen next.'

'Why?'

'Why what?'

'It should say *hair*. There's a haitch.'

'Aitch,' said Martin. 'But it's heir, trust me.'

Noelle frowned, returning her attention to the comic. Over the next two seconds Martin watched as a glow of enlightenment crossed his daughter's features. '*Now* I understand. 'One of them's thrown to the *air* and one of them's heir to the *throne.*"

'That's right,' said Martin, half-remembering and half-guessing the feedline to the riddle.

'Do you want some toast, Mart?'

'No thanks. 'What's the difference between a ball and a prince?' Something like that?'

'Where's your sister, No-No?' asked Robbie.

'In the *lavatoire*. Making herself ber-yood-iful. Daddy? It's a quap joke.'

Martin laughed. 'It is indeed,' he said.

'Don't encourage her, Mart,' said Robbie, buttering the toast. Her back still turned on the proceedings, she added: 'You're not to use language like that in this house, young lady.'

The phone rang.

'I'll get it,' she finished.

But Martin was closer to the threshold. He picked up the white crescent. 'Hello?'

Pause.

Martin seized the moment. 'Who is this?' he demanded, aware that the kitchen's warmth had made his back damp beneath the shirt he would be wearing to the funeral. The phone line went dead.

Martin grinned. Robbie was approaching. 'What's so funny?'

'You.'

'Excuse me?' She aimed her voice up the stairs. 'Katie! Come down now, babe, you're going to be late!'

'Coming!'

'Robbie?'

'What? What do you mean, *me*?'

'Robbie? If it's starting again, I'm leaving. I told you I would and I will.'

'If *what's* starting again?' Robbie protested. The birthmark that punctuated the space between her eyebrows – the pinprick mole that she still found the energy to despise – now dipped as she frowned. 'Are you serious?'

Katie was descending the stairs.

'You louse,' said Robbie, matter-of-factly.

'Later... Katie?'

'Morning, Dad!'

'How could you?' Robbie whispered.

'It'll be a cold day in Hell, my darling,' said Martin, the grin on his face fixed, 'before I let you go out in *that*.'

'But Dad! It's dress-down day. It's for *charity*.'

Robbie walked off.

'Dress-down,' said Martin. 'Not dress-*off*. Remove that shoelace and put a proper skirt on. It's winter!'

*

There were three speeches at the crematorium: one from each of the sons.

Clamped between Marlin's father's eldest sister and a young man whose identity he never learned, Martin listened to the first two with the retention of a spinal injury patient; it was like catching smoke with a pair of tweezers. To the third speech – to Marlin's – he paid attention.

'You could tell Dad's mood,' said Marlin, 'by his handshake.'

The handshakes! Ingratiated, Martin had been, into the world of adult protocol and demeanour – by the very existence of his best friend's father's handshakes. Come rain or shine, whatever the hour, Marlin's father had greeted Martin at the front door with a stern grip and a muscular pumping of arms. On the hard bench, now, Martin was shooed back through time.

After the service, talk – laughter even – on the pavement outside the hall. Flowers had been constructed into the appearance of a dartboard: a reflection of Marlin's father's chief preoccupation and income. In his day the man had been good. On the proceeds of past winnings (and with his eye on the till of the future), the family had moved over from New Zealand, thirty-three years ago. Marlin's mother had died soon afterwards: the only thing she hadn't brought with her was her health. Aged seven, Marlin had entered Martin's school; the pair had been friends from that day. *Separated only by a consonant*, Marlin had liked to joke. *Separated by continents,* it had later become, once Marlin had returned to the motherland.

'You look troubled,' said Marlin.

'It's your father's funeral,' Martin replied.

'So take my mind off it. What's up?'

'It's Robbie.' The two words, and those alone, felt like releasing a recovered animal back into the wild. 'She's seeing someone else.'

Hours later, in the garden of the pub holding the wake, Martin added: 'Just wish she'd be honest. She wants someone new – I can live with that. Painful. But a fact of life. It's the *lies* I detest.'

'Flimsiest of evidence,' Marlin said.

'As before.'

'True.'

'Can I have one of them? I'm cold.' Martin asked, pointing at the box of cigarettes in its paddling pool of spilled drinks.

'Your funeral.'

*

You can't call me on the landline, she says. *What were you thinking of?*

You weren't answering your mobile.

Which means I can't speak! You won't believe the grief it caused.

I wanted to see you, he answers.

I've explained…

I don't care.

I demand that you care. If you loved me, you'd care…

I'll make it up to you. Tonight.

She pauses.

Are you there? he asks.

Yes. It's possible. He's gone to a funeral, up north.

*

On the train, Martin imagined an existence free from electricity and phones. Mobile phones, particularly... Weren't there tribes – weren't there *histories* – that managed without microwave ovens and texting?

Ticket displayed, he stood up as his station approached. Robbie was waiting to meet him. She was parked in the bus bay, listening to Radio Four.

Martin slotted the seatbelt clip into its socket.

'How was it?' Robbie's voice sounded clipped. She engaged first gear.

'As well as expected.'

'...Thought you might have called,' Robbie told him, indicating right as she stopped at the lights.

'Why?' Martin sounded like Noelle, whose curiosity alone might have earned her a job with NASA.

'To tell me you're okay, perhaps?'

'I'm *not* okay,' Martin replied. 'I just watched my friend's dad get burnt.'

'I know. But he was seventy-five years old, Mart.'

'Thanks.'

'Martin... You're really pushing me here. I'm trying to help. Why are you loading everything against me?'

'I've said.'

'Yes. And we have to talk about this morning,' Robbie added. 'About what you said.'

Martin turned to her profile. 'What *I* said? Robbie. *I'm* not the one whose boyfriend calls every ten minutes.'

'Neither am I.' Robbie shifted the stick into first gear and then enjoyed the rare privilege of second before encountering the next set of lights. She neutralled; yanked on the handbrake. 'I'm not doing anything wrong, Mart.'

'Define *wrong*.'

'...You're impossible.'

*

Unusually, Katie was the first of the girls down.

Martin could see that she'd had a bad night: her eyes appeared sunken and piggy in soft bags of lightly seasoned flesh. She had about her an aura of irritability. She greeted her father with something forced.

'So have you worked it out yet? I heard you arguing last night.'

Martin made it his way not to lie to the girls. 'We're in bother.'

'What she done?'

'Toast or cereal?'

'Both. What she done?' Katie persisted.

'I can't tell you.'

'Another *man* then.'

'How old are you again?'

'Thirteen. The *same* man?'

'I don't know,' Martin conceded.

'I hope not. He was a creep.'

'Who was?' No-No was entering the kitchen, wearing a stripy leotard and pink flip-flops. Once she had crossed to the draining board, she picked up a bread knife. Manically she slashed at the air. 'Don't worry, Daddy,' she said, panting. 'I'll kill him for you, whoever he is.'

'Put that knife down.'

'I'll poke his eyes out!'

'Put it down! Dangerous!'

Noelle pointed the blade at her father's chest. 'Do you want some, *Daddy*?' she asked, stepping closer.

'What's got into you?'

'Or maybe I should cut my wrists,' said Noelle.

'You'll do no such thing. You'll put that knife *down*.'

She threw it at Martin's face.

… And he woke.

The bedroom was the brownish-grey of advancing dawn, as warm as a gymnasium locker-room: just the way Robbie liked it. In her salmon-coloured slip, she was lying beside him; her breathing was harsh and gulping. She's getting a cold, thought Martin, gently stroking his erection. Is it time to get up?

His tongue was sore: Martin had taken to biting it in his sleep. Over the last few months he had been endeavouring to convince himself that this was not a worrying development. Something was bothering him.

Last night they had feebly squabbled; Martin's heart had not been in it. Too drunk to offer anything more than a weary swipe, Martin had snored into a sofa cushion, convinced there was nothing more to say. But there was plenty more to think about. Who *was* he, for example; whose *body* rolled over Robbie's? Whose lips kissed the mark above her navel? Martin built him up, a composite of Robbie's favourite actors. He moved them into a hotel room and slowly closed the curtains. The lover was thin; thin, toned, pale-skinned and handsome, he watched as Robbie sat on the edge of the bed. The lover approached. Robbie tickled the end of his shaft with her tongue…

*

Do you like that? he asks.

I want more, she tells him, running her fingers through his hair.

He kisses her thighs, before moving his tongue back into her folds. He is slow. By moving his jaw he squeezes pulses into her nerve endings.

I love you, she says distantly. Her fingertips follow his hairline; the onset of baldness has left him with fifty pence-sized gaps, to either side of his forehead. She savours the aftertaste of his semen.

After she has wriggled herself into an uneasy orgasm (she is worried about the time), he pushes her legs up and back; she is bent almost double. He laps at her anus like a thirsty animal at a stream.

She knows what he wants: it's the one thing she hasn't given him.

What's wrong? he asks. *Don't you like it?*

Not now, she says softly.

You promised me.

I have to get home… Don't be cross, she adds, lowering her ankles back onto the duvet. He crawls up the bed to lie beside her.

I'm not cross.

It's a big step for me and I don't want to rush it. I have to go.

I'll miss you. When can I see you?

At the weekend. I'll 'go shopping'.

He laughs. *I'm cheap at half the price,* he says, and he watches her as she swings off the bed and picks up her brassiere.

*

Having left it as late as possible to exit the house (hoping for the phone to ring and for the caller not to speak to him), Martin sat in his comfortable, lounge-sized car, four back from the red light preventing him access to the ugly bridge. The traffic was murder. It made him sad; *everything* made him sad. The red light made him sad. The steep slope of the bridge – this also made him sad. The argument with Robbie and his hangover made him sad. The people made him sad. *Guilt* made him sad. Even fear – so frequently and reliably sadness's antidote – was making him sad. Martin had lost his immunisation against sadness. It was a stark realisation.

Green light. First gear. Get a grip. Up the slope. Fucking *move*. The funeral. Robbie. No-No's eyes are getting worse. I said *move*. Flimsiest of evidence: Marlin. As before: that was me. And Marlin had said: True. One of them is thrown to the air. As if... You're not going dressed out like that. Was that it? As if he'd *known*. And the other one is heir to the throne. Crest of the bridge. Bloody traffic. Down the slope...

Marlin.

'Oh God,' said Martin thinly.

Triumphant and afraid, he honked his horn. One of the items in his life he most despised – his mobile phone – he made rare use of, once he had crossed the bridge, laboriously turned around, and crowned the bridge's slope once again. He felt sick. The contents of the call that he put through to Hermione, the team's secretary, were by no means a lie. Nor was the statement that he was going back home. 'The funeral's left me drained.'

Marlin. Back for the funeral; phone calls start. Coincidence? History... He'd forgiven the guy before, but now he'd had his right to remain revoked.

In this direction the traffic was better. Martin was making good time. He winked at a traffic warden, and then later at a lollipop lady, helping school kids across the road. Martin wondered if he should pause – take a coffee, buy cigarettes, even – in order to allow his notions to take shape.

No. Martin pressed on.

Home loomed. A cloud above grew bored and offered a judgement of rain. To the sound of straining wipers, Martin arrived and pulled onto the drive. Shoulderblades pinched, he followed the path to the front door. He was surprised – horrified and appeased – that Robbie's car was not here. Perhaps she met him at motels; it was a relief to learn that their marital bed did not keep a third party. Unless she's gone to the shops, or to work.

Martin waited on the doorstep; his key was pointed at the lock, divining the door to swing open magically. Perhaps I've got this wrong, he thought.

Then he heard the phone start to ring.

As swiftly as he could, Martin entered the house. He snatched up the receiver; he barked out his hello. And he waited into the silence...

The phone hummed into his head. He slammed it down. Panting like a show-dog, he called out his wife's name: once, twice...

*

Come on over, she says. *I'm alone.*

How come?

I'm ill. I've got cramps.

You're turning me on, he tells her.

That's the idea.

Are you sure? he asks. *Risk, I mean.*

She chuckles. *I'm sure you won't be missed for a few hours.*

I meant your *risk.*

*

'What the hell's going on?' he was asked.

'What are *you* doing here?'

'I live here,' said Katie. 'Why aren't you at work?'

Martin started to climb the stairs. 'Why aren't you at school?' he replied. 'And why aren't you dressed?'

'I'm ill! *Hello?* Were you awake this morning?' Katie asked sardonically, pulling together the lapels of her dressing gown. '... What are you doing?'

'I thought it was your mother.'

'You thought what was?'

'But it was you...'

Barefoot, Katie took two steps back. Her spine was against the wall on the landing.

'Where is he?' Martin asked, achieving the staircase's pinnacle. 'I'd like to slap his head for him.' Martin brushed past her.

'*Who?*'

Whoever was calling, thought Martin, immediately acknowledging his error: the paramour could not be in two places at once. Why would he have called the house's number from upstairs?

Into Katie's aromatic bedroom Martin thrashed. The posters; the mirror; the fleets of beauty products: these Martin ignored.

The man, Martin guessed, was approximately his own age. Stunned into silence, Martin took an unashamed look at him, from head to toe. His hair was receding; he had an umlaut of razor scratches to the left of his chin dimple. His chest was shallow, sloping down to a paunch; rubbery and wet from recent work, the man's penis performed a contrite quarter-circle.

'She's thirteen years old, pervert,' said Martin, ebullient with loathing. But his voice was threadbare and weak. He realised that he had never viewed another man's erection before. 'I'll see you locked up.'

I haven't done anything wrong, the other man replies, reaching for his underpants.

'Statutory rape is wrong. Five years' worth of wrong.'

There's been no rape, the man answers.

'She's thirteen years old!' he repeated.

'Dad!'

Martin turned, pointed at Katie's nose. 'And *you* can stay out of it.'

'*Dad!*'

'Shut it, Katie.'

There's no one there, she states.

When Martin returned his attention to his daughter's seducer… there was no one else in the room. No pigeon-chest; no shave-cut; no semi-thawed hard-on. The fear that struck Martin's sternum made him sit down on the bed.

'Get dressed,' he said quietly. 'Now.'

*

'You've shaved,' he remarked. 'I like it. But what will *he* say?'

'Won't notice,' said Robbie. 'He doesn't look at me below the elbows. That's where I stop functioning. If I'm not serving dinner I'm not of use.'

'Sorry to hear that.'

'I'm sorry to say it,' Robbie told him. 'Is it how you remembered?' she asked him, patient for his exotic Kiwi accent.

'It's raining,' he replied.

*

We have to be more careful, she says.

No one knows.

But Dad suspects. He drove home early and surprised Katie. Lost it. We're safe. I wouldn't let him hurt you.

I know.

…Turn onto your front, he says.

Okay, she answers, doing so.

It will only hurt for a second.

I know. Go on… says No-No.

*

He heard her scream. *One of them is heir to the throne,* he heard her say. *The other one is thrown to the air.*

'Dad?' said Katie. 'Who should I call?'

'I told you to put some clothes on.'

'I'm sick!' Katie protested.

'So am I. And *I'm* dressed.'

'Do you need a doctor?'

'No. Who is he, Kate?'

'Who?'

'Your sister's boyfriend,' said Martin.

Katie frowned. 'I thought it was you,' she told him, starting to dress.

The Soloists

These days the launderette's a safe place to work.

Not much of a job, I'll give you that, but it covers the rent and a drink on a Friday night, and I've usually got a few bob to spend on the kids every second weekend – that is, if Debbie ain't creating and making life prickly for us all and saying I can't have 'em at the last minute. She's like that sometimes. But I wasn't going to tell you about her. I was going to tell you about my job, and about the trouble it got me into, roughly this time last year.

Logically speaking, I should be able to pinpoint the exact date, but I can't. It was around the time of the third anniversary of Sammy's death. That's my brother – or it was. He died doing those silly bloody stunts that the telly's made popular. Extreme sports they call 'em. But what's so sporting about having your fucking leg nearly wrenched from its socket? Bungee jumping. The heart attack took nearly twenty minutes to kill him off stone.

Around this time it was that Ralph Marrison came into the launderette one night, around two. Forgive the vagueness, but the hours blur. You won't see the job title 'Admissions Executive: Laundromat Services' in the top ten of most exciting occupations in the land. And the title's a joke anyway. I'm a bouncer, that's what I am. Admissions Executive my arse. I turn away those who want a warm place to crash for a couple of hours – and I've done a decent job over the last eighteen months. We don't get many junkies or drunks or prozzies anymore; just the spirits, wraiths and insomniacs who choose to avoid the day and do their washing in the midnight hour.

Ralph Marrison I should have kicked out straight away; but he looked the part. He really did. Jeans too short for his lanky legs, and oil-spotted too; also he wore a dark green shirt and a battered black leather jacket. He was carrying a floppy maroon bag, in which I assumed he held his dirty pants. But smalls were not what he wanted to launder that night.

I have a table near the door. My accoutrements on the shift from nine p.m. to six daybreak are as follows: packet (one) Bachelor Cigarettes; lighter (one), refillable; sandwiches (six), ham and Brie or Marmite and marmalade – a much maligned combination; Thermos flask (one), black coffee, sixteen sugars; book (one), most often Psychology-Lite or dumbed-down universe physics; and that's me for nine hours. I do not get sleepy. I used to, but I don't anymore. I don't even sleep much during the day. I watch the Nature Channel.

His first words to me were: 'Blimey. Is it bright enough in here for you?'

I looked up from the book and said through a mouthful of smoke: 'You get used to it, chief. Any machine'll do, just not the last one on the left. Engineer's coming in tomorrow.' I had already put a note on the glass eye of the door to this effect but you'd be surprised how many visitors I get who can't read English. Or read anything. Some, you'd swear, can barely walk and blink at the same time.

'Nice and warm,' he goes on.

'Yeah.' You get suspicious of conversation: it always masks something that is *not* being said. 'Do you need a hand?' I asked.

'How much is it?' the guy says.

'Eight quid for a full wash. Pound coins only. Do you need change?'

'Yeah, I do.' He drops the bag on my desk and works the zip open. 'See, I've only got notes,' he added.

'You can say that again,' I told him.

The bag was full – completely stuffed – with tens and twenties. Not in the neatly counted decks that you see in the films where the rich couple has paid the kidnapper. The bills were scrunched, mangled, folded, torn.

'You'd better leave,' I told him, thanking my stars we were alone. My thought was that we might not be for much longer. Anyone could walk in.

'My name's Ralph,' the man said. 'I have ten thousand pounds in this bag and I need to get rid of it.'

Call it human instinct, but what do you do when you're fed a line like that. You suck it and see, don't you? You roll it around your tongue.

'Leave it here,' I told him. 'I'll dispose of the article for you.' I trust there was plenty of sarcasm in this but Ralph only looks at me and nods.

'That's the idea, pal. What's your name again?'

'Chris.'

'Chris what?'

'*Ralph* what?' I asked.

'Marrison. Chris what?'

'Chris Newman. Bouncer Extraordinaire. And what's your gig?'

'Chris. I'm a flight attendant. Now listen. I've got ten bags of sand and I can't be doing with this stuff around. It's yours. For eight.'

'Okay,' I replied, 'I'll see what I've got in my wallet.'

'What's in the till?' Ralph wanted to know.

'Half a mill in sparklers. Come off it, mate. This is a launderette, we don't carry that sort of cash. And anyway, I don't get it.'

Ralph nodded his head. 'The bills are marked. Can't be walking 'em.'

'Marked?'

'UV pen, mate.' He laughed. 'I hope I won't be losing your respect if I say I haven't earned it ploughing the field. You get me? So what I'm saying to you is, I'm giving you an investment opportunity. *You* get ten, stuff it where you will; and I get eight and a clear conscience…'

I closed my book. I extinguished my cigarette.

'You don't understand. I ain't got it, mate. Even if I was interested.'

'Which you are.'

'Which I am.' How could I not be? But I'd never done anything illegal in my life… 'Where did you get it? Seriously.'

'On my window-cleaning round. Are you in or out?'

'I'm stuck here till six,' I told Ralph, hoping for an easy out.

But what Ralph said back was this: 'I'll come back then. Breakfast?'

'Listen. Are you a copper? Is this a fit-up?'

'No. Do you know Cooper Street?'

'Yeah.' What I didn't mention was that I *live* on Cooper Street.

'Six thirty, let's say, in the Roll With It caff. Okay?' Ralph coughed.

'One thing,' I added. 'Why me?'

Ralph's reply was simplicity itself. 'Because you're open,' he said.

Once something has shocked you, you can't become unshocked; that's my belief. I am still shocked that Sammy doesn't answer the phone. I am still shocked (though God alone knows why) that I've ended up here.

That was a clue that was. *Of course* I went. What did I have to lose? I hadn't committed to anything, and I definitely didn't take along eight thousand pounds. Where was I going to get eight K in the middle of the night? I repeat: I work in a place where people wait for muck to be crushed from their fabrics. Eight grand? I was even hoping that coffee would be Ralph's treat. I never eat breakfast – or any other meal – with people I don't know, and even with my own family it's a struggle... the Christmas morning scrambled eggs at the ex's place, for example. But I'd have a black coffee and hear him out, I decided.

Reassuringly for me, the Roll With It was already busy. I liked the noise. Ralph was sitting at a table near the lavatories, and this was when you could still smoke in public places; when I arrived he was reading a red-top and rolling a snout of Robinson's tobacco. He bid me welcome and then went back to finishing off the Problem Page.

'Silly bastard,' he muttered, eventually closing the tabloid.

'Who?'

'This guy: shagging his own mother-in-law. Thinks he might get caught but can't stop himself. Apparently the sex is *electrifying*. Ever happen to you?'

'What? Doing it with the ex's mum?'

'No; electrifying sex. Sounds dangerous rather than anything else. I'd rather it keep it *nice* or at best *exciting*. Joyriding's electrifying. Bungee-jumping's *electrifying*...'

I asked him: 'What made you say that? About bungee-jumping.'

Ralph shrugged his shoulders. 'Just an example,' he said.

An example; I let it go. 'And what about this?' I said.

'Electrifying?' He snickered. 'This is business, mate, nothing but.' He leaned a little closer, revealing stained molars, a twitchy smile threatening to break out. 'The truth? Not even stealing it was electrifying, Chris.'

'Whose is it?' I asked.

'Was it. Whose was it?'

'Whose was it?' I asked.

'You don't need to know. I've given you the facts. Do you want some food? They do a good egg and bacon bagel.'

'I don't like bagels.'

'Sandwich then. On me.'

'I'm not hungry, thanks anyway. You're asking me to trust a lot, Ralph.'

He shook his head. 'On the contrary, mate, I'm not asking you to trust me one iota. The bag's in a safe place. Nod your head and I go and get it. I've made it quite clear it wasn't mine to start with but it is now. Your only involvement is raising eight-tenths of it to hand to me.'

'At which point I'm carrying marked notes.'

'Indeed you are, chief. That's the gamble.'

My coffee arrived; I thanked the foreign waitress and took a pause to pour in the equivalent of about four sugars from a round dispenser.

'And what if I get caught?' I asked next.

'Chris, listen. After this morning I don't know you. That's your own business. This business breakfast never took place. I was never here.'

I smiled at him. 'Ralph's not really your name, is it?' I said.

'Yeah it is, funnily enough. That was an error on my part. Still wasn't here, though, if anything ever came out. Listen. You'll have the bag; as long as you don't go down to the Peugeot show-room and pay in cash, or be a *dick* about it, who's to know? What do you buy every day?'

I held up the packet from which I was fishing a cigarette.

'Little shop?'

'Yeah.'

'Fags and papers? Bit of blue on the top shelf?'

'That kind of thing.'

Ralph inhaled sharply. 'Just keep it that way,' he advised me, 'or sell it on yourself – it's your money, do what you want with it. We got a deal?'

They crashed through my mind, the years, the jobs... Sheet metalworker, trolley collector, *debt* collector, leaflet distributor, hopeless barman, lazy driver, launderette bouncer... Was this the best that I could hope for for me and my kids? An ex-wife who hated me for the misdemeanour of never making much of what little I ever had. A future of grey and beige. I was forty-one years old, damn it, and I had little to look forward to other than the first smoke of the morning, self-improvement via library books, and sleep.

'I'll get you the money, Ralph.'

'When?'

'What about quality control?' I ignored his question. 'How do I know you're not passing me a bag full of toilet paper with important faces printed on?'

Ralph was drinking tea. He placed his Mr Tickle mug down in the rainbows of grease on a plate – the grease being the only evidence of a vanished breakfast. 'Mr Anorexia there behind the bar just accepted one,' he said.

'The fuck does that mean? *One?*'

'Lower your voice, please, Chris... It's as I said: caution's the operative word. But it's fine. Run your fingers along the watermark; do what you want. I repeat, only when?'

'Three days?'

Ralph shook his head and rinsed his mouth. 'Burning a hole in my carpet, mate.'

'Two.'

'Including today, I'll go with two,' agreed Ralph. 'First in line when the Shabby National opens, okay? Where do you live?'

'Nine buildings away,' I answered, sniffing. 'Above the key-cutting place. And you?'

'Shut up! Where I got the keys cut for this creeping? Small world.' He seemed stupefied by the coincidence.

'And where do *you* live?' I try again.

'By the rivers of Babylon, mate...'

He had keys cut, so at some point he'd had access to the original keys – even if he'd stolen them to begin with. But why were the bills marked? (And was he telling me the truth anyway?) I'd lost grip on the notion that Ralph had burgled a mansion or something. Not even millionaires keep ten stashed in the cookie jar, do they? Or UV-light their banknotes.

So... a kidnapping? That seemed real; this idea returned, again and again, like a malnourished cold. He'd got away with it: implication being nobody hurt. Fair and decent enterprise, then... As long as I broke it down, say, to one note spent a week, in different establishments... I was thinking like this as the banks opened. Not that I went in: this is the 21st Century. Back in my bedroom I picked up the phone and tickled a few credit cards, claiming to operators I had a new carpet to lay, and that some repairs needed doing to a car I don't even own. By noon I had three collected assurances that a total of eight thousand would be in my account and available to spend on the following day.

The handover was easy. I had worked myself up into a bear with nits – jumpy and restless as I was. But it went like a charm. I'd like to say I never saw Ralph Marrison again, but that wouldn't quite be the truth; there you go...

Bobbie and Trina were at first the only suspicious parties, and that was shortly after I collected them from their mother's house the following Saturday. They might have been eleven and nine respectively, but they had the instincts of private investigators. 'You've hoovered and washed up,' said Bobbie.

'Thought I'd make an effort, girls,' I replied.

'You *never* do the washing up,' Bobbie either complained or accused.

I confessed one fragment of the truth. 'Okay. I've got me a cleaner.'

'Blimey. What's her name?'

'Rita.'

'And what's your new girlfriend's name?' asked Trina.

'I haven't got a new girlfriend.'

'Then why are you cleaning up?' she continued. 'Win the Lottery?'

'Something like that,' I answered. 'Do you fancy the ski slopes?'

A week passed, and then another, and then one night, around eleven o'clock, with the lion's share of my shift still to serve, I was at my table, reading *Coping With Bereavement* and keeping half an eye on the five customers on the long wooden benches who were watching their machines with nothing more than low-grade territoriality, when the door opened and in walked Ralph. He looked a little... *ferrety,* unhinged; he was nervous.

He told me we needed to talk. It would only have wasted time to ask what about so instead I left a silence. We hadn't even said hello to each other.

'I need to buy the money back,' he said. 'You don't need to know why. I'll give you my ten for the marked ten.'

'You're not making sense, Ralph. Why would you want to do that?'

'I'm in a bind,' he said. 'Can we do this?'

'No.'

'Eleven then. Help me out.'

'I can't,' I admitted, 'I don't have it.'

'What? You've spent it in *three weeks?*'

'Not all of it.'

'Christ. What did I tell you about being prudent, Chris?'

'I have been. I've bought some new clothes, not a yacht. What I mean is, I don't have all of it, not to hand. I treated myself here and there and I've stashed some in a brand new bank account and set up a debit to pay off the interest and monthlies on the credit cards I ransacked.'

Ralph was shaking his head. 'What did I say about *banks* fuck's sake?'

'Nothing! You didn't mention banks!'

'Well, you should have worked that out, common sense...
How much can you get your hands on? Tonight.'

'None. I've got to watch this place,' I said. 'It's my job.'

'How much is left at home?'

I pretended to do a rough mental calculation, although I
knew the precise amount I'd scattered around, in the pages of
books, in my breadbin, in the cardboard packet of a Dover sole
readymeal in the freezer. I said, 'Six.'

He paused. Then he told me: 'Get it, Chris. I'll look after
the till. You can be there and back in fifteen minutes.'

'I don't *want* to be there and back in fifteen minutes,' I argued. Immediately it was as though someone had twisted a dial
and turned him jerky; it wasn't just the heat inside the building
that was making him sweat.

'Chris, please. You have no idea of the sort of scum I'm dealing with.'

'Are you in trouble?' I asked, stupidly. Of course he was!

Sparing my blushes, he declined to answer. He made an effort
to control his breathing; he sort of patted down the air at his waist
with his fingers splayed out, as if he was smoothing out a pillow.

'Chris. I am offering you ten thousand pounds for your six...'

'But you haven't answered my question!' I protested. 'Why
would you-'

He cut me off. Not aggressively. 'You gambled before,' he
said reasonably, 'so why don't you gamble again? Did I let you
down?'

'No.'

'Am I an honest man?' he continued.

'Apparently not.'

'But to you I have been.'

'Yes... to me you have been. Where's the ten?'

'Where? Same place as before,' Ralph told me. 'What's that
got to...'

Stay steady, I was saying to myself; but my scalp felt tingling and feverish, my pulse quickened. Call it greed. Call it luck. *Call* it a sensation that for once in my crummy last few years I was doing something right – even if to achieve this goal meant doing something wrong. No-going-back style of wrong. Maybe-go-to-prison style of wrong. The fuck-it-let's-chance-it kind of wrong. I picked up my half-eaten sandwich. I chewed, deep in thought. Turning my attention away from him, I watched the customers. One of them, only one, had started to read a magazine; the others were staring, sudblind.

I'd made ten, and here I was noodling over a further four. For what? Was there any possible reason to *want* to be caught with bent money? Obviously, yes; the shivering wreck to my side told me so.

If he's got the marked notes, I thought, even three-fifths of them, he can claim to have stolen them. He can say he was *there.* So where *wasn't* he? If things get so desperate that you're taking the bite for a robbery, what the hell are you trying to escape from?

'The marked bills are an alibi, aren't they?' I asked, turning back to him.

Ralph seemed unwilling to go as far as this. 'Will you do it or not? Here…' He plucked a chain of keys from his jacket pocket. 'Here's my house keys. This is trust. You can go and get the bag yourself. I'm letting you in.'

I finished a mouthful of sandwich. I told Ralph that that was trusting all right but that it still didn't help me: I still couldn't leave my post. If my manager came in unexpectedly – a chance in a thousand but it had been known – I'd be for the chop.

'Let me go to yours, then,' he answered. 'Tell me where you got it.'

'Compromise…' Thoughts were racing ahead of me; they came in pictures of me scissoring up a credit card, its value now nil, paid off; of a break in the sun – I was due some time off, and with Angelo, my boss, when it came to paid leave, it was a case of use it or lose it, and I'd always liked the Algarve – and I thought of the girls, their birthdays, a better Christmas. 'Why don't you fetch the ten *then* go to mine for the six?' I suggested.

'I'm touched.' He accepted my offer of a bunch of keys. Nodding his head – I'm tempted to say *sagely* – he also accepted my directions to the flat.

And then I waited. Fortunately, to kill the time, I had a fight outside to observe, on the pavement, near the bus stop. A youth wearing, of all things, a Take That sweatshirt – he attacked an older guy who was withdrawing money from the cashpoint. I stepped out into the chill. When you work a graveyard shift, a good scrap is street theatre. I lit a cigarette and egged them on. I didn't really care who won as long as neither of them spilled into the launderette. Arms and fists were flailing; it was like watching two octopi knocking it out for a lady octopus or for a bit of sea territory. Quite amusing.

The nerves settled in shortly after this welcome interlude. Fact, 'nerves' might be selling the emotion a bit short – like saying Jack the Ripper could get a tad cross from time to time. Fucking *shitting* myself. Where *was* he? Ralph, I mean, not Jack. It didn't take the better part of an hour to walk half a mile and back... but I tried to console myself with the thought that he himself might live a good distance away. Like Scarborough, for example... At one o'clock I rescued my mobile from the inside pocket. Chance in a million, I knew, but I was going to call my home number. The mobile was dead. Sandwich-mush wriggled in the pit, in the gut. Breaking wind, I walked to the payphone. Dropped 20p into the slot. Called the flat. When the machine kicked in with the message that had once been humorous – *If you're not selling something, leave a message,* my voice instructed me – I could have winced at the irony.

I'd been sold something all right: I'd been sold a sucker's punch.

The night moved slowly. Pictures haunted me – threatened me. I could see Ralph trashing the flat. Once he'd found the money he would leave the taps on with the plugs in the sink; the water would be soaking through to the locksmith's below as I sat there, impotent. He would set fire to my kitchen. He would break my crockery, pinch my laptop... He would...

I was tempted to call Angelo; explain that I needed to abandon the shift. I even sorted out, in my head, a good reason to do so: one of my girls was sick with a fever and was calling for me because Debbie was at the casino. (This last part was probably true. My ex often worked late ones as well; she did bar work sometimes, on top of her day job in a chemist, ringing out receipts for paracetamol and johnnies.) I could say that the babysitter – whose first child, incidentally, I'm sure, was conceived on the sofa I used to own in that house – had called because she hadn't been able to reach Deb...

Nothing of the sort, of course, did I do. No; I simply waited, hoping that my radar hadn't failed me. I *had* trusted Ralph, there was no way around that. Now I felt like one of those people you read about in the red-tops: the ones who give thousands of nicker up front to door-to-door *arrivistes* and chancers selling driveway repair and guttering overhaul, who then bugger off before they've unloaded their shovels from the back of the van. Fucking duped.

Didn't matter the dough wasn't mine to begin with. I tried to be philosophical in that way, but it didn't work. Another failure, was all I could think, after a while. Hours earlier than it would have been normally, I finished my flask of coffee, I finished my food, I was in no mood to read; I had nothing to do. Wait, wait, wait... Two o'clock, three o'clock, four o'clock more. The beginning of the time when traffic denses slightly; the first bus pulled up outside, in the rain. Umbrellas led passengers on board. I watched. There was no one in the launderette; I could risk it, run home... How much money was in the till? Surely it could be left. But I didn't dare.

Perma-tanned, bleach-toothed Beverley arrived punctually at ten to six – for her go behind the table. Now me, I'd never been one to dress up for a job such as this, but Beverley always made the effort. She wore a suit and sensible shoes. More often than not she brought along textbooks, intending to study for the Economics degree she was taking at what used to be the 'Tec. She was nineteen, in her second year, and I'd sported a hard-on for her for months, but not this morning. 'Gotta dash, Bev,' I told her and started to run.

Other than the fact that my front door was open at the top of the flight of metal stairs, there was nothing to suggest anyone had been in my flat. Not at first, anyway. Tribute to Rita, the place still looked more ordered than it had since the day after I'd moved in – intending at that time for it to be no more than a temporary bolt-hole. Not a cushion out of place; not a nick-nack broken. Nothing. No, not nothing, I realised; there *was* one thing – one thing that only an anxious fellow like I am might have given any credit to. The kitchen light was on. Debbie had termed it neurotic, but I prefer the word fastidious – the description of my ritual before I leave home. I check the plugs are out the wall; check the taps are off tight; check the fridge door is properly shut. And I turn all the lights off.

Ralph hadn't left a bag stuffed with fifties, twenties and tens. I felt sick. He'd cleaned me out... But when I checked on the money I'd left in the breadbin, it was still there. The money in the freezer was not. The money inside the pages of paperbacks: not. Confusion and relief boxed and sparred. I emptied the breadbin on to the top of the washing machine, redundant as it was for any other purpose as I laundered my clothes during the quiet hours at work. As soon as I'd counted past six thousand and still had a good pile to go through I knew that Ralph had honoured his side of the bargain, just changed the arrangements slightly. Instead of handing me the money at the launderette, he'd left it here. Come to think of it, it made better sense. Nine grand and counting... Perhaps I slipped a note or two because it came to nine-nine-seventy. Close enough.

I needed a leak. I often pee in sinks to cut down on water bills from the flush mechanism, but today – after all I'd been through, and more importantly, *made*, money-wise – I decided to treat myself and headed for the can. Nonetheless I noticed my bathroom sink in passing, and it wasn't empty. The water filling about one-third of the volume was by now only lightly flecked with suds, but it *had* been soapy – and hot. It was only tepid now, as I discovered when I reached down to the plug for my keys. It had all worked out.

Copies? I thought then. After all, he'd done it once, copied keys, or so I believed, in order to steal the cash to begin with. What might have stopped him making copies of everything on my ring? I laughed aloud. The logical side of my underused brain suggested that the fact that it wasn't yet seven a.m. was a fairly serious rebuttal of this kind of crazy talk. It was over. And I was fourteen sheets proud. To celebrate I strolled down to Roll With It, after visiting my local newsvendor for a paper and a packet of tobacco. It was gluttony and not hunger that made me order the breakfast that was three up from the 'Full Fucking English': top of the tree was 'Colon the Barbarian'. Starving survivors of plane wrecks would struggle with this beast. And it took me nearly an hour and a half, but I ate it all and then went for a nap.

Mid-afternoon, and I'm watching the Nature Channel: a documentary about bison. The front door rattles on its hinges as a heavy fist pounds upon it. The doorbell had broken in earlier times, but I hadn't had it repaired – no one visits. I got up from the armchair, prepared to have a few words about unnecessary force against lifeless pieces of wood.

The fist that struck my face struck it *hard*. That burning sensation of nasal cartilage being compromised – this was the sensation that dwarfed any other, as I stumbled back from the door and bumped into a stand-alone lamp. The bowl of the lightshade wobbled. Though I took the first kick offered in my direction – it connected with my outer thigh – I dodged the second by stepping to my right. Through the blurriness of tears in my eyes I saw two men, not particularly well built or well dressed. Both had now entered my flat, and whether or not they were in the right place they meant business. The second one closed the door.

I'd retreated to my lounge. 'What do you want?' I demanded. The first man through the door was shaved, scalp, face and eyebrows all (he resembled a baby whose appearance only a mother could love), and as he asked me 'Where is she?' I attempted to take stock of my situation and my opportunities.

'Who?'

What appears from the second intruder's left trouser pocket is black and cylindrical, about the size of a mouth organ. To start with. Its wielder is pock-marked, face and hands both, with uprooted spots; he's an ugly bit of work, and he's getting closer... With his thumb he sprang a catch of some kind and the harmonica jettisoned forth another section of what looked like solid rubber. The baton, by this stage, was approximately a foot long; instead of hitting me with it, or trying to (I was ready, I thought), he swung the weapon at my widescreen TV. The glass did not break, but a crack was formed that looked like a child's drawing of a stick-man, minus the head. There was a crackle, a spit of sparks, and then my bison education was abruptly culled.

It wasn't the thought that I could buy a replacement easily enough that prevented me from complaining – I had already concluded that the money wouldn't be mine for much longer – but it was the terror welling up that caught my tongue. Give me a pissed-up headcase at the launderette any day; this was *calculated*. A leather-skirt offering a blowjob in return for half an hour of sleep on the bench and fifty pee for a plastic cup of sweet tea is a doddle in comparison. Child's play. A second or two passed before the first man said:

'Do we need to ask again?'

'No; you need to explain,' I told him.

The baton-whacker mumbled 'Dear oh dear' and took a swipe at a photograph of the girls, taken at the zoo six months earlier; the picture left the windowsill and fell to the floor, the glass breaking.

'I don't know what you're talking about,' I went on, trying to stay calm, 'but let's talk about it instead of breaking things, shall we? A drink?'

Amazed as I was, this seemed to put the alpha male's temper on ice for a few beats. 'All right,' he allowed, 'I'll have a Scotch if you'd be so kind.'

'Um.' I made a move for the kitchen. Billy Bollocks with the stick gave a twitch, not having expected sudden motion. *And a saucer of milk for your kitten?* I wanted to add. 'I don't think I've got any. Don't drink much myself.'

To the doorway and no further they followed me. The cupboard under the sink was where I kept such booze as ever entered my home, which wasn't much. I have nothing against the stuff – as I said, I like a pint on a Friday night, my one night off work – but I don't hoard a lot of it away. A swift inventory followed, the running commentary going, '...gin...nearly empty, mind... Bailey's... half a bottle of cooking sherry...'

'I'll have a sherry,' the two men said, more or less in stereo.

I poured. 'Fuck of a punch,' I complimented Raider One, the blood that I had no intention of staunching now spoiling what had been a perfectly decent T-shirt. 'Now...' handing over the tumblers '... would you mind telling me what you're doing here and why I'm getting a thumping?'

'Marriott grassed on you, son,' said Raider Two, sipping with the surreally placed politeness of one at an art exhibition's opening night.

Gently I shook my head. 'I don't know anyone by that name,' I said, quickly adding: 'And while we're on the subject, what're yours?'

Raider One finished a mouthful – most of the glass's contents. 'I'm Pinky and this is Perky,' he said. 'Now where is she, now we've had a rest.'

'Where is who?' I tried again.

Perky threw his tumbler at the oven. Not only did it break, but the glass of the oven door cracked and sherry licked over the linoleum. The moment of manners exhausted, he transferred his baton back to his better hand (the right) and swung it full pelt at my ribs. Only instinct forced my arms forward to block some of the blow's force, but the strike was still painful.

'Chris Chris Chris,' said Pinky, shaking his head. 'If I look in this breadbin and find money I'm going to know you're lying, aren't I?'

That was when I turned chilly as the lakes of damnation. Words spluttered from my mouth – or sounds did, rather. How exactly it came out I don't know but I think I was aiming for something like, 'Well you *will* find money, but that doesn't prove anything...' A sentiment to that effect.

'Bingo.'

Why hadn't I hidden it somewhere? After counting it, it might have been placed *anywhere*... so why did I leave it where I'd found it? I held out my hand to Pinky. A tad confused, he did what I wanted and handed back the tumbler he'd been drinking from. I turned my back on my tormentors. What else was there to say? They'd known where to find the money; I was busted. Sighing, I filled the tumbler all but to the rim – not for a second helping for Pinky but for myself. I turned back around and leaned against the sink, drinking. As I spoke I eyeballed them one at a time. 'I don't know a Marriott but I know a Marrison.'

Pinky cocked his head to one side. 'It could have been Marrison,' he conceded, 'the line was bad. Bottom line being, he's dropped you in the shit.'

'Hasn't he just.' I drank again: blood and sherry – copper and sugar – in my mouth, disgusting. 'But I don't know what she you're talking about. Swear to God. He's set me up. It was him, whatever it was…'

I forced myself to stop talking. You can't become un-shocked, as I've said before, but you can change that shock into something like revelation. My lips and vocal cords were digging a bigger grave than my silence ever could. The truth was filtering through. What I had were the *unmarked bills*: ten grand's worth of the buggers. Did I *really* have anything to fear? I finished the glass of sherry, saying, 'Truce, lads; I was naughty. I robbed, okay? But you're here about something else, I think, and it doesn't concern me…'

Perky had not stopped staring at me since he'd flung away his tumbler; even now he refused to speak – he was staring at me, blinking fast, the muscles in his jaw as tensed as those of any Dobermann. It was Pinky who'd assumed the duties of spokesman. 'Oh you're wrong,' he told me, 'it's very much about the money as well. Mr Herman was clear about that. You know and I know that ten large is a night out for a man of his stature, but that don't alter the fact that it's his money and not yours, sunbeam, to piss up the wall.'

'I don't know *anything*. I don't *know* a Mr Herman!' I protested.

'Where is she?' Perky demanded, breaking his monkish vow of silence.

'For the last time, *who?*'

On this occasion Perky doesn't take it out on my cooker: he takes a step forward and kicks me hard below my left knee. Punches and baton strikes find me: three, four, five of them, and then I start to fight back, pain and anger my spurs to creative violence. Still sipping sherry, Pinky moves not a jot in my peripheral vision as we go for it, tooth and nail. I land a good one on Perky's chin; I slam him fingers first in his windpipe, a blow that winds him and makes him crabwalk to the left, gasping a rattle.

'Enough of this,' said Pinky, his left hand going into his jacket. Though I couldn't be sure of what I'd got into, I knew this move couldn't possibly signify good news. I pictured a gun emerging, a knife… it was a lighter. What looked like a normal cigarette lighter. I could've offered him a light without all the bloodshed. 'It seems a bit unnecessary but let's test the money anyway.'

Salvation! *'Yeah*. Test the fucking money!' I told him, my attention between him, flicking flames now, and Perky with the damaged voicebox – damaged if I had my say in the matter. 'You won't find no UV on *that*.'

'Who said I want to? How old is your patter, mate? *UV?*' He opened the breadbin and pulled a note out at random – a fifty. 'It's almost cute. Ultra-violet went out with the Ark.' At which he set fire to the bill.

'…you *doing?*' I demanded.

The fifty pound note quickly took, yellow flame; a spiral of brown smoke transfixed us all – before there was a flash of white light. Pinky dropped the cinders into my kitchen sink, on top of a dirty cup or two.

'Which proves what?' I asked, my face furrowing up in bewilderment.

'See the flash there, pal? That'll be the magnesium deposits. Burns with a bright spark up, see? And Mr Herman had the bills dusted in that shit. Come on. You wanted to talk. Let's talk – you and me. Bring your bottle. Is there enough for a second one each?'

'Just about…' I was trembling. In itself this wouldn't look good; it would look like I was guilty; it would look I'd been caught red-handed. 'Do you mind if I just clean up first?'

'Yes I do. Grab a tea towel.'

While I mopped the blood from my face I assessed the damage with careful ministrations, using fingertips. Not broken; that was a relief. The one I called Pinky pulled a chair over from my small dining table and twisted it round so he sat on it back to front. He was higher than I was on the sofa. Perky took himself off on a reconnaissance mission of my home.

'He was here,' I said quickly. 'Marrison. Ralph Marrison. He tried to wash his prints off my keys – that's why they were in my sink – but there must be some way of getting to the bottom of it. *He was here.*'

Pinky shrugged. 'I have no doubt he was. You were in it together...'

I was shaking my head. 'I wasn't in *anything,* believe me.' And I scampered through a précis of what I knew – in doing so I was able to convince myself of just how ridiculous it sounded.

'But he's played his part; he's learned his lesson. I don't frankly give a monkey's toss *whose* fingerprints are on the notes. They're in *your* kitchen – ten thousand pounds for the ransom – and you didn't have the common decency to return she,' was what I heard him say.

My face screwed up. 'Wait a minute...' I capitalized the first letter of that 'she'. 'She's a name? The *name* of the girl is She?'

It was Pinky's turn to look baffled. 'What girl?' he asked.

'What kind of a name is She? Sheila?'

His pause told me a lot – as indeed my ignorance told *him* a lot. I could see him doing his arithmetic there, his chin now lowered down to his folded forearms. He said 'She' once more before his spelling it out made it clear. He said, 'Ess. Eye. Dee. Aitch. Ee. *Sidhe.* It's Irish. Like *she* is... It means spirit.'

'Found her!' cried Perky from my bedroom.

'It's not me!' I shouted, panic laced into my words like veins in skin.

'You sick bastard!' was Perky's next statement. 'Let me do him, Al.'

'How is she?'

'I haven't done anything, I swear on my mother's life...'

'Sit down, Chris. Sit *down.*'

As I poured myself the rest of the sherry – fuck protocol and social niceties, no one else was getting any more – Perky returned to the lounge, holding a baby-shaped parcel, swaddled up in my summer duvet.

'Dead. Filthy bastard hid in a drawer under the bed.'

He was talking about me! Me! Me, who up to a month earlier had never put a foot out of step in his life. A *filthy bastard?* But what were *they* talking about, if not a missing child? Perky deposited the package on my pouffe. Inside its wrapping… was a dog. A puppy.

'Irish Wolfhound, Chris. Impeccable lineage and pedigree. You sold yourself short at ten grand, son, to be honest. Mr Henry pays ten grand in *tips* when he goes abroad for his summer break.'

'Really?'

Pinky laughed. 'Nah, not really. Just a family pet. But true, the tips.'

I tried to keep my voice as level as possible. 'This,' I said clearly, 'has nothing to do with me. This is the work of Ralph Marrison.'

'Then why's it under your bed, prick?' asked Perky.

'He planted it there!' I shouted. 'May God strike me down if I'm lying.'

Sarcastically, Pinky looked up towards the ceiling. When he gave me his attention again he said, 'Well *that* seems to have worked, Chris. Tell you what: you're off the hook with our blessing.' He snapped his fingers: a 'great idea' expression on his face. 'But we better be sure, though, innit? May God show a sign if you're telling the truth.'

'All right…' he whispered.

'Not very conclusive, that, Chris,' said Pinky. 'Not *scientific*. But do you know… What amazes me is the stupidity of it all. You had the money, so why not give back the dog?'

'You're asking the wrong person. I'm a launderette bouncer. That's it.'

I might as well have not spoken. 'The money was *yours.*'

'Oh sure. That's why he put magnesium on it.' I closed my eyes, but I couldn't keep them closed for very long. The dead dog on my furniture – that was all I could focus on. My voice was lower. 'Ralph did it. Ralph screwed you on the deal, not me. I thought I was in for a bit of easy money for a change.'

Pinky nodded. 'But you see, Chris, Ralph couldn't have ballsed up the deal – he was too busy at exactly the same time, robbing the betting agency.'

'Then he's in it with someone else. It ain't me.'

'You're convincing,' said Pinky, 'I'll give you that.'

'It's the truth.' I was spent. Resigned, flat and spent; I had no energy left – and besides, the sherry was starting to bring down my mood, even if it was helping to anaesthetize the bridge of my nose. 'Can I get this straight, please?' I asked. 'He steals a puppy and holds it for ransom, right?'

Together Pinky and Perky nod their heads.

'This Henry guy agrees to pay, but at the same time the deal's going down a bookie's joint is being robbed. Is that about the size of it?'

Pinky nodded and Perky agreed verbally.

'Well, couldn't it be a coincidence?' I asked. 'Bad luck?'

'But you just said that Ralph came into the launderette…'

'I know what I said.' Was there something in the Psychology-Lite books that I read in the wee hours at work that could help me now? 'But *couldn't* it be? *Couldn't* you have made a mistake – or someone else made one?'

'Be clear about what you're saying,' Pinky said haughtily.

'I'm *saying,*' – I'm saying, what the hell am I saying? – 'that aside from a torched fifty quid note, there's ten bags of sand in my kitchen. That's five each for the two of you. And your story? You came here. You didn't find dick. You roughed me up and I didn't know nothing. *Ralph gave you the bum steer.'*

The silence is almost painful. Beats of time, in counterpoint to the throbbing in my nasal gristle. Lay it on, I thought.

'Money's yours, gentlemen,' I added.

There was a shift of power, or so it seemed, for it was Perky who asked me: 'What about the dog?'

I remembered a line that Ralph himself had fed me.

'The dog was never here, my friend.'

'But what *about* it?' he pressed.

'I'll take care of the dog, Perky. Claim your prize.' I was smiling.

In my short relationship with the two hoodlums, ever the pragmatist, it was Pinky who mentioned, 'We might have to rough you up a bit more. For the sake of appearances. You've only had a slap, mate...'

Still smiling, I said, 'It'll be my pleasure. Where would you like me?'

And that was it. Believe it or not, I say to myself, that was a whole year ago. Time flies when you're having... fun? Fun I guess. Sure; why not? Not once since that time have I seen Ralph Marrison; nor have I seen Pinky or Perky. Or the top joint of my left pinky finger: something of a speciality of Raider Number One, he led me to understand as he was disinfecting a carving knife in kettle steam. You can live without it. The four grand I had that Ralph couldn't get his hands on – well, that money went a long way, really. As Ralph had said: caution is the operative word. A ten here, a ten there. And unfortunately, with caution or not, sometimes dogs do fall into rivers...

These days the launderette's a safe place to work.

Humiliation Days

Joanna dived into the swimming pool naked. On this warm, scented night, she'd woken after barely an hour of sleep (another bad dream about Scott), and had felt in need of a splash. Water was where she felt most at home; now that life with Scott was approaching the unbearable. Knowing he was sleeping, the covers tangled round his slim limbs, she would swim to forget him.

A few lengths completed, she stopped in the shallow end, standing up straight. The water came up to her waist. She pushed back her hair, shivered at the breeze on her skin. She listened to the night traffic on the road beyond the perimeter wall. Joanna sat down on the pool steps, feeling dirt specks on her buttocks. As the wind picked up and whistled, she peered into the darkness.

She gasped as her breath caught.

Somebody was coming over her wall.

Joanna squinted, the streetlights eclipsed by the figure now sitting astride the wall. Joanna didn't know if she was more frightened or furious, but it took only a second to learn that fear had won the struggle. As quietly as she could, trembling, she lay down on the steps, and slid close to the wall tiles, her chin to the surface.

Was he looking at her? Acutely aware of her nudity, Joanna covered her breasts with her arms. He couldn't *fail* to see her in the dark water. She wanted to scream at him, but would this make him run or get angry? And would her scream be loud enough to wake Scott? Would he even be able to respond quickly enough?

The intruder was moving. He swung his other leg over the wall, and dropped down into the flower bed. As he hit the soil he emitted a grunt of lost air.

Joanna watched as he walked slowly through the stalks and petals, his body bent low. A few steps took him over the low wall between garden and the pool's concrete fringe. He was wearing head to toe black; his face obscured but for his mouth and the skin around his eyes. When he took his first steps on the concrete, his footfalls were barely noticeable. Soft-soled shoes.

Burglar's shoes, Joanna thought. If only he would get in the house and steal what he had to steal, so as to not see her. But instead, he walked the wrong way around the pool – in the direction of the deep end, the diving board, taking no notice of the house.

Joanna's scalp was beginning to freeze. With confusion she observed the intruder mount the diving board. He walked along it and bounced on the edge, testing its spring. Joanna couldn't believe he'd trespassed to go for a *swim*... Sure enough, the intruder backed up off the diving board back on the pool's fringe, walking round; a full circuit, every step bringing him closer to where Joanna was curled up next to the tile wall.

As he approached, Joanna held her breath. Her lungs ached; her eyes burned. But it appeared – by the grace of God! - that the intruder was losing interest in the pool, instead he was trying to look through the blinds into the spare bedroom. If only I'd turned on some lights, thought Joanna. As still as she could be, dimly aware of the cramp gaining solidity in her left calf, she listened to the lapping of the water beneath her chin, hoping that it wouldn't disturb the burglar.

Past the spare room, the intruder walked up the single step on to the covered patio, with its potted plants, and the sun-loungers folded up neatly. Joanna cursed herself for having closed the kitchen door: she'd been worried about a gust of wind slamming it shut and waking up Scott. Why hadn't she left a light on in the kitchen? The house was thief-bait.

Yet the thief turned away again! *This* time he'd see her, she was sure of it ... But to Joanna's relief, he walked back around the pool the same way he'd arrived, peeking again into the gloom of the spare room, his narrow back to her as he strolled with more confidence past the board. He used the path through the flowers, and leapt up against the wall, catching the top and squeezing it with both his gloved hands. He kicked against the brickwork, and soon he'd levered himself up.

When he slipped out of sight Joanna remained in the water, shivering. Perhaps her eyes were deceiving her and he hadn't really left. What if he was behind her? She had her arms wrapped around her body. Then she heard a noise. At the sound - like that of a safety catch being released - Joanna shrieked. She let go of her hold on herself and began slapping the surface of the water in a panic, even after she'd registered the sound to be that of the kitchen door opening.

Scott.

Joanna twisted herself in the water. Her husband was by the side, saying something to her, but she couldn't make him out through her tears and the panic that flowed through her. Without his help she didn't think that she'd be able to get out the water, so she was most relieved when he did help her.

*

'I can't believe you're serious! You think I *imagined* it?'

'I didn't say that,' Scott protested calmly. 'I said it's *possible* you were tired - it was the middle of the night - and you may have dozed off for a few minutes lying there in the water. When you woke up it was still dark, and you couldn't tell you'd been dreaming.'

'I wasn't dreaming,' Joanna said.

Scott nodded. 'We'll register it with the cops first thing tomorrow. How's that?'

It was probably the best Joanna could hope for, yet the offer didn't satisfy her. The lights in the house were now all on (she'd seen to that), and with that she was sure the intruder wouldn't return; this was starting to calm her down, thanks also to a few stiff brandies and a couple of aspirins. She was trying to be more logical. Wouldn't the police tell her she'd been lucky nothing had been stolen or damaged? Wouldn't they take prints of the shoe marks made in the flower-bed soil and just say the shoes worn are sold at every shoe store, in this size? And wouldn't they warn her not to swim naked?

'Can I have another brandy?' she asked.

'One more. You know you and alcohol.'

Joanna sighed. 'I *want* to pass out. I won't sleep any other way tonight.'

'I could give you something.'

'No medicine. But, you know what I'd really like?'

Scott looked up from behind the kitchen counter, and even from the heavy sofa in the lounge Joanna could see the unambiguous gleam in his eye. He couldn't be serious!

'I'd like to hear some classical music.'

*

Joanna was informed by a young female officer that the precinct was comparatively quiet this morning. To Joanna it looked chaotic. Cops were moving quickly, pushing people in handcuffs in front of them, or carrying sheets of paper, cups of coffee. Having to raise her voice occasionally to combat the din, Joanna gave her statement. On completion, the A4 form slid through the printer. The officer skim-read what she'd typed. 'Honest with you?' she began.

'Not much you can do, is there?'

'Afraid not, Mrs Winter. If the intruder had even broken a *window* we'd have something. But to tell the truth, even with a good footprint, we got nothing.'

'I understand.'

'Best we can do is have a car cruise London Drive for the next couple nights, looking for anything. Other than that, I'd advise you to have the pool light on and not to swim naked.'

'Even though it's my own pool.'

'Even though it's your own pool.'

*

The lack of sleep was catching up on Joanna by the time she was halfway home. Even if she hadn't called in sick, she could not have gone to work now. Her eyes itched, she squinted. Driving into the sun perched on the far line of the highway, she began to feel dizzy... The garage door opened by remote control. Joanna stepped into the sun. At the end of the drive she took three letters from the mailbox. Two were for Scott, official-looking, but the third was addressed, in an ornate hand, to:

The Lady of the House,
1526 Pembrook Avenue.

Delivered by hand – there was no post mark. Joanna tore open the envelope as soon as she entered the house. The paper inside was thin and cheap. And though the missive was only two sentences long, it had the impact on Joanna of making her legs go weak.

I saw you in the swimming pool last night and you are very beautiful.
Please swim again when it gets dark.

'Well, this puts a new light on things,' Scott said that evening, the paper between thumb and forefinger.

'I haven't been able to go out all afternoon. I'm frightened.'

'Let me think a minute.'

Tight lines of concentration poked up from the top of his nose; the slight wrinkling his brow. Married three years next Thursday, thought Joanna, Scott had never been good in a crisis, unless it occurred at work. She had met him when she'd been training to be a nurse, and her work assignment had taken her to his clinic. Impressed by his proficiency - the way he dealt with the beaten, the slashed, the wounded - she'd fallen in love. It wasn't the same now.

'Do you think we should have a gun?' said Scott.

'Seriously? I thought you were against them.'

'Well, I was. Till my wife was threatened.'

'I haven't actually been *threatened*...'

'Spied upon then.'

'I'm not sure.'

Scott hardly heard her. 'I want to protect you. I won't let him do anything...'

'He hasn't *said* he'll do anything.'

Playing the game wrong. If she carried on she'd be accused of fighting for the other side. By the virulence rouging his earlobes and cheeks she could tell Scott was finding her reticence beguiling. 'Do *you* want a gun?' she added quickly.

'Not a question of wanting...'

'You need me to approve...'

'I'm trying to *help*.'

Joanna was standing behind a chair, her hands on its back. Now she bent her head slightly, tired of the fight. 'Sorry. I'm worked up.'

'I could give you something to help calm you down,' Scott said.

'A few drinks will be enough.' Negotiations into weapon-buying were thereby postponed, and there was no further communication as the evening rolled on. They watched television together, a hundred miles apart.

*

Joanna did go to work the next day. As one of the two secretaries in the Sociology Department's Office at the University, her days were spent typing and dealing with the administration. Dull work, too easy; but to stay home all day would be worse. She had always liked to earn her own dollars.

Barbara asked, 'Feeling better?''Thank you.' Joanna had told her nothing of the peeping tom. As far as Barbara knew, Joanna had missed yesterday's thrills at work because of a twenty-four hour bug that had confined her to bed. Joanna was thinking of telling the truth. Barbara was older and wiser... Barbara was a large Oriental woman, hair long and dark. She knew about her marriage: she'd deduced it on her own, confronted Joanna about it one lunchtime. Barbara was a veteran of failed (and 'abusive?') marriages. She knew the signs. 'I don't want to talk about bastards,' she would say, 'but trust me I know the signs, hon.'

'Joanna?' The voice belonged to Professor Wearth.

'Hello, Craig.'

'Big favour?'

Wearth was disliked. It wasn't just his voice: a wheedling sound, that of a puppy given speech. Everything about the man was vaguely unpleasant. His talking-down to the mere *doctors* of the Department; his patronizing manner in general. Underlings should know their place. He was fifty-four, and God's gift to women.

Even *Big favour?* took on a deeper meaning when Wearth said it. Joanna had known for some time that he liked her; but the favour was typing. It always was.

*

The student canteen was bustling, but Barbara and Joanna would rather eat there than with their academics in the staff room. This was not unconnected with the fact that much of their conversation revolved around Departmental gossip.

They had just settled when Barbara said, 'He's after you big time.'

'Leechy Craig?'

'Mm-hm.' Barbara said swallowing a spoonful of thick soup.

'Repulsive... He already asked me out once.'

Barbara's face lit up and seemed to expand with the shock. 'Why didn't you tell me?' she asked excitedly.

'Long time ago. When I first started here. Before he knew I was married.' Joanna lay down her knife and fork on her salad. 'We met by accident in the mall. I tried to get away quickly but he kept me talking. Would you like to maybe go out for a drink or dinner some time. I told him, Craig, I'm a married woman. We'll go out as friends then...'

'And he took no for an answer?'

'Not exactly. I told him I was in a rush. Go to work Monday, there's a letter on my desk. Dear Joanna, I hope you didn't mis-construe my intentions. I hope our working relationship won't be affected. Then he has the gall to make a pass at me in the elevator a day later! *Swear*. We're in the elevator and he's all, *Joanna*, you're *quite* the most beautiful woman I know. Won't you let me get close? He was *already* close - breathing down my neck. Again I say I'm married. He doesn't care. He says he *wants* me...'

Barbara laughed. 'That man will do anything to get laid...' She bent her head over her soup again, not waiting to see Joanna's reaction.

*

All evening Joanna pottered nervously around the house, trying to think matters through. After a while Scott had become dis-turbed by his wife's hyperactivity. She was in the kitchen now, on her hands and knees, scrubbing the floor. Scott leaned against the cooker, a glass of mineral water in his hand. 'You've been knocking yourself out all night,' he said.

Joanna gave him a half-smile. Then she gazed at the cloth in her bucket of soapy hot water. 'Just being the obedient wifey,' she said. It had meant to be sarcastic, but Scott, pleased, gave her the benefit of the doubt. He placed his glass on the hob and gave her a smile of his own. 'Have you been drinking, Scott?'

'No. A question for you. How far would you take this obedient wifey bit?'

So that was what he wanted. She couldn't help but be surprised: quite some time had passed since Scott had last been so up front. Here she was, in her scruffiest clothes, her hair lank and sweaty from working, and now Scott wanted her. It was a change from their recent pathetic two a.m. gropes. He was kneeling behind her, his groin to her backside; she could feel him through the fabric of her jeans. 'You'll ruin your suit,' she said feebly.

'Don't you want to?' He had her hips in his doctoring hands, and was swiveling her backside in a small circle.

What harm would it do? 'Yes,' she said softly.

Scott needed no second invitation. He reached underneath her and tugged at her belt. Joanna closed her eyes. In seconds he had tugged her jeans and panties to her knees. Not wanting to stand up, Joanna lay down on her belly, to make the removal of her clothing possible. Scott yanked at her jeans, inching them down her legs. Joanna's bare legs were on the cold wet floor, and she thought of herself lying by the side of the pool, pressed up against the tile wall. She pushed Wearth's creeping face from her mind, closing her arms in an embrace around the bucket. The dirty water inside slopped.

Joanna felt Scott's tongue on her flesh, licking all he saw. She closed her eyes tighter. His tongue was teasing her anus; she hoped she was clean, then she hoped she was dirty instead. He lifted her up off the floor by the hips, though she continued to clutch the bucket. All she could smell was floor cleaner. Scott's erection nudged against her, wrongly angled for either aperture. Teasing; the zipper against her skin; too much in a rush to remove his clothing, he had just opened his fly.

'Come inside,' she said.

'Where?'

Joanna gasped as he shoved her forward. The water in the bucket slopped up and over the sides. A splash hit her face; salty and chlorinated it felt like semen. Every push Scott made slopped more water on to the kitchen floor. Joanna breathed in the scent; sliding her cheek against the spilt suds. Squeezing the bucket harder; bending the plastic out of shape... Shortly before Scott came, the bucket fell over. Her remaining clothing already wet, Joanna slid her upper body in the spillage, while Scott drove into her. Under him, she slapped the layer of water, delighted by the sound.

*

Two days passed before the second letter arrived.

Joanna had been feeling better, and had almost given up the idea of the intruder being Professor Wearth, when she discovered the envelope. On seeing the handwriting she went cold. She took the letter inside, as before.

> *I came to see you swim last night, but you didn't.*
> *Why won't you swim for me anymore? I love you.*

This time she didn't feel weak. She felt flattered; she was a mass of contradictions, and wished she could get matters straight. She'd hated the man coming into her back yard, yet she didn't mind him admiring her. Right. Her imagination had conjured up a picture of a harmless weirdo, who had perhaps had robbery on his mind at first. Then, in order to keep her still in the water, he'd pretended not to notice her.

It couldn't have been Wearth. What did Professor Wearth have to gain by creeping onto her property? Even if he *had* a good reason, would he have been able to climb the wall? Did he have the guts or the strength? Besides, she'd typed up his letters often enough; she knew Wearth's writing as well as she knew her own. She decided not to tell Scott about the second letter.

*

Scott was watching the game and Joanna was doing the ironing in the bedroom when the doorbell chimed. Scott got it: 'For you!'

The officer who'd taken her statement.

'Hello there,' said Joanna.

'Good evening, Mrs Winter. I was in the neighborhood, thought I'd drop by to ask if there'd been any more trouble.'

'No trouble.'

*

'Well you're certainly in a good mood this morning,' Barbara said at lunch, in the queue.

'Feeling good.'

'I better not ask...'

'Had a good night's sleep.'

'And how are things at home?'

'Okay.'

'Truly? You've been distant; I didn't know if things...'

'I'll tell you a story,' Joanna said. 'As soon as we sit down. Make that straight hair of yours curl.' She raised her eyebrows. 'Intrigued?'

Ten minutes later Barbara was all in. Joanna looked at her expectantly. She wanted to be told she was a fool for submitting to the flattery, or a fool for keeping the second letter from Scott. But what Barbara said was: 'My Lord...'

'Meaning what?'

'I don't know. Why dump this one on me, Joanna?' She laughed. 'If you want my opinion, I think you're right about it not being Leechy Craig. Not his style. Couldn't possibly be. But Scott's a doctor; there's drugs in the house. Maybe this guy's...'

'I thought of that too.'

'You be careful, Joanna.'

'I'm always careful.' She ate a few fries with her fingers. 'Wanna hear something crazy? I've been having bad dreams about Scott recently...'

'So things *aren't* great!'

'I never *said* great. I said okay...' She swallowed. 'I even thought that Scott had *arranged* for someone to climb over. This guy could come into the house, and Scott could be the macho protector. To impress me. Stupid, I know.'

'Far-fetched. Probably true.'

Joanna shrugged. 'Can I bum one of your cigarettes when we go outside?'

*

That night she went swimming.

Few drinks earlier, she woke after two a.m., needing the lavatory. Scott was snoring gently. Joanna slid as easily from the sheets as she could, and dressed in a long t-shirt, she walked through the house to the back door after she'd peed.

Outside was cool. For a minute she listened to the traffic on London Drive. She breathed in the early morning air and stared at the wall. She took a walk around the pool and stood on the diving board... and felt strange. The intruder was the last person to have stepped here. And then she was startled by a noise.

The sound of climbing: toecaps against brick.

And what do I do now?

Swim! was her answer. But her heart was beating too fast; she'd drown. God forgive me, she pleaded, and fell to the side -

into the water. Cold; she was shocked by its stunning chill as she sank to the bottom. Too late! She stayed under, the t-shirt having ridden up. She blew the air from her lungs so she wouldn't float to the surface, and she kept herself stationary. Shouldn't she have left a light on *this* time? Joanna started swimming for the far end of the pool, nearer the kitchen door. When she'd reached it, she stood up, the t-shirt clinging. She pushed her hair back from her face, her eyes burned to the sting of chlorine.

When she opened them again, like before, she gasped.

There! On top of the wall, the silhouette... Her breath caught. This is what you wanted, she thought sourly. Barely conscious of what she was doing, she dipped down into the water. The t-shirt bellied out; a pocket of air raced up her belly, over her breasts, and popped out of the neck hole. It's what *he* wanted. *Swim.*

Joanna pushed off from the side, taking her eyes from the intruder and gliding. She'd chosen the middle of the pool: should her instincts be proved false and this man be a psycho, she wanted to be where it was hardest for him to reach her. She got to the other end, under the diving board, and turned to see her admirer.

He dropped to the flower bed. The intruder was standing by the wall, making no attempt to get closer. As she swam again, Joanna kept an eye on him in case he made a sudden move, and she was taking care to swim slowly. The last thing she wanted to be was exhausted if matters turned unpleasant. Perhaps he's scared I've set a trap for him. How she wished she could see his face!

In the shallow end again, standing up... when the intruder walked through the flowers, over the short garden wall, on to the concrete. More scared than she'd ever been, she watched him as he moved closer. He was barely six feet from her when he stopped. Joanna was powerless but to wait, blood thumping in her ears.

I'm a whore, she told herself. How can I be doing this? - as she lifted up her t-shirt to the maniac in her life. It peeled from her skin like a huge Band-Aid: a relief in itself. Guilt coursed through her. The t-shirt was collected and crumpled around her neck. Joanna was oddly frightened to take the garment off completely, but knew such misgivings to be ludicrous. She'd come this far...

She tossed the t-shirt in the direction of the peeping tom. The two occupants of the dark continued staring at one another, Joanna's body pocked and ruffled with gooseflesh. But despite her chill (and the likely prospect of a sniffle tomorrow morning), she stood her ground, naked, her arms by her side. The intruder picked up her t-shirt. A second's hesitation was all it took - with Joanna thinking he was about to throw it back again - before he began wringing out the excess water. Joanna's bladder gave a twinge. Through chattering teeth she asked, 'Can you hear me?' – her voice the most fragile of whispers. She was frightened of waking Scott. 'You must go, do you understand? You can't come back here anymore.'

No reply. No movement.

'You can't speak, can you?' said Joanna.

The man shook his head.

Joanna lowered herself into the water, circled her arms - both to generate heat and to hide herself from him. 'You have to go,' she said softly, a catch in her voice. Eyes felt hot. She felt like somebody had died. By way of response the visitor held out the t-shirt. 'That's yours,' Joanna said. 'If you want it. But go now... Leave me.'

*

The next day, crying in bed, Joanna felt a strange, potent mixture of emotions. To Scott, who always left the house first, and who got from his wife guilty frustration and anger before tears, she was being 'hormonal, and unreasonable.' He wanted to know why, once again, she had no intention of going to work. She wouldn't tell him; she was lying about this anyway. Scott slammed all the doors as he left.

What did *he* know! They were strangers, overlapping in place only... Late to work, she was obliged to perform her apologies to Oscar-winning standards, for she was apologizing both for herself and for Barbara, who was yet to show up. Professor Wearth, as he stated in his office, was not a man who appreciated sloth.

'I was unwell.'

'And Barbara?'

'She complained of a cold yesterday,' Joanna lied. 'Lot of it about.'

Wearth nodded. 'We all get ill, Joanna; it's not that you're both under the weather that galls me. I'm not a monster. What I object to is neither of you calling in to tell me this.'

'It won't happen again.'

Dismissed, Joanna took her seat, thinking it wasn't like Barbara not to phone in. A road accident flashed in front of Joanna's eyes.

She kept making mistakes: her head was not working properly. How could she ever have thought Leechy Craig might be her suitor! Wearth knew no more of her world, and no less, than did her husband.

Hours passed, no call from Barbara. Joanna ate by herself in the student canteen, and when she'd finished she couldn't remember tasting anything.

A summons from Leechy Craig came directly after lunch. It was on Joanna's desk when she returned. In the professor's office she was instructed to close the door, which as far as she could recall was a first since he'd interviewed her.

'Please sit down, Joanna.'

'Something wrong, Craig?'

Wearth looked at her over the top of his silver-rimmed spectacles. He was reading something on his desk. 'I'm afraid so.' He sniffed, cleared his throat at astonishing volume.

I've been fired, Joanna thought numbly.

The piece of paper was handed across the desk. 'Please read this, and tell me what you make of it.'

Thin paper, Joanna noted as she took hold. Her mind was blank, frazzled away to nothing at the thought of losing her job. But instead she read:

Leave Joanna alone or I'll make you leave her alone.

Joanna recognized the loopy writing from the two letters the peeping tom had sent her. Now he knew where she worked too?

'I've asked you to explain this.'

'I can't.'

Wearth cleared his throat again and patted his lanolin-slicked hair with both hands. He looked not at her but at the window when he remarked, 'I hope this doesn't refer to our little misunderstanding some time ago, Joanna. I assumed I could trust you not to tell anyone that I... was *interested* in you, at the time.'

Joanna's face drained of colour.

'What is it, Joanna. You've gone...'

'*Jesus*!' She was on her feet, at the office door before Wearth could offer a complaint.

The drive home, she barely heard anything. Blood rushed in her ears; she couldn't hear the traffic. Like being underwater; being naked, alone, in the dark, underwater... There was a letter in her mailbox, as she'd expected there to be.

*

Last one, I promise. I won't write to you again.

Thank you for last night. I will treasure the memory, the t-shirt and the trust.

I have some explaining to do, I guess. Why I barged my way into your life. I always vowed I'd not let a man take advantage of me again. And haven't I been good to my promise? You bet I have!

When you told me about the difficulties you were having with your marriage, it riled me more than it probably did you I thought you meant knocking you about. Been through that. Couldn't bear to see you suffer, Jo. Forgive me.

There's one thing I never came clean about. I'll hope for your forgiveness in time for this as well. When I told you about my abusive marriages, I really only gave you half the story. 'Abusive' can go both ways. I wasn't always the victim.

Clear enough?

I crept over your wall that first time to 'scare' Scott. Let's keep this non-committal... Would I have done it? Done what? No idea. I was gonna 'steal' from you, the bungled burglary. He'd be protecting your house and something would go wrong. You'd be free. Then you told me you and Scott are getting along okay. I hope you weren't lying. You confused me.

I'm sorry I was cowardly enough to disguise my writing and pretend to be someone else. But we all have to be people we don't like from time to time. Ask my ex-husbands. These are our Humiliation Days, baby. You and me.

Take care of yourself. Think of me always as Barbara.

Love, B.

*

Joanna knew she'd take care of herself - whatever that took. She'd do it, for the woman she'd never see again, whose name, whose real name, she evidently had not even learned. Joanna removed her clothing on the short journey through the house. It wouldn't be like when she was swimming at night, but the next best thing.

The blazing sun torched her body as she wandered up to the diving board, white under the solid blue block of sky. Crying as she dived into the pool, Joanna's tears touched the cold water first.

Estate

A neighbour called it in and I was seven blocks shy.

'Fifty-two sixer Lancot response.'

I hit the blues and spun it round before Ops confirmed.

'Roger, Fifty-two sixer. We await.'

The address was on the Plowberry Estate, but now wasn't the time to worry about damage to my windshield. Ops had rung a 197. Child at risk.

I climbed the stairs and copped a few puzzled looks. A few hostile ones, too.

A girl answered the door, opening it a quarter and peering through the gap.

'I help you?'

I badged her. 'Your parents home? Had a call about a baby screaming last night.'

She raised an eyebrow. 'You get lost?'

'Excuse me?'

'Baby screaming *last night*? It's nearly dinner time!'

'I got here as fast—'

'Well, I can't hear no baby screaming. Can you?'

'I asked if your parents are home. I'd like a word.'

'They don't live here.'

She was fourteen or fifteen. 'You live alone?' I asked, trying to see past her.

'Ain't a crime, last time I looked.'

She closed the door a fraction.

'I'm not the law.'

'Your badge says Police.'

'My badge says Police Doctor. And I can tell you, Miss, I been shifting eleven hours straight, so could you do me a favour and lose the front? Wanna tell me what's wrong with your child?'

She slammed the door.

Two hours late already, and Percy would be pacing, waiting for me. Probably scratched the place up, which he does when he's distressed. He doesn't like to be alone.

Back in the cruiser: 'False alarm.'

'Roger that.'

It didn't explain why the girl was on her own, baby or no baby.

'You get a name or address on the shout?' I asked Ops.

'That's a negative. Anonymous call. Coded.'

'Roger, Ops. Over.'

I spun it round and drove back to Plowberry. Something didn't taste right. Funny the glimpses you get that you don't understand until a short time later. When I was trying to see past the girl, into her hallway: it hadn't struck me as funny at the time.

She took longer to get the door.

Though I'd been gone about twenty minutes – if that – she looked older. Considerably. The first time I saw her she was fourteen or fifteen. Now she'd graduated to the looks of a twenty-one twenty-two year old. Hair was shorter, figure fuller.

If I didn't know better I might have assumed sisters.

'I won't ask to talk to your parents this time. They don't live here.'

'As I said before.'

'Nor does a baby.'

'As I said before.'

'No you didn't, matter of fact, but let's move past that. You live alone.'

'Bingo.'

'Wanna know how I know?'

'Oh, I'll *sob* if you don't explain.'

'One coat on the hook behind you. Just the one. And where's the buggy?'

'Bravo, I don't have no baby. Can I get back to painting my nails?'

'But it was you called it in.'

She frowned. 'Called what in?'

'The 197. Child at risk. It was you, but not as you are now, right? Gonna let me in?'

'…You're a doctor. Ain't no one here sick.'

'You will be in a couple of hours, I reckon. You're getting older by the minute.'

'We all are.'

'You know what I mean. You were a teenager half an hour ago; you'll be an old girl by the end of the day. And then a baby again, screaming all night and waking up the neighbours. On a loop.'

Now she knew I knew the score she seemed relieved – less defensive. She even opened up the door all the way. She still didn't invite me in but it was a start.

'I can help you with whoever you're running from,' I told her.

She lifted her chin. 'What makes you think I'm running?'

'A hunch. Plenty of Loop Girls created for men who sold them by the hour to other men, so would I be way out of line if I said so? The sort of men who kind of like an eight year-old. Sort of men who like an *eighty* year-old… Yeah you're running all right, sweetheart.'

She paused. 'What did you mean about a call?'

'My best guess? Cry for help,' I said. 'Sometime when you were a kid this afternoon you coded a call and pretended to be your own neighbor. Said a child's screaming all night. You were trying to get noticed, so you don't need to go through the darkness as a baby one more time.'

For the first time the woman smiled. She was mid-twenties now, getting a few more interesting lines on her face; a little fake tan – or maybe real tan. I couldn't help liking what I saw.

'So what are you then, by preference?' she asked me. 'Eight or eighty?'

'About *forty*-eight.' I snickered. I didn't sound like myself. I took out my wallet and pressed the buttons: invisible to both of us, my business card buzzed into her inbox.

'That's usually around nine p.m. Give or take... You could bring some wine.'

'I have a dog to feed.'

She shrugged. 'After that then. Where do you live?'

I told her. I could easily be back here by nine. Take a taxi if I was going to stay.

'I scream loud,' she warned me.

I copied her shrug. 'I snore like a gibbon... Red or white I should bring?'

'Red. Good for the heart.'

'That's a myth. From *prehistoria*.'

She smiled again. 'I'm an old-fashioned girl,' she told me as shading appeared under her eyes. Her arms had developed muscles, toning; she worked out when approaching thirty.

Some kids had done the windshield.

I drove home with the evening wind in my face. Smelt of dust.

I cut my hand on a piece of glass when I reached for the gears. Hardly felt it.

Lapsus

'He thinks I should change my name. He says Carol isn't classy enough. Not sexy enough.'

'...What does he suggest?' asks Dr Bruce-Sange.

'*Lamella*, believe it or not. It means a layer of bone tissue.'

'I know... Your hour's nearly up, I'm afraid.'

'Okay. But do you think I should change my name?'

'It's not what *I* think, Carol. What *I* think is irrelevant.'

'Explore it at least for me, would you?'

'Your hour's nearly up. We haven't got time.'

'Then explore it in two minutes for me, or I'm deducting *pro rata* from your fee.'

'No you're not. I can't answer: I don't have all the information.'

'Such as?'

'Such as: what do you mean by *change your name*? Change it *legally*? By deed poll? Change it for the hour you're with him? What?'

'Legally.'

'Such as: change it to what, if you can't agree on Lamella? Such as: why would you even consider it? Why has it played enough of a part in your week that you'd bring it to me?'

'...I'm not in love with him, if that's what you're suggesting.'

'I'm not suggesting anything, Carol. Why do you mention love, do you think?'

'Oh *now* you've got time...'

'No I haven't. It's the question you can take away with you. Now if you'll excuse me... Until next week.'

'If I come back.'

'Indeed – if you come back.'

'...But you know I will, don't you?'

'You sound defensive, Carol.'

'*Don't* you.'

'I don't know anything.'

'The thing is, I don't know *why* I should return.'

'Yes you do.'

'...Yes. Yes I suppose I do.'

*

It is not a precarious industry – the industry is as old as mammals – but careers within it burn bright. Lives are driven at weird velocities – gluey periods of boredom, synapse-flares of unpredictable danger – and it is only the practitioners themselves who are precarious. They spend their working hours in full awareness of programmatic self-destruction... unless they are lucky.

Carol Hayes is one of the lucky ones. Having passed her thirty-fifth birthday, she is two decades into the game, and longevity in any industry earns benefits. One of these, for Carol, is financial stability: this she has achieved via the establishment of a reliable client base (this in turn the result of word of mouth, as much as anything) and long gone are the days when she was obliged to work more than two appointments per evening. As time has moved on, Carol has felt confident in the escalation of her hourly rate; more sure of herself when no means no (she does not enjoy anal); and convinced of her skills and abilities, as all good professionals, in any field, must be.

One of the lucky ones. Never tempted to try heroin and never coaxed into making movies, Carol engages her mind and body, telling both herself and her psychoanalyst that she is in control of her workflow. On the subject of her appointments and her crimes, she even keeps notes in an A4 ledger. One day she will write a book about it all, she says: once she has made enough to retire. In her mind she has named it *One of the Lucky Ones*.

She has devised a typology of the men and women who use her services. Scottish Tony, for example. It is Wednesday, and therefore he is on her mind. Unless he specifically decides otherwise, the appointment for Carol on Wednesday nights is a man named Scottish Tony. Carol does not know if Tony is his real name (nor does she care to guess). She has worked for him for four years and his name doesn't matter anymore. Barrellish, square-headed and rigid-bearded, Scottish Tony is meek and remains in awe of the potency of the fifty-pound note. He cannot believe that he gets what he gets for a mere two hundred. It delights Carol that when he finishes on her buttocks (he always withdraws), the next ten sentences or so that he utters are due an exclamation mark to top them off, one by one.

'It was me, by the way,' he tells Carol, to her surprise (he rarely speaks until Beethoven's Fifth is concluded: she knows that he times himself to its rhythms). 'The one who recommended Giorgio to you. Or you to Giorgio, I should say.'

Carol is rinsing the taste of his cocksweat from her mouth. At Scottish Tony's insistence, she keeps a bottle of mouthwash at his flat for this purpose. She has long since ceased believing that he will drug it between appointments. He doesn't need to. Carol is already hooked on his cash.

She spits. 'Who's Giorgio?' she asks.

'The European. The musician.'

'...Oh, *Andreas*.'

Scottish Tony laughs. 'That what he's calling himself, aye? Okay: *Andreas,* if you'd be so kind. About as Greek as whelks and cockles, though. From further east'd be *my* bet.'

Carol returns to the bedroom. Scottish Tony lies supine, wet with her spit and sick. 'Recommended me how?' she asks.

Scottish Tony needs vodka before every appointment. Ordinarily this is not a problem. Now he slurs: 'Met him at the gym I manage. He was after a no-strings – we got talking... Man's as rich as an *actor*. You should be saying thank you!'

'I *am* saying thank you. I didn't know you were acquainted, or I would've said it earlier.'

Curious about the Andreas/Giorgio name change, Carol takes the night bus home. The smoothness of the journey feels awkward and oppressive; it feeds the headache that has grumbled for several hours, and makes it grow. She longs for an incident, a bit of night drama to witness – a singing alcoholic will do. Nothing happens. Back at home, as ever, she bathes and scrubs herself, inside and out. She is two hundred pounds richer, and sadder. She cannot recall a single time she used the man's name. (As far as Chaz was told, the punter's name is Thursday.) Sadder still, perhaps, is the fact that not once has Thursday used Carol's name either.

*

If Carol is not in love with Thursday (as she made clear to Chaz, although why she did so is something of a blur), she is certainly fond of him. Apart from anything else, he makes business a pleasure. With his quirky European accent and infrequent failures with English grammar, his longish white hair, his tough fingertips and his whisky paunch, Thursday is somewhere in his mid-sixties, looking good for his age. Often when Carol visits, she will linger a few seconds on his doorstep and listen to the music that he is playing on the piano that he keeps in one of his back rooms. Other times, her ringing on the doorbell interrupts a symphony in mid-eruption. As far as Carol knows, it is no exaggeration to suggest that Thursday's life revolves around classical music: and although she likes a good proportion of it as well, she is ignorant. She is into jazz.

She wonders if Thursday might be trying to improve her mind; to induct her into a world of powerful music, of emotions trapped and then released in strings and cymbals. After her third visit, when a pattern began to develop (a pattern of sore knees and two pieces of gum on the night bus home), Carol asked him what the music that had been playing throughout had been. He told her Mahler – 'Mahler's final Budapest triumph! *Don Giovanni!*' Standing up from her nest of cushions on her fifth visit, she wiped her chin and told him: 'I recognize this! It's Mahler again!' And Thursday smiled so beautifully, so kindly, that Carol almost invited him to keep his money. *Almost...* If nothing else, Thursday is simple in his complexities, and to Carol this is a positive factor. Whether it is a melancholic second movement that guides their movements and timings, or a Strauss with which to waltz, Thursday usually favours her mouth. Carol believes that she is getting better at predicting when the piece is coming to an end. Sometimes, for variety, Thursday wears a cape: he wraps it around her head when it is time for her to go faster.

Thursday pours Carol a glass of peach schnapps.

'Thank you. The Shost, by the way, before you ask.'

'Excuse me?'

'Our musical accompaniment is Shostakovitch: *Lady Macbeth of the Mtsensk District.* 1936, I think. You played it to me three weeks ago.' Carol sips her schnapps. 'The Shost fell from favour as a direct result of this. It put him under pressure to simplify his *groove.*'

Thursday stares at Carol for so long that she suspects he might be offended. Then he laughs so hard that his penis wags and bows in appreciation.

'*Bravissimo!* You've done some *research,*' he says.

'I went to the library – the first time in five years. I checked it out and played it at home.'

'Ah!' Thursday sits down beside her; they are comfortable together in their nudity and the temperature is pleasant, even with the patio doors slightly ajar. 'Carol...'

She flinches slightly at the sound of her name.

'I've been thinking,' he went on, '...about the matter we discussed last week.'

She interrupts his flow of thought. 'So have I... Andreas.' *His* name merely sounds ludicrous. 'I'm not sure I'm comfortable with Lamella.'

'No, not that.' Thursday swats the idea from the air. 'What would it cost me to make you give up your other clients?' he asks.

Carol flinches again; disguises it by transforming it into a cough. 'What do I earn, you mean.'

'Precisely.'

'Fifteen hundred a week. Cash.'

'...I have money.'

'Is that an offer?' Carol feels slightly giddy.

Thursday turns away from her and teases his moustache while he thinks. 'It's a proposition,' he replies. 'Eight thousand a month and you don't see anyone else. If I find out you've betrayed me, I'll say you burgled me after I'd fallen asleep. Your fingerprints are all over the place.'

Feeling inexplicably let down on some level, Carol says, 'You don't need to play rough, Andreas. The threat is totally uncalled for.' She wishes she had a robe or something to wear: something to pull tighter across her chest to show him how he'd upset her.

'Of course it is,' Thursday tells her, turning to face her once more. 'Do we strike a deal?'

There are bound to be ramifications to the new arrangement, Carol knows; but for the moment, all she can see is a life without visits across the town every evening; a chance to see the world before midday; a lunchtime catch-up with friends...

'We do.' Carol holds out her right hand and lifts her glass of schnapps a few centimetres. 'Toast? Or shake hands?' She waits. 'Or do you want me to suck you again?'

Thursday reclines into a barge of cushions; his bald white thighs yawn apart. 'Why not combine the alternatives?' he suggests.

*

Carol sits down outside a café at twelve-thirty. Her lunch date is Lorraine, a friend of nearly a decade standing, and Lorraine is a few minutes late. Carol doesn't worry. She orders a cappuccino and watches the world as it falls past… Lorraine is one of the practitioners (rare breeds) who fall in love with one of the men who presented his erection to her. As a late teenager, Lorraine escaped the care system (and an unpleasant incident about which she refuses to speak) via a fondness for anal and watersports; at the age of thirty-nine, she claims to be mended, body and soul, her teeth as flawless as a dolphin's, and in love with an American businessman named Den. He is fifty-two, visits Europe for work appointments, and has an office and desk in the City. Lorraine likes to joke that his nickname is Den of Iniquity.

So it *could* work, Carol reflected while pausing to call Lorraine; it *could* work with Andreas. He could save me… Does he want to?

Neither woman being hungry for carbs or protein (and Lorraine shining in a tight spring *ensemble* that must have cost a grand), Lorraine orders – of all things – an ice cream sundae, the sort that two adolescents might share on a nervous first outing without a chaperone. It is topped with a diadem of pitted cherries.

Eyeing the dessert with something akin to disgust, Carol sips her blackcurrant tea and says, 'Don't tell me. The doctor says you're not lactose intolerant after all.'

'You could have had one, Purple! I offered!'

'I don't *want* one! Not one that size anyway…'

'They come in Thin Bitch varieties as well – you saw the menu.' Lorraine sucks her spoon clean of a mouthful. 'And speaking of not wanting one *that* size, Purple, I hear you've found a provider. Spill.'

Carol smiles. She doesn't ask how Lorraine knows: the streets between Thursday's house and her own flat are not tar and stones – they are a network. Secrets last no time at all in their profession. Naturally people talk: if a fresh disease is rumoured, a commentary beats like jungle drums – who'd become sick? to what extent? Similarly, the new recruitment, say, of a zealous Chief Inspector in the area – one with his feelings known on the subject of soliciting – is a sure bet to get tongues wagging.

'His name is either Andreas or Giorgio. We're not big on names.' Carol shrugs, wrapping her hands around her mug. 'No, that's not true. Actually he wants me to change mine. He says Carol is not fitting for a muse.' She smiles again. 'He's a musician, you see; a composer. Piano.'

Lorraine nods. 'So I hear. Change it to what?'

'Lamella,' Carol answers, a little sourly; she cannot shake the sensation that this has happened before. Then she makes the connection. 'My psychoanalyst tells me it's *pertinent* that I'll bring something like this to the session. It says more about me than about Thursday – Andreas, I mean.' Carol is getting muddled. Perhaps she is not as rested and well-slept as she imagined herself to be. Perhaps she is perturbed that her regular Monday appointment – a man named Barry – took the news of her temporary holiday from the scene so well. He neither fought her on the phone nor begged her to reconsider. Carol took his nonchalance to bed with her. She dreamed about Barry. Someone was pinching her skin, rolling his fingers through her organs…

Carol rallies. The adjustment was always going to have affected her more than anyone else, she reasons. It is nothing to worry about, a few nights of getting used to new sleep patterns.

Lorraine looks sceptical. 'And what's *his* name?'

'I told you. Andreas.'

'*No*. The psychoanalyst proffering his wanky-woo ways…'

'Oh. No, it's a she. Her name is Chaz – Charlotte, presumably. Chaz Bruce-Sange.'

Lorraine blinks and pauses. For a second it seems as though she is going to struggle for something to say, but she recovers. Carol is well aware that Chaz Bruce-Sange is an odd name, but Lorraine's reaction is more than she would have expected.

'Hell's teeth... Purple, are you serious? Serious about the Lamella bit?'

'Well, *he's* serious – that's the point.'

'*Lamella*, though? There's a brass works the golf club bars,' says Lorraine, sucking her spoon clean once more. '*She* caught a dose of lamella the other month. Tell him no. Names are different.'

'Says you, who still calls me Purple after ten years!'

'Purple Hayes,' Lorraine replies straightfaced and deadpan, 'you're in my brain... Do you want some of this? I'm starting to feel sick. My eyes are bigger than my belly.'

Carol is happy to change the subject. 'Which seems to be bigger than I remember, if you don't mind me saying so.'

'Seventeen weeks. Hence the sundae.'

'Ah! The old eating-for-two excuse.'

'For three, actually.'

'...*Twins?*'

Lorraine nods. 'I won't say I'm unhappy about it... but it wasn't planned.' She shrugs. 'Marital security if nothing else, I hope. He'll have to put a ring on it now.'

'Or buy you off,' Carol adds – there is no room for sentimental falsity in their world.

'Or buy me off,' Lorraine agrees. 'Will you be moving in with him?'

'I hope not. Intense is not the word, babe! He makes Joseph Stalin look like Tommy Cooper.' Carol smiles fondly at a recollection. 'And then he can be a real sweetheart. Calling me his muse, that kind of thing...' She wants Lorraine to pick up on the muse reference.

Lorraine lays down her spoon, defeated by half a pint glass of remaining ice cream and diced bananas. 'My advice? Buy him the occasional gift with what he's paying you. Don't go mad, just show gratitude... What's he into?'

'Classical music.'

'Yes I know that. Specifically.'

'Mahler. Shostakovitch.'

'Try to find a rare recording. Or get him tickets to a performance. Something off the beaten track. Unusual... and special.'

Carol cannot wait any longer. 'He says I've inspired him to compose something new on the piano,' she says. 'The first thing he's written in thirty years.'

*

'I want to learn about classical music,' Carol announces.

'Well, you've come to the right place,' says Darryl Carbrini, behind the counter at Octaves. They are surrounded by musical instruments, by racks of CDs and even vinyl copies in square transparent sheaths. 'Do you have a starting point?'

'A *starting point?*'

'Yes. Or I might as well say find a fish – here's the ocean.'

'No I don't have a starting point. I know Mahler – and the Shost.'

Carbrini fingers his blue bowtie; the smirk on his lips appears superior. 'Then you *do* have a starting point,' he remarks, ignoring the diminutive of Shostakovitch, as he might a tasteless joke in the presence of an archdeacon (as Carol compares it the next day in her weekly session with Chaz).

Specificity will help them both, Carol reasons; they have got off on the wrong foot. 'I'm trying to impress my new boyfriend,' she says. 'What he doesn't know about classical music you could sign on a cornflake. Can you help me?'

'A present?'

'...Yes.'

'Your estimated price range being...?'

Carol has used Uncle Google for some light research. The figure seemed outlandish but she vocalises it anyway. 'Up to five hundred.'

Delightedly smirking, Darryl Carbrini strums his bowtie once more. 'I'm seeing Elgar.' Italicised by this fresh mission, he abandons Carol and forages among the racks, his plump backside swollen in beige slacks. As far as Carol is concerned, it is all the man can do to repress a howl.

*

Carol has received enough surprises in her life (and work) to be cool towards their dubious appeal. She comes right out and describes what she is handing to Thursday.

'I've bought you some Elgar. A rare one from 1967.'

'Elgar? No I never had the pleasure. Shall I do the honours?'

'Please.' *Never had the pleasure of what?* Carol wonders.

The opening bars of *The Enigma Variations* sound. As is customary, Thursday stands close to a waist-high speaker near the drinks cabinet. Carol settles on her knees and opens her blouse and Thursday's dressing-gown.

She is in the bathroom when she hears him play. Although she cannot know for sure that this is the piece that Thursday claimed that he has composed with her in mind, it is nimble and sprightly; it feels flattering to have inspired such a prance. She is one of the lucky ones indeed! Not even Lorraine's sugar daddy has given her a piece of music!

Pleased that Thursday has enjoyed the gift, Carol dresses in the lounge and joins her benefactor in his practice room. First she lingers on the threshold. 'May I?' She has never been in here before and it is smaller than she expected, more or less overwhelmed by a three-quarters size piano and a bank of recording equipment.

Thursday nods and continues playing, complete as his recital is with ill-picked notes. He is not proficient. 'Do I make you feel good?' he asks her over a particularly bum chord.

The question does not surprise her as much as her answer does. 'Yes you do.'

'And who have you told about me?'

'My psychoanalyst for one.'

'Ah! I've tousled with Sigmund in my time, I can tell you.'

'...Sigmund?'

'Sigmund Freud. Golden Siggy, his mother called him, the spoilt bastard. Almost totally unmusical, or so he claimed; but I happen to know he could squeeze out an ounce or two of enthusiasm for *Don Giovanni* and *The Marriage of Figaro*. He is an interesting man.'

'...My analyst's a Jungian, I'm afraid.'

'Oh.' Thursday's fingers trip over a sequence. 'Never knew Jung...' He stands up and pulls his dressing-gown cord tighter. It is apparent that he wishes Carol to lead them out.

'You never *knew* Jung?' Carol asks.

'No. It's time, Carol.'

Because Thursday has already has his second helpings this evening (he is never good for thirds), she assumes that this is her cue to walk to the bus stop. She is correct. But before she opens the door in the hall, she hears him mumble something behind her back. When she asks him to repeat himself, he says, 'Katalina. What do you think of the name?'

Carol riffles through the possibilities. 'For me, you mean? Well it's better than Lamella.'

'Which means you'll consider it?' Thursday looks hopeful.

The evening has been pleasant. Why leave on a curdled note? 'Sure. Of course I will.'

'That's my muse.'

She steps outside into the early morning air. A cat prowls the wall at the end of the short garden; at the sight of Carol it turns tail and runs away, spitting curses over its furry shoulders.

*

It is while she floats in an overfilled bath, roughly an hour later, that Carol wonders if Thursday has slipped something into her drink. She feels odd: overwhelmed by light-headedness and euphoria... Is she *ill*? Well, if she is, it is not like any indisposition that she has contracted in the past. It is pleasurable, she feels young... She swears aloud and sits up quickly, crashing waves up and over the bath's slopes. She breathes deeply. '...No. No I won't have it. *No.*'

She does not fall in love anymore: it is a rule; she is immune. In the same way that she doesn't catch chickenpox or mumps. Too much has happened.

'No.'

But the feeling won't leave her, and she interrogates her memory. Apart from Thursday's semen, she had nothing to drink at the man's house, so he cannot have slipped her a happy pill, could he? She turned down his offer of his favourite tipple, peach schnapps.

And then she hears his voice.

I knew them all, the voice says into part of her brain.

Am I dreaming? she asks herself. She splashes water into her face; sits up straighter, her spine as stiff as the head of a rake. Her heart pounds.

I knew them all, Thursday repeated. *I was there, inspiring them... Do I surprise you?*

Surely standing up will break the spell and shut him up, Carol reasons. She must have dozed off in the water – dangerous business – but then she hears her own voice answering him.

Not at all.

Carol stands up, knee-deep in hot soapy water, and the drama in her skull has not faded out.

I should. I was present at the birth of some of the most important music of all time. I was a muse. I helped them get what they wanted... and they all betrayed me.

*

Thursday is in a good mood, in high spirits, the next time Carol pays a visit. In fact, she suspects that he's had a few schnapps before she arrived. She wonders if he will offer her a glass.

He does not. But he offers her something else instead. 'Do you know what this is?' he asks her, his voice slurred.

'It's a CD.'

'Containing what, do you imagine? Take hold of it. And this.'

Thursday hands her a pen.

'I'm told this will write on the material the disc is made of. I would like you to write the word *Lapsus* on it, and then my name.'

Biting hard on the urge to ask him the obvious question, Carol remembers the lessons she learned from Chaz. She repeats what she assumes is the work's title.

'Lapsus?'

'Yes. The return of the repressed.'

'Spelt?' she asks smugly.

'*Spelt?*' The goodwill seeps from Thursday's features; a smile decays on his lips. 'I have just composed my first new work in three decades, and you ask me to *spell. I can't write.* We didn't learn in those days.'

'...Sorry, Andreas.' Carol's ears feel bruised by the thunder that has left his mouth. Thursday has spun on his heels – the pirouette so melodramatic that Carol would have sniggered, if only she could edit out her sudden fear – and now he stomps away from her. He makes Carol think of a bull. Perhaps it is the snorts of anger that splutter at his nostrils.

Feeling foolish, Carol stands her ground with the CD and the pen in her hands. The least she could do is write LAPSUS: unless it has a double-pee in the middle, it is simple enough to spell, isn't it? And who cares anyway? Thursday has just confessed that he is illiterate.

In the practice room he strikes a chord on his keyboard, and Carol follows him along the hallway, intending to say sorry – albeit as much out of a fear of not being paid as out of consideration for the man's tortured but prissy sensibilities.

He does not look up from his fingers when he speaks.

'All of the great composers needed a muse,' he says. 'Shosta-kovitch – the Shost – had a woman named Katalina. Mahler was in love – chastely so – with the infant daughter of some well-to-do neighbours... None of these facts will you find in the biographies.'

Carol recalls the weird vision she had in her bathroom. A premonition? 'Well, how do *you* know?' she asks, stepping closer.

'I was there. In spirit, you might say.'

'...I don't follow.'

'I was to Mahler and the Shost – and a host of lesser-known names, talented mediocrities as the past has judged them – as you are to me: as a muse.'

Carol is getting sweaty. '...I still don't follow. When you say you were there...'

'I inhabited the space between Katalina's mortal breaths. I created the smiles on the little girl's face; I deepened her dimples and made her cuter. I made those composers love something in those females – a quality that would inspire them to create wonder.'

As a fantasy, Carol supposes, it is harmless enough. Thursday wants to take credit for some of humanity's finest (and most enduring) classical music. So what? Let him have the last word. What harm could it do? Egocentricity is not a crime.

Looking up from the keys, Thursday says, 'You don't believe me.'

'...I'm finding the concept difficult, I must admit.'

'I helped them create masterpieces, and what did *I* get? A soldier's wage, a servant's wage – whatever job I happened to occupy at the time. But I wanted to *write*. I gave them tunes and melodies and the best I received was a bit-part in their dreams. Well. Well, I've waited a long time for my turn – and then I found you. You, Carol. And I promised myself that I would never treat you in the way they treated me. They didn't even know my name!'

Perhaps it will help to anchor the conversation down to the now, to the present – to this room. 'What is it, by the way?' Carol asks. 'Your real name.'

'It's whatever you want it to be... I owe you that much.'

'What's the name on your passport?' she persists. *'That's* what you owe me.'

Thursday looks confused. 'You want my passport?'

'No; I want to know your name, that's all.'

The man shrugs. 'I've had many names. You choose it,' he offers.

'No, that's not good enough. Who is Lamella?'

'...Pardon?'

Carol takes two strides to the piano. As hard as she can she slams the keyboard lid down on Thursday's fingers. His immediate scream and her ferocious demand – *'Who is she?'* – are of an equal decibelage.

'She is the little girl that Mahler thought inspired her. *But it is me!* The little girl is just the human form. *It is me in his head*, in his hands...' Thursday breathes, ragged and hoarse.

Carol does not understand but she lifts the keyboard lid. If she hasn't broken one or more of the man's fingers it will be a miracle. What has she done? This man has volunteered to take her away from a tough life, and she might have crippled the only tools he used. She has not even thanked him for the CD that she has apparently helped him to create – she has undammed his creative juices. 'Oh God, I'm sorry,' she breathes.

She crawls under the piano, thinking of two things. The first is that she only knows one way to apologise – only one way to do most things, it seems – and when she drops her lips into his lap she hopes he will play the tune of his forgiveness. She wants *Lapsus*: the return of the repressed. Does that make *him* the repressed that has struggled to return? Or is it her? She works. Blessed relief it is when she feels his skin twitch; when she tastes sweat; when he tickles a chord from the ivories.

The second thing that Carol thinks, kneeling beneath the piano, uncomfortable and happy, is ironic in tone and texture. *If this isn't love,* she thinks finally, *I don't know what is.*

She needs to be punished, she understands. By cancelling the weekly appointments with her clients, she has missed out on their unvoiced resentment; she has lost their anger, which she has taken a long time to build up. Too much happiness is a poison: even Chaz seemed disarmed by her sunny demeanour and her failure to fight, scratch or moan. She works. She is a worker, a working girl, a practitioner; she is one of the lucky ones, is she not?

It is in the following moments, while trying to choke herself on Thursday's erection, attempting to stab herself with his weapon, that she realises that his money is not enough. She longs for bad nights and disappointment. She will return to Scottish Tony's place, to vomit on his chest if he wants her to. She'll go back to listless Barry, and to all of the others.

She loves her European; his name is not important. She'll know it one day. For now, she is his muse: that is what he said.

She owes him the gift of the rage that other people brew within her. She wants him to create; she is no use to him happy. But when he starts to play a piece of music that she does not know, she is sure it is *Lapsus*. It is her tune.

Given time, Carol will learn how long to take to its accompaniment.

Strokes

I.

Steve Bitch was a hard man, even into his seventies. I've seen him take on two Chinesemen carrying machetes. Seen him pierce a guy's lip with a dart. Seen him get shot in the buttocks and keep on fighting. And I once saw him punch out a *horse*. But I never saw anything come as close to laying him low – as Cheryl Abbey.

Cheryl was his weakness. He doted on her, although I didn't always know that at the time. And I was with him in the lanes when he got the call. This was in 1980. I was keeping my eye on a bunch of lads in lane five. The previous week they'd had too much in the bar and got a bit beautiful. A fight had kicked off with a group of students using lane four. Brief and vicious. I could hear someone saying 'That's *my* fucking ball' and then there was a flurry of fists and feet – you know how it goes. Lenny and I had to wade in with the truncheons while Julie called the filth.

So anyway, the next week they're back. As Julie hands over the bowling shoes, I wander over. All I say is 'Good evening, gentlemen,' and the geezer with the red hair and the West Country accent says: 'It's okay, man.'

I nod my head. 'So there won't be any repeat of those high-jinks, will there, lads.'

'No. We were out of order. Sorry about that.'

'Have a good evening, gentlemen.' But I'm keeping them peeled, just in case. They're noisy as fuck as they have a laugh and a carry on, but they're not doing any damage; they're keeping themselves to themselves. All is well. All fifteen lanes are busy and everyone's having a good time. Bar's packed. It's the sort of night that keeps Steve happy: low maintenance and high profitability.

He appears at my side in that uncanny way that he's always had. No one else could ever do it. As Head of Security, I'd long since developed a kind of radar; I *always* knew when people were getting close to me. Apart from Steve. What was it? Did he *float*, for fuck's sake? Or use an atomising ray on himself and then reassemble at his chosen location?

'The fuck are *they* doing back?' he demands.

'It's okay, boss,' I try to assure him. 'I'm on it. I've let everyone know.'

Steve takes this, but grudgingly. 'If one of 'em so much as flicks the Vs at another punter, Gal, I want you in there. Okay?'

'Yes, Steve.'

'And send him home via A&E.'

'Yes, Steve.'

'In two separate fucking ambulances.'

And that's when it happened: Julie's voice came over the tannoy. 'Telephone call for Steve,' she said. And off he went, over to her shoe-desk. I watched as she handed him the blower. I watched as he mouthed 'Hello?' And then he didn't say anything for a good few seconds. But his face, as the saying goes, spoke volumes.

I'd seen it before, of course: that look of sadness and panic. It was on his features when he told me about his mum being committed; when we found that starving dog, left to die in the bins round the back; and when his dad contracted cancer. But it was stronger now. It wasn't just that his face lost colour, because that never fucking happens in real life, unless you're losing blood quickly; it was more like whoever had been squatting in Steve's head had finally been booted out by the authorities, and all that remained was a shell, littered with beer cans and johnnies. That's what it was: Steve's face *hollowed.*

Out of professional duty (and nosiness) I moved on over. The phone call was winding down, and Steve had barely said dick to a nun. What the hell was going on?

'Boss?' I said.

'Fuck. Me,' said Steve. A few seconds passed, and then he made a decision, and some of the light returned to his eyes. 'Gary, I need a drink,' he told me, and I nodded.

'Let's go to the bar,' I suggested.

He shook his head. 'I wouldn't wash me dishes in that baboon-piss, Gal,' he said matter-of-factly. 'I don't know how we get away with, I really don't.' A hysterical smile flashed across Steve's features. I'd preferred it when he was more obviously disturbed. 'My office,' he said. 'Proper drink. Who's on?'

My team, he was referring to.

'Cliff, Errol, Elvis, Jack, Bill and Maggot,' I said.

'Leave 'em. They can manage.'

*

I wasn't allowed to drink on duty – none of us were – but on this occasion Steve all but wrapped my fingers around the glass and lifted my hand to my mouth. It was whisky: about eight measures of a treasured malt that cost more than my monthly take-home.

'Bewful, innit.' Steve asked.

'Yeah, boss. What's *wrong?*' This behaviour was well out of character, and I was worrying myself into a state of high blood pressure.

'Do you remember, Gal, I went to the States last year?'

'…Yeah?' A bit of nonsense and snuff, as I recall. Michigan. A bad debt had done a runner back home, and had foolishly assumed that Steve wouldn't bother to incur the expense of a plane ticket just to get back what he was owed. It wasn't a whole lot of money. But Steve *liked* to go against expectations.

'Well, while I was there I got myself a girlfriend for the night. Her name was Mitzi.' Steve sipped on both the malt and the memory. 'When I woke up the next morning she was still there, and so was my wallet. I'd left like a hundred dollars in it – for her – and hidden the rest. But there she was, having a bath.'

Steve was digressing and it was doing nothing good for my temperature. 'And that was Mitzi on the blower, was it?' I asked, eager to get the story back on track.

'...Yeah.'

'How did she get your number?'

Steve shrugged. 'I give it. Told her to gimme a chirp she's ever in town.'

'Jesus, Steve, what were you gonna do? Go out on the tiles with her on one arm and Julie on the other?' I was talking about Julie, Steve's wife of ten years, not Julie who worked downstairs.

Again, Steve shrugged. 'I never expected her to take me up on it, did I? Thank fuck I didn't give her my *home* number! I can't imagine that going down too well with the chain.'

'Woe. And now she's here.'

'Yeah.' Steve was smiling again. 'And she ain't alone.'

I frowned. It was getting worse. 'What, she's not brought her husband, has she?' I asked. I tried to make it sounded as though it was something to have a good chuckle about, under other circumstances.

'No,' said Steve. 'She's brought our daughter, Cheryl. She wants her to meet her dad. Tomorrow.'

*

Obviously, I wasn't there for the meeting. Equally obviously, with the benefit of hindsight, a fight sparked up that night: the same bunch of clowns as before. And believe me, I was in no mood for any fucking nonsense. Cliff had asked one of the group, an Irish fella, to extinguish his cigarette while he was on the lane, and the Irish fella had thrust a ten-pound bowling ball against his ribcage, the silly cunt. I mean, it's bad enough picking trouble with a total stranger; it's total fucking lunacy to do so with a member of Security – a man who fights people for a living. I saw it happen. And listen: you don't touch a member of my team; and you definitely don't touch my brother.

Julie was picking up the blower. 'No filth,' I told her as I ran past. By the time I'd made it to lane five (by sheer coincidence it was the same lane as the previous week, as if it was haunted or something, by a poltergeist of violence), Bill had also got involved. It was five against two in their favour. Cliff was on the floor, and three of them were laying into him with their bowling shoes. The other two were taking turns with Bill, who was a short man (dead now: a motorbike accident in '87) with the temperament of a pitbull terrier when the urge was upon him. He was putting up a good struggle. I picked up the lightest ball on the rack (a weapon is no use if it's cumbersome) and I clocked one of Cliff's assailants with it: the right side of the cunt's head. The *back* of the head is more effective, but I didn't want him falling on top of Cliff; you have to consider these things, and quickly. The cunt fell to the side, squealing like a piglet, his fingers up in the mash that I'd created, while the other two bandidos took steps backwards.

The one with the red hair was grinning; he reached for a tiny knife in the breast pocked of his blue-and-white striped shirt. The blade clicked up like a freed erection. I couldn't help but see the funny side.

'Are *you*, Mr Ronald McFucking Donald, threatening *me* with that toy?' I asked. To my left, Bill had been joined by Errol. And Errol was a tasty little fucker: whippet-thin, fast, and as determined as a sixteen year-old is to get laid. So I knew that that was all in order. It was me that I was concerned about; me, the burger billionaire, and the other stroker – an Italian-looking fella with cow-eyes and an uneven 'tache.

Ronald made his move as Cliff climbed up to his feet. I managed to get the ball between the blade and Cliff's right ear, and Ronald was thrown slightly off balance. I used it. As Ronald half-presented his back to me, I hoofed him – good, hard and clean – in the spuds. He bent over. Tache punched the side of my head but I barely felt it. I brought the ball down on the base of Ronald's spine, aware that our spectators' noise had alerted the rest of the team. Elvis was running over to join in the fun; so was Maggot.

Sensing this fresh disadvantage, two of the bowlers made tracks. They ran for the door, followed briskly by two more of their party... Only Ronald had been wounded sufficiently to prevent an escape; it was therefore Ronald that we used as an example – a deterrent, if you will: a warning against any further likeminded tomfoolery. We dragged him out to the yard behind the kitchen. Julie's voice over the tannoy informed people that it was safe to return to their games; that the police were on their way. Cliff, meanwhile, did most of the work. He used a truncheon to break Ronald's fingers. He applied some hot fat from the fryers to Ronald's shins. And once he'd lost consciousness, it was Cliff who tried to set fire to his face.

*

But I wasn't there at the venue for the meeting.

Steve was, and twice. Once, a full three hours early, in the sun-washed saloon, at eleven a.m.: opening time at The Ferret. He was there with his pint of ale (or *owl*, as Steve himself would have pronounced it) – with his tabloid, his fresh pack of fags, and his impatient indignation. Knowing, however that he had an important rendezvous later, Steve kept it simple and restrained himself to a cautious seven pints and four pork pies. He left at one-thirty, the better to sober up before the two o'clock assignation.

The second time, he was late. Sobering up had involved sitting down on a bench outside the agricultural museum; and sitting down had involved falling asleep. Nevertheless, sweating like a monk in a brothel, Steve arrived. *En route* he had procured an expensive posy of inexpensive blooms, which he handed to Mitzi during their kiss-filled reunion.

'How you been?' he eventually asked.

'The truth?' said Mitzi. 'I been depressed, Steve.'

'Oh?'

'Baby blues,' she elliptically explained. 'This is Cheryl.'

*

I didn't know dick about it for several weeks; and it took a crisis to convince me that Steve Bitch had lost his minerals, big time. Steve had turned into a different animal. Let's not forget that by this point Bitch was fifty. His first wife, Greta, had given him two sons, Mark and Jerry; and Julie and Steve had conspired together to make Ethan. So maybe it was the thrill of having his first *daughter*; I didn't know. I had my own kids in my twenties – Orlando and Fresco, at their mother's insistence – and I'd never wanted more. But some men are different, aren't they?

Understatement of the millennium.

*

The crisis in question went like this.

We had a system: the Security team always left the building en masse, along with Steve and with Julie, if she hadn't left much earlier. Usually, it was just a precaution, but we'd all witnessed occasions on which the operation had made sense. You got it from time to time: a bit of naughtiness from the kids doing glue behind the swimming pool. The odd drunk chancer. Some jaded silly sausage whose bird had just given him the elbow. You know how it goes. To this day, Lenny – if he's still alive – probably sports a scar on his neck from the night when he was attacked by a guy with a screwdriver. We drowned that cunt in the duck pond, and then gave Bob Forrage – the cabbie – fifty notes to dispose of the body. At the time I didn't know what he did with them. It was none of my business to know. As long as he let the old rats have a nibble, and that it wouldn't get back to the lanes, that was good enough for me.

Let's just knock on the head the notion that people 'appear out of nowhere', shall we? That's fiction. (Apart from the in the case of Bitch. And I said, some words ago, I don't know he performed that party piece.) No. The cunts didn't come out of nowhere; they came out of *somewhere* – the top right corner of the car park, near the tennis courts. There were eight of them: five of us. Me, Bitch, Lenny, Maggot and Cliff. A slow night: we were always understaffed on Tuesdays – and dangerously underprepared, as it turned out. Here they came. Tooled up; perky teeth like pinpricks in the night.

Lenny spotted them first. 'Timebombs at two o'clock,' he said, and we all turned our gazed towards the coordinates.

'Fuck,' said Cliff.

'Keep it all in your pockets,' I said for everyone to hear. 'Who's carrying?'

'Me.' That was Maggot.

'No one else? Jesus.' I was stunned by the team's laziness.

Steve interrupted. 'Sweat not, Gal. Stay flowing. What are they, after all? Fucking amateurs. *I'll* talk.'

I must admit, this made me feel better: his power of seniority rarely failed to impress me. The sense was warming. We all approached one another, and I recognized Ronald McDonald. Revenge hump, I thought.

It ignited like woodchips. It was rectum-hot, and lengthy. Lenny went down: a mallet to the left temple. The moon was briefly stained by a web of non-adhesive airborne blood. But if those strokers had expected us to curl up like plastic in smoke at the sight of one of our number disintegrating, they were about to be disappointed. We became *more* violent. The debris said it all. An hour later, I found a tooth by the wheel of my car; my bumper had a nosebleed's worth, a skull's worth of blood acting as an anti-rust agent.

Steve rose up above the only member of their clan still present. 'Your *name*, cunt,' he said – as if he'd already asked the question seven times.

The rest of them had vanished. And the lurker, who was neither Ronald nor the Paddy, was seven foot two with eyes of blue. The guy had already pissed himself baggy. I don't blame him.

Steve Bitch was revelling in the moment. To look at, despite his wounds, you wouldn't have thought that he was a fifty year-old man who had recently spent sixty minutes being stabbed and kicked. He had about him the look of a stallion, after a steeplechase; he was sweating profusely, but the guy was a picture of grace under pressure.

'I won't ask you again,' he said as he stroked a hot flush of blood up his right cheek and into his greying, thinning hair. I wished I could look as cool. The truth was I'd taken the teeth of a handsaw into my left wrist; I was bleeding quite badly. I didn't hear the answer to the question.

I woke up as a doctor was applying stitches.

*

That night I suffered a panic attack.

Call the fucker what you will, but to me it'll always be a panic attack. The full wax. In hospital gloom, I dreamed that I couldn't rise awake, and red rats were chewing my front door. I was trying so hard to wake up – in the dream – that I woke up in reality, or so I thought; in fact, it was just another chamber.

A woman was naked in my bedroom. 'I have something to show you,' she said, pulling the toggle of a zip down the centre

of her face, from her forehead. 'What?' I asked. She kept on un-
zipping. She pulled the zip down to her crotch, and her flesh fell
away in two perfect leaves, like the skin of an overripe banana. A
child of about nine – a girl – stepped out of the pink puddle.

'Where you been?' she asked me sulkily.

II.

Given my painkillers and antibiotics, I was staring at Steve
with the grimmest example of astonishment that I could muster. 'You draining my worm, mate?' I asked. I couldn't believe
what he'd proposed.

Three days after the injury. My wrist was half again its usual
girth; I appeared to have an extremely long hand, the wrist now
beginning four inches back from its previous origin. Five stitches.
Clouds of purple-dotted bruises the length of my forearm... Padding, gauze and bandages.

It takes a lot to sever the major vessel in the wrist. It's not
a piece of piss. You have to dig deep for the cunt, and fortunately
my attacker hadn't known that, or hadn't had the right opportunity to put his knowledge into practice; I'd received what the
doctor called surface wounds. There'd been plenty of blood but
there had been no lasting damage, as the various prods for feeling
to the fleshier part of my hand had proved to the medical body.

'Mate. It makes *sense*,' said Steve. 'You're in no fucking state
to return to work and the favour would make me smile. What's
the damage?'

'The damage? The fuck do I know about looking after a
little girl?' I said.

'You've had kids!'

'*Boys*,' I protested. 'And do you honestly think I did most of
the work? That was Annabella's project.'

Steve sipped at his whisky. It was the second time in recent
days that I'd been invited to share a snifter... so I should have

known that change was in the air. 'Well, Gal,' he said, watching me take a pull on my own glass. 'Here's the news: the principle's the fucking same – girls and boys. Keep her warm and cosy but don't roast her alive. Give her some food – Mitzi'll tell you what. Obviously not mussels and innards.' Steve was speaking patiently: a sure sign that he was becoming aggrieved. 'When she cries you plug a bottle in. Of milk,' he added quickly.

'Well I weren't gonna give her a fucking brandy, Steve,' I said sourly – a way of admitting, by the way, that I'd already accepted the challenge.

Which was what? Well… to help Mitzi, basically. She was suffering from post-natal depression, at a time when I don't even know that the condition had been christened with this name. And Steve was spot on with his earlier implication (not statement): it was too early for me to return to work. I wasn't ready. His suggestion, therefore, was to take a sabbatical from the lanes (on full pay) and help Mitzi out for one or two days a week, with Cheryl.

'Anyway. She'll probably have a kip most of the day. It's all she ever does.' Steve paused. Then he continued, in a ruminative fashion: 'I wonder why they sleep so fucking much, Gal. I mean, they do fuck all all day; you'd think they'd have a bit of fucking energy, they're so *new*.'

'One of life's mysteries, Steve,' I said, my voice oozing sarcasm. I couldn't stand to relinquish hold of the lanes. As it turned out, I didn't have to. Two decades later and I couldn't really inform you, with any degree of accuracy, how the whole thing came about; but the gist of it was this.

Steve wanted me to help with the baby. I took this to mean that he was not paying up his equal ante, which was not true, as the matter turned out.

Other matters – practical matters – were more on my mind at the time. You'll have guessed the outcome, of course, and the futility of saying no to Bitch, but I can only stand by what I said at the time: the fact was that this was a *very bad fucking idea*. Half an hour later, and I'm saying things like:

'I'm not doing nappies, Steve. Fuck that.' Firmly.

'You'll do what I fucking tell you to do, Gal,' he replied, pointing a meaty finger at my nose. 'Or do I need to remind you that for the moment you're still on my payroll...'

'Jesus. I'm not *comfortable*, okay? I don't like the idea of seeing your little girl in the nod. It's fucking weird.'

Steve tutted. 'You disappoint me, Gary. What does it say in your job description.'

'Nothing about babies!'

'What does it say?'

Sighing, I quoted: 'Head of Security.'

'*Exactly.* Think of it like that. Protecting all that's mine. And for Christ's sake, take it as a compliment, Gal. You think I'd just let any old stroker take care of her?'

It wasn't working. I remained unhappy. But do you know what I said? Of course you do. I said, 'I suppose not.'

'You bet your fucking *arse* not!' Steve smiled. 'Can you imagine Lenny with a baby? Wouldn't know which way up to hold the cunt!'

I laughed. 'All right, Steve,' I said. 'No more butter, okay? I'm fucking soaked. Trial basis. Don't work, I want my position back. Deal?'

'Dealypoos,' said Steve.

*

In that painkiller blur, I found myself travelling to Mitzi's gaff. She'd holed up in a room above an offy called Unicorn Wines – except Mitzi called it a liquor store. Bless. 'Like attracts like,' was one of her earliest sentences to me, and with it I realized, sadly, that although she would often attempt to be pithy, amusing and wise, those goalposts were too far away for a woman with clinical depression as a round-the-clock job. She'd never make it. She wasn't strong enough.

'A cup of tea?' she inquired, soon after our first introduction, 'or are you typically English, Mr Nash?'

'Typically English, I'm afraid. What you got?'

'White or red?'

'White, please.'

'Right up. Take a seat. There's an ashtray on the radiator.'

Being the person I'd ended up being at the time, my first reaction was to reach for the heavy glass cube with one hand and my lighter with the other. But when Mitzi returned, carrying two glasses of (what turned out to be) excellent Colombard, I explained: 'I didn't think I should smoke with Cheryl in the room.'

'That's very kind. But *I'm* going to. I'll open a window,' said Mitzi. And then added, as if to try to justify her instinct. 'Children are a lot tougher than adults give 'em credit for.' Cool air smoothed the temperatures in the room. 'My old man smoked three packs a day in front of me until I was twelve. And then he quit. Overnight.'

I nodded. 'Heath scare?' I asked.

'New woman,' said Mitzi. 'The bastard left us. On Thanksgiving. Thanks. He carved the turkey and went out for a packet of smokes. The next time I saw him was five years later, and that was by accident. The piece of crud was buying *sheets*: with her. I introduced myself. I almost started singing 'We've Got So Much In Common' but it smelt of a cheap shot. I thought: Fuck it. Left with my head held high. Ignoring any questions about my mother. Like he gave a fuck.' She exhaled. 'The point being, there's a lot of nonsense talked about addiction.'

I can now, at the age of fifty-two, confirm this opinion. I quit booze and fags at the age of forty-eight: doctor's orders. But I lit up in Mitzi's flat; I directed the streams towards the tacky chandeliers, half convincing myself that I was contributing something towards the good.

'About Cheryl,' I said, sipping.

'*Yes.*' Mitzi's voice, all business.

'Steve wants me to take some of the weight off your shoulders.'

'Oh does he now? Who says I've *got* any weight on my shoulders? Or that I'd be willing to hand my offspring over to a total stranger? No offence.'

'None taken. I'm not exactly over the moon about this myself,' I told her. 'But he's my boss.'

'Funny: he introduces you as his friend.'

'Steve doesn't have any friends,' I said. Then I softened my approach. 'Boss first. Mate second. Business being the operative word. Seriously,' I added, going back a step or two, 'didn't he explain why I was coming.'

'All he said was he had a *mate* that I'd like to meet.' She did more than sip on her wine: she drained the glass. Then she reached for the bottle for a refill, asking: 'Are you married, Mr Nash?'

When Mitzi had said *Mr Nash* the first time, I'd assumed that she'd been working on her irony: overdoing it for comic effect. You know: an affectionate piss-take of the stereotyped view of England – genteel England – with its scones and urbane good manners. No. That wasn't the case. I realised that she was waiting for permission to call me by my first name. Had Steve even told her what it was? 'Call me Gary,' I said.

'Gary.' Mitzi nodded. 'Are you Gary with one R or two Rs?'

'One.' And I added, smiling ruminatively: 'Actually, I've never met a Gary with two Rs who wasn't a wanker. Just like I've never met a Steve who wasn't an alcoholic, funnily enough.' A step too far? I wondered. 'Most people call me Gal,' I said.

Mitzi took no notice of the slur against the man we had in common. I couldn't think why I'd said it, other than to break the ice, I suppose. 'Well, *I* can't call you Gal,' she told me.

'Why not?'

'Because Gal means girl where I come from.' She puckered her lips. 'Unless you want me to take the more dominant role in this relationship.'

What was that supposed to mean? 'Call me Gary,' I said. 'That's fine.'

'Gary,' Mitzi repeated. 'Would you like another drink, Gary?'

'Yes.' It was good to know that Mitzi wouldn't be scrimping on the piss.

'Yes *please*, Mr Nash.'

'Yes please.'

She smiled and leaned forward. I took the opportunity to glance down her blouse. Red brassiere. Mitzi poured me another and asked her question again.

'Separated. Divorced,' I answered.

'Seeing anyone regularly?'

'Not really. Thanks.' I had the feeling that I was going to need a fair amount of the old *vino*. I didn't like answering too many questions at the best of times, but it seemed to be Mitzi's way.

I was getting ready to learn a lot more about Mitzi's way.

*

Cut a long story short, we agreed to a trial basis. I endeavoured to persuade myself that this was all for the best; and that, even if it didn't quite work out, the arrangement needed only to last until I was back to my full working capacity. The morals of it all? I still don't know. I still don't know if what I was doing – what *we* were doing – was moral, but I became a kind of surrogate father. My weeks took on a different shape and flavour. Even a different texture. I would wake up to Cheryl's cries, and warm and soothe her against my chest; I'd feed her a bottle. Before long I'd even got to grips with nappy-torture.

This was how it went. Mitzi had Cheryl for the weekend. I reported in for duty, prompt and usually hungover, on Monday morning and kept her till Tuesday lunchtime. I picked her up again on *Thursday* morning and delivered her back to her mother at twelve noon on the Friday. Simple. But as I say, what a change to my lifestyle! For a start, this was 1980: there were none of those groovy little baby-walker pushchair things; Cheryl's pram took up half my lounge. And the child within seemed to emit a kind of attention-demanding forcefield. Every couple of seconds, I would find myself looking at her lowered eyelids, or wiping some gooey mucus from the corner of her mouth. Like her mother, she was beautiful. And I had to protect her. So I ran a check on all the things that I wouldn't be doing while Cheryl was in the flat. Smoking was out, naturally, regardless of the free spirit on this matter in her mother's premises. I didn't drink plonk – just in case. I didn't even feel comfortable with the idea of a bit of porn and a strum. What I did was sit a few feet from the pram, drinking water and trying to read some old bollocks about the ghost of a famous jockey haunting a racecourse: a book I'd had on the go for months. Every time Cheryl sniffed I had a heart attack. Regardless, we went on that way for several weeks: and then my arm was back to its full strength.

*

Other things happened in the meantime.

The first, exactly a week after the attack in the car park.

*

One of the very many reasons why my marriage turned to soot was the phone call that would arrive in the early hours of the morning. It didn't happen often. But by then, I think Annabella was prospecting for any reason to leave me – or any reason to make me leave, to be more accurate – and business conducted when honest folk should be sleeping was certainly an accusation that was lev-elled against me: a pointed finger that I couldn't deny.

I thought of Annabella on this Friday night as I picked up the receiver. 'Hello, Steve,' I said.

'Sorry, mate. I know it's late but I just got a call from the filth. The lanes've been torched.'

I drove quickly. The streets were sibilant with fallen rain, but above these sounds I could hear a constant ring: an alarm. As I passed the swimming pool, the early aroma of smoke and burnt plastic filtered through the car's air ducts. I parked up.

The fire was out but the authorities were still on hand. A dinosaur-large fire engine was at rest at an angle to the blacked front doors. All of the glass had shattered; the bricks were caked with black. Desultory firemen were wandering around, their work largely done; and Steve was giving a statement to a police officer who resembled Peter Cook.

'How bad?' I asked Steve.

'And you are?' asked the officer, clearly coolly perturbed at having his line of questioning interrupted.

'Gary Nash. I work here.'

'As?'

'Head of Security,' I replied. We could all feel the irony in *that*.

'Mainly Reception,' said Steve, 'and lane one, the drinks ma-chines and the shoes. We don't know about the smoke damage yet.'

Keen to re-establish his role as the leading man, the officer added: 'Have you any idea who might have wanted to do this, sir?'

He was talking to Steve but I didn't like his tone. I said, 'Sorry, I didn't catch your name.'

'Sergeant Gerrard, sir.'

'Thank you –'

'It's okay, Gary,' said Steve. 'Yes, Sergeant: there was an in-cident this time last week, roughly.'

Exactly this time last week, I thought, starting to see a pattern emerging. It wasn't difficult, after all. One Friday night, a group of lads gets pricklish with some other punters; the next they get a kicking; the next they retaliate; and the next the lanes get incinerated. It didn't take Poirot to work out the connection, or to see the implications.

Who *were* they? Who was Ronald McDonald? Who was the Irish guy? What did they have against Steve? And why in Christ's name was Steve now revealing everything about them?

The answer to this last one was now clear: Steve wasn't. Perhaps he had also added up four ones to make four. He was saying: 'Two guys had too much beer and started arguing. Then fighting. We had to step in before it got out of control.'

'I see.' Sergeant Gerrard scratched notes into a tiny book with a biro that he'd chewed at the end into some sort of minuscule biscuit-cutter. 'And your staff will be able to corroborate this, will they, sir?'

'Certainly. Those that were there at the time.' This I took to be a cue to get on the blower as soon as possible: to call Julie, to call Cliff, to call Errol and so on… we had to agree on our story. 'I'm not sure what they were arguing about,' Steve finished, pre-empting the filth's next line of inquiry, as they pompously refer to it.

'I'll need to speak to them, of course.'

'Of course,' agreed Steve in a voice that said: stands to reason, like; common sense…

Eventually Gerrard seemed satisfied, and he walked away. His optimistic air was not shared by the two men that he thereby abandoned. I said:

'You had me worried there, Steve.'

'Yeah? Why?' He gave me his most gruesome grin. 'Don't tell me: you thought I was gonna talk about those clowns last week. Do me a favour.'

'Sorry.'

'You should have more faith in me, Gal.'

'True,' I admitted, but not wishing to dwell on the point, I added: 'What are you gonna do now?' I should also remark that in the week since the ambush, even though I'd had the injury to contend with, I'd been keeping tabs on progress. And I could not say that I'd been startled by Steve's efficiency. I'll come back to this in a minute.

'How's your arm?' Steve asked.

'It hurts like a bastard. What are you gonna do now?'

Steve faced me, looking up slightly as most people have to do. And I was ready; I was ready for anything – any response that Steve might make – except for the one that I received. *Hunt 'em down, Gary*, I was expecting to hear. *Tickle 'em till they bleed.* But what Steve said was frightening. It was the last thing I could have hoped for:

'I don't know,' he mumbled.

And I began to revise my opinion of how I should have trusted his decision. He didn't *know?* Steve Bitch always knew; that was one of the ways that he'd become the man he'd become.

'You do know what this is, don't you, Steve?' I asked. Could he have missed the punchline? 'This is strokework, mate. This is strokes.'

'I know.'

'Well I'm glad you know something,' I told him bitterly. *'Jesus.'*

Steve closed his eyes. Now I'm for it, I thought; I had overstepped the line. But his voice remained muted and more importantly his arms remained by his side. All he said at first was, 'Listen, Gary…'

Then he left a good long pause. I was aware of the flashing lights above the fire and filth vehicles; the throat-rouging stench of burnt offerings in the air.

'…I need to think. My business has just gone up in flames and I'm tired. Is that okay with you?'

'No.' But I caught my tongue swiftly enough before it could offer anything else too recriminating. I even managed a clause of demure politure. 'Do you mind if I speak freely, Steve?' I didn't wait for a response; I had something to get off my chest. 'Since Cheryl arrived, you've been a bit…'

'Slow?' Steve guessed.

'Yeah. Well no. Indecisive, was what I was gonna say.'

'Well fuck yourself, Gal. You have *no idea* of what's going on in my head, do you understand me? *No idea.*'

'That's true,' I allowed.

'So I'd be *grateful*, Gary, if you'd do me the courtesy of keeping your fucking lips together until I ask you a direct question. Is that clear enough?' he asked. 'Is that *decisive* enough?'

'Clear enough,' I answered deliberately. That was me put in my place; and that was me, blood rising, already rehearsing my letter of resignation at the back of my mind.

'The stuff I have to juggle you wouldn't believe,' he continued, unbearably. 'You think I couldn't work it out that this was strokes? Gimme a fucking break. We'll confer on the matter in the morning. Go home. I don't know why I called you out in the first place. Get some rest. I need you in for nine.'

*

The second thing that happened during those early weeks with Cheryl was this: I bumped into our one-time regular informer and information-gatherer.

Osman the Snail was a grass from Somalia. He spent all of his grass money – on grass. Therefore, with predictability, Osman had been of decreasing practical use as time had gone on. For I don't care what you say: that stuff will eventually rob you of sense. By the end, a few years later than the time I'm telling you about, Osman had been reduced to statements like:

I've heard there's gonna be a robbery, soon.

Oh yeah, Doris Stokes? When? And where?

Man alive. *But*: on this day in 1980, the Monday after I'd received my bollocking from Steve, I was nostalgically pleased to receive Osman into my company. I had little Cheryl in her pantechnicon pram, and I was buying slabs of beef from a guy we called Sniff – an unfortunate name for a butcher, I thought – and I met Osman in there by accident. He'd seen me through the window.

'*Easy,* Bertie,' he said – a phrase that he'd appropriated from one or more of his Caribbean compadres. Osman was a magpie for slang, and he used it *all* incorrectly. 'I hear some jiggy about you, sar.'

'Is that right? Fuck off, Osman,' I said playfully.

'No, man. This the full deck. You got some money out against your hide. What it worth?'

I weighed it up. Was I more inclined to believe him, given recent events? I thought so, as scary as that made things seem. Did Osman *mean* against me, or did he mean against the lanes in general? I wasn't the owner, after all. I only had enough money for shopping, so I said, 'A gammon joint, mate, if it comes to more than peas and carrots.'

'Throw in a chop.'

'Get cunted. What is it?'

'Man. You got one fucking evil wasp – ' to rhyme with asp ' – to contend with now. You a statistic.'

'And who's my enemy?' I asked.

'Where that joint?'

'Fuck me. Sniff,' I said to the butcher, 'put a gammon steak on that fucker, would you?'

'A gammon *joint*, man.'

'Joint. And this bear be fucking worth it, Osman. Telling you.'

'Okay. Outside, guy.'

And outside – in the plump air of a summer rain – we discussed the situation. What he opened with was: 'America. You know it, man?'

'Sure.'

'You enemy a *Yunk*. And he vicious, like a piran-ha. Yat.'

I was frowning, probably. 'Talk specifics,' I told him. 'Don't want no more fucking bullshit. Don't waste my time. Who's the arrow?'

'A guy called Corbett.'

'Christ. This is dog-dirt, mate.'

'This is true!'

'I don't doubt it. But it's still dog-dirt.'

III.

The third thing that happened in the early weeks was sex.

There were very real and very practical reasons for me not to attempt to seduce the mother of Steve's fourth child, but the third thing that happened was sex. You see, there seemed to be no analogous obstacles from Mitzi's point of view. As soon as I arrived – a lunchtime drop-off in the third week – I could all but smell the desire on her breath. At first I thought it was garlic, the better to repulse me. But no: a lust and vodka cocktail. Dangerous. A minge-Molotov. And I was in the direct line of sight.

'I can't, Mitzi,' I tried to explain. 'Steve's not only my mate – he's my boss. I couldn't touch you any more than I could Julie.'

'So that's her name, is it?'

'Yeah. It's not like I don't fancy you. It's just...'

'I know. And it's quaint. The *chivalry* of it all...'

Was she drunkenly mocking me? I had a good mind to rip open her blouse then there, but I didn't. She did. Or at least she started to unbutton it.

'Don't, Mitz,' I said.

'All this could be yours, Gal...'

Well, I'll keep it brief – but I didn't at the time. She was playing a Bruce Springsteen album for the third time; again it jumped on the loud bit in 'Candy's Room' and I gave her what I owed – right into the back of her throat. I'd already been minge-bound and up between the spokes. And I collapsed. Laughing. Laughing like a brook. Laughing like a man who'd just been tricked into signing his own death warrant. How funny was that?

A few minutes later she asked: 'How long do you usually have to wait before you can go again?'

'Excuse me for a second,' I replied. I got up and walked into the bathroom. The tap water was cool and calmed me down for a second or two. Then the panic returned. What the hell had I done?

Wait. Examine the facts. Mitzi was not Steve's girlfriend. They'd had a one-night stand a year ago, and she was a grown adult, capable of making her own decisions. Yeah. I liked that, but...

Wait. Steve Bitch could get psychopathic. I didn't like that quite so much.

All the while I stood there, and then sat there as I evacuated my bladder, the tap water gushed on. I found it soothing, mind-emptying...

There was a knock on the door. 'You have a *bath*, Gal?' Mitzi asked.

'Nah. Just a slag's wash.'

'...Just a *what?*'

'I'll be out in a minute.'

'Well hurry up,' she added brightly, as if the prospect of learning some new slang had warmed her soul. 'Your meal's getting cold.'

Meal? The word had the opposite effect on me than my terminology had had on Mitzi. I leaned closer to the mirror. Don't do it, I mouthed; but my advice was *well* late. I'd already done it, and now Mitzi was saying thank you with some grub. Too cosy. I gripped the sink harder, convinced that somehow Steve Bitch would have picked the information from the air: the knowledge of what his ex and I had done. I emerged.

The meal was cheese on toast, sprinkled with black pepper. I ate my two slices in the silence of a monk who had taken his vows. (Bad comparison.) Inferring that something was wrong, Mitzi said:

'You seem uneasy, Gary.'

'I've got some work to do,' I lied.

'*Oh!*' said Mitzi, uncurling a forefinger from around her wineglass and waggling it in my direction. 'Liar liar, pants on fire. You've got a bad arm!'

'Okay,' I admitted.

'I know what you are,' she added girlishly. Had sex made her *drunker?* 'You're guilty.' She smiled. 'Don't worry about it, babe: it'll pass.'

Babe? For Christ's sake, I thought, don't ever call me babe in front of Bitch. I stood up as Mitzi said, 'I've done *thousands* of bad things. Over the years. And I've forgiven myself for almost all of them...' Whether my face was still wet from the spruce-up in the lave, or whether I was sweating, I didn't know. But wet it was; I was hot and bothered. Even more so, I reckon, on seeing Mitzi's sudden snakey fever; her reptilian panic.

'Where you going?' she asked, no trace of the girl in her voice now.

Well. I've been called — I have to admit this — heartless in the past. No, I have; it's true. In particular, Annabella would make good use of this frequency. But eyes have accused me of the crime much more often: the eyes of wide boys that I've been obliged to render a spanking to; the eyes of men that I've dragged along behind my car... So did I leave her? Did I fuck. I didn't have the heart. In the final analysis, I didn't have the heart to be heartless.

'For a lash,' I offered, as romantically as I could. From the next flat along I heard a door behind slammed. The noise seemed appropriate.

'Again?'

Vowing to get out of the flat as quickly as possible, I rattled the chain once more. 'I'm leaving,' I would tell Mitzi's face the next time I saw it. Back into the living room I strode. Mitzi was lying on the small table, naked again. 'Are you ready yet?' she wanted to know.

Maybe Cheryl sensed my panic. She awoke, at any rate, and demanded attention. I stepped into the July sunshine with blood on my hands, and I vomited brown bread and melted cheese into a hedge.

*

'Soft' was what I'd really been intending to say on the night of the fire, not 'indecisive'. Steve's coil, his spring, had relaxed a jot; his muscles did not seem quite so flexed. But he hadn't actually done anything *wrong*. Indeed, if it had been only me who had noticed a melting-away of the man's faculties, perhaps I would have put it down to the fact that I'd been with him too long and that I could do with another job. But it wasn't. On a drink out with my brother Cliff, for example, I heard sentences like this: 'He'll be shaving his legs soon.' Or: 'Don't pinch his lipstick, whatever you do.' Typical Cliff-like overstatement, of course (one of the family characteristics; we'll get to the others in due course) but I was both chilled and appeased to acknowledge that I wasn't alone in the boat. Others had noticed.

'Don't let *him* hear you say that,' I'd warn – only half joking.

'Why? You afraid he might pull my hair?'

'You haven't got any hair, you bald bastard.'

And on we'd drink. Only once, again in the company of Cliff but with Errol also present, did I hear something like this from the latter's well-wetted lips: 'Spineless littulw minget ee is.' Errol couldn't handle his beer, I should explain. But that wasn't the reason that I felt compelled to intercede.

'Less of it,' I said, pointing a middle finger.

'Why?' said Errol, amused.

'One: because he pays your wages and you'd be in prison now without him. And two: because if you insult Steve you're insulting me too.'

'Eh? How does that work?'

'It just does,' I said firmly.

And there of course was a third reason. Three: because I didn't want the fabric of the unit I'd helped to shape, to mould, to unravel. That prospect was too ghastly to contemplate. Rebuilding the unit would be like stomping up treacle-coated wooden steps in diver's boots, carrying a tea chest of fifty pee coins. Fuck that.

On the morning after the fire, I was at the lanes for nine, as had been requested of me. Several matters were on my mind, and one of them was the following: a clutching at straws. Steve's philosophy on the subject of forgiveness was that once you've apologised, or otherwise proved yourself to be contrite (an important sub-clause to the contract) then that was the end of the matter. Asked his opinion on any of the phonebook-long columns of names of people (usually men) on whom he'd executed punishment over the years, he would invariably shrug his shoulders and say something like: 'Old dinners, Gal'; 'Water under the bridge, matey'; or something like that. It was finished business. Steve refused to harbour grudges.

To me, the next morning, this seemed like good news. I knew that I had upset him in the early hours, and I was eager to redress the balance. Nor was this simply my own idea: I had telephoned Cliff at eight and he'd urged me to do the same.

Little Claire had answered the blower. 'Hello, it's Claire,' she said as soon as she'd lifted the receiver to her mouth.

'Hello,' I said, 'it's Uncle Gary.'

'Uncle Gary. What did you have for *breakfast*?'

'For breakfast, darling? I had me some toast and juice.'

'Well, I had baker negs. It was yummy.'

'Was it, darling? That's handsome. Can I speak to your dad?'

Although I always enjoyed talking to my niece, I made certain I finished that part of the call as briskly as possible. There followed a long hiatus full of mumbles while Claire dragged her old man from the pit.

'All right, Gal,' he'd eventually said. 'Who's ill?' A reference to the early hour; Cliff liked to sleep until about ten on a Saturday, while Lisa did the supermarket shopping.

I explained about the arson.

Cliff exhaled into my ear. 'This sounds like strokes, mate,' he said.

'That was my diagnosis, too.'

So I stepped over the broken glass and kicked up thick low clouds of carbon, in order to enter the building. Inside, the smell was worse than I'd imagined it might be: maggoty chicken flash-fried on a bed of kerosene-soaked dishcloth. And Steve was there, as I'd known he would be.

'Wanna borrow a gasmask?' he joked.

I smiled, relieved at least that my day wasn't starting with a solid reprimand. 'I could do with one,' I said. 'You could bottle this up in a test tube and sell it to Handjob Harry.' Referring to a furtive drugs dealer on the peripheries of our circle. I'd bought gear from him on a few occasions.

Steve nodded. 'I might have to, mate. Won't be earning much from this gaff for a while. The bastards...'

'Look Steve...' I began. '...about last night. I was out of order.'

He held a hand up. 'Forget about it. A moment of high anxiety.'

'But I really think we need to discuss this,' I pressed on.

Steve indicated the lanes, empty behind his back. 'Do you wanna game?' he asked. 'And yes, we *will* discuss it: when the rest get here.'

'Rest?'

'I've called a full staff meeting for eleven o'clock. A few have made their apologies – previous arrangements. I accept that. Jack I couldn't get hold of...'

'It's the weekend, Steve. He might have gone away.'

'He's on the rota for today.'

'Surely,' I said, 'you don't suspect *Jack*...'

'I don't suspect anyone yet,' Steve replied. 'I got your brother a few minutes ago. He was still in *bed*.' A disgusted tone.

'He hates mornings. That's why he always requests afternoons and evenings.' It sounded rather defensive, I thought. 'Let's play a few frames.' Get him relaxed, or slightly calmer at least; more loquacious. Then start spooning.

As it turned out, Steve bowled a spare and reopened the negotiations himself. 'This is a conspiracy, Gal,' he said.

'No, mate. This is a vendetta. This is pre-arranged and calculated. You've spat in someone's eye and that someone doesn't like it. Think. Who'd have the patience to work like this?'

'I don't know.'

'*I don't know* is gonna get us all fucking killed, Steve. It's not good enough. Make a list.' I paused. 'I don't suppose you keep a diary, do you?'

Steve shrugged. 'Only for dreams and sex.'

The latter didn't surprise me, but it did intrigue me; I was interested in comparing notes – although not about Mitzi: that hadn't happened yet. 'You keep a dream diary?' I asked.

'Yeah. You can learn a lot about yourself from your dreams.'

'I don't doubt it. What did you dream last night?'

'I didn't dream last night. A list of what?'

'All the people you've damaged.'

'Gary. I haven't got time to write fucking *War and Peace*...'

So we carried on bowling – I could manage nothing better than an eight; my mind wasn't on it – and we talked retaliation times. Those unaccustomed to our lifestyle and the kind of work that's our charge – the amateurs, in other words – are getting out of hospital and getting on the blower the same morning to round up a team. No think-through. Even if you've been discharged, you're not in tip-top condition; you're weak. The worldlier, the wiser – they take their time. They wait. They clip their nails and feed the fish; they kiss their wives' left cheeks before they leave for work in the morning. They buy petrol for the car. And at no point do they let on that what is roaming the prairie of the imagination is revenge – or a debt of culpability.

Steve bowled a strike and we had a coffee.

*

The essence of the meeting was this. We would all remain on leave at full pay until the insurance companies got the cheque sorted out and the lanes could open again. That said, we would all be on call for minor chores, as and when.

We knew – or thought we knew – what this meant. I for one was glad to make the inference. Steve was plotting something. He'd been conducting his own investigations. Unfortunately, I was wrong.

'Most of you'll know that we got one of them last week to give his name. The name,' said Steve, 'was Peter Yahweh. Peter, I regret to inform you, is no longer with us for follow-up questions.' His heart had burst while Steve and Maggot had tortured him in the car park. I'd found this out later.

'So Gary...'

'Yes, boss.'

'I want you to get our man on it: Osman. Have him sniff under a few tails, if you'd be so. Okay?'

'Osman? Osman *the Snail*? Are you sure about this, Steve?' I asked, quickly realising that I'd sorely misread his mood. I'd stepped on *his* tail. He had no intention of allowing insubordination in front of the team.

'Are you *doubting* me, Gary?'

'No, boss... but *Osman*! Christ. His brain's virtually water, the amount of gear he gets through.'

Steve held up his mug of coffee. 'Who are we to judge, Gal?' he said with an infuriatingly ruminative smile on his face: designed to make me look as small as a teddy bear's thumb. 'One man's poison, and all that...'

'I'm not saying it from a moral high ground, Steve,' I tried to explain. I could feel the room tense. The entire fucking *room* had pains in the shoulders. Common sense, I thought, and chased its scent avidly. 'I mean, can we trust him? His faculties have been worn down to fucking plasma.'

I hadn't been able to get Osman on the phone before I met the stoned fucker in the butcher's shop. This was good. Planets were aligned, or some such shit; it was fate. It meant that I didn't have to offer the bastard any money. See above. Whoever had answered the blower had told me that Osman was in Amsterdam.

'I can't get him,' I told Steve a few days later. 'He's in Amsterdam.'

'Oh is he? Is he now?' said Bitch. 'Well I'll tell you what, Gary, you wouldn't believe the advances in air travel in the last century. Get the name of his hotel and get on a *plane*, you daft cunt. Go and shuffle his cards a bit. And if he won't cooperate and come back, do him some *Amsterdamage*.' Steve smiled at this one; he loved it when he could make himself titter with wordplay. 'Rattle his dice.' This was in a pub called The Ferret: one of Steve's watering holes.

'Okay,' I said sadly, not relishing the idea of the trip.

'You bet your *cock* okay,' Steve told me.

*

Explanation time.

'Strokes' was a term that covered the notion of repeated and regular assaults on an individual or organisation. Even the *planning* was aggressive. Coined by Steve, 'strokes' was inevitably an ironic word: it was the opposite of the strokes that you'd give a pet, or a lover. The attention was the same; the pressure was different. *Strokes*.

Now, call me a cunt (I called myself a cunt frequently enough at the time) but I was reading all manner of menace into the coincidental appearance of Mitzi – this was before our thrash: it was synchronised with the outbreak of this wave of carnage. Or it seemed to be at least.

'Steve,' I said. 'Let *me* do some digging. I've got a hunch.'

'Go on.'

'You're not gonna like it.' But Steve and I went back a long way, and at any rate he made a point of insisting that a Head of Security shouldn't be keeping work-related secrets from his employer. Yeah: he *said* this but he frequently contradicted himself, as we know. Well, he'd tell me to shut up if the information wasn't what he wanted to hear, I reasoned, so I went ahead and voiced my suspicions, such as they were.

Steve smiled and told me I was talking bollocks. 'A non-starter, mate,' he said. 'Erase it.'

But I couldn't. I can still remember (in my bones, if you like) the uneasy feeling that came over me at that moment. It was brief, it was fleeting, but it was there: a sensory response to the look that twitched for half a second onto Steve's face. It was the same look I'd seen when he'd answered the phone to Mitzi, in the lanes: that hollowed-out, scooped-dry expression. I got the feeling that mentally I'd done what only he could do physically to me: approach without being noticed. Like it or not (and I didn't), I had sneaked up on Steve; I'd found his hiding place.

And Bitch was lying to me.

IV.

Annabella met her second husband in 1982, I could write at this point, and I suppose I'd mean that literally. After all, Joe McHugh was already married at the time. Annabella took her car to him to be fixed; there were several complications following an MOT. They got talking. They got married. I went to the reception and kissed

them both (weirdly, I quickly understood) on either cheek, offering my blessing. Not that I was happy, of course. That night I entered what was then a new pub called The Raven and deliberately
started an argument with the bloke who was reading out the quiz
questions. I took umbrage at the one about strontium, and got
him in a headlock until he agreed to withdraw the question on the
grounds of impossibility and to buy me a pint.

Why is this relevant? A conversation I had with Mitzi, in
bed in 1980, has reminded me of the fact that I can't be friends
with my exes. But could *Mitzi* be friends with her exes? That was
the gold I was waiting for at the time, as she spun out her yarn.
It was six or seven weeks after I'd first met Mitzi, and a lot was
riding on the chance that the three of us – me, Mitzi and Bitch –
could work this out as grownups. It was bound to come out sooner
or later, I guessed. And I have to say that the odds seemed stacked
against such happy families. I *can't be friends* with my exes. I've
tried. My sons I adore – they amaze me, they control me – and I
would attempt to lift a building from its foundations if the clause
was put forward as a guarantee of their continuing love; but I
can't speak with any long-term civility to Annabella. I just can't.
It's beyond me: another language. Not that she has much to do
with me these days; we abandoned each other, and the boys are
nearly twenty. They can make their own decisions, independently
of their mother's enduring rancour.

My arm was back to normal, but for a small residual scar.
I'd been to see Steve, to ask him what he wanted to do about
the arrangements with Cheryl. To my surprise, he had asked my
opinion. 'How do *you* think it's going, Gal?' he'd said. My response was that Cheryl was lovely: a non-committal answer. The
fact was that carrying on with looking after the girl – which had
its own pleasures, don't get me wrong on this – led to other fringe
benefits. Namely sex in the afternoon; and increasingly, sex in
the evening. I'd stayed over a couple of times. A risky business,

undoubtedly (I had no way of knowing if Steve would turn up at any point, although Mitzi didn't share any such concerns) but worth it, I felt. I wouldn't say that I'd fallen in love with her, but I'd become very keen on a good percentage of her character. Her *willingness*, above all else. Steve had suggested that we all continued as we had been, for the benefit of Cheryl.

Without this consent (this directive?) I might never have had an argument with Mitzi. But one night we raised the roof-beams with our voices – or she did, mainly. It was late. The sweat was still cooling on my shoulders.

'When I was fourteen,' she said, reaching for her glass of water. 'I used to go with this guy. Boy, really: I think he was seventeen. I was in lust with him.' She smiled; maybe that was the best way to describe the status of our own relationship, and maybe she knew that. 'I gave him everything he wanted. We explored together,' she continued after a drink. I wondered where this might be leading. Surely I wouldn't be expected to account for my ex-girlfriends... 'Everything. Apart from one thing, which I *would* have given him, if only I'd known how to do it. But he just kept on – kept on saying, 'God, baby. I really want to hear your pussy fart. Let me hear that, baby. Lemme *hear* it.' But I didn't know how to do it. It made me paranoid. Like, why couldn't he be satisfied with oral sex, like the others? This *pussy*-farting business was another league. It was only later, a year or so later, that I had sex with a guy in his twenties: his name was Leo. And he *was* a Leo. He pumped so much air into me that eventually it happened. So *that's* what you wanted.' She was quiet for a few seconds. So was I. In an attempt to avoid further examination of the topic (it had arrived out of the blue) I busied myself with rolling a smoke. I'd bought some gear from Handjob Harry as a favour to Mitzi; I'd learned that her birthday had gone uncelebrated a week earlier. She was thirty-six, and the grass was my gift.

Mitzi then produced her strangest voice. I paused in my licking of the paper, as disturbed as ever, for the strange voice

– offered only when Mitzi was close to catastrophically drunk – always forewarned a dramatic swerving away from the subject in hand, usually in the direction of her personal guilt. She would go on to confess something awful that she had done; tonight was no exception. 'Wouldn't you like to go back and right your wrongs, Gal, if you had the chance?' she asked.

Knowing that I now had a role to play, I told her: 'It was hardly a *wrong*, Mitz.' If I hadn't ejaculated so recently on her left ear, I would have attempted to buy some time by making a pass at her. Sex was one of the few things that could be relied upon to shut her up.

'It was the one thing he wanted,' Mitzi argued.

'Then he was a spoilt, over-privileged sack of horseshit, wasn't he?' I said. 'Anyway, you should never give up all of something – not to anyone. That's what life's taught me.'

There was a pause. Then Mitzi said, 'I think that's sad.'

'Maybe. But it's the truth. I don't believe,' I continued, firing up the joint, and with a cocky swagger in my voice, 'for one second that you have shown me all there is to know about *you*.'

Believe me when I say that I had my reasons for such a conviction; but I don't know why I chose that moment, I really don't. Other than to say, it might have been the drink talking (we'd certainly polished off three bottles of red wine), and that I probably assumed that if Mitzi was inebriated, I would creep closer to my comprehension of something I'd found in the bathroom.

I didn't bank on receiving the reaction that occurred. Mitzi made that noise that only women know how to make well: that noise of disapproval – of self-disgust, almost. In letters, the closest we can get is *HARRUMPH*. But that doesn't do the sound – or the chill it invoked – any justice. 'Well thanks a lot,' Mitzi spat, and turned a fierce stare in my direction.

'I don't mean sex,' I added quickly.

'Neither do I! Jesus, Gary! What's going on in that head of yours? What? you think you get anal sex because you *like* it? Newsflash, bub. You get anal sex because *I* like it. Okay? *Okay?*'

'Yes, okay.' Keeping calm. 'But as I say, I wasn't talking about sex, Mitzi. I was talking about secrets.'

She was angry. She reminded me of a vacuum cleaner – and there's a piece of lint or cloth or bum-fluff on the carpet: something the cunt doesn't like. It's off its nosh. So it snarls at the fucker. It goes back and back again, trying to suck it up. Trying to do its duty.

'Secrets?' she shouted. 'Talk about the pot and the *kettle*. Criminey! You swan around, Gary, like your poop doesn't stink and you have the... *audacity* to lecture me. The fucking nous...'

I sat up straighter. I made a point, as childish as it seemed, of not offering Mitzi anything to smoke. And I said, regretting the remark instantly, 'You used the word nous incorrectly.'

Mitzi was stunned. 'So how's this?' she asked. 'Fuck. You. Gary. Is *that* well-aimed? Does *that* hit the mark?' She was now at the bedroom door. Mitzi turned; I was sure that her eyes burned with more than the effects of alcohol. Whatever the pills were in the small plastic bag in her bathroom cabinet, she had taken one or two before I'd arrived that afternoon. Now she was raging. 'You are a lowlife, scumbag piece of shit, Gary Nash,' she told me. 'I wouldn't cross the road to piss on your face if it was on fire.'

'Nice image,' I said, inhaling some fake breath.

'Cunt,' said Mitzi, leaving the room to check on Cheryl.

*

'I had a dream about you, Gary,' said Steve.

'I bet you say that to all the boys,' I told him, ruffling my newspaper. It was the day after the day after the argument with Mitzi. I had a cuboid headache and for the moment I didn't want to talk. *Talk?* I didn't even want to think. I didn't see many benefits in being able to *breathe* that morning. I was only half listening as Steve said:

'But you were a bear.'

'I'm not sure I want to know.'

'Why not?'

'Because, Steve, it's usually considered inappropriate for a manager to confess to nude dreams about his staff.'

Steve appeared confused. 'But bears are always nude,' he said testily.

I put down the paper. 'Sorry, mate. Did you say *a* bear?'

'Yeah.'

'Sorry. I thought you said I was bare. As in naked.'

'No; you were a bear. An animal. And you went into this river, to look for fish. You were waist deep in the water, stroking the tide?'

'Right. Did I catch one?' I asked, to keep him happy. I was waiting for my chance to say something that was going to make him *unhappy*, after all, so I figured it might be an idea to start the trek on good footing.

'They were queuing up to be caught! All these silver ones. I think they were supposed to be mackerel. What do mackerel look like?'

'What do they *look* like?' I repeated. 'They look like fucking fish! What do they look like indeed!' My resolution had lasted about twenty words.

'Okay. Let's call 'em mackerel.'

'Let's do that. What about 'em?'

'Well, they loved you. 'Sweeping the coin-shiny fish from the waters," Steve quoted. 'That's the sentence I had in me noodle when I woke up. You held a fish up in your hand – your paw – and said 'I love you'.'

'My secret is out,' I said, though I knew I shouldn't be taking the rise. Steve took his dreams seriously.

Was he trying to trap me? I searched – I panned – for meaning in the metaphor. All the harmless creatures loved me. Fine. Did he know about Mitzi? Did he know about the row? Was this Steve's way of saying I'd been busted? It seemed too indirect, too fucking abstract, for Bitch; but given his new way of working, who could tell?

What I wanted to say next was: 'Steve, what's your point?' – but that sounded, I realised in time, too antagonistic, too stand-offish. So I substituted it for the following: 'What did I do next?'

'You kissed the fish,' said Bitch, 'and it grew wings. It *evolved*, Gal; it moved on to the next stage and took flight. It sang to you from a branch...'

'How many pints did you have last night?' I wanted to know.

Steve shrugged. 'Just the nine or ten. Nothing special.' He sneered. 'And what about you? You look like you got *tarnished*. Sure you're up to working?'

The lanes remained closed. The refurbishment was going to be costly – we all knew that – but we hadn't realised how long the operation would take to begin. The insurance companies were happy (a few men had been sent out to inspect the damage and to ask questions) but the filth had applied the brakes. That twat Sergeant Gerrard wasn't satisfied. And okay, it was his job to be suspicious after an act of arson, but the time – the days, the weeks – was dragging on, making us nervous.

All the same, Steve expected everyone in for two staff meetings every week. This was what he meant by *working*: it was my turn to take the minutes.

'Steve. Have to ask you something, mate. Well, several things.'
'Go on.'

'What are we going to do about John Corbett?'

Steve nodded. 'As I've told you before, Gal, *we* are going to do nothing about our boy Ronnie. You leave John Corbett to me.'

'But you've been saying that for *weeks*,' I protested. 'At least give me a clue! The staff are edgy; *I'm* edgy...'

The strokes had not ceased. They had, on the other hand, altered. We were now looking less at violent crime and more at vandalism. After the fire, a *week* after the fire, Steve's car was broken into. It could have been a coincidence, we agreed ('we' being Cliff and I) but we suspected not. Nothing was stolen; it was a prank for its own sake: six windows to replace. The week after that, despite the presence of Lenny and Cliff on car park patrol (the car park also served the swimming pool and the tennis courts) four other cars were slashed at and 50p'd; tyres were punctured. It was *nuisance* crime.

'Leave everything to me,' Steve said, a glint of diamond in his voice.

But you're not doing anything, I wanted to say, *you soft turnip.* I'd pushed my luck on this issue far enough. But… 'If you're trying to protect, Cheryl,' I went on regardless, 'I can do the spadework myself. I don't mind. I'll find this Corbett fucker and put the screws on till he agrees no more.'

'*Just leave it, Gary,*' Steve hissed.

'Okay, mate, okay,' I said. And I think it was at that moment that I set myself the challenge of taking the whole matter into my own hands. 'About Mitzi,' I continued, changing the subject.

'What about her?'

I'd given this one a lot of thought: the problem of the pills. I knew that I couldn't just blurt out: 'Steve, she's off her tits half the time.' He would want to know how I knew, first off; and would my few visits a week to pick up or deposit Cheryl – visits that Steve would have every right to assume were swift and functional – seem enough to justify my worries? Secondly, Steve would ask what concern it was of mine; to which I only had one word: Cheryl. The truth was, Mitzi had entered Mood Swing City, and I didn't like it. But I had an in.

Depression. Steve had told me himself that Mitzi had the baby blues. If I applied to Steve's prurient nature *and* mentioned the pills, faking my belief that they were anti-depressants, I at least had somewhere to start.

'It's a personal question, boss,' I said. 'Are you *fucking* Mitzi?'

'No.' This came as a relief. 'Well, once or twice,' Steve amended, 'but not now. I think she might be happier if I was.'

'I think she might. She's depressed, Steve. She's on medication...' And leave it at that, I thought; don't mention unless you have to...

'I know. I get it for her.'

The admission came as a real surprise. Trying not to show it, I asked, 'From Handjob Harry?'

'Yeah.'

Anti-depressants? Was that all she was on? 'Well, tell him to lower the dose when you see him next, would you? She's quacking like a duck out there.' She needed medical help, I understood at this moment. 'Why ain't she with a *doctor*.'

'She doesn't want an English doctor. She don't trust 'em; she's worried they're gonna put her to sleep and then fiddle with her sixpence.'

'Jesus. What makes her think *that*?'

'They have newspapers in Michigan, Gal. It's not as if it's a secret...'

'One or two bad apples, Steve.'

I had failed to impress Bitch on two counts.

*

After the meeting, Cliff and I went to The Sound of Trees. Despite what Steve had had to say, Cliff still harboured unease about the state of his finances. I assured him – or tried to – that Steve would stand by his claim: nobody would be out of pocket while the lanes stayed unopened. But on the subject of the lanes staying unopened, I had other concerns on my mind. 'They know something, Cliff,' I said as I placed down the drinks.

'Who do?'

'The filth.'

'About Steve?' Cliff asked.

'No, about the Tory Party. Of course about Steve, you stroker.'

'Less of it. What's there to know?'

'That's what I intend to find out,' I told him. Steering clear of Cheryl's name altogether, I brought my brother up to speed with other matters.

Cliff merely shook his head. 'Here we go,' he muttered.

'What?'

'Every time you get that look on your face, Gary, there's trouble.'

'What *look*?'

'That look like you're about to wet yourself. Leave it alone, Gal.'

'I can't.'

'Well it's your funeral,' Cliff replied. 'Possibly literally, given our manager's let's say unpredictable nature.'

'Not lately it isn't,' I disagreed.

Cliff smiled. 'Wait. Wait a minute,' he said, creases deepening in the corners of his eyes. 'You're squeezing me plums, right? Seriously? Tell me you're joking. You expect me *to help you*?'

I didn't say anything. Cliff stood up and assumed the correct posture at the pinball table, a few metres away.

Disappointed? Stabbed through the heart, more like it. I knew that it would be more than a case of pigs merely flying – the pigs would have to fly in a choreographed display like the Red Fucking Arrows – before Cliff saw my point, so I left him alone to play the game that I have never enjoyed. I bought another round when I'd finished my drink, and a bag of pork scratchings. I had a fag. I settled down in a gloomy mood, and waited.

Cliff returned. 'Soz,' he said like a schoolboy. 'I just don't want you getting your worm stamped on, that's all.'

'Neither do I.'

'But you're going to go fishing all the same, aren't you?' asked Cliff.

'I don't see that I have any choice. Stuff's happening here that we could all be involved in. Bitch has lost the fucking road-map and I want to know why. He scored Ronnie Corbett once. The fuck don't he just do it again?'

'It's none of our business,' Cliff said in an even tone.

'It might be.'

'But it might not. And until we know either way, I would *turn your back.*'

'I don't have a choice,' I repeated. 'Not if I want to be comfortable.'

'*Comfortable?*' spat Cliff, his early mood reawakening. 'It would be a routine enquiry. 'You and me. We find John Corbett and get him to lay off. Or at the very least *explain.*'

V.

When I got to the offy over which Mitzi lived, I could hear loud music – the Kinks – coming from her flat, even though the windows were closed. On the pavement I recognised the man who was leaning, with his full weight it seemed, on Mitzi's doorbell. We hadn't been formally introduced or anything, but it was the man who worked in Unicorn Wines – maybe owned it – and the cheeks of his cigarette-filter face had turned an alarming shade of cherry. He recognised me too, of course – I'd got into the habit of buying wine from him before I went up to see Mitzi – and in a fury he said:

'You tell her!'

'Tell her what?' I asked, more nervous than I had been at the thought of our reconciliation. 'What's going on?'

'All day long! All day long she play this bloody bastard song! All day long!'

'Okay, okay…'

'No, is *not* okay! I ring bell, she no answer. I phone, she no answer! You have a key?'

'No.'

'Then I call police. Enough is enough. My customers, they complain. All day long – boom boom boom – through the bloody bastard ceiling. I can't *fink*!'

He made a start for the front door of his business. 'Wait,' I said. 'Maybe she's had an accident.' The little white pills in the little white bag...

'Then I call police and ambulance. Enough is enough.'

'Just give me a minute,' I implored him. 'I'll see what I can do.' Bending over double, I pushed in the letterbox and shouted through the slot. '*Mitzi*! Mitzi, it's Gary.'

'I want her out, sir. I want her *out*.'

'Yes, I hear you. *Mitzi!* Mitzi, please! Answer the door, love. It's Gary!'

The Kinks song – 'You Really Got Me' – finished at that moment. I used the silence to bellow the name once more. Cheryl was crying, I could faintly hear. I could at least take this to be a good sign: the *girl* was alive...

'You Really Got Me' started again. I'd assumed that when the furious proprietor had said song he'd meant music. I'd taken it as a slip of the tongue. But no: at the same blood-racing volume Mitzi was playing the same *track* over and over... This meant that the woman remained conscious. I took what comfort I could from this deduction. She might be drunk or high, but she had to be awake to rewind the cassette or reposition the needle.

'Fuck this,' I muttered. My long legs took me to the boot of my car; the boot swung up with his comedy coffin creak. Now, don't ask me to go into too much detail, okay, but I've had to force doors in my time; on some occasions it's the only option available. Despite what the scum journalistic pissbags of this country wrote at the time of my trial, I have *never* burgled a house; I have *never* robbed a sweetshop: but yeah – I've forced open doors. You take a mallet and a screwdriver... well, ideally you take an electric drill, but I didn't have time to fuck about with extension leads. The mallet and the screwdriver would have to suffice. The bloke viewed my return with great suspicion.

'You break door you pay!' he said, but the words were damp; more regret than perturbation was in the tone of his voice – as if he'd concluded that even if he were to call the filth, they'd have to do the same thing to gain access.

I set to. I got to work... Things are different now, of course: those deadbolts are a cunt. But Mitzi's front door staggered open easily enough. The whine it emitted as it swung wide was in the same key as the one that my boot always produced: backing harmony singers for a garage door diva somewhere.

'Mitzi?'

The song had started again. I kept my fingers on the wallpaper, tracing the Braille of the rosebud patterns as I climbed the stairs. Several of the stairs queried my tread with a cautious creak. I felt the presence of the shopkeeper behind me. I turned. 'Stay back!' I told him. 'Go back to your counter.'

'This is my property!' he protested, but he could rationalize the situation, at least from a business point of view. He had not locked up the offy and thieves could be making away with anything as we spoke.

Again I called Mitzi's name, battling against a wall of guitar, drum and bass. I opened the door that let you into the flat proper.

The noise was outrageous. Up closer to the epicentre, however, I could at last hear Cheryl's crying more clearly: she was in the bathroom. Her face was wrinkled with self-pity and distress, but it appeared unharmed. That was one good thing: I'd feared worse. A battered baby. It was impossible to tell if the girl's body had received any knocks, however, as Cheryl had wrapped her snugly in a fluffy pink towel, and left her to wriggle on the floor, staring up at the bare lightbulb (which wasn't switched on; good daylight flowed through the shadowed glass of the window). Cheryl's forehead was moist, either with sweat or from a recent bath. The room was indeed warm and humid; Mitzi had left the bathwater in the tub. It wasn't all she had left in there either.

Curling lazily in the water was a diluted eddy of blood. My eyes were fixed on it for a few seconds, as my brain limped round the implications. *Jesus! She's cut herself*, I thought. Yet I might have managed to convince myself that it was all in my imagination if it hadn't been for two more bits of bloody evidence. One was a red fingerprint on a wall tile. The other was a red spot that was riding a patch of dissolving foam, like a penguin on an ice-float.

I dashed into the lounge. That ugly taste of adrenalin and despair was in my throat, and my legs were as wobbly as a church made of matchsticks. The music was making the floor tremble too, which didn't help.

Mitzi was sitting on the carpet, in the corner of the room; she had wedged herself into a corner. She was naked. Her bare back was against the wall. Her eyes were closed (did she even know I had arrived?) and she was masturbating with great force, great energy and concentration: both hands. The wrists, I could see, were made up with blood.

First things first. Three quick strides took me over to the record player, and I lifted the stylus off the shellac. The silence was heavenly: a long drink of water to a thirsty man. (I even imagined that I could hear the shopkeeper below me sighing his thanks.)

'Mitzi?'

She had opened her eyes and departed from her fugue state, but her fingers were still keeping themselves busy.

'Stop doing that,' I told her.

She smiled. 'What have you done, Gary? Come to *save* me?' Said with rich sarcasm and dirt.

I crouched at her feet. I tried to take hold of her arms, just above the red wrists, but she shooed me off, she fought me.

'Leave me alone!' she croaked.

What have *you*, done, Mitzi? I thought. 'It's all right,' I said.

'I've orgasmed twelve times,' she whispered. 'I'm a *bad* girl.'

*

'I'm going to have to tell Steve,' I said.

Mitzi's head twisted gently on the pillow; a few strands of hair rippled into a new position: her hair was like waves. She was smiling. 'About what? The sex or the pills?'

'He already knows about the pills. He gets them for you, remember?'

'Oh that shit,' she said in a disparaging tone. 'That goes *straight* down the toilet. I was doing worse than that in the third year.'

We were at my place. I'd had no choice, really: the shop-keeper had started bleating about civil liberties and tenant responsibility, and I'd known that his fingers were twitching to use the blower. Mitzi was lying on my bed. I'd dragged a chair in from the lounge. I suppose what I was doing was the suicide watch.

Something about what Mitzi had just said had alarmed me, but it took me a few hours to pin down the source of my disquiet. It wasn't the message itself – that much I knew at once – for I could easily picture the younger Mitzi at school, in the lavs, or behind the bike-sheds (did they *have* bike-sheds in Michigan?), with her eyes filming over and wide as the capsule was gently laid in her palm with the reverence of a benediction. No. And it wasn't the woman's lack of faith in the gear that came from Handjob Harry, although I remarked on the latter point next.

'Who's supplying?' I asked.

'Nobody you know.'

'Who, Mitzi?'

'Why's it so important to you?' she said, reasonably enough.

Was I jealous? 'Because I'm going to have to tell Steve about this as well,' I said.

'Tell him what you fucking like,' Mitzi replied. 'I feel like shit and you're giving me an interrogation! I don't think much of your bedside manner, I must say.'

'Why did you do it, Mitz?' I asked, my voice softer – I'd actually taken her accusation to heart.

'Are you the good cop now?' she answered, closing her eyes.

I stood up. 'Jesus. You know, you could show me a bit of fucking *gratitude*.'

'For what? For breaking my door down?'

'Hey! I had to write a cheque for fifty fucking notes for that door!' I protested.

'You weren't paying for the door,' said Mitzi.

'So what was I paying for?'

'His silence. You got off lightly.'

So did you, I thought. As I was leaving the room I said, 'You fight me every step of the way, Mitzi. You don't seem to realise that I'm trying to help you.'

She had heard that my voice was a little further away. She sat up quickly, holding her right hand to her temple. 'Where are you going?' she asked in a panic. The question said more about her subconscious state than she would have wished to reveal, no doubt. In spite of her bluff and bravado, she knew she needed me – or needed someone – to be at hand. She didn't want to be left alone.

'To check on Cheryl. And to make some coffee.'

'I couldn't drink another coffee.'

'I wasn't making it for you.'

I didn't really want another cup of coffee either; I simply wanted to be out of that room. Cheryl was dozing in her pram, in the lounge. I moved about as quietly as I could. Poor kid, I thought. What a legacy! A mother so junked-up and nymphomaniacal that she didn't know what day it was; and a dad with the instincts of a rat, who obviously adored her but saw her when *he* was good and ready.

Mitzi had run a bath and used a cheap razor; she'd told me that she'd intended to see it through, but I didn't believe her. Although she'd had no way of knowing that I'd be calling round, she must have expected the loud music to attract some attention. A cry for help. A dummy run, perhaps. It didn't solve the problem but it was a relief, all the same.

The question was, what did I do next? In her flat I'd forced my fingers into her mouth, and because of what she'd vomited up I did not foresee any further complications from the drugs themselves. Given time, the body would heal; but the mind? I wasn't so sure. The cheap razor, with its plastic helmet designed to stop you shaving too closely, had not been the equal of the task. It had failed her, she'd said in the car, like so many other things failed her. At the time I'd been driving like a madman with a full bladder, and I hadn't really taken the statement in. Now I did, as the water in the kettle started muttering. Mitzi was on my bed, with a pair of my socks tied tightly around her wrists, sweating out her mistakes and the last of her self-esteem.

'How are your wrists?' I asked in due course.

'Sore.'

Attempting to lighten the mood (there's nothing like a good suicide attempt to raise your spirits, eh?), I said: 'You won't be trying that again in a hurry, will you?'

'No,' said Mitzi. 'Next time I'll try something more practical. A tall building, maybe…'

'Mitz. I don't even want to *hear* sentences like that, let alone respond to them. We'll get you a doctor – '

'I don't *want* a doctor.'

' – and we'll get you some help.'

'Who's *we*?' she asked.

Good point. 'All right, *I*.'

'Aha! So I'm still a secret, am I?'

'For now.'

'How *exciting*.'

'... I wonder, Mitzi,' I added, vexed, 'if I stay with you for any length of time, if I might get used to this constant piss-taking and sarcasm.'

'You might,' she agreed with a smile.

'Do you need something to eat yet?'

'Is that all I get on the subject of my wrists then, doctor?'

'Yes. Are you hungry?'

'No.'

'I can make you both something before I go out.'

'Out?'

'I'm on shift at six o'clock,' I lied.

She cocked her head. 'I thought the lanes were closed.'

'They are – ' But how did *you* know that? ' – but Steve wants me to do some additional hours. Strategy. Planning.'

'But you're not going to leave me here, are you?'

'I don't need a chaperone, Mitz.'

'But I do! I might steal something.'

'I got nothing worth stealing. How about some eggs?'

'I might steal your eggs.'

'*Mitzi*. Please...'

'Okay. No thank you, pretty please. Have you got any pot?'

'No. And I wouldn't give it to you if I did. Likewise drink.'

She started to unwrap her left wrist; I could see that the black sock I'd given her was damp but not drenched with blood.

'How's it looking?' I asked, stepping towards the bed. I perched on the side and held Mitzi's fingers, to examine the wound.

'All stopped.'

'Good. Why don't you take a shower and change your clothes. Make yourself comfortable.' I was still holding her hand, massaging her fingers and reading her palm. I noticed something.

'What is it?' she asked.

'Nothing. I've got to get ready for work.'

She shrugged and pulled her hand away, but gently. 'Don't let me stop you,' she said. Her voice was different. You might even have described the tone as kind.

Flesh heals. Hadn't I had recent reason of my own to appreciate the fact? The skin moves back into place. Ear-piercings clog over; burn scars vanish... but sometimes there are tiny, almost infinitesimal clues as to how the flesh once looked. And I'd seen one of those clues on Mitzi's hand – for the first time, despite our hours of lovemaking. More specficially, it was on the fourth finger, up close to the webbing: a band of *just* lighter-coloured skin, pressed only a millimetre into the digit – as if she had recently removed a ring. A wedding ring – a ring that had held back the sun's attention.

Mitzi was married.

*

I'd arranged to meet Cliff at seven, near the Chardonnay Pig. I bought a babby – or a kebab, to give it its due – from a spick and span place opposite the language school. I was feeding myself when he arrived. He sat down.

'Do you want some pitta bread?' I offered. I didn't bother trying him with the meat: Cliff has been a veggie since he was twelve (and I was fourteen); he was taken on a school trip to a farm, and that was that. No more meat. And especially no sand-blasted sheep carcass.

'No thanks. Let's do it. Before I change my mind.'

I abandoned the rest of my meal.

VI.

'I called you last night, Gal,' said Steve. It was weird. You'll never know what I fancied: I fancied some *company*, of all things. Julie was out cutting hair. And you know what? I couldn't think of any cunt worth spending time with. So I thought of you.'

'I'm touched.'

'I thought you might like to come over for a game of ping pong.'

What Steve was really asking was: Where were you, Gal? I decided to spin the record. Hadn't I taken as many precautions as I could think of? Ensured that Mitzi knew that she wasn't to answer the telephone? Not mentioned Cliff's name while in the Chardonnay Pig?

'I was with a bird,' I 'explained'.

'Oh yeah?'

'Yeah. At her place. She went – ' And here I thought of Mitzi. What kind of perversity was it that almost led me to say *like a steel band*, as Steve had once said to me? ' – like a bongo player.'

Steve sniffed approvingly. 'Where'd you meet her?' he asked.

'The Sound of Trees.'

'Woe. I hope you wore a marigold, mate. Know what that place is like.'

'Anyway…' I said. 'Steve, I'd really like to know what's going on.'

Immediately Bitch's expression curdled. 'Why? Let's assume a different course, shall we, Gal? Fucking *why*?'

'What do you mean, why? It has an effect on my life, that's why!'

'You've got a job to do,' Bitch said simply. 'I'd a thought you'd be grateful for a bit of a break from the lanes, but not you, Gary. *Oh* no.'

Don't antagonize the cunt, I told myself sharply; but that mention of having a job to do – that put iron filings on my nipples, it really did. I said, 'I'd find it a fuck's sight easier to *do* my job, Steve, if I knew all the facts.'

Steve closed his eyes. 'Working ain't supposed to be easy,' he answered quickly. 'That's why they call the fucker *work*.'

'Please, Steve. I know it's something to do with your trip to America last year. What happened to you and John Corbett? I've always thought that you gave him a tickle and he gave you the money. And now he's back. But do you know what the funny thing is, Steve. No cunt's seen him. No cunt's heard from him. His own fucking cousin in The Sound of Trees maintains that the bastard's still in the States. So do you wanna tell me what's occurring, Steve? This is getting ridiculous.'

It certainly wasn't the first time that Steve had got violent with me. As it turned out, it wouldn't be the last. But it was, I think, the most unexpected.

Without warning, Steve stepped to the side of my chair. Laying his hands on the back, he pushed down, unbalancing me. I was not swift enough. As I toppled backwards, I tried to slow my descent by hooking my row of toes under the lip of his office desk: too slow. I went down like a kamikaze pilot. Could it even have been a full second later that Steve had his foot on my windpipe?

I had never seen him so livid.

'The fuck are you talking about, Gary? And speak quickly. I am in one bastard of a bad mood all of a sudden...'

You can't unring a bell, as someone once said. I opted for the truth – and it was only in the minutes immediately following, when the pressure of Steve's foot increased and it became hard to talk, have I ever regretted it.

'I was at The Sound of Trees,' I told him. 'Doing *your* work, Steve.'

'You dick. You stupid fucking wanker...'

'Go on,' I said. I must have been sweating. 'This is the most animated any of your *disenchanted* staff have seen you for weeks. Get pretty! What are you waiting for? But tick tock goes the fucking clock, Steve. You're losing a good man here, and there are people more than ready to turn against you.'

Steve lifted his black shoe. As he moved away from me – with the grace of a piece of furniture being shoved around, I could add – he expressed the full horror of a man caught talking to his own cock on the Underground. I couldn't recall ever seeing him so tasty, but so *scared*; he even examined his hands. I believed he was going to vomit.

'You total fucking moron,' said Steve. Not a trace of anger remained in the accusation. What was there? Fatigue, first and foremost. 'Get up and unbunch your knickers, Gal. Sit down. John Corbett is not our arrow.'

Rising to my feet I asked, 'Then who is?'

'I don't know. But it ain't John, okay? Grant me your trust.' When Steve sat down behind his desk, the message was clear: he anticipated no further activity in this room. Not today. 'I need to get these lanes open again,' Steve continued. 'This is my first priority. Forget everything else. Without the money I generate from the lanes I will not – ' he spoke slowly ' – be able to finance any kind of return message to *any* cunt. Okay? So fucking work with me, Gal. If need be, convince your *team* to work with me. I know what I'm doing.'

*

'I think you're an interesting character,' Mitzi had told me, before it had been too late to stop dead. How many times had I slept with her by that point?

'Well that's a start,' I replied; then the voice of my subconscious reconsidered on my behalf. That, emphatically, was *not* a start; it must not be a start. This was the beginning of nothing, I vowed. Naturally, I was wrong. 'Mitzi,' I went on, 'just trust me on this. You don't want to get involved with me. I'm a hopeless case. I'm good at sex but I'm an alcoholic.' With the same words I was speaking about her. 'You'll be spending half your life repeating what you told me the night before.'

'At least you're honest. That's another point in your favour,' she said. 'Listen. The first bit you'll have to prove and the second we can work on.'

'The drinking? No. We can*not* work on that. I won't be reconstructed, not by you or by anyone else. It's part of my lifestyle.'

'Yeah.' Mitzi laughed. 'You're an Englishman through and through: we've established that. And it's cool, okay? I hate people trying to change other people as much as you seem to. I like a drink myself.'

'That's not the same thing,' I said.

'Even so. Drinking was a contributing factor in your divorce, wasn't it, Gal?'

'It was at that.'

'Are you a funny drunk or a sad drunk?'

'Compromise between the two. A philosophical drunk, I suppose. Never violent.'

She nodded. Where was this interview going? 'And do you swear more when you're drunk?' she asked.

'I fucking do.'

'"Wanker,"' she prompted, waving her hand.

'I fucking do, wanker,' I said and oh, how we chortled. We were well oiled and it was only just past lunchtime.

'That's my boy,' said Mitzi.

But as always she'd go too far; she wouldn't stop. She'd tumble down the hill and start an avalanche. The sadness was always looming.

'I did a terrible thing once,' said Mitzi: the same old song. It was night, so we must have been drinking all through the afternoon. Her body stiffened as if the headmaster had entered the assembly hall. The effect? It was as though, at that second, she had stumbled upon the decision to forgive herself for something else. I'd become a kind of sounding board.

'Do you think,' she went on, voice lowered, ruminative, 'that it's possible to do a good thing but for it to twist at some point into a bad thing?'

Was she serious? 'The story of my life,' I told Mitzi.

'I'm not joking.'

'Nor am I.'

'I mean… twist in the air like – Do you know the story of the magic arrows?'

'No.'

'Well never mind. Well, yes mind. The magic arrows didn't necessarily fly in a straight line. They flew where the hunter wanted them to fly. They read the hunter's heart. And one day, the hunter was angry and cold inside, and the arrows were confused by his decision – '

'So they stabbed him,' I said.

'Three bullseyes through the breastbone.'

'Nice. What's that got to do with anything?'

'I think…' Mitzi paused. 'I think we can mean one thing but your fate can be… haunted. And the bad vibes can leak backwards. And every good turn you make is made to look, from the outside world, like an act of selfishness – or cruelty.'

'What's your example?' I asked.

'Okay. But let me explain, I meant what I did as a nice gesture; I was young.' I know that she had a drink of something: I can remember that she paused, and if you haven't worked it out by now, our pauses were often punctuated with alcohol. I think she sneezed. And she said, 'There was a death. A boy of thirteen. His name was Ben Barnes, but everyone called him Rocky: he was a boxer. What do you say? Tasty?'

I nodded. 'Tasty. Useful. Pretty.'

'*Pretty?* Well, I prefer tasty. Not that his athletic build did him any fucking favours whatever. He drowned. He was on a class camp in South Carolina – a back to basics, bivouac bullshit deal. You know the flavour.'

'Sure.'

'And he drowned in a lake. Muscles to die for, but he'd never learned to swim. The silly boy did the *one thing* that he wasn't allowed to do, and that he couldn't do anyway, and he breathed in a lungful of water. The story was all over the news, like back-sweat on a fat guy.'

'Another nice image.'

'Thanks. I was broken up, Gal,' she said. 'Like, a million pieces. And so I thought I'd send a message of goodwill. I was sixteen. I wanted to convince the parents that they weren't alone in their ordeal. So I sent 'em a letter. A really cute letter, but heartfelt. I said this – I said: 'I was upset to read about the loss of your son. If it's any consolation, I know what you're going through. I also lost a child to water when I was your age. My daughter died in a paddling pool.'

'You didn't!' I almost begged.

'I did. But I meant it *nicely*. The last thing I expected was a *response*.' She read her palms; she read her elbows. They were red-rough: carpet burns.

'Which you got?' I said.

'Which I got.' Mitzi rose and ransacked the fridge for more piss. A few minutes later, she re-established her position and settled down.

'So what happened?' I asked.

'I received a touching letter of thanks. It made me cry. 'Thank you for your kind words.' 'Thank you for your thoughts and bless your heart.' That kind of thing. And then she asked: 'Did you ever get over your loss? What did you do to help yourself?' Well, I had a choice – right there and then. It's like that song, 'Should I Stay or Should I Go?' it was one of life's sweet decisions, you see, Gal – the kind that teaches you a lot about yourself…'

'Even when you're only sixteen.'

Mitzi shrugged. 'Maybe especially then,' she said. 'And I feel I have to keep saying this, Gary, but I was trying to do something *positive*. How could I leave her out in the dark and the cold? So I wrote back. I told her about an organisation called The Grape Institution. I did my research in the college library. The Grape Institution was a support group based in Maryland, but with branches across the States. And I thought that would be that. Duty fulfilled; time to move on, for both of us. But Mrs Barnes wanted to enter into a correspondence, of all things.'

'And you did?' I asked, already knowing the answer.

'I did,' said Mitzi. 'Do you know how I felt after the initial cautiousness? Flattered. We even struck up a friendship, albeit a friendship based entirely on lies. The disaster happened when she kept on suggesting we meet. What could I do? I met her. I went to the drugstore with my allowance and my waitressing money and I told this beautiful Chinese girl: Make me look older. And she did.'

'So did you travel down to South Carolina?' I asked.

'Yes. I met her on her home turf: a town called Crinton. Rat-infested place. I went on the train.'

'Where were your parents?'

'Well I didn't invite them along, if that's what you mean!' Mitzi laughed. 'No, they were cool. I told 'em I was meeting my penpal, which was true.'

'Weren't they worried?'

'Probably. But I'd been a grownup for a long time by then.'

'By sixteen?' I said.

'Oh sure. I grew up fast, man. I lost my virginity when I was twelve: a so-called friend of the family. I was shoplifting at thirteen. Grass and liquor at nine. That kind of thing.'

'So what happened when you met Mrs Barnes?' I asked.

'She was June to me by that point. But what happened?

She saw right through me, that's what happened. I can still hear her voice: 'You wicked, evil child,' she called me. I learned a lot from that.'

'Like what?'

'Like – I'm incapable of immediate repentance. I can't just say sorry. Even when I know damn well the blood's under my nails. First I have to deny the crime I've been accused of, and excuse myself. Then I have to brood. I have to sit on my branch and watch life passing by me, underneath. Then I pick at my scabs for the rest of my life.'

'Do you want some pizza?' I asked.

*

A few hours later, at two-thirty in the morning, I called Cliff. 'She said third year, Cliff.'

'What?'

'Third *year*. Like an English person does. Not third *grade*, like a Yank… *Third year.*'

'Gal. The fuck are you talking about?'

'Listen, Cliff. Mitzi was describing something about her school days, and isn't it normal for an American to say "third grade"?'

'I suppose so. So what?'

'*So…* I think Mitzi has been here for a lot longer than she's told us,' I said, my voice rising. I'd had a couple more nightcaps since arriving home.

Cliff paused. 'Hang on, Gary. *When* did she tell you that?'

'Recently. At her place.'

'Jesus, Gal: you're not, are you? Tell me you're not.'

'Why not? She's not Steve's bird anymore,' I said.

'No. That'll make it all cosy, won't it? Fuck me, Gary. Did you check your last bowel movement? I think you might've shat your fucking brains out. *Steve's ex!* You might as well paint a fucking bullseye on your chest.'

I waited. I controlled my temper. No one likes to have the obvious stated at them, and especially not by a younger sibling. 'That's not the point of the call,' I told Cliff softly.

'No; but *on* that subject, Gal – I know for a fact you own a clock because I've been to your flat and I've seen the cunt. It's the middle of the night, Gary.'

'But Cliff – ' I started.

'Maybe you wanna tell me her star sign while we're here,' said Cliff. 'Call me when that big yellow thing is in the middle of the sky again. Okay? Not the white one. The fucking yellow one.'

He hung up. I wasn't too upset; I would make it up to Cliff in the morning; we had already agreed to meet. For now, other matters prevailed. Whoever had attacked the lanes – the Ronald McFucking Donalds and the Irish fellas – were more than likely hired thugs. Nothing else. Bought for a few weeks of mayhem and then allowed to return home. Nobody in the Chardonnay Pig had known the strokers that we were talking about – or if they had they hadn't been grassing. I had to accept that the Chardonnay Pig and the John Corbett leads were wastes of time. Someone else was orchestrating the shenanigans.

Who?

VII.

Ernie Gurney's real first name was Eric. We called him Ernie because it sounded funny. He was Bitch's financial adviser. He was a tall, thin man with the type of waxy skin that makes someone look like a mannequin. He had nothing on top, but a narrow path of greying hair stretched grimly around his head. He also had a small moustache that resembled a blocked drain.

I'd booked an appointment with him and I was sitting in his office. I'd accepted a mug of *unreasonable* black coffee and was sipping on it while I waited for Ernie to return from the lav. If I'd known how long he was going to be, I would have gone through his filing cabinets as fast as you could say Jack Robinson. I might have found what I was looking for (whatever exactly *that* was) and I could have aborted the more dangerous part of this afternoon's programme. But there you are: hindsight – life's most beautiful unusable gift.

'Sorry to keep you,' Ernie said as he sat back down. 'Now.' He had the air about him of one who was really proud of the loaf he'd just delivered; here was a man who was *grateful* for the necessity to excrete. 'What can I do for you?'

Tell me all about Steve's financial dealings in the summer of '79, was what I needed to say – it was the truth. 'I wanted to talk about going self-employed,' I said. 'I want to run my own security business.'

'Okay...' And he began: off he went. Ernie told me about premises' rent and tax-deductible materials; he was fluent in his knowledge of employer liability and client insurance. In truth, I really was interested in such matters, only not at that moment; I had bigger plans on my mind. Besides, the way Ernie lectured was such a fucking bore that I was robbed of ambition in two minutes flat.

The phone rang. Cliff and I had arranged for this to happen when Louise, Ernie's secretary, had her lunch break. Louise was a temp, earning a few notes an hour, but we knew (via Osman the Snail, whom we'd paid to watch the girl's movements over the last few days – and paid with a food parcel, by the way: a sure sign of the bad times on which he'd fallen) that she always took her lunch at twelve-thirty sharp. She browsed around the Arndale Centre, or went into the library to read the broadsheets with the old guys sheltering from the rain. And Ernie was strictly a one-man-one-assistant operation. Two decades earlier, he'd been turned over and left to burn by another accountant and adviser with whom he'd gone into partnership.

We knew, in other words, that Ernie would have to answer the blower. By way of an introduction to the call Ernie stated his full name. This wasn't so common in the early 80s.

He paused. His forehead tensed like cellophane pulled over a sandwich. Perhaps he even went a little bit white. He certainly said 'Oh God' and stood up. 'I'll be right down,' he added urgently.

'What is it?' I asked.

'Some wanker's just hit my car. I'll be back in a minute.'

That prediction would have more truth than Ernie imagined. As soon as he reached the car park he would see that his car had not been touched – his car, his beloved B Dub. Personally, I've never been attached on an emotional level to material things (it was one of my quirks, this disinterest, that used to annoy Annabella silly) but Ernie's adoration for his motor was legendary. In his cups, more than once, at one of Steve's Christmas shindigs for the staff in the lanes, he had told me that he would rather have the car than a child, any day. Even so, I had to be quick. He'd give the car a once over, no doubt, and then climb the building once more, puzzled, in the lift. When he returned he'd find me, still in my seat, sipping the last dregs of my cooling coffee.

That was the idea. Ernie would never know about the bit in the middle: my bit. To his dying day (Aids, of all things, in 1991, a few weeks before Freddie Mercury) I don't think Ernie had any notion of the part he'd played, that afternoon.

I can look back now and thank God for the fact that this happened before the computer revolution. All of Ernie's working life was filed neatly in cabinets, in hanging cardboard pockets on rails. Not knowing if Steve would have been filed under 'Bitch' or 'Birch' (his real surname), I rifled in the second of the 'B' drawers and found my employer's notes stored under the former moniker. Tax returns, mortgage statements, even MoT certificates: Steve's approach to most things financial was coolly hands off; Ernie did *everything*... Clock was ticking. I pulled out bank statements, flicking through them as though I was counting cash. Here was one for August 1979. What I was searching for was a hefty injection of money: the reward for whatever job it was that Steve had executed in Michigan. But nothing seemed out of place. Even if he'd been paid in cash, wouldn't he have banked the spoils? Then again, would I have known it if I'd been staring the fact in the face?

I was getting desperate. I reckoned another minute, maybe two, before I heard the suite's outer door click open. But what was this? Paydirt! Behind the bank statements were the pages of Steve's passport, all in order. There was a stamp for 'Immigration & Naturalization Service: Chicago, Illinois': but the date was for July 23 1977. There were stamps for Melbourne Airport ('Arrived' and 'Departed Australia'); for Warszawa and Gdansk; for Egypt ('Registration within 7 Days' and 'WORK IS NOT PERMITTED'). But there was nothing for 1979. And the Melbourne stamps were for January 1980.

Steve had not been to America in 1979. Not Michigan and not anywhere else, unless he'd swum there. I was sweating. I shoved the papers back into the drawer and pushed it shut. I sat down and blotted the perspiration from my face with my jacket sleeve: blotted, not rubbed – red marks. And I picked up my coffee, acting up the aura of one who is not used to being kept waiting.

Ernie arrived shortly afterwards. He was having no such qualms about rubbing vigorously the dome of his skull with his right hand. 'The damnedest thing,' he said once or twice.'

'What is?'

'Car's fine! Not a scratch! I was thinking as I went down: how the hell would he know that it was my car anyway? And where did he get my *number*?'

'Did you recognise the voice?' I asked.

'No. Some Jock.'

'Well that narrows it down. Anyway...'

'Must have mixed me up with someone else,' Ernie was saying.

'Must have. Anyway – ' I was feigning more impatience: Ernie had failed to acknowledge the first helping. 'I trust I'm not going to be *charged* for this time.'

The allusion to money snapped Ernie back to the here and now. 'No, of course not,' he said rather primly. 'Where were we?'

*

'So what?' said Cliff, burping. 'I mean, he lied to you. Big fucking deal. You're not his dad; he doesn't have to tell you the truth about anything.' He burped again: he always did when he'd had a few. Intoxication brought out several of Cliff's talents, proclivities and characteristics – the volcanic eructations, the ability to roll a cigarette with one hand, a fantastic eye for trick shots at the pool table – but this honest sharing of opinions wasn't one I wished for now.

We were in The Sound of Trees – a pub, you might have gathered, whose pastoral-sounding name was famously at odds with its reputation for fighting, dealing and prostitution. I'd wanted to go somewhere peaceful, but Cliff had self-righteously pointed out that it was my turn to do him a favour. For some reason he loved the place. 'It's good to go somewhere where you can feel superior,' he would tell me later.

'I know this ain't what you wanna hear,' he continued, 'but I'll say it again. He's got a secret. Who cares?'

'And I'll say it again as well: I care.'

'Why?'

I paused. 'Confession time,' I said. 'Because I'm looking after his daughter – as a result of *something* that happened back then.'

'You're doing what?'

I sighed. 'I have something big to tell you.'

'Fuck me,' was Cliff's review, a few minutes later. 'Is *that* where you're disappearing off to half the time?' He rinsed his mouth. 'Fuck *me*.' To steady his thoughts he drained his glass of the remaining quarter of a pint of lager, then stomped to the bar to buy us some more.

'And I think she was married,' I continued. 'Maybe still is. She used to wear a ring on her wedding finger.'

Cliff remained both unconvinced and unequivocal. 'Some women do that,' he said, 'to resist the advances of... unwanted attention.'

'Believe me, Cliff, this bird wants all the attention she can get.'

'Divorced, then?'

'Maybe. But follow me, mate: Steve fucks off for a fortnight to do a so-called job in so-called Michigan. We know he didn't go there – '

'We *think* he didn't go there.'

' – So where did he go?'

'Maybe he was just having an *affair*.'

'I doubt it. Christ. We've had staff meetings with the cunt where the only topic on the agenda was what he got up to with some tart the night before. But on this *one* occasion he doesn't brag. Why not? Why do we only find out about it a year later?'

'I don't know, Gal. But I'm reading your smoke,' said Cliff. 'You think she paid him to bump off the old man. *Maybe she did.* It's none of our business, mate. We've both had to wipe people in the past.'

'For work reasons!' I pointed out loudly. 'Never in cold blood. Never unprovoked.'

'Perhaps he *was* provoked, Gal. Maybe Steve was her knight in shining armour.'

*

'I had a call from Handjob Harry,' said Steve. This was turning into a most eventful day. 'About the upward trend in your cocaine consumption...'

About my *what?* I thought. 'Oh yeah?' I said.

I'd arrived home only a few minutes earlier. Where was Mitzi? Wrapped up in a pod of my towels, Cheryl was crying in the middle of my bed. In order to answer the phone in the lounge, I'd needed to close the two intervening doors from the wailing; I didn't want the caller to hear the sobs. Didn't want to get a rep as a bad parent, now did I?

'Yeah. Plotted on a graph, the line would be vertical.' Steve sniffed right into my ear. 'Tell me to mind my own business, but what's up, Gal? You don't *do* coke. I've never known you to touch the stuff, apart from a few lines.'

His assessment was spot-on. As with pornography and chocolate puddings, I was an infrequent but interested user. Nevertheless, I assumed a stance of full non-cooperation, trying as I was to determine if Mitzi might have bought drugs on the strength of my name. 'I didn't say I did,' I told Bitch.

'Then I definitely don't approve. If you're selling it on, sooner or later you're going to bring attention to me and mine. And I don't need that.'

A bit rich, I thought, given Steve's nefarious activities over the years. But I was waking up to the indignance I should feel that my supplier had grassed me up. The last time I'd be dealing with *that* clown. 'I'm not dealing,' I said.

'What, then? Gifts?'

I was angry. Perhaps if we'd been face to face I might have lacked the strength, but a few miles of telephone connections had made me brave.

'Steve. You asked me to hang fire on judgements on your life,' I spoke clearly. 'You could easily offer me the same service.'

He was silent. 'You're not the same man I once knew,' he said quietly.

'Neither are you, Steve. And you're well aware of the differences.'

'Excuse me, Gal?'

'No I don't excuse you. We've had this up to the roof, Steve. Whatever *I* do is not going to harm you. Gives a fuck if I've bought gear? *Your* actions, on the other hand – '

'Oh, not again…'

'Okay. I'll not say it. I wouldn't kick a man when he was down.'

'I would.'

'But you're not, are you?' I said. 'You're not kicking anyone.'

'Gary?' Steve breathed heavily. 'You're becoming a bore.'

I could live with that, but I was still cross with Mitzi. I returned to Cheryl and lifted her to my chest. Only by doing so – by taking her off the bed – did I see the piece of paper that the girl must have rolled herself on top of.

One-handedly I unwrapped its single fold.

'Oh fuck,' I said, having read the short note. Chills were moving with the speed of germs around my body. Sensing me tense, Cheryl shrieked.

Why this next bit comes back to me now, I don't know; but I remember that at some point during the weeks of lovemaking, I had chuckled and said something like, 'I think you're bad news, babe.' Mitzi had also laughed. 'You've only just worked that out,' she'd replied. 'Do you have an attention problem? That's what I've been saying from day one.'

You wouldn't believe some of the bad things I've done, Gary…

The voice is as clear as the daylight on my face.

It was the first sentence of her suicide letter.

*

We've all done bad things, Mitz, I told her once – and told her firmly, the better to erase what was sure to be more than a smudge of self-pity. Me? I'd lost track, mate. The whole lot had blurred. What I knew was that it has been more than ten and fewer than one hundred; though I doubted at the time that Mitzi had had expiration on her mind.

Rereading the letter, I remained in doubt that her bad thing was mass murder; but I knew at that point that she was suffering from guilt. Mitzi had killed her old man.

I've done some terrible things in my time, the note continued. But none as terrible as what I'm about to... commit. None as terrible as that.

By the time you read this...

I placed Cheryl back on the bed. The baby was none too happy with this regression in her status, in her control. Lumpily I ran for the blower.

Bitch it was that I called.

'Steve? Brace yourself, mate. I think Mitzi intends to kill herself. She might've done it already.' I explained.

The tone was Dole office and car-clamp. 'Where?'

'Arndale Centre,' I said.

'And where's Cheryl?' Steve asked, all traces of our argument, it seemed, now forgotten in the beams of a much worse truth.

'With me. I can't leave her, mate.'

'I'll go,' said Steve.

Part Two

I.

I didn't speak to Steve for nearly six months; but I thought about him regularly. I took him to bed with me – in the sense that I dreamed about him often. In these dreams the air would smell of regret and bad decisions. It was clearly unfinished business as far as my psyche was concerned. Steve – you'll laugh – but Steve had come closer to breaking my heart than any woman had ever managed.

The name of my new employer was Dougal Sharty. Funny bloke. He ran a pub called The Shark, which was known to get a bit perky when the last bell rang. I was on a so-so salary to mind the door and give the odd warning look. To be honest, it was easy money. Although confrontations were frequent, they were easily dealt with: the pissed-up, donkey-jacketed losers usually got the message after a couple of shoves. People generally do.

'The Shark' was also the name of Dougal's alter ego. In his spare time he did a touch of wrestling. Leotard: the whole bit. Not the choreographed old wank that you get on the box: proper wrestling. Forearm smashes, a count of three when the shoulderblades had made contact with the canvas. And by all accounts, he was handsome in the ring. But unlike Steve, Dougal wasn't a violent man. Wrestling was a hobby, it was exercise – whether it was sparring in an empty gym or in front of an audience. Why 'The Shark'? Well, it was more than a convenient moniker, given his surname (Dougal 'The Shark' Sharty); it was also a reference to his slight backbone protuberance – and a little unkind, I suppose, but I didn't make the fucker up. One night, it must have been around ten-thirty, with the pub in the loud, proud motion of a liner at sea, Dougal approached me, as he did his other employees on a daily basis, to ask if everything was all right. I told him it was. The evening had been a matter of routine, so far. I'd had to ask two blokes to lower their voices or leave, but they'd lowered their voices and that was that.

'Do you fancy a late one tonight?' Dougal wanted to know. 'Got a party arriving at twelve for a lock-in.'

'Sure. Am I on duty, you mean?'

'No no no. Have a drink with us.'

This sort of invitation had not been extended up to this point; and I took it as a welcome blurring of the manager-employee dividing line. I was happy to accept the offer again.

Now, I wish I hadn't.

*

I'd had to leave Bitch: the house of cards had fallen.

It wasn't just Mitzi's death that cemented my decision, but it was, as the woman herself might have put it, a contributing factor.

Life speeded up. Restoration work on the lanes was allowed to commence, and Steve made his mind up that he had no intention of relinquishing his hold on Cheryl. The latter was the source of another row.

I knew that Steve was riding a wave of acute parental self-disgust, and so I framed my next question – two days after the suicide – carefully. The subject was the bringing-up of the little girl.

'Have you,' I said, 'really *thought* about this?'

He looked at me as though I'd just farted at a séance. 'Of course I've thought about it, cunt,' he replied. 'I done nothing else but think about it. It's on me fucking noodle round the clock!'

'There'll be records, Steve,' I tried to persist.

'… I dream about it. I think about it in the shower and on the yoke.'

'They'll want to check you out, man.'

'Yeah? Fucking let 'em! What's wrong with me, Gal? What's wrong with my suitability as a parent? Eh? I've raised three kids. I got money. Nice pile.'

'That's right. You've also got a criminal record for grievous and a list of fucking cautions as long as a dingo's cock.'

'Is that long?' Steve asked through a smile.

'Long enough, mate. She's an American citizen…'

'Was.'

'No, *Cheryl*. She's an American citizen. They'll at least look into your books.'

Steve made a face. 'So what? The fuck do I pay Ernie Gurney for if it ain't to make the figures add up? Cunt charges me enough for the privilege, don't he?'

'Yeah.' I repositioned a few of my pieces. 'Listen, Steve. Let's suppose it all goes well and you're granted full parental rights – '

'No 'suppose' about it, mate.'

' – Okay. Have you thought about Julie?'

He paused before replying. 'What *about* Julie?' he said. 'She knew what I was like when she married me.'

Did she? I wondered. 'But we ain't talking about slipping a tart a length every now and then: we're talking a new *kid*. And maybe she doesn't *want* a new kid: especially someone else's.'

'Then I'll raise her myself,' said Steve.

'What, in secret? Fuck off!'

Steve waved my objections from the air. 'This is nitpicky stuff, Gal,' he said. 'Let *me* deal with that.'

'Oh, I will. I want nothing to do with it. Just promise me you'll consider it all,' I said to him.

'I promise. Now get your arse back to work.'

*

A few more words about Mitzi...

She tensed at the sound of sirens. Sometimes she curled up into a ball if an ambulance screamed past. She didn't like tomatoes. She smothered her steaks with mustard. She could fix her ankles behind her ears. She feared the onset of diabetes. She had once subscribed to the medicinal theory of drinking one's own urine. She enjoyed English castles. She thought the Royal Family was 'cute' in a two-headed-puppy-at-the-carnival kind of way.

Her political tendencies dressed to the right. However, she despised Ronald Reagan. She fancied the actor Alan Alda. M*A*S*H was her favourite television programme. She adored Adam and the Ants. Her favourite colour was black. Her ambition was to swim the English Channel. She enjoyed the taste of cough medicine.

Suicidal tendencies ran in her family. 'It's a full-time job,' she once told me, 'not to think about suicide. Not to think about doing it. It's on my mind constantly. It's a chance to *connect*. I want to know what Corrine Maltovicci felt.'

'And who's Corrine Maltovicci?'

'Was. A friend from school. Sleeping pills, Complan and rice wine.' Mitzi stabbed a cigarette to death on a tray. 'Full marks for originality. She always had a thing about the Orient. It was her dream. Rice wine was as close...'

'As close as she got,' I fed in.

'That's right.'

As it turned out, Mitzi was the victim of irony. What killed her wasn't intention; it was more like a fateful arbitration, if you can accept that sort of pomposity. She bottled it. Having made the decision not to jump from the top of the Arndale Centre car park, she had wandered, drunken and topless, in the lanes between cars.

The car that ran her down – the car that dissolved her pelvis – the car that ended her life – had been driving too fast.

'I went to a suicide party once,' she had told me, 'in upstate New York. A place called Middletown. You won't have heard of it.'

'Correct.' I took the proffered joint between first and middle fingers: grass, tobacco and cocaine. 'Thanks. What's a suicide party?'

'What does it sound like?' said Mitzi. 'We do the Charleston and some breakdancing, of course. We kill ourselves. Well, not *we*, obviously, 'cause I'm still here. They.'

'What, for real?'

'Yes, Gary, for real. They're surprisingly popular among a certain social set in America. Wife-swapping is considered *passé*: it's so 1970s. So now people kill themselves and we watch.'

'Jesus.'

'It probably happens here, too,' said Mitzi.

'Probably. How many people saw it?'

'There were eleven guests, plus the woman's ex-husband and her new husband.'

I exhaled a hot mouthful of smoke and coughed. 'And they just let her do it?'

Mitzi nodded. 'It was what she'd always wanted. Her last creative act.'

'Was she ill?' I asked.

'I have no idea. A suicide versus the long decline, you mean,' said Mitzi. 'She might have been. Something terminal would make you push the pen down harder on the plan.'

Did I dare to believe her? Did I dare to believe any of it? A suicide party would appeal to the gregarious nature of the victim – or executor. And at least it was honest. I don't like the world and the world hates my guts. Here comes a candle to light me to bed, and here comes a chopper to chop off my head. Poetic, in a sense. 'What happened after?' I asked.

'After what?'

'The act.'

'Oh. Well, in this case I took a wrap of speed in the bathroom and drank until I got shitfaced. There's no actual *protocol*. I just did what I always do at parties.'

*

A dream of melting ice woke me the day after Steve passed on the news. I showered for a very long time; I washed Cheryl. I gave her wet food to eat.

I couldn't take the suicide on board.

Nor could I bring myself to go through her belongings.

Not at first.

*

Steve and the lanes – I left them after one final argument. Casting all of my remaining caution to the wind, I set Osman the task of finding out anything he could about Mitzi Abbey. Anything at all. I should have known better. But in my mind it was all connected: the strokes, Mitzi... Steve's lackadaisical manner. I also wanted Osman to go back to whoever had told him that the arrow was John 'Ronnie' Corbett: to get a name for who had supplied such erroneous information. It wasn't that I was livid about the mistake; it was more that I needed to know who was floating Corbett's name. It hadn't been an accident.

Well, I don't need to elaborate much, I am sure. I was summoned to the office. Steve was in a biting and cynical mood. I was listening, for sure, but in my heart I had already left the job and I was looking for vocabulary for my letter.

'Pardon my memory, Gal,' he said, ' – I'm getting on a bit now – but did I ask you to conduct an investigation, or continue an investigation, or did I ask you to *wash your fucking hands of the whole thing*? Remind me, do.'

It had all blurred into one thing in Bitch's head, too.

I sighed. 'The latter,' I answered.

'The latter: that's right. It's all coming back to me now. So we face a question, don't we? At what point did I promote you to Chief Pain in the Arse for this business.'

'You didn't, boss.' And how I resented that last word; I shouldn't have used it. That said, there was no point in not letting Steve have this moment. I would have been powerless to stop him anyway. The best thing to do, with Bitch, was to lie flat on the raft with your fingers gripping tightly, and pray that the tempest wouldn't last long.

'I didn't. *That's* right. So tell me, Gary, is there any reason – any reason at all – why I shouldn't reward your impertinence by booting your bollocks from arseholes to breakfast-time?' Steve asked.

In truth, even then, there wasn't. You live by the code and you die by the code: all that. I had betrayed the man that I felt had betrayed us all, but two wrongs don't make a right. However, what I said was: 'I thought I was acting in your best interests.' Which had the ring of truth to my own ears.

'Oh you did, did you?' By going behind my back?' His eyes were starting to bulge: in the repertoires of Steve's body language this was the equivalent of the marker that tells you when the engine is overheating. 'What was it, Gal? You can tell me. What? You thought I wouldn't *find out*?'

Come to that, how *had* he found out so quickly? Who was watching me? Watching Osman? 'I was trying to help,' I complained.

Steve nodded as if he'd accepted at least this much (which after all was perfectly true; sorry if I'm sounding too defensive about it all). But he was far from finished. 'Did you ever stop to think that your actions might throw a few stones in the millpond? No. I'll be dealing with these repercussions for fucking weeks...'

With whom? I didn't bother to ask. Who was Bitch trying to impress? The argument was running out of breath. Although Steve was still angry, I could sense that he was moving, in his mind, from the past through the present, to the future: he was dreaming up ways of repairing the damage – of repairing any trust that I had broken. My *own* salvage operation could begin right now, I realised. It might have played heavily with my heart, but what I said was:

'Steve. Do you want my resignation?'

He regarded me with full hostility. 'Don't talk fucking stupid,' he said. 'How's that gonna help? Not only's my back against the wall, but I'm also a man down. Sod that.'

'It would show whoever's watching that you're taking the matter seriously.' I suppose I was trying to talk myself out of a job. 'You could say you fired me.'

The laughter that emerged from Bitch's mouth was like a yelp – callous and cold. 'If I wanted to say that, Gal, I'd just fucking *fire* you. No. That won't solve anything.'

'Then what?' I asked, already knowing the answer.

Already knowing that Steve was mistaken.

II.

I used to take great pleasure in the word *strokes*. It appealed to my sense of irony. I liked the dualism: the sense, as agitated as it might have seemed, of two polar-opposite applications having to live within the same six rooms – the identical six letters. Repeated application of friendly or malevolent force. But now I view that perception as dirtier than two-month-dead carrots. We've claimed the word out of context. We've referred to the applicant and the supplicant. We've been thinking about who did it, and not the one – the many – that it was done to. Re-spin the wheel. 'Strokes' is about giving comfort, unequivocally: comfort to the one stroking, not the one being stroked.

*

Three months after I left the lanes, I had one of those cold mornings of the soul. You know the shake. You're awake and your eyes can see the clock, but you don't believe it's 3.17, or whatever, because you've found a new way of living outside time. It'll be 3.17 forever, or until you fall back to sleep. The problem is, you *can't*; sleep doesn't want you anymore. Sleep's had enough of you. You're as useful as an old prophylactic, a dead firework.

I thought of Cliff. Fuck me ragged if I hadn't tried to convince the cunt to leave Steve as well – not to hurt Steve, I'll quickly add, but because I was worried about my brother. I still am. We were close, and the protective instinct – it doesn't just curl up and die. Although logically I know that I couldn't rush to his aid right now, even if he needed me (not at least without calling in some expensive favours, or laying down some elaborate bribes), the feeling is still strong inside me. And on that night… well. You know when you've had too much sun on your shoulders, and a few days later your skin starts to peel? That *itching* sensation? Well, that's what it was like: an all-over bath of itching. My bones were itching. My *blood* was itching.

Cliff.

Cliff hadn't left Steve, and I'd been wounded, I suppose. Aggrieved, too. Although I had sent a card on Cliff's birthday, and bought him a jar, I had not attended the party at the house: I'd been worried that Bitch would be present. And I didn't know how to talk to Steve any longer.

As it turned out, Steve hadn't gone either. I'd been feeling lousy ever since. But now, in the night, with the yellow digits of the clock frozen at 3.17 for what seemed like the second hour in a row, Cliff greeted me in my head. Yeah: I got paid in the brain. The unwillingness, the *hurtful* unwillingness, to play much of a part in my investigations (if that was a fair charge); the lack of concern for my trials; even the refusal to quit his job at the lanes: all of these things pointed suddenly at Cliff, and a bewigged old dude in a red cloak said, 'Guilty.'

Cliff and Steve were into something together. It had all become obvious. And to borrow the words from the song, it was bigger than both of them.

But what? What *was* it?

Conflicting messages of heat and chill were affecting my skin. I thought I was ill, but now I understand that it was the sort of work-horror that grows out of a simple seed of guilt. It's a very misshapen – it's the ugliest impulse there is: that of guilt. I was suspecting my own brother of a crime that I didn't even know had been committed.

I wanted to call him. I knew I couldn't, or at any rate shouldn't, until the big yellow thing had arrived in the middle of the sky again to say Wotcher! Then the clock clicked to 3.18; my bladder swelled; and out in the lounge my telephone rang. Feeling slimy with panic and sickness, I let my erection guide my way through the gloom. I imagined I was dreaming.

It would either be Steve or Cliff, I knew. I was wrong. It was tears that greeted my cautious hello; a woman's tears. Mitzi? Annabella? No...

'Lisa? Lisa,' I said, 'what's wrong?' Cliff's missus. And I already had the answer to my question, fully formed. 'What's happened to him?' I asked.

'They've taken him to A&E,' she managed, the sentence taking nearly a minute. 'He's asking for you.' A hollowed-out quality to the air behind her words: she was there, in the Accident and Emergency, with my brother. The very fact that she'd made the call, as opposed to delegating the task to a duty nurse, spoke one clear truth to me: she was not being allowed to attend to her husband. The doctors were working on him.

'What did they do?'

'They... they...'

I played music in the car. As soon as I cleared my street, I turned it up loud. Kinks. I edited out Lisa's sobbing, and replayed the sentence, again and again: 'They tied him to the steering wheel and set the car on fire.' Not even 'Lola' could drown out Lisa.

The journey was over in ten minutes flat. I parked up and entered the building. A&E was New Year's Eve busy, although the new year had long since arrived. Some drunks were waiting on the cold red benches; one had brought along a deck of playing cards, evidently accustomed to the inevitable wait. A young couple looked stunned, near the desk; he wore the facial bruise of whatever household weapon she'd employed to clock him with.

'Clifford Nash,' I announced.

I was led down three corridors (well away from the suite of curtained cubicles) which were all identical through my grief – led by a short, plump young woman who bristled with efficiency and doled-out sympathy. Years later I would wear a pair of spectacles just like hers, but her eyeware wasn't on my mind at that moment.

Cliff had been given a room of his own. That said, there were four more beds, oddly empty – perhaps the grim and lucky crew, waiting out there in the angst-scented wings – perhaps four of their number would roll the right dice tonight and receive some medical attention. None of them would have needed it more than Cliff appeared to.

The sight of him was enough for me to reach for my mouth. He was a blister: unpopped, undrained. His face was a plastic mask of reddened skin; his hair had been claimed by the handful. His eyes were the only parts of his head that remained recognisably *Cliff*.

'Just don't ask if I'm okay, all right?' he said. Even his voice had changed: deeper, sandier.

'Nor you,' I told him. 'Fuck, man...'

'Yeah. I have only people's first reactions to go on so far,' said Cliff, 'but I'm guessing I won't be smiling in the school photograph for a while. Pull up a perch.'

There was a chair near the door. I moved towards the bed, carrying the chair, and the relief I felt on sitting down would have been worth quite a high asking price. 'You haven't seen yourself?' I said.

'They're telling me it's not as bad as it looks,' he replied. 'Shallow burns, was how one guy put it. I can't tell you how reassured I was by that.' A winning line; a Cliffy bit of pugnacious piss-taking. It was all I could do, seeing my brother like that and smelling his bravery (the wounds must have hurt like a bastard) not to break down in front of him.

To business, I thought but didn't say. 'How many of them were there?' I asked.

'Six. Two behind and four in front. I was leaving the lanes – '

'Strokes,' I muttered.

'*Oh* yes. It was strokes all right.' Cliff paused for air. He raised his bandaged hands... What was it? What did that futile, gentle, *assessing* gesture remind me of? I know now, but I can't remember when it came to me – not then, I assure you. It reminded me of Orlando, impatient with a piece of Physics homework (force, mass) but returning to the battlefield, the chessboard of scientific knowledge, one more time, such was his hunt and such was his competitive nature.

'Explain, mate,' I said.

'I left the lanes. Me, Steve, Errol, Lenny, Julie and Maggot. By the way, Julie's shagging Errol now. Strike.'

A long-running joke, or piece of speculation. For some months we had discussed among ourselves (never with Julie, and certainly never with Errol) the frankly disturbing way that Julie seemed not to be sleeping with Errol. We couldn't understand it. She had knocked down the pins of all the other members of staff (she'd enjoyed a *spare* for some time); but not Errol, the youngest of us all. Was his age the *problem?* That it might be connected to the colour of his skin held little water, we agreed... So it was good to learn that in one respect at least, the world had reverted to type. Male skittles down: a *strike*.

'That's good to hear,' I said, remembering briefly my psychotic ride in Julie's rocking chair.

'But there were too many cars,' Cliff continued. 'It looked wrong.' He breathed excitedly. 'Steve told us to keep our heads up, but nothing happened. We all got in our cars. Julie was with Errol, the rest of us alone. I was followed.'

You make a swift choice in such a circumstance. Either you gamble that the cunts have done their homework and they know where you live, or risk it and tread down on the pedal. You might lose 'em. You might lose your toes in the resulting pile-up.

'I lost 'em,' said Cliff. I indicated left on Church Street but steamed over. Did a dog's leg over the Downs, past the zoo... anyway, I lost 'em. Except I didn't, of course. I can see that now, the wankers.'

I was nodding in a way that used be called 'sagely'. I couldn't have felt more ignorant if you'd just proved to me that one and one is four.

'They were waiting for you at the house,' I said. 'Lisa and the kids okay?'

'Oh they're fine.' The question seemed to vex Cliff, as though I'd missed the point; but I hadn't. 'Lisa's here.'

'I know.'

'One of the cunts rang the doorbell after they'd set the car on fire. They weren't trying to kill me.'

'Your insurance premiums'll go up,' I told him, aiming for levity. But:

'Nope. Weren't my car,' he said.

'Whose car was it?' This had come as a genuine surprise.

Cliff tried hard with his shrug. It was pitiful. 'Stolen for the very purpose, would be my guess. But there was something: a mapbook,' he told me. 'Opened full frontal to Shropshire.'

'What's in Shropshire?' I asked.

'That's what I'm hoping you'll find out on my behalf.'

'Excuse me?'

'You heard, mate. It was a clue, Gal. We haven't worked it out fast enough and now some cunt is getting impatient. What's strokes if we're all too fucking numb to pinpoint the stroker? Eh? I'm sorry I doubted you.'

'Mate. You got nothing to apologise for. It's me who should be bringing *you* a bunch of grapes.'

Cliff faced me. I didn't much appreciate the tenderised steak of his absorption. 'Gary. Put a penny in the slot, eh?' he advised. 'I'm just the second act, mate. Someone else is the climax. And it's either Steve or it's you. Be prepared.'

Shortly afterwards, I got as pissed as my granny's mattress. I don't remember a good deal of the following couple of days. My loss.

III.

I wasn't lying when I told you that I didn't see Bitch for six months after I left the lanes; but I accept that I misled you slightly. On a couple of occasions I spoke to him. One was the morning after Cliff was attacked. I caught him early, Steve that is, recalling clearly his once-given advice that phone calls are most effective if made first thing in the morning or last thing at night. Julie sounded odd. No doubt she had heard of my defection; for all I knew, Steve was tossing a dart at my photograph on the board as part of a new a.m. ritual.

Or maybe Steve had forced Cheryl into Julie's life. After all, the girl had been snatched from me, and who else was going to take care of her?

'To what do I owe this?' said Steve, deliberately leaving off the word *honour*, the word *pleasure*.

'I have some news for you,' I said. I took a deep breath, whatever that means, and told my former employer: 'Cliff was assaulted last night. He's in the L&D.'

'Really? I have news for you, Gal. So was Errol and so was Julie. And so are they.'

'So what are you doing about it?' I asked. 'You can't leave this to fester any longer.'

'Gary. Do yourself a favour, eh?' said Steve. 'Stop telling *me* what I can and cannot do. You left! You sacrificed any favours or influence you had when you slammed the door.'

'Cunt, I fought for you, I stuck up for you – '

'And then you left me. Your membership entitlements have been cancelled.'

I was sad. 'What business do you conduct in Shropshire?' I wanted to know.

'None.'

'Oh Steve…'

'Oh-Steve what?' said Bitch.

'You don't remember, do you?' I asked him. 'Your advice – your précis of all that life has taught you. In the realm of inter-rogation, a second is acceptable. Half a second is not. Remember? You were too quick, Bitch. You know exactly what's going on. So what? Drugs? An automatic or two?'

'Nunna your biz.'

'Not ordinarily, I agree. But thank you,' I said, 'at least for conceding I'm not going mad.'

And Steve paused again. 'No, you're not going mad, Gal,' he said.

'Shropshire.'

'No dice.'

'*Shropshire.*'

'No.'

'I know you killed Mitzi's husband,' I said. 'Or you were part of it.'

'Yawn.'

'What I don't understand is why.'

'Gary. This is going nowhere.'

And he hung up.

*

Sergeant Gerrard informed me that the next question was merely a matter of routine, but: 'Where were you last night, between midnight and four, sir?'

'At home. Alone. Followed by the hospital.'

He wrote this down, as if he wouldn't recall the response. Then I asked the typical of my own. I was unnerved, I think, by the silence.

'Am I a suspect?'

'Sir. The world and his wife right now are suspects,' said Gerrard.

'Any clues?'

'Yes, sir. There's a burnt-out shell of a stolen Volvo Estate. That's our biggest clue so far…'

Wrinkle-browed I stared at him. 'Are you wanking in me mittens, mate?' I asked.

'Sir?'

'I *know* about the motor! I mean, anything else? Like, who tried to barbecue my younger sibling, specifically.'

Gerrard was giving me a look that said: Don't tread on my toes, Charlie; so I did something completely out of character. I apologised to a member of the constabulary. This didn't much appease him either.'

'We have some lines of enquiry that we're following,' he told me.

'Smashing.' I tried to say it as if the guarantee had built my confidence. Then I realised that the word was all wrong.

IV.

I didn't go to the funeral. I wasn't invited. Mitzi's, I mean.

I worked. I worked at The Shark, worked harder than I think I'd ever worked (but I was soon to work even harder). I put in the hours. I came home and I slept in the lounge, with a beanbag for my pillow and a sleeping bag my quilt. I couldn't bring myself to go into the bedroom much. Although I'd had a perfunctory tidy-up after Mitzi killed herself, the room was much the same as when she'd lain on my bed, my black socks tourniqueting her scratched wrists.

The room held too many memories. Every time I opened the wardrobe to reach for a fresh shirt, I saw Mitzi's handbag. In the intervening weeks, I had not had the courage or front to open it. I didn't want to know. The only reason that I hadn't thrown it out – the only reason that I hadn't thrown *any* of her belongings out – was that I kept expecting the filth to want to see her stuff.

I worked. I came home. I drank.

I worked, I came home...

Life was thinner without Mitzi. I started to imagine conversations with her, but conversations that were easier to predict than they had been in reality. Not *nice* conversations, for neither of us were nice people, but honest ones.

You're a liar, darling, I said to her one night when I'd had a lot of brandy. *I don't trust a word you say. You're a bad dream looking for a head. You need audience participation.*

Is that so? she asked me.

That's so. And I'll tell you something else –

If you must.

You've latched on to the wrong bloke. I'm every bit of a nightmare as you are. I'm a bastard.

Well, I agree with that bit, said Mitzi.

Good. We have a launching pad...

I couldn't even ask Steve where she was buried. (I couldn't ask him anything.) Had she been flown back to America? Had she been cremated? Had Steve scattered her ashes on the duckpond near the lanes?

One night, in frustration, I punched the bathroom mirror.

I barely dented the glass. I broke a bone in my little finger.

*

Late evening, and I'm at The Shark. Dougal has just asked if I'd like to join him and a party of friends who would shortly arrive for a late one – a lock-in. I've accepted the offer. I'm tired but I don't want to snub the invitation.

By eleven-thirty the regular punters had left. There were a few pavement scuffles – nothing serious – and behind the bar Mags turned off the music and some of the lights. (I had my eye on Mags – the Chief Barmaid – from day one, but nothing happened.) The staff – that was me, Mags, Clive, Ruth and the bottle-boy, Ferret – sat with Dougal in one of the snugs. I was sipping a whisky and coke. We were all in a good mood, even when Dougal produced his guitar from the shelf above the deepfreeze in the kitchen and started singing 'The Rocky Road to Dublin' in an accent that always deepened on such occasions.

The guests arrived on the stroke of midnight. There were five of them: 'old friends', Dougal had explained. Two of them had just returned from their honeymoon in Tokyo. Their names were

John and Claire. There were two more men, called Ralph and Eric, who worked in finance and had the aftershave to prove it.

The fifth member of the group was Mitzi.

*

At first I could only stare. Apart from a couple of half-pint freebies throughout my twelve-hour shift, I'd had nothing alcoholic to drink until the double whisky that I'd yet to finish. My heart was hurting. I doubted my own eyesight.

Dougal caught hold of my horrified expression; not mirroring it at all, but rather offering an amused-cum-disgusted one of his own, he took mine and shook it like a dog with a rat. He sniggered. 'What's up with you, Gary-mate?' he asked. 'You look like you've farted and then followed through.'

I ignored him. 'Hello, Mitzi,' I said.

'I'm not Mitzi, but I get that a lot. I'm her sister.'

'This is Wendy,' Dougal clarified.

The woman was frowning. 'Did you *know* her?' she asked me.

Inadvertently, we had stolen the show. I don't think I've ever wished harder for a sudden eruption of music from the sound system in a pub. That said, if fucking Bananarama or A-Ha had come on at that moment, I might not have discerned the subtle difference in voice-tone that Wendy had from her sister. Emphasis on subtle. But the *visual* effect was astonishing. My youngest brother, Colin, had twins, but Mark and James were nowhere near as close to being mirror images as Wendy and Mitzi were.

'I knew her quite well,' I said. And then added, eager to smithereens the mood: 'Who's for drinks? I'll be Mum.'

Why hadn't Mitzi told me that she had a twin sister?

I proceeded to get very drunk.

And later that night, I was attacked.

V.

If you called Osman the Snail at home, you didn't get him; this was a hard and fast rule. Although we're discussing a time that was pre-mobiles, it wouldn't have made a blind lick of difference if the communication revolution had been and gone: Osman refused to answer the blower. It would be answered by a man, or at least a male (there were no women in Osman's life) – sometimes the voice was very young. A son? I never asked, to tell you the truth. Nor, apart from once, did I ever ask why it took him so fucking long to reach the phone. This was that time. I imagined Osman being dragged from his rack (it was only *noon*, after all, and grasses don't get out of bed in the morning) and extinguishing his snout, or his joint.

'What you doing?' I asked. 'Painting the fucking office?'

'Being happy, man. What up?'

'I've got some work for you. If you can keep your mouth shut and you can open your eyelids for half a day,' I said. God knows why we all treated the poor bastard so badly; his usefulness was definitely on the slide, but he had done good work in the past and he didn't deserve such contempt.

'They open!'

Then again, one of the *benefits* of having such a malformed piece of waste on hand was that it gave you a repository for your sarcasm. It gave you somebody to shit upon. I continued: 'You got a pen?'

'It *all* up here,' said Osman.

I gave him the name: Mitzi Abbey. 'Anything and every-thing you can find,' I instructed, and waited while Osman made the calculation.

'Okay, man. Forty ladies.'

'Fuck off,' I said equably. 'I'm not giving a hanky of smegma like you two hundred notes. You can fucking whistle. Ten ladies.'

'Frankly speaking,' said Osman, 'you do be shitting up-stream. Twenty ladies and me *expenses*.'

'Deal. By the end of the week,' I said, content to have reached the compromise that I'd firmed up with myself, beforehand… and ready at last to tackle the problem of Mitzi's belongings.

'Salutation,' said Osman.

*

Not that the night in The Shark had been a disaster. Far from it; meeting Wendy was quite an achievement, if looked at in universal terms. *Of all the bars in the lands*, and so on… Wendy had to stroll into the one in which I worked. Who said that there is no such thing as an accident? Everything is wished for, hoped for, pre-decided. If I thought that at the time (and my memory of much of the conversation of that night is understandably blurred) then I reckon I would have been halfway to believing it… The attack occurred after I'd left – when I'd been swaying around, looking for a taxi. After nine or ten whiskies I didn't feel able to drive. Besides that, I had too much to think about and a walk to the taxi rank near the NatWest bank would clear my head, I thought.

It cleared my head, all right. Blows to the cranium will do that.

But I remember talking to Wendy. She told me about her work in theatrical costuming. She told me about her little red car and her little lilac flat. She told me that the family had not grown up in Michigan.

We were getting on rather well, all things considered. Much of the shock had passed and I'd kept my lips sealed effectively. It was only late on, when the drink had taken over my conscience and when the two of us were speaking alone at a different table, that I ruffled my bravery, took my vitamins, and said:

'Mitzi.'

'No, *Wendy*,' she answered with a smile of reproof on her lips.

I nodded. 'Oh I know what you're thinking, Mitzi. You're thinking you've bought me with this Wendy bullshit, but you haven't. Okay? Even if you don't understand anything else, understand that.'

'You're drunk,' she said winsomely.

I pointed at Mitzi's face. 'Correct. And close to getting drunker. But that changes nothing. You see, I know your *body*, Mitzi. And I have a good memory...' The skin of her wedding ring finger, I thought; but the light was too poor to get a good look. 'I can remember what you look like, under your clothes. You have a birthmark above your navel. You have a small scar at the base of your spine. And I might be no *expert* on the subject of identical twins, but I'm shertain – I'm *certain* – '

'Gary.'

' – that it's *impossible* for two twins...'

'Gary.' She turned her attention away from me. By this point, as I say, a number of conversations were in lucid, vibrant flow; social factions had formed. She was checking to see if anyone was watching us. She leaned in closer to my ear. 'Meet me in the ladies in two minutes,' she said.

I nodded.

'Subtly,' she added.

'I'll meet you as subtly as I can,' I assured her.

The following one hundred and twenty seconds were painful. I had time to drink most of my beverage (I didn't want to finish it in case someone offered me another) and to examine my fingernails. Through the booze I sensed my subconscious, sending up warning flares.

Then I walked to the passage that led to the lavs and to the room marked 'Staff Only' (an office for Dougal). Pausing, I realised, would have been a bad idea. If I was caught in the wrong bathroom, I'd simply blame the scotch and the dope.

I pushed the door open. The white insides held no mystery for me as I'd been in there before, and more than once: Dougal exercised a system of staff egalitarianism in The Shark. This meant that although I was principally a doorman, and others had their own roles in which they majored, we were all on call to step into another's shoes if the demand was there – if someone rang in sick, for example. So yes, I'd cleaned the ladies' loos on three occasions. Not something I'd wish to do again, for sure, but it was gainful employment, and we all got paid the same.

'Quickly!'

I stepped into Mitzi's cubicle. I abandoned the quip about this all being rather snug. Mitzi pulled the front of her shirt from her skirt; she didn't unfasten the buttons but she lifted the fabric to an inch below her brassiere. The light beige skin seemed darker when compared to the pale hand that I placed above her hip. I only looked up into her eyes when she said:

'The belly button, Gary.'

As best as the limited space of the cubicle would allow, I bent at the waist. I'd been set a challenge – the hunt for the birth-mark – and my face was close to her skin. Both my hands were now on her hips.

'No birthmark,' I admitted, breathing in the warm, fresh smell of her upper body. I touched her navel lightly with my tongue; I licked her salt slowly; suddenly I was carving her flesh with the care of a sculptor chipping granite. Her bulbous pucker seemed to make me suck harder...

'Now the scar,' she said quietly, a few seconds later. She turned around; and although she remained standing she straddled the toilet and bent towards the far wall, her elbows on the cistern, presenting her backside and the slope of her back towards me. That's it, darling, I thought; let the dog see the rabbit.

I pulled out what had remained tucked in of her shirt. 'No scar,' I conceded. I pushed it up the incline and massaged her lower back. That was with one hand. The other hand I used to lift her skirt; I folded it neatly up the slope. Then I eased the legband of her underwear, from left to right, from one smooth buttock to its twin, revealing the crease that went some way to finishing the job of preparing my pole.

'I'm messy,' she said. 'Go upstairs.'

She was on, in other words, plugged and insulated, or so I concluded as I unzipped my piece. I was snakey, not rigid; but I pressed the gap against the one I was about to create. I worked some drool into the spokes...

'So what's worse,' she had asked me once, 'a spank or a tickle?' One of my favourite topics – that of violence – was being discussed.

'A tickle,' I'd said. '*Immeasurably* worse. A tickle is where you leave the guy alive... but he's wishing you'd polished him off. A spank is merely a severe beating. It's line-of-work; it's routine.'

'I see. And where does a *slap* fit into all this?'

'A slap is largely cosmetic. It's damage to the face. It's a warning, usually. Give us what we want or we give you more of this. All that.'

'Fascinating,' said Mitzi, taking in her language lesson. 'And what's worse: getting *handsome* or getting *pretty* with someone?'

'The two terms are not graded on a scale,' I'd told her. 'It would depend on who you're giving a seeing-to to. You get handsome with a woman. You get pretty with a man. Or groups thereof. Or you might get *attractive*.'

'Okay. So do *you* ever get handsome with women, Gal?'

'No. I make it a point never to offer more than an opening punch. A woman rarely wants more than that – despite what she thinks. Men are less keen on personal failure. So you have to get pretty. It's common sense.'

With Mitzi, in the toilet stall in the restrooms, I got... I'd have to say that I got handsome with her. If it lasted five minutes I'll be a Dutchman: I hadn't ejaculated since early that morning, and when we were finished we dressed in the sober but harried manner of honeymooners peeking out for breakfast.

We hadn't even kissed.

Except, of course, we had: only not recently. 'Thank you, Mitzi,' I said. *Thank you for the pipework,* I'd intended to add.

The gratitude appeared to overwhelm her – but it was the mention of her name that had done the damage. Very swiftly, to give her credit, she regained her composure. '*Wendy,*' she corrected me.

'Nice try. Shall we go?' I asked. I snapped back the lock.

'Wait!' she said. Her panic was the final proof, but I was actually disappointed. I'd expected, I suppose, one last argument. 'No scar!' Joyful tone. 'No birthmark!' She showed me the palms of her hands – *how can you top this?* – and her smiled was brittle and ambiguous: precisely how I recalled it.

'Neither did Mitzi,' I said. 'I was *lying*, Mitz. But it was a bloody good try. Not bad. Now. Do you wanna tell me what the fuck is going on?' I asked. 'Or *what?*'

She was shamed. She didn't even think to call me a bastard, even though I'd clearly used her. She'd been caught with the safe key in her hand; and it was as if she had a moustached, for all the fuss she made with her upper lip: the typing away of moisture. Shame on *me,* I know, but for a few seconds I gorged on her discomfort.

At last she said the following:

'I thought you'd mixed two people up.'

'Well I didn't,' I told her.

'No. I guess not,' said Mitzi.

'The sex was the final straw,' I said. 'No one is as good as you,' I said, now lying. What I meant was: no one is as dreamily enthusiastic.

'So what happens next?' said Mitzi, after a breath-clutching pause, obviously chuffed. 'I'm *Wendy* to these people.'

'And I won't fuck with that,' I informed her. 'I promise.' I sniffed a lot of dead thought down into my throat. 'But you understand how much I'll need an explanation –' I warned her ' – and soon. I mean it.'

'I understand,' she told me, voice muffled.

'Like tomorrow. Don't make me find you.'

'Okay. Give me your number.'

'You've *got* my number,' I told her.

*

The lads that did me were beautiful. They were young and saucy. Nervousness didn't come into it: these fuckers had run a mile before.

They reminded me of myself at their age.

VI.

I didn't hear from Mitzi for four days, and that was all right with me. I kept myself busy by recuperating. When I made it back home, I slept for sixteen hours and called in sick to work, already five hours late for the start of my shift, in the middle of the afternoon. Dougal wasn't best pleased with my behaviour, I should say; he assumed that I was suffering from a hangover. Which was true.

But no bones had been broken. And flesh heals.

She called me at The Shark. 'I was getting a tattoo up north,' she told me. Recalling her Miss Marple euphemism for anal sex (if Miss Marple ever employed such a euphemism: now there's a thought) I wondered if Mitzi had had the ink drilled in on her Aris. Painful. But no: she meant the north of the country.

Shropshire? I wondered. It was then that I realised that I didn't actually know where Shropshire was.

'Don't they have working telephones up there?' I asked.

'I didn't take my address book.'

'Directory Enquiries?' I pushed. I wanted her to notice that I was chagrined and that I had the upper hand. I *didn't* want her to notice that I'd been in a fug and a heated-up panic (partly down to the injuries, admittedly) since we'd parted. Apart from anything else, who could I talk to about Mitzi.

Only Cliff.

'Stop nagging. I'm here now, aren't I?'

'I suppose. Where's 'here'?'

'About ten minutes from you,' said Mitzi. 'Can you get a break?'

The answer was yes. 'Well Dougal's in Ireland on a stag do. I'll have to clear it with Mags,' I said.

'Do that. You know the fountain by the art gallery?'

'Where the tramps sleep.'

'Right. I'll meet you there.'

She was dressed for the winter but the weather had turned mild. Perhaps this was the source of the discomfort that I read on her face. Or perhaps it was the prospect of meeting me. Perhaps she had assumed that I would have finally gone through her belongings.

'So what were you doing up north?' I asked her after I'd kissed her cheek.

'I told you: getting a tattoo.'

'Why really?' I was conscious that I only had an hour to spend. I was on thin ice as it was, with Dougal; my illness had not been appreciated, to say the least. I didn't want Mags to grass me up for being late back from my break.

'Don't you want to see it?' she said.

'Maybe later.' I took a gamble. Sometimes, with Mitzi, you had to be a catalyst; you had to provoke a reaction – to get the next thing to happen faster. 'Are you running from someone?' I asked. I was thinking of the faked suicide; the abandonment of Cheryl… and of what I'd found among her possessions.

'Yes,' said Mitzi. The weight of the confession was heavy on the back of her neck; she bowed her head.

'Is it Steve?'

'Indirectly.'

'Well who is it directly?'

'My husband's family.' She looked around, as if for an eaves-dropper. Tourists were entering the gallery, consulting maps and taking photographs – with cameras larger than frying pans. Pigeons were digging at the concrete, for treasure; they were fighting over cigarette butts and dropped gobs of ice cream.

'Go on...' I urged her. 'You had him killed, didn't you?'

She nodded.

'How did you choose Steve?' I asked.

'Steve?' she repeated, blinking.

'To kill him.'

'*Steve* didn't kill him,' said Mitzi. 'My brother Joseph killed him. Steve was my alibi. We booked into a room in St Andrews for a fortnight. It cost me a fortune.' She smiled. 'We spent all day in bed or playing golf.'

'But how did you know him?'

'Okay. My husband's name was Barry Andrews. He was a gambler.' She raised her eyebrows. 'And I don't mean a fiver on the gee-gees from time to time. I mean a classic, compulsive, burn-your-home-down-for-the-insurance-money gambler. The concept of rags to riches was alien to him. If he ever did make any money, he just kept going until he lost it all again. I met him in New Jersey.'

'Not Michigan.'

'No. Michigan is where Mitzi Abbey comes from. My real name is Amanda Andrews, nee Cash. I was working on the black-jack table at a place called Magic Wheels. I worked in The Worm Room. I was off duty but still in uniform, just wondering around the casino. I had a coffee or two: I didn't want to go up to my room, you see, 'cause I was covering for a woman named Wendy in an hour's time. Her little boy was having an operation. And I saw this man – Barry – at the roulette wheel, doing *well*.' She chirped in amusement. 'So you might say the bastard was lying to me from the start. From the *off*, as you guys would say. Can I have a cigarette?'

'Good call,' I said, producing what we used to call, as kids, Benny Hedgehogs: a packet of Benson and Hedges. I sparked two up in my mouth, and handed one to Mitzi... or Amanda.

'Thanks. Amanda didn't smoke,' she said. 'I only started when I was twenty-nine: when I became Mitzi. The bottom line is, I fell in love with the turd. I was a country bumpkin – a hayseed. Raised in this wide spot in the road called Crackentoff. Lot of *Dutch* people there. And I saw Barry, winning, and I saw a jumbo jet *out* of that fucking burb. Out of the country, even.'

'The grass being always greener,' I interjected.

'Exactly.' Mitzi seemed impressed by what had been, at best, a minor surge of inspiration: as if she'd learned something about her motivation at that time. 'So what can I say? I pursued him, relentlessly. I took him up to my room. He bought me a necklace on our first proper date. I would now regard that sort of extravagance with caution.'

'Just as well I bought you fuck all.'

'Damn straight. And he said: Why don't you try six months or a year in Nottingham.' She pronounced it in the English fashion: *Notten-num*. 'Although I didn't know what the hell he was actually saying. It was a while before I realised he was saying Notting-*ham*.' She laughed again. 'And I went. My sister was miffed – jealous – but everyone else gave their approval. After all – Barry was only thirty-eight, apparently successful...'

'What was he doing in America?' I asked.

'Gambling. Fighting.' She shrugged as though attempting to dislodge a koala bear from her shoulders. 'I never thought to ask, more fool me.'

This, I didn't believe; but I decided to leave the subject alone, like a puddle of nuclear waste – like poodle piss. 'So you moved to England,' I said. 'To Notting-ham.'

'True. But he was a shite in shining armour, Gal. He stole from me. He poked a lipstick in my eye once! Slapped me around like he was tenderising steak. He was a bastard.'

She paused. And I smiled.

'What's so funny?' she asked me.

Wondering just where to begin, I paused and I sniffed in the fresh smell of the fountain's waters. 'Got me feathers ruffled the other night,' I said. 'I'm now a six-foot-two bruise.'

Mitzi made a good show of appearing alarmed. 'Why the hell didn't you say something sooner? They didn't mark your face, though…'

'True enough. Not that that felt like much of a consolation at the time, I can tell you. It was after our evening in the pub toilets. They jumped me.'

'My God…'

'And funny things have been going through my head, Mitz.' I lit another cigarette. 'Do you know what my first thought was? That you'd arranged it.'

'Me?'

'Life's been very different since you arrived,' I told her.

'For the *better*, I'd hoped!' Mitzi was getting cross.

I was keen to dispel any anger. I still had an ace up my sleeve, after all. 'Don't worry, Mitz,' I said. 'I know it wasn't you. It was just the series of *coincidences* that made me think it. And things you told me, before: all the bad things you've done. At that moment I wouldn't have put it past you.'

'Well thanks a lot,' she answered sulkily. 'So who was it?'

'That set it up? It was *Bitch*.'

*

There were three of them, and one was wielding a cattle-prod.

I was shocked into the back of an old blue van that had recently driven dogs – or at least one dog – to its destination.

The smell was not offensive; it was puzzling, more than anything else.

They sellotaped a bobble hat over my face. One of them pulled it down (I could see through the stretched woolly mesh) and another one taped the frayed hem to the bristles on my throat.

We disembarked at the Community Hall in Marsh Farm. I made a token show of resistance, knowing that the odds were stacked against me.

Very early on, when one of the cunts was noisily in the lav and the other one was brewing *tea*, of all the strangest things, I tried the one I'd been left with – the youngest one – with a bit of rationale and reasoning. I was after answers; but I was also after a swift denouement. By that stage they had only worked on my chest and shoulders, and I was hopeful that I'd be emerging from the ordeal in the next few hours. It was Cliff I thought of. The attack on Cliff had not been intended to kill him; it had been strokework. It had been *strokes*. I was clinging to the hope that my attack, too, was indirectly on Steve Bitch.

'You wouldn't let me go to the grave,' I said, 'without knowing the name of my enemy, would you?'

'I'm not your enemy,' I was told. He had a squirrelly voice and persona. 'I don't care about you one way or the other. This is business.'

'I'll buy the contract. How much you getting?'

'That's not how it works, and you know it.'

'How much? Ton? Ten tons?'

'Five. But I have to say, I'm disappointed in you, Mr Nash.'

I laughed. '*Mr* Nash. Love it!'

The little boy continued: 'I'd heard you were a cool head on calm shoulders. I didn't expect to be *bargained* with.'

'No. But I've got your attention now, haven't I?' What was that *stinging?* Oh yeah; it was pride. 'Jesus. Five tons. Is that all I'm worth?' I asked.

'No, that's all *I'm* worth. I'm new to this. I don't have a market value yet.'

'You've got a future in this industry, it's obvious, okay? You're suave and you're tasty. These are both important attributes, believe me. I get the impression that when the filth starts sticking its snout in and sniffing, you're going to carry on watching the cricket or whatever and not look like you've just been having a wank. Am I right?'

My assailant looked nervous. I was roughly in the middle of the hall, on a chair, and I posed no physical threat to the lad; but it was plain that he hadn't been anticipating a *conversation*. He was glancing at the lav-door, at the kitchen; being alone was not a comfortable state of affairs...

Nonetheless, he said, 'You're right.'

'Good. We've got a launching pad in that case. Listen. I'll give you and your men...' Pump him up a bit, I'd thought; make him feel as though I believed him to be in charge. '...a K each and I'll fuck off to Edinburgh or something.'

'Can't do it, mate. I've got instructions to bring back your tongue...'

My *tongue?*

The system was appallingly symbolic – and even more appallingly simple. The punishment, according to some *faces*, should fit the crime. If you rape my sister, then I find you and I harm your genitals. If you steal from me, then I damage your hands. The fire-theme (the lanes, my brother) had evidently been done to exhaustion, I thought. And the notion was a bleak one: it implied, now directly, that *I* was the mark. The strokes were all for me.

But why? The removal of a tongue signified that someone thought I'd been saying too much of what I shouldn't have been saying. What was I supposed to have blurted?

Bitch's face was in my mind.

Trying to sound contained, I went on: 'That's not a problem. We can find a tongue in about twenty minutes. What do you say?'

'Sugar, mate?' called the cunt in the kitchen.

Good, I thought; if they don't know how many sugars they each take then maybe they don't know each other very well. A better chance of betrayal.

'Four!' was the reply.

'Righty-oh. Nash?'

I was frowning beneath my bobble-hat mask. 'You're making me *tea?*'

'Course. We're not *animals*, you know. Thought you could do with it.'

'Thanks. Two lumps, please.'

'Right. Then we'll start working on your legs and your bollocks. Okay?'

'Oh fine…' I mumbled.

The young man approached me quickly, a smile on his face. 'Just out of interest,' he whispered. '*Where* would you get a tongue in about twenty minutes? I'm curious.'

What I was about to say would do little for my reputation as a blabbermouth, but I was in very deep as it was. How could matters deteriorate?

'My ex-employer was a guy called Steve Bitch. Maybe you know him.' I searched for a reaction on his face, through the wool. 'Anyhow. Whenever things got a little bit carried away, we would have to deal with the body, right? You can't just leave them on the tennis courts and hope that no cunt notices. So we'd give this taxi-driver a call, right? Called Bob Forrage. And *he* dealt with…'

And that's when it happened. My attacker's face formed the self-same expression that Steve's had, when something that he hadn't wanted to hear had been heard. The words *Bob Forrage* had stretched the elastic.

It was a gamble; it was a guess. 'Maybe you know *him*,' I said.

'Tea's up,' said the voice of the man who was now leaving the kitchen. 'What games have you two kids been playing?' he asked cheerfully.

At no point up till then had Bob Forrage featured seriously in my estimations about anything that had occurred. After all, who *was* he? A taxi-driver who collected meat. But *then* what did he do with it?

I followed the crumb-trail. 'I'll have to take this hat off,' I said (they had not tied my wrists together); but a fresh brew was not uppermost in my mind. Bob Forrage... So the corpse went to Bob, and then he passed it to someone else. Who then passed it to someone *else*. Who then passed it... Was it possible that the same parcel of bones that we'd played with could make a long journey to Shropshire? What other connection to that county did Steve have?

The tea was hot and sweet. I drank it slowly, savouring my time. The men who then got to work on my knees, thighs and gonads – they didn't seem particularly bothered that I'd seen their faces. It was all in a night's work.

VII.

The call to Steve Bitch was one of the hardest that I'd ever had to make. And I made it after a call to Handjob Harry: a man who sold more than narcotics.

I'd expected it to be anaemic and sour. But when the time came, it was fraught with coked-up energy. The conversation *itself* was a drunken maniac.

'Steve-mate,' I said, and didn't falter. It spilled out. 'It's about Mitzi,' I went on. 'She's the pus. There's no easy way...'

'Gary?' said Steve.

'Yeah.'

And I heard – I actually heard – his eyebrows rise. 'Well well well,' he singsonged. 'Kicked your ball into my back garden, have you?'

'No. I have something important to say.'

'Is that a fact? Is that why you're bothering me now?'

'Steve. It's Mitzi... Are you ready?'

'Mitzi's dead, Gal,' said Bitch, very coldly. The words had been intended to finish the conversation; but they only served to make me more contrary.

'She's the filth.'

'Is she fuck.'

'She's a badge! I've been through her stuff. I swear to you...'

'...*What* stuff?'

'Her things at my place,' I strode boldly on.

'*Excuse* me?' said Bitch a second later.

'It doesn't matter. Please, Steve...'

'The *fuck* it don't matter! What you not telling me, cunt?'

Thinking that there was no worse that this could become, I lit the fuse and said slowly: 'Mitzi *stayed* here a couple of times.'

'I see. And you expect me to be happy about this, do you?'

Did I sigh? Did I squirm? I think I can recall squinting hard at the refrigerator. One of Orlando's paintings, dating back to when he had attended nursery school, was still sticky-taped to the white door. It had been known to bring me comfort in the past; but it didn't now. 'You're missing the point, mate.'

'Am I? You were feasting on *my bird* and I'm missing the point?' Steve said. 'Jesus, Gary, what is it with you? Do you reckon that tyre marks are gonna make an attractive addition to your face? This season's *look?*'

For a second or two he breathed like a bitch-dog in oestrus. I chose the silence, but perhaps I should have waited for him to finish. I said:

'Two things. One, you told me you weren't nibbling anymore –'

'That don't mean that you can, cunt!'

'And two, the main point: she's the plod.'

'Mitzi's *dead*. You had a bump on the yed or summing?'

'I *have*, as a matter of fact. But I'll come to the clowns you sent in a minute. She's plod. And those strokers were cut-price. *That's* why I thought that you couldn't have had anything to do with it: you'd a bought a better team. Then I realised that's what you *wanted* me to think. And it all added up.'

Steve laughed. 'P.C. Mitzi,' he tested out. 'Yeah. So likely.'

'I know you arranged it all, Steve. The attacks, the vandalism, the fires… Cliff and me. Julie, Errol… But I also know the filth is on to you, mate. That's why that Sergeant Gerrard kept holding back from letting you work on the lanes. I don't know how or why – and I'm not at all sure that *this* bit was intentional – but you've allowed the dog to see the rabbit. The filth are closing in. What I *think* is going on is this. Whenever we've had to snuff out some cunt's lights, we've given the body to Bob Forrage. I think it's finally *disposed of*, though, in Shropshire. Maybe they shred it up for chicken food; it doesn't much matter. Plod *knows*. And they've traced the line backwards – back to you, Steve. So what better way of blindfolding the powers that be than setting up this *strokes* charade?'

'Hurting valued friends in the process,' said Steve.

'If need be.'

Steve sighed. 'Cunt, that's fighting talk,' he whispered.

'Whenever you're ready,' I replied. 'No. Whenever *I'm* ready. When I'm healed. When I'm good and strong and able to give you a race.'

*

Don't assume from my silence that Mitzi's reference to playing golf at St Andrews had gone unnoticed. I phoned the course. You can't just turn up at St Andrews to play golf – not unless you're a celeb on the Pro-Am circuit, or at the very least a member – and again I'd caught Mitzi out.

Why was she still lying to me? What was she still covering up?

*

Or are these stupid questions?

By then, and because of an hour-long conversation by a fountain, I already knew a great deal more than I had previously known. And that's the tragedy, I suppose: that the big events, the main, the pounding, are so easily doled out, in portions a mere hour long. So life really *is* a soap opera!

The badge? Pure nonsense, of course. What I'd found among Mitzi's stuff had been worse – totally, immeasurably worse – than a copper's shield.

I'd found paper. A small hardbacked notebook, stuffed with writhing notes and doodles – in Mitzi's hand. It was Mitzi's work in progress. Mitzi Abbey – or Wendy, or for that matter Amanda Andrews – was not the filth. Mitzi was a *journalist*, and she was working on a book about criminal behaviour.

'Here's this,' I said, by the fountain, and gave her back her writing.

'Thanks. I'd been wondering where that had gotten to.'

'I've copied it, of course,' I told her.

'Of course.'

'Did you *mean* me to find it?' I asked.

'No. But it's worked out nicely, I guess.'

'For you maybe.'

'For all of us,' she insisted. 'What? I would have been allowed to get all this great material if I'd asked *nicely*? Dream on, Gal.'

I looked at my watch. I could spare another five minutes, but that was it. 'I need to know. Call me stupid. But did you feel anything for me at all?'

'Of course I did. I told you: you're an interesting character.'

'And I said something like: Don't get involved. I'm good in the sheets but I'm a soak. And it should have been *me* who didn't get involved.'

'Well, Gary, take this back to work with you this afternoon, okay?' said Mitzi. 'You *were* and *are* good in bed; and you've got nothing like the drink problem that I've got – or that Steve has. Stop sweating about it.'

I nodded. 'Which brings me,' I said, 'to the question of cocaine. Did you buy a load of gear and say to Handjob Harry that you were getting it for me?'

Mitzi looked embarrassed. 'Ah... I owe you an apology for that,' she said. 'Entirely for personal use. Sorry.'

'Mitz, I wouldn't have *minded*. I would have spent the afternoon doing it with you – happily. But why does *everything* have to be a lie?' I asked.

She screwed up her face. 'I told the truth sometimes.'

'When? The depression?'

'Real. But not baby-related.'

'... Where *is* Cheryl, by the way?' I asked.

'With my sister, in Northumberland. That's where I was going – or where I went – when I got my tattoo: to see my sister. Or Cheryl's mother, I should...'

'*Excuse* me?'

'You heard.'

'You faked a *baby?*'

'I did what needed to be done,' she said. 'I needed an in. I thought I'd appeal to Steve's paternal nature.'

'Well, you did that all right! And it cost him his empire! Are you even *American?*' I asked.

'Of course I'm American. What do I sound like?'

'A liar,' I told her. 'I've got to get back to work.'

'I'm not stopping you.'

'But how did you get your sister… is her name Wendy, by any chance?'

'It is. You're catching on.'

'… to agree to giving you her *baby?*'

Mitzi cocked her head. 'It wasn't so difficult,' she answered. 'Wendy was depressed and here was an offer of help. She went to France for a few months.'

'And how much does Steve know?'

'Steve knows everything.'

*

Give me an hour alone in Steve's study, I thought (some prayer!); and let's see what worms I dig up in the tines of the fork… But of course this would never be; not again. And you can teach yourself to live with frustration. I came to comprehend that. After a while it doesn't even sting too badly. Besides, whenever I thought of what I might find in Steve's safe, I heard Steve's voice, in a gruesome chuckle, saying: *Gal – do you think there's a fucking audit trail for this shit? Why don't you weed out your noodle from time to time? You're becoming a liability…* Or words to that effect. And besides the besides, what else could I do but what I did? This is what I did. I arrived at The Shark at ten every morning and left at midnight, or thereabouts. I wanted all of the hours that I could get, and Dougal was cool with that: as he said, it gave him a chance to sit around in his Y-fronts every morning and practise the guitar. 'You're a man a soul can trust,' he once added. That didn't help, but I was grateful for his faith and the opportunity to blot out the non-working world.

Mags – the chief barmaid – had a sister, a younger sister, called Sasha, who lived with Mum and Dad, doing her A-Levels. Sasha Hurley thought it was cute that I didn't mind being called her boyfriend, despite the age difference of fifteen years. But what else could I have been? A Sugar Daddy? A Love Professor? Sasha was sweet. She had only enjoyed a few bedfellows before me and it was a grand experience to instruct her in the ways of my favourite stunts. At the same time I was still seeing Mitzi, now and then. (I even once, for old times' sake, took Julie – Julie from the lanes, not Steve's wife – for a film and a fuck. Call me, neither of us said at the end of the date. We simply wiped ourselves off with a pillowcase and returned to our existences.) Nor was seeing Mitzi any great feat of quickstepping philandering. I said to Sasha that I could not in any conscience relinquish my responsibilities to a young child – yeah, I used Cheryl as well – and to my relief she was dandy with that. I didn't mention the sex, though; it didn't matter that I suspected Sasha of having a college man.

I was waiting.

And that was how it went on. I learned to cook more adventurous meals; I bought a new car; I exercised more (when my bruises had healed) and started to take care of my teeth and hair. I was beginning to recede. I went to the pictures more often.

Throughout this time Cliff's health and appearance improved, but his mood decayed. As the burns healed and were administered to by our faithful healers, his conversation – if you could call it that, 'opinion donation' was better – would turn again and again to the subject of revenge and retribution. Nothing could dampen his fervour – not even the very real obstacle of our having no one directly to *blame*. I hadn't told Cliff what I suspected about Steve… And if I say that Cliff was becoming an *understandable* bore, you should take from that that an understandable bore is still a bore.

Not that I wanted to react any differently, of course. My body was an Underground guide of scratches, scars and burns (it still is): and every one of them tells a story – a revenger's tragedy. Revenge *is* tragic; the necessity for it is tragic. You complete the mission, shower off, spruce up, and make a value judgement on whether your clothes are worth saving from the incinerator (or in my case, the oven). You settle down with a brandy, the better to review your performance. And you descend from your kicks-high, your violence-high, in a mood of sombre reflection: regretting that the whole sorry business should have come to what it had recently come to.

Yet I was waiting.

VIII.

Osman was twenty minutes late. He sat down heavily.

'What's up?' I asked.

'Johnny Nectar, man – he is a *bad* way. He come back – *slice up!*'

'And who the fuck is Johnny Nectar?'

'He my assist*ant*. Man! He look like a *quilt*. They do him goodly.' At which Osman reached across my table to grab my pint, half-finished. But lacking the confidence to raise the glass to his lips with one hand, Osman smothered and cradled it with all ten of his fingers, and still his arms shook as though he'd overdone it on the weights.

My eyes, I am certain, would have revealed at least a smidgeroo of displeasure. 'If you're telling me, Osman, you're sub-contracting with inferior workers, then you're the one's gonna be in a bad fucking way.'

Osman rarely *did* angry. A clear indication of what he had recently endured was that he now fixed me with a stern gaze. 'I tell you, man: I say my *assistant*. I mean it.' I shrugged. 'As long as you're paying the cunt, then fair do's,' I said. At which mention of money Osman removed and flipped open a tan leather wallet and pulled out some notes.

'What's this?'

He held out some money. 'Your ladies, man,' he said. 'I don't want *nuffing* to do widdis. Me, I can't breev.'

'The paper's yours, Osman.'

'No,' he protested. 'Dam wun it. Take it.'

'It's *yours.*'

Osman was shaking his head. 'If I stay omviss payroll, I'm a mark, man. I'm a target-to-be. A statistic. And fuck *dat* for a game of shoulders.'

'...What happened?'

*

'You asked me once,' said Steve Bitch, shortly after I'd told him that I was going to kill him, 'if I kept a *diary.* Do you remember, Gal? Right here in this room. D'you remember?' We were in his office, at the lanes. 'Christ, mate. I coulda shat for fucking England that day. Fought you had me, see? Though I couldn't see *ow.* Remember?' He smiled. 'You're very *quiet* tonight, Gal.'

I said nothing. But words were burning in my head.

Steve had stood up.

'Stay away from that dartboard,' I told him.

Bitch looked at me with regimented arrays of disgust oh-so clear on his face. 'Oh Gary. You disappoint me, mate,' he said. 'As if I *would.*'

'Just sit down. Please,' I said.

'And what makes you think I ain't got a piece in me desk?' he asked, complying, but with far too much brass for my liking.

'I don't. But I've got a more powerful one.'

'Ooh. And my dad's bigger than your dad. Jesus. What you wielding?'

I showed him; my jacket flapped open like wings.

'Erotic. You sure?' he asked, nodding. 'There's no passport back, Gal.'

'I'm sure,' I said.

'Then *point* it at me. Make me do what you want. Which *is,* by the way?'

'What?' I asked, squinting. Did I mention that my eyesight was failing?

'I *said:* what is it precisely you actually *want?*'

'A full story,' I told him. 'Jackanory, mate.'

'Okay, Gal,' said Steve as I removed my pistol from the left inside pocket of my jacket. Steve raised his hands – and then folded his wrists behind his neck. His stomach swelled out like a riptide; my first thought, as he re-settled, was that he'd put on weight. Then I thought: No. He's *lost* weight. He's *lost* it.

'Starting where?' he wanted to know.

'The diary, as you've brought it up,' I said.

'Oh yeah. This is a piquant story. I told you about the dreams and sex.' Steve was amused. 'But it wasn't quite the whole and nothing but. I could have elaborated a bit on the reference to *dreams*. See, Gal – I wasn't talking about nightdreams. I was talking about *daydreams*. Mine. The imagination taken flight, as some cunt put it. And you're *in* them, Gal. You're *in* the fuckers.'

'What do you mean? Gimme a gargle on that,' I said, pointing towards his bottle with my sovereign ring.

Leaning across the desk, Steve poured me out another snifter. More likely, an octuple measure of hardcore, expensive Scotch.

'I *mean*… Gal. I mean I took one or two fucking liberties when it came to the truth. Okey-doke? I've recorded your actions for posterity–'

'*My* actions?'

' – and some things are spot-on and some are somewhat fucking embellished,' said Steve, now retying his arms behind his head.

I was shaking. I said, 'Why, Steve? Just make me comprehend.'

'Because… you were right about some things,' he answered. 'The swine need a scapegoat,' he said, beautifully candidly. 'An' *I* ain't gonna take the fucking lowbrow for no cunt.'

'Swine?'

'Yeah. You were right: Mitzi's the blisters. She's pork soss-arge. I knew that all along,' he lied – he *must* have lied. I couldn't deal with another twist.

My head, my body – my voice was cold. 'I ought to kill you now on general principle. You're worse than Osman the Snail!' I said.

'But *that* stroker's got much less to lose,' Steve answered. 'For what it's worth, I'm sorry, Gal. But I couldn't be put down again. You were right – you were *scarily* fucking right. I don't know how you did it. Arsehole Gerrard is getting perky with me on a daily basis. Thinks he smells Bermuda. I'm his ticket to an early retirement.' He barked out a laugh. 'Like *I'm* gonna give that cunt the gum off me shoes. Breakdance on that, Batman – you know what I mean? He can fucking well fuck off, can't he?'

'Jesus.' I said it and then I waited. 'Give me one good reason,' I said, 'why I shouldn't throttle you right now like a wolf with a lamb.'

'I'll give you two.' Bitch paused. 'One, because you're soft and I could break you like a piece of polystyrene.' He hadn't acknowledged the irony of my asking him such a question. 'And two, because the filth'll be here any minute.'

It took a second. And then: 'You've set me up!' I screamed. 'Put your hands down. Put 'em down!'

'I'm your prisoner.'

'No. Put 'em down or I'll shoot you, I swear.'

'Yes.' Steve's voice was more on the level; but he didn't do as he'd been asked. If anything, he went on looking *more* worried, *more* contrite...

'You're a cunt, Steve...'

'Again, I suppose, yes. But someone had to go. Filth're sniffing around the operations.' He regained his Don-like composure. 'Gary, *someone* had to go. I'm sorry it had to be you.'

'But *why* me, Steve?' I begged. 'Been good as gold.'

'*Because* you're good,' Steve replied. 'You're beautiful. No one'll doubt you've got the onions – got the vitamins. You're the only cunt I'd trust to take the medicine.'

'To go down for you, you mean?'

'Precisely.'

Hope springs eternal, as they say, and so I fused with the belief that Steve still meant me well. Call me naïve. Fucker was just building up to it. 'And what awaits me,' I said, lips rising, 'if I take on your burdens? What's at the end of the tunnel?'

Steve squashed it. 'Nothing. It's all over, Gal.'

That was when I started to attack him; and that was when he failed to defend himself. Not from any punch. And not from any kick.

That also was when the pus arrived.

Batons, smirks. And parrotty indignation. It took two men to prise the phone cord from my fingers, and as they dragged me away I took what solace I could from the sight of the red welts I'd created on Bitch's neck.

Part Three

I.

'*Stop talking, Steve,*' *I said.* '*That's enough.*'
    '*So go for it.*' *And Steve shrugged.*
    I paused, but not even for a second.
    I squeezed the trigger and his face exploded.

And then I woke up. Not once, but twice, three times — even four. My dreams, from the start, took on this kind of violence and this kind of internal structure. My dreams resembled my prison: Sugville West. My dreams were hot and sweaty; my dreams were rooms inside rooms – and then a cupboard would open up to reveal a brand new suite of doors and grey and beige.

One thing, and one thing only, was clear.

As soon as I got out... oh, yes. As soon as I got out I was going to kill Steve Bitch. I was going to point a gun at his face and I was going to shoot.

Nightly, he detonated in my head.

And then he would pick himself up like an atomised cockroach. I would watch as he reassembled himself. I would load the weapon again. But something different – something other than a bullet – would fly out of the nozzle on the second, third, fourth and fifth shots: something that would change the scene to pure slapstick. A lightbulb would emerge; some custard; a mouse's nose and whiskers; a placemat...

Listen. Don't trust Trust.

Trust is an unreliable little fucker. The cunt'll let you down every time.

Believe it. The bastard is irresponsible.

Trust?

Trust, my arse.

I trusted a man called Stephen Birch, once upon a time. I believed that he was worthy of my faith and dedication. But he wasn't worthy of a dicksplash of come in an eggcup, the piece of dirty sanitex. The crow. The cunt. Sooner shit on you as a matter of fucking principle than do right by your morals.

So I don't trust trust anymore.

It's not worth it.

But all of that said, I ended up trusting a tranny named Zsa Zsa. God knows why.

*

I should probably step back in time a little bit. But to where?

Okay. To the beginning of my trumped-up sentence. Where else?

I was Nash-G4785. To start with, I was an A-Cat-Base.

That is, I was an A Category prisoner – a danger to other prisoners and to the staff, and possibly even to myself – on the Basic tier. Ironically, I suppose, this did not mean that I was regarded as the lowest of the low. No. But I *was* the darkest of the dark.

I was plute, I was trite. I was the fucker that your mother warned you about; I was the one who'd been caught lighting matches.

Figuratively speaking, you understand.

That was how Sugville West operated: a system of hierarchies and strict distinctions, wherein any movement could only be as a result of behaviour maintenance and mood reparation. But where you started — well, that was no fucking choice that you could make. That was made on your behalf.

Your so-called crime made that decision for you.

There were nine possibilities. A-Cat, B-Cat and C, inside which a prisoner was designated the status of either Basic, Steady or Enhanced. A-Cats were murderers, and Basic meant that for my first year I was banged up for twenty-three hours of every day. Suicide watch. Supervised meals. And the chance of some exercise was as likely as the Easter Bunny farting 'Rule Britannia' on my oat flakes of a morning. Like, *forget* about it.

My cell was exactly twice the width of the narrow bed on which I developed sores and strummed myself to sleep every night. Even then, when I was snoozing like a leopard, I was watched. Observed. *Clocked*.

Not to mention, taunted and verbally abused.

Was it simply the case that the men who locked my door were afraid of me? What else could have explained the nastiness of those fuckers? After all, I was charm personified — or at least I tried to be. Very early into the sentence I asked one of my gaolers what I should call him.

'You should fucking well call me sir,' was the answer.

So I called them all *sir*. To be honest, it did me a favour: it took away any responsibility for learning names. Not that my courtesy was rewarded in that first year: not even once. On more than one occasion, the door was opened — and I'd be standing at the far wall, as per instructions, with my hands neatly folded over the pyjama-ed sack of my crotch. You were supposed to show that you hadn't magicked up a weapon from somewhere. And I would do just that.

And then in they'd come. A group of the black-uniformed little cunts, with revenge (for what?) scribbled over their tidy little faces. Bearing arms, as they say: truncheons and prods. What a spanking I'd receive, just for minding my P's and Q's. The first time I fought back, despite the odds: it was a reaction that was built deep down inside of me. It wasn't logical behaviour. It was instinct. On that one occasion, I managed to get a pillow partway into one of the guard's mouth. Not much of a reaction, I'll accept, but the fight died down when that bastard started to turn a shade of blue that should only be seen on currency.

That first year – fuck it – was a nightmare.

Regularly, I would dream of Mitzi, as well.

Mitzi. She was going abroad on business: to Helsinki. Fuck knows why the capital of Finland. Never been, although I've always fancied it. I've always fancied Northern Europe. Is it any fucking use? Is it tasty?

There are no clocks in A-Block. Routines, oh yes; routines are the order of the day (shit joke), but clocks are a privilege reserved for B-Cat offenders and higher. Possibly for B-Cat *wardens* and higher, too: I have no idea by which criteria each screw gets a gig. But what I *do* know is this. Learning to tell the time again, without any instrument to help you, is part of the punishment. Addiction – any addiction – is a way of stepping outside time; and imprisonment is a monkey on your back without an equal. Harsh mistress, and all that. The idea being that the punishment fits the crime, presumably. And maybe so...

Predictably enough, the night-time is the worst. At night, simultaneously combating and courting sleep, a thought is like an infection. Digs in, roots – it breeds in the ordure of your past. You are obliged to fight it: an almost-contractual agreement. No Thinking. Banned by order of the establishment: official. So you wait for the fever dreams that signal that sleep is on its way.

You wake in a cold box. You are trying to tell the time. Only by making yourself get up to use the lavatory are you able to get a fix on your tiredness quotient, and with this information are you able to make a stab at the hour.

The thought might be that A-Cats will use a clock to kill themselves, or each other... or a screw. What they don't seem to grasp is that the absence of a known passage is what makes us so murderous in the first place.

But why am I writing any of this? Because since I've come in here I've had the *time.* Perhaps I should be grateful. If I can't trust Trust, perhaps I should trust Time. I have spent a lot of it in here already, and I'll tell you about it in just a bit; but my question (to myself) remains unanswered, years later. I started writing as soon as I learned how to do so, in my classes – primarily – with Grassy Noel, who will always be an inspiration to me. But *why* am I writing this? *Why* did I start? *Why* am I writing any of the words that tumble and scratch from biros that I now need to save up favours for to buy? And something else. Despite the company that I have but no choice to keep, why haven't any of my thoughts been defaced? Why no threats? Why no strokework on my *notions*? No strokework on my *memories?* Easy fucking target, I'd have thought, with the manuscript growing like mould.

But my pages are pristine.

Which is more than I can say for anything else.*

Should I bore you with what you don't need to know?

Prison was... I'm tempted to say *a nightmare* – but everything's a nightmare these days. The traffic is a nightmare; the price of petrol is a nightmare. Relationships, journalism, the NHS: nightmare. A prolonged stay in chokey is what happens *after* you're endured the nightmare: to discover that the cunt doesn't end. Chamber after chamber – with fearsome, sap-sucking vestibules in between – *that* is the prison experience.

By local standards, though, I did okay. It was hardly a picnic, but it ended up as well as it might. Not at first: being an A-Cat

Base was just awful, but once I'd earned my wings… well, things took an upswing. Fairly swiftly involved in the redistribution of mind-altering substances, I was able to forge an *identity* in the nick. (Riskily, that might qualify as irony; but whoever claimed that I didn't indulge in an ironic existence, eh?) Not much of an identity, granted and true; but enough to topple myself from the top of the arse-hunter's tree: the prime fruit. I was windfall. Not that shit didn't happen, *bien sur*. *Shit* being the operative word… Receiving, as I did, very far from my (what-proclaimed?) 'fair share', I nevertheless was required to keep my wits about me, and other clichés. Keep 'em peeled… But I'm getting ahead of myself, am I not?

Sod it. This is what's on my mind right now.

Basically, I was handed a pass; I was given a get-out-of-jail card. (Joke.) The let was provided by Zsa Zsa: the guy who co-ordinated all of the buggery rotas for the showers on C Block. If you wanted a workout, you booked it through Zsa Zsa; you chose your chicken and you stumped up the price (tobacco, a violent favour… a bit of skallywaggery). But I realised, see, that I could *work* with Zsa Zsa, and I bartered: a smoke or two, a pill or three, and leave me off the list, okay? Unfortunately, not everyone listened to Zsa: not even to a shiny-skinned, gnu-muscled hulkcock like him. Perhaps it's better to say that not everyone *knew* about the appointment book. Either way, in such cases, I'm afraid it was a touch of the therefores, mate: what came to pass – it came to pass, and woe betide the poor sod who'd bucked the system…

Good old Zsa Zsa.

His *name*? A cluttered etymology; a word-stew, if you like. See, Zsa Zsa said *shower* a lot, as you can imagine: it was the nexus of much of his business. But the problem was, he couldn't pronounce the *ow* diphthong correctly – not unless he was aiming for the long *a* in, for example, 'ale', at which time we would get 'a pint of owl', 'five minutes, without fowl'. When Zsa Zsa said 'shower' he said 'shah'. *Shah*. And over the years, it must have stuck as a nickname: *Shah*. And then some wag went for *The* Shah. And then it reached, inevitably enough, for The Shah of the Shah, as you might say The Shah of Iran. But some of the lads whose English wasn't so frisky started to shrink it down to Shah Shah, not understanding the rich history behind the moniker.

'Zsa Zsa' stuck.

All the same, let's not be coy: it happened once or twice. More specifically, over fifteen years, it happened *eight* times. What stopped it – I would adore saying otherwise, to endorse my rep as an upstanding pugilist, but rightly or wrongly, this was not the case – what *saved* me was my work ethic, and (together, now) my *connections*. Even rapists get scared.

My *official* job, eventually, was in the kitchens: anything to get me out of that fucking box every day – even a five o'clock rise and shine to the get breakfast ready for fellow lags. I'd mentioned my background in pub catering (well, I'd helped out from time to time, chopping vegetables, flipping steaks, so I wasn't *lying*) and the word had got around. Soulless work, of course; but once an active man, always an active man. The days I *did* have to spend in the cell – for no one man was permitted to hog all of the cooking shifts – were anathema. Once I'd learned to read well (of which more later), books helped me to pass the time. Writing what you've just read – that helped, too. But Sardineville (one of my co-resident's coinages, once I'd graduated out of A-Cat and was no longer regarded as a menace to prison society) was a grim place to be. I sat on the lavatory a lot. I exercised. I argued with Dean Bolt (the aforementioned cellmate) on the subject of politics. Well, on the subject of anything, really. I became interested in football – more or less as a matter of survival. But to start with – and for a long time – I was alone. Alone.

Most of my creative thought was spent on deals and smuggling. But not at first: at first my creative thought was spent on revenge and lust.

Long before I was allowed into a classroom, I began my new education. I tried – and tried hard, tried *desperately* – to rationalise Bitch's behaviour. And there *were* some interesting findings, there in the middle of the night, with the walls breathing cold dust into my sinuses. When a beast is wounded, it hides, I found out: a fact that led me closer to my full comprehension of Bitch. 'Strokes' had sent arrows into his rump, and all he'd wanted to do was to find a nice pile of leaves under which to bury himself and bleed. It still didn't seem right – it remained a moral turnaround on his part – but I learnt to live with it.

In the daylight, at least, I learned to live with it.

At night I was crueller than ever.

*

There have been too many characters in my life. It has been a heavy span, portly and jowelly (and needing exercise); and one good thing you can say about incarceration is this: it forces you to put your life on a diet. People drop away, and leave your lifeskin sagging. Eventually, you tighten up like a drum. And your note is now different when someone hits you.

But I couldn't lose Steve and I couldn't lose Mitzi; I certainly couldn't lose Cliff. Not only was the wait – the time inside my cell – truly foul, but so was *their weight*: the spare tyres they had formed around my lifehips, the stones they had added to my dimpled lifebuttocks. My lifemuscles were still strong, but my lifetonnage sometimes made my lifelungs groan in the wee hours.

Mitzi…

Her lifetongue probing around my lifehelmet; my lifenose nudging her lifeanus… *In abstentia*, that woman had never been more alive. I would try to get a flavour of her guilt, just a taste. Lipsticky, floury; coppery and rich.

'Stop talking, Steve,' I said. 'That's enough.'

'So go for it.' Steve shrugged.

The gun trembled. It was wriggling in a more pronounced fashion in my grip. There was sweat running over onto my teeth.

'What's stopping you, cunt?' Steve asked.

Goading me, leading me on. I wanted to pick at this fantasy as though it were a scab. It wouldn't heal because I wouldn't let it heal.

*

None of which is to suggest that I personally, as a human being – if you could have called me the same – was becoming skinny. Not personally. Quite the opposite, in fact. From the very beginning, in my rise to grace – from A-Cat to C – I always made sure that I ate all of my meals, obediently, and chewing thoroughly: even when the evidence of tampering and interference was plain. Oh yes: the result of that noseblow that seethed on my mashed potatoes? I mushed it all in with the gut of my soupspoon and waited for my stomach to cease its disgusted contractions. Then I ate it. I ate it all up. While not stupid enough to risk the guards' ire by sarcastically asking for more, I would nonetheless move onto the coffee: the salty coffee, laced with urine, or the coffee capped by an archipelago of rampant spittle. My lot in life.

Sooner or later, I guessed, these taunts would settle. And I was right – but they took their time. Indeed, for a while I think that I was the subject of appalled fascination for my tormentors. But I acted as innocent as I could, and never complained. As I spooned in the flakes of excrement that had found their way into my ice-cream, I could feel – rather than risk seeing – pairs of eyes at the peephole on my door. It wasn't so much that I was pretending that no one was watching me; nor was I daring them to go further, and yet further. It was more the case that by acting naïve – by swallowing my repasts and then doing my exercises – I was hoping to give the impression that nothing was wrong; that I was contrite. That this – this blood goulash, this vomit risotto, this cigarette stew – was clearly the best that a stroker like me could hope for. It was my penance. Even when the game became vocal – dirty chuckles at the slit, and for the love of God the sound of some gambled money changing hands – I kept my eyes on the wall, and grew porkier. Who'd have thought that bile could be calorific? And I was A-Cat Enhanced before it stopped.

*

'Sir?' I said. 'Sir, I think it's time for my recreation hour.'

Half a foot of grey-painted steel separated us, so I know why the guard on duty thought it wise to be a bit cocky. Or safe, at any rate.

'It's recreation hour when I *say* it's recreation hour. Got it?'

'Yes, sir.'

It was what I lived for. One p.m. to two p.m. was when I was allowed out of my cell. You got a belt thrown in. You donned it and pulled it tight. You were then invited to face the wall while a brace of officers approached. Not once did I make any trouble. When you're sent down, you know, you are the subject of a series of in-depth tests, one of which gauges the right-arm/left-arm preference. It is important that everyone knows your strongest arm. So in my case, my right arm would be reached for first. A cuff would be snapped around the wrist. The other cuff was slipped through a loop on the front of the belt and my left wrist was similarly clinked shut. My arms were out of action.

Then I would be led, by six men and a dog, to the Muster Point.

The air was like nectar. The air made me drunk.

Six months into my stretch I asked a question.

'Sir?'

The entourage of screws would have a leader. One of the less brutal of the cunts that I had to deal with was called Snow. He was on duty, feeding me a cigarette: I exhaled and said, 'Sir, is it possible for me to get a job?'

'Not until you're out of Basic, Nash.'

I nodded. 'And how do I get out of Basic, sir?'

'You don't. We decide.'

I paused. It was no more and no less than what I had expected. Nevertheless, I had a script. 'I would really like to do something, sir.'

'As I say, Nash…'

'I know. But may I ask you a personal question, sir?'

Snow looked around, as if scouting. 'What is it, Nash?' he asked.

'Sir. You've known me for six months now.'

'Yes.'

'Do you honestly believe that I'm a danger to anyone?' I said.

'It's not my diagnosis to make, Nash.'

'I'm an innocent man, sir.'

'Of course you are, Nash. So's everyone.'

*

But that was not true. Not everyone was innocent.

This might come as a surprise, but we had some *thieves* in Sugville West. I know, I know – it's a mad world. We had a bunch of criminals in there. And what? Steal a worthless commodity from a breach of gurgling villains, and you'd be all too forgiven for thinking that a twinkle-irised and ultimately sarcastic 'Say it isn't so' would be the outcome. Correct me if I'm wrong. Indulgence, you might think – you might have thought – indulgence in the palaver in question would have been the searched-for gold. Who cared? The way it was and the way it would always be…

Not so.

Theft was taken seriously. Why? Because when you've got less than you need two hands to hold, whatever you *have* got is worth its weight in… bronze, at least. Which is not to say that there weren't ways and means of going about a spell of rampage. Sorry. *Revenge* is what I meant to scribble there.

Revenge.

*

Let me give you an example.

It is Christmas 1987. No longer am I an A-Cat Base. No. I am now a B-Cat, and eligible for education (of which, more later). I was still Nash, prisoner code G4785, but I didn't need to go crazy in my coffin for twenty-three twenty-fourths of every day. What's more, I was allowed to work. See above.

But it was Christmas: the time of the year that prisoners fear most. Visits are prohibited and there is an inverted sense of jubilation about the whole nick, as though we feel that the command to be joyous is one that will instigate a serious spanking if we defy it.

Define depression.

Depression is a prison's worth of lags, all pretending to be happy and grateful. So what you do is keep busy, or as busy as you are allowed to keep.

One Christmas Eve, I was having a perfectly decent row with Saturday Dave and Tarzan Burser (two Welsh fraudsters), when a squirmer called Billy Sharron idled past, having a spazzy because someone had pilfered his toothpaste. So what? Possession being nine-tenths and all that, you might imagine – as I say above – how we weren't paying him much of never mind: at first. But some people just don't know when to *stop*.

He kept on, long after I'd determined to myself to ignore him.

Billy Sharron was by far the pikiest of the C-Cat pick-pocketing little bastards. You could smell the cunt with the cell doors closed. Quite why he was getting so uppity about some *toothpaste* was beyond us. He had teeth like chunks of chisel. And Saturday's giving it, *'Jupiter.'* Tarzan's giving it, *'Saturn.'* We were arguing about what was the best planet in the solar system, and why. Propounding our theses, as it were. My money was on Mercury: cold as tits. I think. And that silly billy Jitter, Billy Sharron, should have respected our rights to a festive disagreement, he really should have. But no; he lays in with: 'One of you cunts a nick me toofpaice.'

It was Christmas. It was the season of goodwill. Forced or not forced. And so I said, as politely and slowly as I could, 'Excuse me, Billy? What?'

'*Jupiter.*'

'Me toofpaice. Someone *nick* it,' said Billy Sharron.

I raised a muscular eyebrow. 'Do you wanna moderate your tone, cunt?' I suggested, continuing with the old polite game.

'It's fucking *Saturn*,' says Saturday. 'Inhospitable atmosphere int it.'

'But Jupiter has fucking *electrical* storms. It's a right cunt. Hard as nails,' says Tarzan, who had learning difficulties and who had yet to catch up, luckily for Billy. Tarzan hadn't got his name by being able to swing from vines: it was because he'd once been caught trying to steal semi-precious birds from a zoo. He'd got himself lost, or bored, or something, and he'd ended up getting chirpy with a *leopard*. Straight up. Or so the story went at any rate. Apparently he'd brained the cunt with a piece of birch, although I have my suspicions as to the validity of the anecdote.

Anyway. Forget this Yeehah for Yuletide nonsense; Billy had put my back up. I was cross. I was feeling undrunk and unfriendly: in no mood not to have a fight, despite my good behaviour over the last long time. Or maybe, because of it. What I have to admit was that I *could* have let it go… but I didn't. What I have to admit is that I started – or at least catalysed – what followed.

'Ladies,' I said, and waited for order. 'Twitchy here is giving me brain damage about some missing fucking toothpaste.'

Invitation enough. Invitation *plenty*.

Saturday Dave put on his Queen-Liz-having-a-plop type of face. 'He's fucking *what*?' he exclaimed, the outrage – as they say – palpable.

'I know. Beggars belief, don't it,' I continued. 'But for the record. You wouldn't happen to have been advised, would you girls, as to the whereabouts?'

Dave had stood up quickly. His chair squealed like train-brakes.

'Dave, Dave,' I said calmly. 'Peace. I'm sure the little Pikey is half a second away from apologising. Ain't that right, Wriggly?'

'No.'

Satisfied, I was shaking my head. 'In that case, do you wanna borrow me biro?' I asked.

'Why? I can't write,' said Billy, effectively destroying my punchline. I had to dig deep to recover. I'd expected him to ask why. *So's you can write your fucking will in the presence of witnesses,* was what I had planned.

Can't write, my scrotal lance.

'Kill him, Dave,' I wanted to say. But I had no time to say anything. Dave was attempting a dive across the table, towards Billy. *At* Billy. The resulting scrap was not what I wanted, and not what I'd hoped for, but at least I was not directly involved in the physical action. It was Dave, not Tarzan and not myself, who ended up getting restrained and being denied Crimbo lunch the next day.

II.

'Hello,' I said into the telephone receiver that Julie had just handed to me.

It was Bitch. 'Get your arse into my office *right now*, Gal,' he said.

But it was a dream.

And do you know something funny? I was grateful to receive it. For the dream was like a lasso, pulling me back to my old world.

Not referring to the memory of Steve, because he wouldn't leave me alone, even if I had wanted him to. No. The dream was welcome because it reminded me of my first name. No one used the word *Gary* in Sugville West. It was a community of surnames and Sirs. First names were old currency.

'I'll fly back home via Hell before I fall in love with you, Gary. I'll *swim* back home via Hell,' said Mitzi.

'You're too kind.'

But this was also a dream.

And I was as thankful for it as I was for any of my others.

Gary. My name is Gary. My name is Gary Nash. Not 'Nash' and not 'Nashy' or 'Nashers'. My name is Gary Nash.

*

'All right, Gal?'

'Never better, mate,' I answered. And I would mean it. Banalities are what you look for when everything else is mad around you.

This would be the typical consistency of an early phone call – with Cliff. He would ask me how I was doing. I would tell him that things were okay. Visits to A-Cat Bases were not permitted. It was a case of a call or of nothing at all.

They were my lifeline. Zsa Zsa might well have been my saviour on the inside, but I still needed a lifeguard to stop me from drowning. It was Cliff.

There were jokes: early jokes. 'So Gal,' he would say, 'going anywhere nice on your holidays this year?'

Sooner or later, as surely as night follows day, we would end up talking about the past – the lanes, the Bitch... and Mitzi.

'Yeah... I see her last Thursday.'

'And was she...?' These conversations: oh man, they were so full of pauses. So full of uncertainty. Mine, in particular.

'Was she what?' Cliff would ask, for the first few of my monthly calls. After that, he knew exactly what I was about to say.

He would intercept the question and give me both barrels. I'd like to think that he was trying to spare me the pain that would be there for me in the asking.

'Was she alone or was she with someone?' I would say.

'Well, she wasn't alone.'

'And you're not talking about carrying some *baby,*' I wanted to clarify.

'No I'm not. Sorry, Gal.'

I have to say that this first time was the only occasion on which the following discussion took place. While it's true to say that in Cliff's opinion there was rarely an instance in which Mitzi remained unaccompanied, we did not have to do what comes after this more than once. And only on that once was it to salve me, to soothe me. Only on that once was it to save my sanity.

'Who is he? It's Bitch, isn't it?' I declared.

'No, mate. Why should it be?' Cliff asked.

'It *shouldn't* fucking be. That's the point.'

Could I actually hear Cliff's brow pinching together like cut pork getting stiff in the refrigerator? I fancied that I could. And that pleased me. It didn't make me think that he was struggling with *answering* the question; it made me think that he was questioning my logic in my having posed the bloody thing.

'Well no, Gal, it's not Steve. It's Errol.'

I paused before replying. '*Errol?*' I eventually said, aghast.

'Yeah.'

'Errol from the lanes?'

'No, Errol from Hot Chocolate. Errol Flynn. Of *course* Errol from the lanes. How many other Errols do you know?' Cliff asked.

'I don't even know that one, it seems.'

'I don't understand you, Gal,' said Cliff.

'I know…' I muttered. Because it was a pride thing. That a toady little scrote like Errol could function as my replacement was hardly likely to do positive things for my self-image, now was it?

'What's the matter, Gal? You're better off without her, mate.'

'Am I?'

Mitzi… Mitzi, darling. I would have crawled ten miles over broken glass, just for the *chance* to wank on your shadow. Why'd you do it, babe?

But what bad thing that she had done was I referring to?

'*Yeah*. She's bad news, Gal.'

'That's *my* line,' I complained.

'Eh?'

'Nothing.' I don't now remember what I actually meant by that. At that point I had next to no writing skills – or reading skills, come to that – so I had certainly not started to write this account. Had I ever called Mitzi bad news? Had I used the insult *about* her while talking to my brother? Don't know.

'Gal. Are you sure you're all right?' Cliff asked me in this same conversation. Bless him for the note of concern in his voice.

'I'm bearing up,' I said through a sigh.

Bearing up under the strain, as we used to say.

*

'Weirdest fucking dream,' I said to Zsa Zsa. The discussion took place at the Muster Point during one of our guard-accompanied recreation hours. Well, *I* had only one hour. It seemed to me as though Zsa Zsa could pretty much come and go as he felt like it. He was privy to extraordinary privileges. And how was this? It certainly appeared improbable that his actions – his business – was totally unknown to the staff of Sugville West. An official blind eye was turned.

On one occasion I ventured to ask him about it. In essence, this is what he replied. Pent-up frustration is not a good thing for a prison. And so if a trade was made that didn't actively *harm* any of the staff was underway… well, where was the damage? And besides, even gaolers got lonely sometimes…

'It's started giving me earache,' I continued, referring to one of my many recurring dreams. 'Brainache, even.'

We had nothing else worth talking about so Zsa Zsa said, 'What is it?'

'It went like this. Very simple. I had a cup of black coffee but despite how much I poured milk in – a thimble-full, a pint, a gallon – that drink stayed as black as a badger's cock. If a badger's cock is black. I just couldn't make it turn to the colour of pissy rainwater puddles. Try as I might.'

Zsa Zsa sniffed. 'That's all about revenge, that is.'

'How so?'

'It's your subconscious, darling. Telling you that you want to do something but you're totally unable to do it. Trust me: it's revenge.'

'I wouldn't argue with that. And actually, while we're on the subject...'

'Yeah?'

I turned to the guard called Snow. 'Sir?'

'What is it, Nash?'

'Can I speak openly to Zsa Zsa?' I asked.

'I don't know anyone by that name, Nash.'

Pedantic twat. 'To Hazelwood, sir.'

'You can speak to him any way you please,' Snow replied. As reasonable as the staff got, was Snow; but on that day he was evidently in a funny mood.

'And what I say won't get either of us into trouble,' I persisted. It was never a bad idea to cover all of your bases.

Snow shrugged. 'I couldn't give a fuck what you talk about,' he said.

I turned back to Zsa Zsa. 'It's about a little tramp called Billy Sharron.'

'Oi, Nash,' said Snow, and when I turned back to face him I could see that his features were balanced on a fulcrum: amusement and distemper. Which way would he fall? 'Don't fucky say fankyou or nuffing woe ya.'

'Thank you, sir.' Jesus. It comes to something when you have to give appreciation for the gift of freedom of speech.

'What about him, love?' said Zsa Zsa.

I approached with caution and not a little bit of trepidation. But then I thought: Sod it. 'He's opened an account with me. Christmas Eve,' I said.

Zsa Zsa nodded. 'What did he do?'

'Verbal.'

'On Christmas Eve?'

'Yeah.'

'The toerag.'

'Exactly,' I answered, pleased for the understanding, and growing in confidence. I hadn't had a beating from the guards in some time. I couldn't imagine them getting saucy just to repay the simple matter of a bit of payback-speak. *No one* – not lags and not screws – liked Pikeys such as Billy.

Zsa Zsa shrugged. 'Verbal him back,' he suggested. I declined to take offence… but I *was* rather hurt and disappointed. However, I was aware that this was part of Zsa Zsa's way: non-committal lack of interest at the opening.

'In front of Saturday Dave and Tarzan Burser,' I continued. 'Cunt needs a shave. Face it.'

Coolly Zsa Zsa added: 'I don't argue with that.'

'I'd like you to be the razor.'

Zsa Zsa nodded. 'But you can handle yourself. Why me?'

'Because…' Here I sneaked a look at Snow. The other guards on duty at the Muster Point were Brookfield, Japp and McDevitt: all packing. But not, in truth, giving much of a toss about Zsa Zsa and me. As long as we kept a distance between one another, they were happy to leave us be. Sure: they could probably *hear* us, but they were busy smoking cigarettes – as grateful, no doubt, as we were for the fresh January air. New Year's Day had been and gone. Snow was looking at me. The flame from his lighter danced in the breeze.

'It's got to be anonymous. He can't know it's me.'

There was a pause. 'Interesting, lover,' said Zsa Zsa, exhaling. 'Let me guess. This is practice, right? This is not about Billy Sharron. 'Cause who gives a monkey's about someone like that.'

'Well, we all need someone to shit on, Zsa Zsa,' I interjected.

'True. But you're exercising some new muscles, Nashy. What you're doing is what that guy who put you in here used to do.'

I sniffed. 'You're not going to endear yourself to me by comparing me to a bastard like Steve Bitch, I can tell you that,' I said.

'I'm not trying to. I'm explaining your motive, sweety. Steve Bitch got people in his employ to ruffle feathers, didn't he? And now you're learning to do the same,' said Zsa Zsa. 'So do you know something. This stretch might be seen as a kind of *promotion* for you, lover.'

'Well, it doesn't feel like one,' I answered.

'Not yet, maybe. But there's a good chance that it will. Getting me to arrange a fall in the showers for Billy Sharron is your way of becoming a boss.'

Considering this, I turned to Snow. 'Sir?'

'What is it, Nash?'

'Would you light me another cigarette, please?'

Once he had done so, and once he had stepped away (by this point I had earned the right to hold my own cigarettes, although I was still cuffed) I went on: 'So you think that deep down I might be practicing a long-distance return assault on Steve Bitch?'

'That's not for me to say,' said Zsa Zsa, smiling. 'But the answer to your original request is yes. Now. Let's discuss terms and conditions.'

'Okay. But the thing is, mate, I want it soon. Soon.'

'Me?' He laughed. 'I don't work on any other timeframe, babes.'

The toothpaste, by the way, was never found.

*

'You set me up,' I breathed again and again, and quickly. 'For Christ's sake, Steve, *you set me up*. Why?'

And I didn't know or not if this was a dream.

'In a manner of speaking,' said Steve Bitch, sniffing. 'And you needn't look so shocked. Fuck did you expect, strokey?'

No. It must have been a dream. It must have been.

I was honest. 'My broken heart,' I said. 'Why, Steve?'

'Why what?'

'Why betray me like this?'

'Oh excuse me. I must have lost my copy of the family tree: I completely forgot that you were my *dad*. Jesus. How old are you, Gal? You had a job. You got paid. Now move on.'

*

I left Sugville West on many occasions.

Not physically, of course; but my mind took wing and I tasted clouds and sunlight as I flew. It was beautiful. Usually.

Most of the egresses were calm enough. Once, however, in a while, I got stroppy: on my exit I'd be carrying a samurai sword or a hedge-trimmer; I'd hack of a guard's feet as I swept past. As in a cartoon, he would merely sink four inches, but stay upright. He'd wriggle a fist in my direction. Sweet dreams...

Someone nick me toofpaice.

Yes. It is sometimes the smallest misdemeanours that can lead us into moments of madness, such as the one that Billy Sharron was shortly to regret causing. Steve had once said something odd: 'Gal?' he said, and settled back into his chair behind the desk at the lanes. 'It's sometimes the eyelid that spasms. Not the leg.' And he'd sipped on a brandy. 'You with me?' he'd asked.

'Not really, boss,' I'd admitted.

He'd also been smoking a cigar. Steve had had a habit of blowing smoke rings when forming his opinions on life and violence. He had nodded. 'When you're *hurting* someone, Gal,' he had taught me – 'when you're quizzing them or putting car tools into their mouths… don't always look for the *obvious* signs of distress. Okay? They twitching eyelid might suggest guilt. Just as much as the leg that's quivering like a shitting wolf. Look for the little things…'

Zsa Zsa had *also* provided a valuable lesson.

Why wait until I got out of Sugville West before wreaking revenge on Bitch? Which led to a question. How did one go about arranging a long distance attack? Even better: How would I *stroke* him from afar?

Zsa Zsa was true to his word.

It was on the afternoon that the comedian Frank Carson did a show for the boys on B, amongst whose ranks I now numbered. The concert was a cracker. I made that up myself. Unsung hero, Frank Carson. Liked the pop in his time, but who didn't, eh? Who didn't?

Anyway. The next thing we eardrum is that Billy Sharron has been seen falling over in the library: a room that he would never have entered of his own accord. A *book* or something – Shakespeare's Quartos: something weighty – has toppled from the uppermost shelf. Bonced the cunt. And Billy's in the infirmary, trying to remember what 'Billy' is short for and how many fags there are in a box. Spaced.

As free from worry as *I* was when I flew beyond the walls. And do you know what I found on one trip out? I found a beach. It was a beach, not of sand, but of a black emotion called woe. I started digging. And I did so happily. 'These castles,' I remember saying, 'won't build them-bloody-selves.'

*

'Smatter? You sound like a lumberjack gargling spunk.'

'I'm ill,' I told my brother on the telephone. 'I'm poorly sick.'

'What? The lurgy?'

'Yeah. It's a peach, mate. Everyone's got it.'

'Well you will insist on keeping bad company.'

'Thanks. Maybe humour will save me.'

Cliff snorted like a donkey. 'Seriously,' he said. 'Unlucky. Here's one. Two lobsters walk into the pub…'

I said, 'No.'

'No? What, you heard it already or summing?' Cliff asked.

'It's not that. I haven't got long, that's all. And I need to talk to you about Bitch. I need to ask you a favour.'

'Gal. We've done this before,' he answered, fairly enough. 'Whether you like it or not, he's still my boss. I've got a *family*, Gal.'

'Yeah,' I said bitterly. 'And I'm in it too.'

'Don't *do* this.'

Uncontrollable crying jags. Dysentery. Squabbles. Rat-like protests… These are the right ingredients for a truly terrible time in Sugville West. I had left them behind me – a long, long time ago. I had been behind bars for five years, four months and three days. I had *evolved* into a B-Cat Enhanced. And I had made it my ambition never to feel sorry for myself again. To achieve this goal I made sure that I sampled freely of the drugs that I used the kitchen in which I (by now) toiled to distribute and deal for. I was high a good percentage of the time… and *time*? Well, time was flying. And if things were sometimes going wrong in my head, what of it? Listen. What follows is a bit of lag philosophy.

There was a small toilet block by the gym, okay? Now that I was B-Cat, I was allowed to visit the gym (when chaperoned) and I went in one afternoon. Two Trinidadian brothers were already in there (again, chaperoned). This was our first meeting (I don't think I'd ever even seen them prior to this encounter) but we came to be friends a little while later. So. One of the brothers (and the guard) was waiting for the other to come out of a cubicle. Watched by *my* guard (Japp), I took my place at the porcelain receptacle. The second brother came out and he moved to leave. The first one started the conversation:

'No, man! Warsh yands!'

'Why? It me own dick innit.'

'It the jarms!'

Indignantly the offender rejoined with: 'Nain no jarms on me, man! Me dick he spotless! Youn eat you *dinner* off this dick!'

At which point *their* guard said, 'Wash your fucking hands.'

But I felt for that guy. *It me own dick innit.* That was how I felt about my head. If I wanted to scramble it like eggs in a pan, that was my own lookout.

You could say, therefore, that I was treating my incarceration resiliently.

The one thing that I couldn't help loathing, however, was Cliff's inability to see things my way. Not in person and not on the phone. Despite the fact that Bitch had set me up and had me put away, he would not leave the lanes (where he had been made the Head of Security as soon as the judge's gavel had hit the wood, apparently). Cliff was of the opinion that Steve would do right by me in the end. Cliff opined that for me this should be regarded as a test.

Strokework? Oh, I had sent Bitch some reminders of his crime, don't you worry about that. In fact, setting things up had not been so difficult. Since the brain-damaging of Billy Sharron (which he recovered from, by the way; and Billy and I even became friendly, amazingly enough; I took him under my wing, on the understanding that he would wash occasionally), Zsa Zsa and I had been in a sort of partnership. We both had *connections.* So the lanes had been visited by the paraffin angel again one evening. The lanes had been visited by the lachrymatory gas angel one lunchtime. Steve himself had jumped free of a hit and run (sloppy work, that one; and I'd registered my displeasure with Zsa Zsa). *Strokes.*

Cliff knew full well that I was responsible. 'You'll never guess what happened last night,' he said once.

'The lanes were roasted. Yeah, mate. You underestimate me, bruv.'

Which brings us to the current conversation.

'Mate. I'm not doing *nothing* to fuck things up with Steve, okay?'

'Not even for me.'

'Not even for you,' said Cliff. 'It's too risky.'

'Jesus. Not you as well,' I replied in disgust.

That got him bristling. 'What the hell is that supposed to mean, Gal?' he demanded.

'You and Steve,' I told him. *'Cowards.'*

*

Have you ever played What Would You Do? Someone poses a question along the following lines: What would you do if your twelve year-old sister announced that she was pregnant?

'Kill the cunt,' said Zsa Zsa, on one occasion when we were playing the game at a party to celebrate the Bar mitzvah of the Governor's grandsonBilly Sharron gave a twitch and said, 'Which cunt?'

'That breached the barricades, darling. What you think?' said Zsa Zsa.

Billy gurgled for a second. 'I thought you might've meant your sis.'

'Oh, grow up.'

'Ladies,' I warned.

Well, I used to pose similar questions to myself on the nights when I was too wired to sleep and too bored to wank. What would you do if you brother suddenly – no, *slowly* – showed signs of imminent madness? I wish I could say that Cliff was his normal self after that phone call, but I can't. Things had changed – and badly – but I couldn't or wouldn't see why.

It took me a long time to work it out.

III.

Grow up.

In Sugville West, there was no insult, no put-down, that was more guaranteed to cause offence, perturbation, outrage and fear. It was a terrible thing to hear. In a funny sort of way, it was a terrible thing to *say.* You always felt guilty after you'd told some lag to grow up. Why? Because it was one of the very real things, inside, that one wanted to do but couldn't.

We couldn't grow up. But we *could* become educated. Eventually I was allowed to study: by keeping my nose clean I'd graduated out of Basic and into Standard. I wanted to better myself – to improve my saleability on the job market, if you will. And besides, you got 80p an hour for every class you took. There was a strong financial incentive. You had to earn your place, earn your desk, earn your biro.

My first teacher was a guy called Noel Winnet. We called him Grassy Noel, or sometimes Tammy – after the country and western singer. He was a good old boy, but an odd choice for such a gig. He was an NQT: a Newly Qualified Teacher. I felt nervous for him as he entered the classroom, accompanied by two guards who were carrying rifles. Grassy stood at the front and the guards flanked him, eyeing us all suspiciously. They moved with him when he approached the chalkboard; it was like a little ballet.

Be stronger, I urged him silently. If I could see the poor cunt's leg shaking, then so could everyone else.

'You can call me Noel,' he said, adjusting the neat piles of paper on his desk. 'And what do I call you?'

Mistake, mistake...

'You can call us fucking scum, like the rest of 'em do here,' said a loud and bolshy Irishman called Barsnacks. The observation earned him a titter. I held myself in, praying for Grassy's composure.

'Okay, Mr Scum,' said Grassy, smiling horribly. 'Have it your way. What about the rest of you?' He looked around the room.

Grassy Noel Winnet was my favourite teacher, and I will remain indebted to him for the rest of my days. Grassy Noel taught me how to read and write properly. There were other tutors who gave me the dates of the famous battles. Others still who taught me about foreign places, rice yields, sediments and economies. I studied hard for my O Levels in English Language, History and Geography. They took me seven years to pass (grades C, B and D, respectively). But Grassy made me understand sentences: the kind that are spent on paper, as opposed to the kind that are spent on wasted hours.

As one class finished, I stood up and approached the teacher. His minders, be-rifled and humourless, tensed. I remembered to observe politure.

'Permission to ask Mr Winnet a question, sir,' I said to Snow's successor. (Snow had been okay to me in the end; he'd retired after a heart attack.)

'Ask him from there,' said Grove.

'It's personal, sir.'

'*Ask him from there.*'

Grassy held up a hand. 'It's okay, Mr Grove. I don't mind.'

Oh, but Grove did. Not that it mattered much: inside the classrooms, the teachers were like royalty. The guards worked for *them*. I walked closer.

'Noel,' I said as quietly as I could without risking him having to ask me for repetition. 'I'm worried about my brother.'

'Your brother.'

'Yeah. You see, I think he's going a bit...' But I couldn't find the right word; the moment had robbed me of vocabulary. So what I did was point at my left temple and move my finger around in a circle: the evergreen mime, that.

'Mad?' asked Noel.

I nodded. Was I as uncomfortable as Noel appeared to be?

'Well,' he said, 'I'm sure you have my sympathies, but I don't see…'

'I can't,' I interrupted.

'Can't what?' said Grassy.

'I haven't got the *skills*.'

'Well, I'm afraid I haven't either, Gary. It's not my field.'

'The *reference* skills,' I clarified.

'Excuse me?'

'I want to research his symptoms but I don't know where to start.'

There was a pause. In the corner of my vision, there was Grove, smirking. And then Grassy said: 'You want me to help you use a library?'

'Yes. I need *help*, Noel,' I said.

'Of course you do.' And he smiled: encouragement and fairness. More than I could have hoped for, looking back on the matter. 'And of course I will.'

'Thank you, sir.'

'You don't need to call me sir, Gary.'

'Thank you. But I can't pay you. Obviously.'

'It'll be my pleasure.'

*

Unlike a lot of the characters in my life, who are good for about ten per cent of their promises, Noel came through. And I think it would be fair to say that a bond of sorts formed in the following weeks. He might even have become my best friend, whatever *that* means. As well as teaching me to better my reading and writing, Noel also obliged me to strengthen my social skills and improve my conversation. I owe that man a great deal, and one day I'll find him to say thanks. Grassy gave me the gift of words. And along with Cliff, he also taught me to respect the power of will: that one can *will* events along.

We can make our own coincidences.

*

I couldn't believe my eyes when I saw him.

I had been in Sugville West for seven years and I couldn't believe what I was looking at.

Fortunately, we were having our dinner at the time. By this stage, of course, I was allowed to take meals (under armed supervision) with selected crowds of violent and pseudo-violent B-Cats. Blurrily I turned to Zsa Zsa.

'Getting his meal right now,' I said. 'Who's that little rat?'

'Which one?'

'*Getting his fucking dinner, mate!*' I shouted, and then said quickly: 'Sorry. But I know the little fucker…' The dolphin teeth; the rudimentary features, as near as damn it cartoonish; but above all, the turf of red hair. I had seen the wriggler before, although not recently, of course. He had gained a pound or two, but it was definitely *him*.

'Don't know him,' said Zsa Zsa. 'But I can find out for you. Do you want a bite of him?'

It was Ronald McFucking Donald.

You can hide anything if the other cunt don't know what he's looking for, Steve had told me once. But now I can update that. *You can find anything if the other cunt don't know you're looking…*

Delivered onto my doorstop, as it were, was one of the bastards that had been part of the attack on the lanes, way back when. When the strokes had started, seven-and-a-bit years ago, a tit that I'd known only as Ronald McFucking Donald had been part of the clan.

And now the little stroker was inside. With me.

The next morning, I emerged from the kitchen after helping to prepare the breakfast, and one of Zsa Zsa's boys, Tom Calcinnin, approached me holding a bag of sugar. We were of course being observed. Tom handed me the sugar and said, 'For the cake. From Zsa Zsa.' *What* fucking cake? I wondered.

'Whose birthday is it?' I asked.

Tom squinted and told me: 'His name is Frank Gerkin.'

Not exactly subtle. But it was all I needed.

*

Messages from the other world came my way, every now and then.

Errol lost his footing on the path of the straight and narrow; he was sacked from the lanes when his third (and only incontrovertible) accusation of car theft arrived. At which point, I thought I had a yet-clearer picture. Errol had stolen the car in which Cliff had been ignited. Even if this would turn out not to be the case, it was true to say that the young man returned to what he knew best. Rumour has it that he porridged in Welly Nick for a spell… And that he split up with Mitzi.

Lenny? Lenny left the lanes and stayed in his job with a freezer firm (delivery man) until the point where he slips from our radar.

Maggot died: electrocuted while attempting to enter a farmer's property – the horse-scaring wire. I felt for the fucker, I really did.

I greeted these old signals with the fondness of phone calls from ex-girlfriends.

*

But I must go back to a time before most of these things happened. I've been putting it off, but it's time to come clean. Mitzi visited.

Thing with a raid, yeah, Steve had said to me, a long time ago, *is silence. But not yours; it's the other cunt's you gotta worry about. You've gotta keep everyone* quiet, *mate. Imperative. See, there's a good chance that if you've thought of raiding a place then they've thought of defending the fucker. So you've got to seal their lips every step a the way.*

That's right from Stumpy the Ape on the door, if there is one, to fucking Trish in the office. Show her what's what. Make it worth her while not to phone the pus. They probably won't show up till the fucking funeral but you can't take that chance, mate. You never know.

Mitzi had crept up on me from behind.

I had been in Sugville West for four years, I'm sure of it, and six months. And all that Mitzi could say at first was: 'Gary. You're looking well.'

'Mitzi. You look like the million dollars that I would have given you. Or worked to find you. Before you shafted me,' I said.

'I didn't shaft you. I loved you, Gary… I'm here to tell you about our daughter.'

'Our daughter. Sure.' I was playing with a cigarette as though it was a miniature flute. 'And you're some sort of blue whale, are you? That you need *four years* to gestate the fucker.'

'I went home,' said Mitzi. 'For the early years. I'm sorry about that.'

Carefully, saying nothing at all, I rolled a cigarette. Thoughts and fears were riding around a circular track in my head, and getting faster, like scrambler motorbikes.

'Cheryl's yours, Gary,' said Mitzi.

'You called her Cheryl.' I sipped delicately on my burn. 'You can't have two cousins with the same name,' I said.

'Whyever not? It's a perfectly good name… She wants to see you.'

The feeling that I experienced – the twang, the heartburn, the seething oils that were oozing through my organs – what *was* that feeling? Shame? Loss? Or the revivification of my buried paternal instincts?

'So what have you told her?' I asked. 'About me.'

Mitzi shrugged the shoulders that I had down on a mattress, a long time ago; the shoulders that I'd slobbered on and initialled with my sperm. 'What else could I tell her?' Mitzi asked – just as I was undressing her, in my mind; just as I was saying hello to her nipples... 'I told her that you've been in hospital for a long-term stay.'

'*For years?*' I shouted, standing up. 'What've I done, eh? Broken every fucking bone in my body and head?' I was leaning forward.

'A coma, Gary. I told her you've been in a coma.'

'I'll give *you* a fucking coma in a minute!' I hollered.

'Step away from the table, Nash,' said the duty officer, now raising his baton. 'I said *away from the fucking table...*'

IV.

She had very strange lungs, as I recall.

This sentence kept spinning in my head as I infected the life of Ronald McFucking Donald, a.k.a. Frank Gerkin. Apparently he was also called Hormones, due to his seeming absence of any. September, 1987; and for the first time in a while I started to think that life was playing into my hands again. Just like in the old days.

We were in the Recreation Room.

'Remember me, strokey?' I asked, putting my hands down onto the jigsaw puzzle that Hormones was laboriously complet-ing. Buck Pal. Corgis.

'Can't say I do,' said Hormones, amiably enough. 'But you're on my bits.'

'I'll *be* on your bits in a fucking second, sunshine,' I told him. 'But we'll come to that shortly. *Think back.* Reminisce. You were part of a squad that attacked a bowling alley seven years ago.' I attempted to portray a man in the throes of hilarity. 'We all got a bit of a fucking spanking, tell the gospel.'

But Hormones remained unimpressed. He said, 'I'm really sorry, I don't remember. And anyway: ancient history, mate.'

I frowned. 'Curious,' I said. 'What you in for?'

'It's none of your fucking business. Get off me jigsaw.'

After a few seconds, I nodded and I stretched erect. 'Forgive me,' I said. 'You got a biro?' And I gave him *that look*. It had always served me well.

'No. Why?'

'You've just signed your death warrant,' I told him.

'So why do I need a biro *now*, cunt?' he asked.

Shit. Provided the wrong punchline, hadn't I? Swift to recover, as always, I said the following: 'Listen, mate. Two years ago, there was a bloke in here called Ashton Forley. Now Ashton was a skinny little wriggler with muscles like knots in a rabbit's cock, okay? His forehead was a map of scars and abandoned subcutaneous. And *he* was the cunt who'd poked his own wife. He'd *stroked* the geezer, and good. Right?'

'Right,' said Hormones. 'So?'

'So… She'd been painting the town with another cunt's brush. You with me? She'd been spending another cunt's currency. Unforgivable.'

'She'd been having an affair, you mean.'

'*Yes.*' I clasped my hands together. 'Which is not to say that his crime was met with a block's-worth of open arms and understanding, you see.'

Confused, Hormones said, 'Yeah. I see.'

'But you want to ask me *so*, right?' I smiled. 'Well, this is the fucking *so* about it, pipsqueak. We have a game here, mate. It's called What Would You Do? Okay. It's a quiz about dilemmas. Do you know it?'

'Can't say I do,' said Hormones, displaying no emotion whatever.

'You can't say you do.' I paused. In truth, I was well pleased by his show of restraint and calm. I was impressed that he wasn't folding up like a piece of pre-formed origami. I sniffed. 'Well, allow me to put it this way, strokey,' I said. 'First and foremost: I'm going to make you fucking *sorry* for what you did to me and my brother and my crew. But secondly, I'm going to tell you why.

Fair's fair. I can't say fairer than that. We played a game of What Would You Do? What would you do if you caught your missus on the alleycat with the bloke next door? And do you know what the consensus was? It was this. *It's all about trust.* So we wouldn't stripe the missus. We would stripe the bloke who was doing the dirty *with* our missus, if he knew what the situation was. *Trust.*'

I waited.

'Trust, you see,' I repeated.

'Yeah, I got it,' Hormones told me. 'What's it got to do with me?'

'It's simple. Are you listening? A man named Steve Bitch fucked me. But just like the woman that strays, I have to accept that he had his reasons, even if I don't agree with them. My *job* is to handle the middle man, with the middle man dreams. And that means you, Dick Turpin. You're as dead as a turbot's piss. You have *no idea* how many people I know.'

And then I walked away.

*

'So what you been up to?' asked Cliff.

'Ha ha,' I told him.

'Going anywhere nice for your holidays?' he continued, his face a brick wall of lines as he grinned from ear to ear.

I had long since tired of the script. 'Jesus. Anyone would think you were *enjoying* my misery,' I said.

'You don't look miserable.'

'Try it through my eyes,' I answered haughtily. I was having a bad month. In Sugville West you didn't have bad days; you had bad weeks, and if you were especially unlucky, you had bad months...

'I would if I could.'

'Would you?' I asked, surprised.

'Of course! Give you one of me fucking livers if you needed the cunt.'

'Kidneys. But thanks.'

Cliff pointed at my nose with a bent lovefinger. '*Or* livers,' he repeated.

Exasperated, I shook my head. 'You only *got* one fucking liver!' I protested.

'Well that's more'n you fucking got,' Cliff protested right back at me.

As I've made clear up above, it wasn't the first time that Cliff had been known to baffle me. *Baffle* me? Looking back even further, for a while, in our teens, it was like he had discovered – or invented – a new sport. Baffle Gal. Bamboozle the Bastard. Send him reeling, like a twisted coin: heads or tails.

Nevertheless, in spite of a fruity few years of precedents, I re-acted. 'And what's *that* supposed to mean?' I asked, parenthetically wondering if he'd been on the pop all morning. *I* certainly had.

'You and your fucking potions.'

'Me *what*?' I asked.

'Your Mad Hatter. Your Gutflakes. Your March Hare –'

'Cliff.'

' –Not to mention the lakes.'

'*What* lakes? Cliff, please…'

'No, mate. I'm angry,' my brother said.

'Okay. You're angry. Just remember, slang's moved on and I haven't. What are you talking about? What's Mad Hatter? What's March Hare?'

'Are you serious?' Cliff asked. 'Coke and pills, mate. Coke and pills. And various other oobie-doobies. You were off your tits a couple of years.'

'*When*?' I challenged, but I immediately wanted to retract the question.

Cliff frowned. 'Gal. Gal,' he said, and his whole face tried to read the whole of mine. It was a terrifying scrutiny to behold. 'Jesus, Gal,' he went on, and the meniscus of dammed tears was in itself a painful mirror, up to which I was now coerced to hold myself. For *I* had caused this. Me. *I* had been the instrument that caused my own brother such pain, such regret. *But help me*, I wanted to say. Show me what the instrument *was*...

'Gary.' Cliff wiped his nose with his shirtsleeve. 'This is horrible, mate. This *burns* me... But you really don't remember, do you?'

'Remember what?' I pleaded. 'Remember *what*, Cliff?'

*

'You had a job. You got paid. Now move on.'

I nodded. Moving on, evidently, was what I was now in the business of doing. I squeezed the trigger.

The room folded in on itself.

Blue light and blue smoke.

And then Steve clicked his fingers, and the blue light receded. We were sitting in his office, drinking brandy. 'Cigar, Gal?' he asked.

I was sitting in the chair across from him. As Steve was, I was dressed in a tuxedo: this was clearly a special occasion. Then, from without, the ripple of hilarity: a collection of voices, raised in laughter and good cheer. With the passing of several seconds, the sound changed into a song. It was Auld Langs Syne. We were having a business conference on New Year's Eve.

Gal, said Steve. *You make quick decisions.* But I had to wait for the next sentence to work out if he was referring to me directly, or was offering a piece of homogenised advice. It turned out to be the latter. *You do that. You wait for your medicine from whoever's got to the punchline faster than you've done.*

I wrote that two weeks before I left. On my face was a smile like that of a wanking Arab. I was going home. And I knew where I could buy a gun.

*

'So how's it all going?' asked Grassy Noel.

The good thing about a question like this from Grassy was that he was never referring to my general well being. Instinctively, that guy knew that there was no point in the posing of such a query. The answer refused to change.

When Grassy wanted to know, he was talking about my relationship with Cliff. He was talking about my quest into the world of *Cliff's* well being.

With no little regret I answered: 'Well, there's a newsflash, Noel. I don't think he's mad anymore. Not at all. But I think he's trying to make *me* mad.'

Noel nodded. We were to be found in the prison library. I had just made A-Cat, and I'd celebrated with fourteen lines of cocaine. This lunchtime meeting was one of the very few that I had approached with cynicism, awe and sickness.

'Which in itself is a form of madness,' said my teacher.

'In what way?' I asked, quite nauseated, although not by the statement.

'The reprogramming of the will, isn't it?' Noel was not looking at me. He was looking into a tender-bound volume on the subject of human behaviour. And how did I feel about the fact that some lag had obviously taken great care, in the past, to colour in his favourite words on every page. He had also written *I agree* and *Good point* at strategic points: on the title page, for instance, against the author's name, and in the References section, by every ISBN.

Noel continued, looking up now. 'It's a tattoo on your own choices.'

Killing time, I cleared my throat. '…I don't follow,' I admitted.

Noel nodded. 'Think of it like this. You have a set of opinions and memories, do you not? Right. And now, as you say, your brother is trying – quite subtly and without coldly – to *fuck with them.* Believe me: that says a lot more about *his* state of mind than it does about yours. Megalomania, one thing.'

'Hadn't thought of it like that.'

'So what's… what's the game?'

'I wish I knew, Noel, I really do,' I said. 'They keep telling me I'm not in prison, I'm in a hospital. By… by *implication*, I'm in a mental hospital. But I'm not, am I? This ain't a fucky *'ospital*, is it?'

'No, Gal.'

'It's a *prison.'*

'Yes, Gal.'

'Definitely. Right.' *Definitely. Right.* 'It's a *prison.'*

'It's Sugville West,' Noel said slowly. 'It is a place of incarceration.'

'Good. Well not *good,* obviously. But… it's not for the criminally insane or nothing, is it, Grassy? I mean, you'd tell me if that was the case, wouldn't you?'

Grassy Noel did something that I had not expected him to do. Dipping his face forward and leaning towards me (his nose was nearly touching the top of the table) he reached out and took hold of both of my hands. Reflexively I looked about me, but the shelves were not being browsed: those prisoners who had been granted the leisure to do so were crammed – packed – into one of the three television rooms. England was playing Finland: the football. Because of this welcome nod of chance, there was no one to watch Noel's gay clasp. Tell me it wasn't so: just be so kind as to *inform* me that Noel hadn't twisted poof for yours truly. That would have been all I fucking needed.

'Gal. What you've done… by asking for my assistance in this project…' Grassy didn't usually sound quite so pretentious. '…is this. You've awakened my interest in psychology, albeit on a minor scale. And I hope this doesn't seem like too much of a betrayal…' Oh, Christ. '… but I've been doing some work on my own, without you. Call it a solo project. You're not upset, are you?'

Was that all? I couldn't give a fu-

'Noel. If I've helped,' I said as diplomatically as possible, 'to stimulate a hobby, if stimulate's the right word, then I'll take that as a compliment. Okay?'

'Thank you, Gary,' said Noel, weirdly glassy-eyed (he was evidently in an odd mood) and released my hands and put them back in his own lap.

'Chief amongst your discoveries being?' I asked.

'This,' said Grassy. 'If you're sane enough to jump through the hoops necessary to convince yourself that you're not in an insane asylum, then you are almost certainly not in one. That's if I've understood what I've read.'

Deep in thought, or shallow in thought to be honest (it lasted about a second), I pouted. When I spoke all I said was: 'Well, that's all right then.'

That's all right then. Despite everything I'd learned, that seemed to be pretty much the best I could produce. And I wasn't even gassed and stoked. No. I might have been on the cocaine for a couple of days earlier – it might have been rattling my rump and squeezing the old beatbox – but *on that particular morning* I had scored neither drink or drugs, for once.

I remember thinking at that moment: I could *murder* a pint. Ah well…

Nightmare?

Let me tell you a little something more about nightmares, if I may? Shame that I couldn't have exorcised my *own*, but I learned more than once over the years, with more than one cellmate, that I had a good voice for banishing – or exorcising – nightmares. Somewhere up in the heavens – in the cluttered skies that represent all of this narrative that has already gone to pass – I mentioned that describing the prison experience as a 'nightmare' was sadly inadequate. But in one way, it *was* a nightmare: or a series of them.

The ones that you actually have at night; the ones that make you wriggle and kick out and speak slowly and shout for mother. Bad dreams: I was the eavesdropper on *plenty* of those fuckers over the years. But Dean Bolt had taken the prize for the worst night fears. Christ: he was like a cunt possessed, he really was – the full epileptic seizure and opera singer warm-up scales of a guy in mortal conflict with the sneezes of his own imagination.

When the fucking bunk is shaking like a lifeboat in a tempest, there is no point shouting: '*Dean! Fucking leave it out, cunt!*' Because it is not the words – not exactly – that they are listening to: it's the tone of voice that appears to be all-important. Most effective, I found, was a softly worded but easy-to-hear *Dean? It's just a dream, mate. Just a dream, mate…*

Slowly but surely, Dean (and the others) would calm. Half asleep still, they would say things like 'I can smell the fear' and 'It was moving'. For the next few minutes, as I reached for my own sleep, I would assure them that all was…

Noel had been waiting. Now he said: 'So what's *in it* for Cliff?'

'I don't know.'

'What are we missing, Gal?'

We? I thought. 'I wish I knew, mate. I just don't get it. What's in it for the cunt to try'n convince me I had a drink and drugs problem? What's *in it* for him to try'n convince me that there are bloody great holes in me memory?'

'And who are *they*, by the way?' asked Grassy.

'Sorry?'

'You said: *They keep telling me I'm in a hospital.* Who are they?'

Nodding my head, I sighed and gave in. 'Cliff and Mitzi,' I said. 'They're together, I think. Well, c'est la vie, I suppose. But there's *no* fucking way that her baby – if there is one – is mine. It's *Cliff's*. I can feel it in me water, I really can.'

'But you still can't answer your own questions, can you?' Grassy asked.

I frowned. 'The main one being?' I said.

'The main one being why. Why *bother*?' Noel ran a hand through his crow-wing-greasy hair. 'I mean, seriously,' he followed on. 'If they've turned against you… why even bother keeping in touch, let alone make you crazy?'

'No. No I can't answer that,' I told him. 'Mate? That's the biggie.'

But during the night, I made people feel better. I had proved it. What if it was true that I made people feel better during the day? The only reason that someone stays with you – in a business sense or in the bed – is if they are getting something out of it. Let's be *honest*. Staying with anyone is on the trust that that some-one is going to provide at least some of your work or love needs.

Naturally, there are other forces at play; but you take the point, I'm sure. Because I'm confident that the other will *want* to provide those needs – and have their own proffered back with due haste. Reciprocity. And *strokes*.

Cliff wanted something from me. *I had something*, even if I didn't know what that something was. Did Mitzi, too? Want something, I mean, not have something? What about this cock about a second Cheryl?

What did I have that would cause her to potion up such a lame lie?

Well… I had been in Sugville West for a long, long time. And the answer was perfectly clear. In hindsight, it had been ap-parent all along. What *else* did I have… except for Steve Bitch himself? I didn't know *how*, but he was mine.

*

'The word is divided into men who stand up to wipe their arses, and men who reach down below their bollocks,' Bitch had told me once. 'Which one are you, Gal? How do you clean yourself up, eh?'

It was another of the lags' Christmas parties: *that* much was for sure. And it was certainly towards the end of my incarceration. Not that I was feeling in any way festive, but at least I wasn't boycotting the fucker. However, my only concession to the reality of the season was to don a paper party hat.

I had a job to do: but not in the kitchens.

That year, the Christmas karaoke – which had come to be as regular as a morning motion – was a particularly bitter chore: Zsa Zsa's voice taking a run-up at his chosen song: 'Eee YAP tan gelw… she been livin inna…' You get the picture. But I chose to steer myself well away, for a while. Job to do.

As, in fact, did Zsa Zsa.

The usual air was festively usually thin, as usual diluted by the usual good usual feeling and usual goodwill. Things couldn't have been more fucking *usual*. A lag from C Block was even *singing* 'It's Not Unusual.' A lag from A Block had just finished, in a voice that spoke of impeccable irony, 'Heaven is a Place on Earth.' You developed a sense of irony in Sugville West. No choice.

Zsa Zsa said, 'Gal, mateypoos? We're nearly there. Snearly *time*.'

'All right, Zsa?' I answered. 'I'm ready. Also here to ask a favourette.'

'Speak freely,' said Zsa Zsa seigniorially. He reminded me, as he had – and often – in the past, of Bitch at that moment, but it was a reminiscence that had not occurred for some time. Despite my getting closer to the date of my release, I had at last learned something of the skill of letting the past *be*.

'I need something.'

Zsa Zsa smiled. 'We're just about to do it, darling.'

'Something else.'

'I see. Well.' Zsa Zsa smiled again – or maintained the one that had been there for a couple of seconds. Philosophy time: 'We all of us need *summing*.'

'I need a weapon,' I clarified. 'I need a gun. For when I get out.'

'Impossible.'

'Not for you, chief,' I said. 'You get in drinks, you get in drugs. You smuggled in a *pizza* for Amatrano's birthday and no cunt batted an eyelid.'

Zsa Zsa – Christ – wouldn't he doing anything else? – Zsa Zsa smiled. As he said: 'Buns. Think. Bit of a difference between a peetz and an AK.'

'But I don't *want* an AK. I want summing simple. Concealable,' I said.

'It's still impossible,' said Zsa. 'Although I think I know your M.O.'

'I'm sure you do, mate. And I repeat: not for you. Not for you it ain't impossible. When I was on the outside, there were people that I could call.'

Zsa Zsa sniggled and giggered. 'Ask *them* then.'

'Too risky,' I replied, having expected this. 'Most of the people that *I* know, know him. Or know someone who knows him. It'll get back.'

'And you want to approach with stealth,' said Zsa Zsa. 'Appreciated.'

'That's right. As I have been, once or twice, over the years.'

Zsa Zsa held up his very white palms. 'None of my business,' he said.

'Well, technically it was…'

'I was never *there*, baby. But about this gun: why in here? Why not collect it when you get out and do what you have to do?'

Such a see-through solution was (to be blunt) no better than the successful application of tinkertoy psychology. I'd scarcely dare believe that Zsa Zsa would *suggest* this, given my prompts; by satisfying me, funnily enough he'd ended up disappointing me a little bit too. I'd thought him cleverer.

'Fuck. Good idea,' I said, a smile on my face. '*Thanks*, mateypoos.'

'Sure. It's still not exactly a pizza or a balloon of heroin, Gal,' said Zsa Zsa. 'There are… shall we say?… some considerable risks involved.'

Sombrely I nodded. 'I respect that,' I answered.

'Yes,' said my barterer, 'but how much, Mr Nash?'

'How much would you like to respect that?' I asked back.

Zsa Zsa shook his head and went silent. When eventually he spoke he said, 'I'm sorry. It's too risky.' And then he went pensive and speechless.

I waded into the resulting silence. I tipped my head. Truth to tell, I embarked upon – probably – the biggest gamble of our professional relationship. I decided – and you don't decide this with a figurehead like Zsa Zsa, not without a glut of pre-planning – I decided to *take the piss out of the cunt.* Nodding, 'Oh, I see,' I added, 'it's the parole you worried about. Well, knife me and tell me to get fucked if you're scared.' But I should explain. In addition to dealing out such wisdom as this – 'Can't drink champagne, mate. Can't drink it. Can't drink it. Makes me fart like a fucking panda. Fart like a warlord' – Zsa Zsa was content to reveal other matters about himself. Zsa Zsa was one of the rare ones: that fucker didn't much give a monkey's if he was inside or outside: it was all part of the grand plan. Work was work.

'…I ain't *scared*, Charlie.'

'Then what?'

Zsa Zsa was tempted, I could see. 'How much you offering?'

'Open the negotiations,' I told him.

Less than half an hour later, we managed to persuade Frank Gerkin, aka Hormones, aka Ronald McFucking Donald into the prison gymnasium.

It was time.

*

'You know the Romans. They had a punishment for cunts like you,' I said. 'They used *mice*. They fed the fuckers on a diet of detergent and bullshit. Waited till they died. Then they minced 'em up like filigree and fed 'em to the ones at had tripped the switch. At first they thought they'd got some rough flesh – a dodgy bit of meat. Then the poison comes through the cunt's *organs* and you've got yourself a passport into a world of strife. That's regal, boy.'

Ever the flid, and despite his indisputable disadvantages (the fact that he was currently hanging upside down from the wall bars, his knees bent over one of them and his arms grimly grasping a medicine ball), Hormones was curious. 'Why?' he asked. 'Why not just give the bloke the poison?'

'Because,' I answered, snottily sighing, 'that. Is not. *Creative*. It's like anything,' I continued, already knowing that in fact I was rehearsing a much later conversation – a discussion for the future. 'The best results come after the best prep. It's how it goes. You wanna play, you gotta pay. Put the time in, strokey. Think about it till your bonce is *satisfied*.'

'You're a dirty little wriggler, Franky,' said Zsa Zsa. 'What are you?' Zsa Zsa was bending at the waist, the better to look into Hormones' eyes.

'A dirty little wriggler.'

'That's right. And what do we do with dirty little wrigglers?'

Hormones coughed. 'We give 'em a blowjob?'

Zsa Zsa answered: 'We give 'em a tickle. Tickle him, Dave,' he instructed Saturday Dave. 'Tickle him in the fucking solar plexus. Until he's ready to talk Bitch. Until he sees which way up his bread's buttered, the dizzy twat.'

'Fuck you,' says McFucking.

Our other compadre, a Northerner called Russells, whom we also called The Thief of Badgag, whistled through his all-but nonexistent, Pogues-singer teeth. He said, 'Ee. Listen to the fockin turd on this un's tong. You'll kiss your mother wi' that fockin moath? Nor. Din think saw. So shot it, you cheeky *gundt*. Aright?' And he turned to Zsa Zsa. 'Shall I 'elp?'

Zsa Zsa nodded. 'As your heart sees fit,' he replied coolly.

V.

'Thing about a gun is, mate – you gotta know you've taken your vitamins.'

What had the years taken from me? What had it taken *for* me to get to this place, at this time? Dawn. At a location that had once seemed like home.

And what of Steve Bitch?

Looking oh so much older – looking, actually, like the actor that Bitch had once been, but with geriatric makeup on – it was all I could do not to think of him as the heir, not to a throne, but to a wheelchair somewhere.

Until he spoke.

The gaze hadn't changed, and the voice was still – it seemed – to be treated as as much of a threat as I ever had. He was still speaking:

'Because I tell you, Gal: if you point that cunt at me and you don't mean it, it's gonna go off in your fucking face. You hear me? In your *face,* mate. So the question is this. Are you prepared to step into the clock?'

'Don't jiggle me, Steve. The fuck are you on about?'

'A clock, Gal; you step into a clock. And you can ride the stream backwards or forwards. But you're gonna arrive at a destination, and you've gotta get ready for the blowback. You're gonna examine your thought processes and find a different shadow you didn't even know was there.'

Steve was into his seventies. And he was still a fucking hard man. Stoic, too: *oh* yes. Steve, as you might imagine, remained stoic. 'Well, Gal, If you're gonna shoot me, allow me the equivalent of a last cigarette. Shoot me *twice,*' he requested. We were on his turf: it was the lanes. Not even the sight of a pistol being pointed at the bridge of his *nose* could make him act any less cockily.

More worryingly, I suppose, I was not feeling as *strong* as I'd imagined that I would. A bad night's sleep – as predictable as it

was unfightable – had followed my emergence from a lengthy incarceration in Sugville West. The buddy programmes and support
groups had led me to believe that a bad night's sleep was but the
first of the expected consequences to follow a stint behind bars.
But this fact did not make me feel any better. In a fit of boredom
and fear, I burned the page of phone numbers that I had been
given to ring, if things ever got too bad. Then I had drunk the
remains of a small bottle of vodka, diluting it with orange squash
and water. Disgusting. This morning – only this morning, a mere
two hours earlier, at four a.m. – I had collected my purchase.

Taken the taxi. Shot a friend.

I laughed. 'I can imagine more times than that: I've got
refills next to me bollocks.' This was what I said.

'Imagine?' asked Steve.

'What?'

"I can imagine more times than that,' you said.'

'I said *manage*. I can *manage* more times than that, you
little squirmer.'

Steve sighed heavily and rolled his eyes. 'You said,' he said,
and clearly, deliberately, 'the word *imagine*. Cunt, you're losing it.
Losing it expansive. You nutter mean? It's like, how the fuck did
I ever trust you to keep your flaps together. You're all over the
fucking shop. You're a *joke*.'

The Killing Joke, I thought.

'Is this,' I asked sadly, 'what it all comes down to?' I paused.
'Trading insults. Gaining points. Touching tips. Is this it?'

'I agree. It's sad,' said Steve. It was the first time that we'd
agreed on a single point for a good, long time. 'So maybe I should
give you some change, eh? What do you think, Gal? I should move
things along? Allow me. Allow me. The obvious question is: 'Isn't
that rather uncomfortable?' Bullets next to your knackers?' He
leaned back and started to pick at a blackhead under his eye.

I was grateful for the re-railment.

'Yes,' I told the fucker. 'But not as uncomfortable as they're going to be for you.' Could it be that even despite the evidence he didn't believe me?

Steve laughed. 'Good old boy,' he praised me. 'You wanna drink?'

'I'm already drunk,' I confessed. 'Steve, it's six in the morning and I've just destroyed the face of someone that I used to work with...'

And yet his smile lingered. 'What better reason do you fucking need?'

'Fair comment,' I answered.

Steve nodded his head. 'Shall I lead, Gal?' he asked.

'I think you'd better...'

The lanes. Ah, the lanes hadn't changed all that much. An *institution,* mate: that's what they were. An institution; and they don't change, regardless of the forces that act upon them. Or so it seems... As I entered the lanes, I recognised a face from the past: his name was Bill. For a second my enjoyment was the greater of my trepidation. Despite the situation, I said:

'Hey Tax Bill!' as I approached.

Bill nodded respectfully, but that was all he did. 'Gary.'

He was standing outside the lanes at six in the morning. Bitch had loudmouths and grasses all over: they would have known, if they'd been paid to know, that I'd been released. Bill was expecting me. Bitch, too.

'I can't *believe* you're still here,' I said. 'How long has it been?' Stupid question, but I asked it.

'You're not coming in, Gary. Sorry,' said Bill.

I ignored that. 'Remember this? Your birthday, twelve years ago...' *Twelve years*, and the bastard was still guarding doors. For a second I even felt sorry for him. Then I thought: And what's so high-flying about *your* life, chump?

Where did *you* go on holiday this year? '*I met him on a Monday and my heart stood still...*' And I made a sort of palms-up flourish, grinning.

Sourpussily sour-faced, Bill deadpanned: '*Da Do Ron Ron Ron, Da Do Ron Ron...*'

'*And somebody told me that his name was...*'

'*Bill.* And that's all you're getting, Gary,' Bill said. 'I'm sorry.'

I made a sour face of my own. I'd identified at least part of my irritation. 'Is it just you, Bill? *Seriously?*' I asked. 'I been in the fucking hole for more than ten years – not that any a you cunts came to visit – and the best I can expect is one person to protect your beloved leader? Don't you think I might be *angry?*'

Had I managed to confuse our Cheerful Charlie?

'I heard you'd been in a loonybin,' said Bill.

'From who did you hear that?' I asked.

Bill shrugged. 'Tongues wag,' was all he would say in his vague fashion.

'Well I haven't, all right? It was Sugville West.'

'Okay.' Bill shrugged again. 'Maybe Steve's got in more troops upstairs.'

'I only count two cars in this car park.'

'Maybe they've chained their bikes by the dustbins.'

'Sure. Step aside, Bill. We go back. This is nothing to do with you.'

'I can't allow it, Gary.'

Nodding, I acknowledged his commitment and faith, such as these qualities could be valued in the blindness that was the collection of lies with which Bill had been educated as to my past history. Simultaneously I acknowledged that we have ways of making you walk...

The pistol was in the right pocket of my leather coat. I pulled it out.

'Do you know what this is, Bill?' I asked, raising it up.

'Yes I do, Gary. And do you know what'll happen if anyone finds out...'

'Cunt? My life's already over,' I said. 'It don't matter now.'

'Over?' As rare as the look was, Bill smirked: even now. A sign of madness, I thought at first; and then I realised that *everyone* knew more than I was currently privy to. But even Bill? 'You've only just begun, mate!'

'What are you talking about?' I asked.

And then a conversation that I'd had with Cliff returned to my head.

*

Always leave the house while you can still focus: that's my motto. That way it's unlikely (it's not impossible, but it's unlikely) that you'll leave a fag smouldering in the eiderdown. That you'll leave the iron burning a hole down to China. That you'll finally return to the bones and the turnips of a battlefield.

Leave sober. Leave *safe*.

Kids, this is my message. It is also a piece of advice that I ignored in preparation for my release from Sugville West. *Did* I. For four days straight I was cunted. I'll tell you how. I relied on Zsa Zsa to open any booty – or I should say bounty – and to cream off the top. Example: Dean Bolt's prepubescent missus sends in a bottle of scratchy red wine. Fine. It's his birthday, and he's a C-Cat. It's the anniversary of his first shampoo. Whatever the celebration. As a matter of course it is decorked – defrocked, devirginised – by whatever lowly shepherd of a twat is working in Admissions that day. *Routine*. Then it gets to Zsa Zsa, who has arranged the shebang (and offered, and probably provided, said Admissions guy a bribe: a favour, a loan of muscle, an Oxo eye-job). But *then* – Zsa Zsa also skims. And keeps it all stored in a vacuum flask. Wine. Red, white; a glass or two of veluvial rose. Then the beer: all together in the altogether. Wine, beer, spirits… hash. Though it cost me a lot, a lot of stuff that I'd have to do on the outside, I was cunted for four days.

I was happy. *This* was the life. Harshness I was spared. Everybody understood, or at the very least pretended to. Me? Me,

I was *getting out*. Nashy's getting out in four days. So excuse me while I talk to the brick-mites. Excuse me while I go a bit loco.

And then the day arrived.

How many days had I wasted in a succession of cells?

*

It was Christmas morning, and all through the house, no cunt was stirring, not even a mouse… Another Christmas. Another year – bye bye. Bye bye. My final Christmas in Sugville West, praise the Lord – God bless Him and shine Him… Just before noon I used the phone privileges that I'd been saving up and called Cliff. His little girl answered the blower. I identified myself. In lieu of saying hello or asking me how I was doing, or any of that old wank, she immediately said:

'And what are you having for dinner?' Her voice, much older – much.

'I don't know, darling. Some chickeny bollocks, probably,' I answered.

'Well, we're having a goose.'

'Is that right, darling? Your dad home, is he?'

'He's here,' she said very properly, 'but I should warn you. He's had a few. Me mum brought him Bucks in bed. And he's been on the vino since…'

'*Who is it?*' I heard.

'It's me,' I said, but much too early. I could hear the receiver being handed over. And then I said, 'Cliff chief. It's Bro.'

And what did I hear?

'Oh, it's you. Y'all right, Gal?'

'Well, many fucking Crimble to you an' all.'

Cliff cleared his throat. He said, 'Gary. I have the family here – everyone's here this year.' His voice dipped. 'It's Stress City, mate. Sorry.'

'Let's try again. Happy Christmas, Cliff,' I said.

'Merry Christmas, mate.'

'Thank you. I'll keep this brief. It's about Mitzi.'

'No, Gal – it's time to stop torturing yourself.'

'Did she ever go out with Ernie Gurney?' I asked.

Cliff's pause was all that I needed. However, he confirmed it in words – or in a single affirmative – a brief second later. And that was when I knew what Steve had planned, and what others had helped themselves in the planning of thereafter. 'So how much are we talking about, with Steve?' I asked.

'Gal. It's Christmas Fucking Day!'

'Don't take our Saviour's Day's name in vain, bruv. *How much?*'

Cliff sighed. 'I don't know exactly,' he said. 'But a lot.'

'Thank you, Cliff. And goodbye.'

'Wait! Gal,' said Cliff. 'Something you ought to know, mate.'

'And what's that?' I demanded. Was he *crying*?

'You were always his favourite, Gal,' said Cliff. 'Always.'

*

I left Sugville West on the first day of May. Quite frankly, I don't know how I got home. What would *your* expectations be, let me ask?

Allow me to speak the truth. For one thing, you don't get an armoured limousine with motorcycle outriders. You don't even get a fucking taxi.

What you get is some pocket money and whatever you've managed to save, over the years, in the prison's banking system. All those lessons, and all of those hours in a dripping kitchen, and all of that dope traded – it added up.

Added up. I emerged, a free man, on a pricklish, clear day. Not rich but not poor. Not happy but not sad. There were no extremes. I was numb.

The train services were having a Mr Magoo day and I ended up on a bus at close to midnight, there having been no service north for part of the journey. The good thing was, I sat next to a guy who managed a sex shop. And you wouldn't *believe* what these people earn - for two days a week work!

I made it home. And I had a nice kebab. While I was waiting for my food, two girls came in; they couldn't have been more than thirteen, wearing tiny skirts and bikini tops. One of them was visibly shivering and had chattering teeth. I was *that* close to asking them why they felt they didn't need a jacket at one in the morning in England! But I didn't. None of my business. And then they ordered the largest kebabs, which were surely physically impossible for any human beings to eat. These girls were tiny. But me, I needed my strength.

Be careful, Cliff had said to me once, way back when. We'd been heading towards the Chardonnay Pig when this had all kicked off: that ridiculous raid for the ridiculous prize to divvy up. *We don't want to offend him.*

Offend him? Are you...? I'd replied. *Listen, mate - I'll offend the cunt all right. I'll offend his fucking arse off. He's not worth a piss in a fucking ashtray.*

But I'd been wrong... oh so wrong. My anger should have been directed elsewhere: at Steve Bitch. And it would be, there was no doubt of that.

As I ate my kebab, I realised that the first strike that I'd been asked to make – back on the Chardonnay Pig, to get John Corbett's address in America – that was one of the things that I simply couldn't forgive. An innocent *man*...

I knew what it meant to be an innocent man, falsely criticised.

And understood the meaning of the word *calumny.*

VI.

Reading the first edition of the day, he was waiting by the bowling ball rack on lane five. A nugget of news had caught in his teeth, and he was chewing it as if it were a toffee. Though he didn't move an inch, I knew that he knew I'd arrived.

'Good morning, Steve,' I said. I was still holding the gun. Some of Bill's blood was on my fingers. The last thing I'd seen outside was the man's right eye imploding, and it would be an image that I'd take to the grave. 'Welcome back.'

'It's been a while, Steve,' I said as he laid down the newspaper.

He indicated the lane. 'Fancy a frame?' he asked. 'Old times' sake.'

'No thank you, Steve.' His voice sounded tired and scratched, like an old piece of vinyl beneath the needle. For no obvious reason I found myself thinking of the time that I'd spent in Mitzi's flat, trying *not* to listen to the Kinks. I could see her clammy wrist-blood on my hands... but it was Bill's blood, Bill's.

As far as I knew or cared, Mitzi was still alive. It wasn't important.

'Take a seat, Gal?' Steve asked.

'No thank you, Steve.'

He nodded his head, asking, 'Well. How do you want to do this then?'

'Answers first,' I replied. 'I know why you did what you did.'

He smirked. 'So what do you want answers for then?'

Not even ten sentences in and Steve was running rings around my lack of logical thinking. In part I was distracted by the fact that no other staff seemed to be in the building. Had he *wanted* to get me on his own, I wondered?

'What are you doing here so early anyway?' I wanted to know.

The question seemed to throw him off guard. 'Meeting you,' he replied, as though I'd just asked if this glass of milk was white.

'But you didn't know I'd be coming.'

To which Steve smiled. 'Oh Gary,' he replied, disparagingly. 'Have a word with yourself, eh? Plug the moss from your ears. You were *followed*. You've been monitored, mate – every step of the fucking way.'

'Oh Christ. It's the same word, Steve. *Why?*'

'Why what?'

'*It's too late for this, Steve!*' I shouted. '*Talk to me!*'

'Why did I have you put down?' Steve suggested.

'Yeah. Start with that one, although I've got my own theories.'

Steve sniffed. 'Why else, Gal? To toughen you up. To get you ready.'

This time I fought with my temper. 'To get me ready for what?'

A shrug. 'To take over, Gal,' he said. 'I'm dying, mate.'

*

Less than ten minutes later, we had repaired to Steve's office. Together we had pulled Bill's body into the building and left it for the time being in the Ladies. Steve had promised to look after things 'on that score'. Then Steve had offered me a coffee in more comfortable surroundings. Having declined the refreshments, he led me upstairs, as a lover will, but there was no erection pointing into the small of my tormentor's back. The only hard thing between Steve's back and my front was the pistol, held out as levelly as I could manage.

Apart from the lines on our faces, it was just like a scene from old times. Do you have *friends* like that? Friends you don't see for years on end, and when you finally hook up again, you re-light a conversation that might have been left *mid-sentence* a decade earlier. Well, the feelings, I'm sure, are the same as they are if the other person you have met is someone you've vowed to butcher.

It was certainly not the case that I trusted Steve – far from it: I had made him open all of his desk drawers, just in case – but at least I had managed to convince myself that we were indeed alone in the lanes. For now. I'd already made the assumption that staff would be arriving in an hour or two... and I still had a lot of ground left to cover. Starting with the start...

'So when we went to the Chardonnay Pig to get Corbett's address, that was all a waste of time, was it? That's one of the things I can't forgive, Steve.'

'Probably. But what else were you gonna do that day?' He was smirking.

I was not interested in joining him in seeing the funny side. I said, 'Jesus. Talk about missing the point! We got loud with those fuckers and they were completely innocent!'

'No they weren't,' said Steve, a tone of ribald protestation in his voice. 'They wouldn't give you what you wanted, and I know your work, Gal, I know your style: you wouldn't've got loud unless they opposed you. Which they did.'

'But what we were after was a useless commodity!' I shouted.

'But you didn't know that. And lower your voice. Anyway, it *weren't* useless. To you it was, maybe, but you got paid, didn't you? Listen. I needed you to *think* that address was what I needed. Okay? So what? You feel duped? You feel *betrayed*? Clever up, mate! *Grow* up! Use what's been plonked on your shoulders. It was a business decision, I made it, and it suited my purpose. End of.'

'No.' It wasn't the end of. It wasn't the end of *anything*. Struggling to keep my temper I said: 'I used to have it as something to be proud of, Steve, that I never hurt someone who hadn't hurt me, in one way or another. And now I can't say that.'

'Diddums. So I made you bust your cherry,' said Steve, remaining (as he always would) unrepentant. 'You've become a man. You've cut the apron strings.' His eyes were twinkling; they were mocking me. 'And what you give them boys anyway? A bloody nose? Horrors! Oh Gal, you *didn't*: you didn't actually… *break someone's finger*, did you? If you did, I think you'd better find me a priest to confess to!'

I struck him. I tightened my right fist, and struck him with all that I could manage: about fifty per cent of my strength. Guilt, fear and tension had eaten away the other half. The chair, nevertheless, rocked backwards: a less exaggerated version of what Steve's head did on his shoulders. I was stunned. Appalled by my own behaviour (and the predicted outcomes), I took two steps away from the seat of my crime, my left hand to my mouth.

Steve placed his own an inch higher. Blood was flowing from his right nostril; he examined the flow by eyeballing his fingertips. Then his delighted gaze me my own more terrified example. It was as if *I'd* sustained the injury. In a way, I suppose, I had: certainly with the benefit of hindsight I had.

'Mate, I'm sorry,' I began.

'You're beautiful, Gary,' Steve replied, oddly. 'Come closer.'

'Why?'

'Just come closer. You've drawn first blood. Now follow through; have the courage of your convictions, Gal. What's an old man like me gonna do? I'm seventy-two, mate.'

'Oh I know how old you are,' I said; but I closed the gap, regardless. 'Your arm. Give me your arm, Gary,' said Bitch.

Again I asked, 'Why?' – like a schoolboy at the board, being urged on by a ruthless mathematician to complete a calculation that is beyond his powers.

'Do you trust me, Gary?'

'No.'

'Good. You were always too bloody servile,' he told me. 'So whatever happens next is the result of a *lack* of trust, right? Which means you do it *knowing* that you're in the driving seat and not because I've asked you for a fucking favour.'

I was reminded of the Steve Bitch of old: the Bitch who thought fast and could out-weasel a fucking weasel. Strong Steve; Diamond Hard Steve. The Bitch that had left me was back, just like in the Elton John song... except he'd never really gone away. He'd merely wanted me to believe that he had.

Steve took hold of my left arm. Having picked up the gun again, I was standing to his right, prepared. With his right hand he held my wrist; his left supported the elbow.

What he did next bemused me rather than upset me. Lowering his head (I thought he was going to kiss my sleeve) he ran his nose along the length, like a pianist performing a high to low roll. He wiped his nose, smiled and looked up again; the blood, though still flowing, had been smeared across his lower face. He was a pirate; he was Redbeard.

'That's for not offering me a tissue,' he said, letting go. 'You've forgotten your manners, Gal.'

'Fine.' If a dry-cleaning bill was all that I had to be nervous about – well, I could deal with a trip to the launderette.

Steve was brightening up. 'What's next on the agenda?' he asked. 'What's the name of the game?'

'The name of the game is Cheryl. Cheryl Abbey,' I said.

'What about her?'

'She's not your daughter.'

'I know,' Steve replied.

'She's mine.'

Steve frowned. 'Well, you helped to bring her up so technically…'

'No, Steve,' I interrupted. 'I don't mean in the pastoral sense. I learned a new phrase while I was inside. Do you know what palliative care means?'

'Yes, Gal. My dad died of cancer, remember?' Steve voiced this question as if it was a weapon: by now, of course, we were indeed engaged in mortal combat, so perhaps the aggressive tone was correct. 'I heard it every time I visited.'

'What does it mean?' I asked.

Steve shrugged. What harm could a simple definition do now? 'Temporary relief.'

'That's right. *Strokes.*'

He laughed – and yes, I suppose I also saw the funny side: finally. What was I *doing* at the lanes? Brute force? This was turning into brute *farce.*

When he stood up quickly, the mood evaporated. I tensed. It was only a fifty-fifty chance that I didn't accidentally squeeze the trigger.

'Woe, Gal...' said Steve. 'Easy, tiger. I'm going to the filing cabinet.'

'Why?' Suspiciously.

'A wee nip, mate. Want one?' And he pulled open the top drawer. The cabinet was the same one that I'd known back in my heyday... back in the halcyon days of our friendship... Friendship? Had it ever been quite *that*?

The bottle of Scotch was brought out. I both did and didn't want a drink. I both did and didn't want *Steve* to have a drink. I had the notion that we both needed to be as clear as a diamond for this denouement. This decision had been made, however, even though I was of course nursing a hangover that resembled the Battle of Stalingrad. I suspected that Steve was, as well.

For the first time I noticed that there were already two glasses on the desk. There had been nothing seen or felt so far that would make me draw the conclusion that Steve had been lying about having had me watched. But I wanted to know just how deep the observations had gone. More than this: not only did I want to know what about me Steve had held to his chest; I wanted to plane at *this* cunt's subconscious. I wanted to teach *him* a fucking lesson.

As Steve poured two half-pints of Scotch for us – a half-six session! Jesus – I played a dummy card. I sniffed to indicate that I wanted his attention, and then I said: 'Steve. There was a bloke in there called Dominic Hurley. Can you think of one reason why that name might have pushed me into a panic?'

'Here you go.'

'Cheers.'

'Dominic Hurley, Steve.' Scotch in my left hand, a pistol in my right: try and tell me that it gets any more butch and carefree than that. So why was I shaking like I remember Grassy Noel shaking on his first day in the classroom?

Taking his time, Steve sat back down and shuffled his back into the leather – the old, worn leather of the old, worn chair. Like owner, like possession. He took a good swig on the tan. Leaned forward. Gagged. And I felt that peculiar mixture of revulsion and delight that we experience when we are certain that someone else is about to be sick. But Steve wasn't sick. He composed himself and repeated the surname.

'Hurley,' he said.

'Yes, mate. The *surname* was what sprung to mind, at the time.'

'*Hurley*? I don't think I *know* anyone called Hurley.'

'Think harder. Maybe he's in the back of your skull some-where...' What was I hoping to achieve? What I think I wanted was for Steve to snap his fingers and agree that he'd known the geezer... whereupon I could pounce. 'He has a sister called Sasha,' I said slowly, carefully, as though instructing a four year-old on how to take telephone messages. 'Whom I was *banging*, Steve, when I left you. And an older sister called Mags – or Margaret, presumably. Who was my staff team leader at The Shark.' I took my first tentative sip on my pre-breakfast whisky. Not even a long stretch could demolish my appreciation of the good stuff. I could still tell the good from the ropey. 'And you know something? I'm not much of a gambling man, as you know, Steve, but here's the poser: What are the cunting odds of meeting their *brother* while I'm on the porridge, eh?'

Fair do's to Steve, I thought. He went at his impersonation of a man confused with all of the high-spirited dedication of a prossie claiming a pube from her gums before the next trick ar-rives. If that's not too coarse a comparison. In fact, he even started to roll his tongue around his mouth – a more direct comparison. That was when the cool façade – it started to thaw.

Again, I swift to pounce. Steve's brow was getting heavy. 'What?' I said – 'is it all coming back to you now, is it? Talk.'

'No,' Steve stressed. And once more I was reminded of the scandal of Steve's getting older. It occurred to me that he was not scared because I might have turned over his rock; he was scared because he thought that he couldn't remember what I was talking about. His face – those lines – it all appeared hollow once again; it was all desiccating. Even at this moment, when it seemed that my small-time bluff appeared to be doing *something*, and when my lust for the kill should have been at its most pointed, its perkiest, I couldn't bare to see Bitch so reduced, so fallow... He kept vacillating between strength and weakness – bodily, mentally. Strength and weakness of the soul.

'I don't know anyone called Hurley,' he told me. 'You gotta believe me.'

'Believe you bollocks!' I muttered, chasing the rules of a game that I didn't have a grasp at understanding. 'Steve? You wouldn't know the truth if it was fingering your ring. You sad. Old. Geezer.'

'That's right!' Steve sat up suddenly. Some of the Scotch that he had yet to demolish slopped over the gunwales of his glass. 'Other fucking men of my age are allowed to go bowling – on a *green*, Gal – and moan, and fart without an apology. And what do I get? Imprisonment! In me own place of work!'

I smiled. Call me perplexed, but it was good to glimpse of the Steve of yore. 'Not a bad line, Steve,' I said.

He looked down into his lap. 'Now look what you made me do,' he muttered, as though he'd wet himself. 'That bottle cost me eight hundred fucking sheets, and I'm spilling it all over myself like a tramp with his meths.'

Sarcastically, I added: 'Did you get it in especially for me?'

'I did, as it goes,' Steve answered, swiping at his lap with his free palm. Then he licked the hand. 'Waste not, want not. But malt and polyester don't go.'

My head was such a maelstrom. 'I missed you,' I found myself saying.

'Likewise, Gal. Been a long time.' And our eyes met across a crowded desk. He lifted his glass and took another drink.

I remembered how to be angry. 'As I was saying, Steve: not a *bad* line. But your intelligence lets you down. That line was too constructed,' I said, 'for a man who fancies dribbling his cereals and having his nappy changed by a fat nurse.' And I took a drink. Something rolled around in my stomach acids.

'Well, in fairness I never asked for *that*.'

'No you didn't,' I conceded.

'And besides, the fuck you know about constructing a sentence and what it means, Gal?'

'*What?*' Seeing red again, I'm afraid. 'The fuck do you I think I *did* for fifteen years, Steve? I read books, mate. I bettered myself.'

'Yeah? To what end?' Steve asked. 'So's you could give an old man a decent pasting? Stroll on.'

'You think I won't do it, don't you?' The sentence – no, the sentiment – no, both – amused me more than anything else had for a long, long time. I laughed like a swashbuckler. And I enjoyed the moment, making him wait; I enjoyed his expectation of the ragged return – mine. The *Look here, sunshine*; the call *To business*…

But his words took a second to beam their way through the mist. In a disgusted voice – as though I'd just found droppings in my *lasagne* – I said pointedly: 'What the hell did you call yourself?'

'Drink up, Gal. We got places to be…'

'We're not going anywhere, mate. *What did you say?*'

Which was the point at which Steve grinned his widest.

VII.

When I was forty – happy birthday! – in the nick, Dean Bolt said something that I'll always remember. Chronically unreliable though his intestines undoubtedly were (his guffs were room-clearers, which is no fucking joke when you share a room with the cunt), Dean had got to the point where he felt that he could at least control his bowel movements to seven or eight a day. Then one day, on my birthday, he said: 'By my age, Nashers, a man ought to be able to rely on his innards.' Shamefacedly, he had shat himself during exercise a few hours earlier...

Comment came back to me now. By *my* age, I noted with a twist (I had entered my fifties), a man ought to be able to rely on his *memory*. Such a certainty had now had gloss paint slung all over it, and a conversation now rewound and played in my head.

Gal: He's senile.

Gal2: No, *you* are.

Gal: He's forgotten everything.

Gal2: No, you have...

The light was bad, suddenly. Perhaps it was the accumulation of fear and booze; perhaps it was my *imagination* that was creating these dark splotches and asterixes. I had an image – I *received* an image, delayed by fifteen years or so by the Royal Mail – of a staff team meeting. There was Bitch: Big Daddy at the head of the table, all but carving the turkey. Foot Soldier Gary is to his right as you look at the picture from the far end of the table. Cliff is opposite me.

It was a *business* meeting: an ordinary team meeting. But Steve was looking at Gal and Cliff with a light-on-glass gleam in his eyes...

Physically impossible as it was for me to have been holding that pistol any tighter, I stood up and leaned slightly over the desk. I was dangerously close, I realised, to Steve Bitch's face. With only a lazy swipe, he could have knocked the weapon away for a fraction of a second. But Steve appeared comfortable in that same leather chair: staring into the deep black eye.

'Say it, Bitch,' I demanded.

Steve made a face, as if he'd noticed a parking ticket on his windscreen on returning to his vehicle: minor irritation. 'Oh put it *down*, Gal,' he said, and drained the remainder of his glass.

'*Say it.*'

'Please. Don't make me think that I've made the wrong choice, Gal,' he replied. 'Don't tell me you hadn't even *considered* it. Christ. What other reasons did you think there were for all the privileges you've received?'

I was all but apoplectic. '*Privileges*? Fucking *hell*, Steve. What privileges? What have I possibly got to be thankful for you for?'

Glass in one hand and nothing in the other, Steve raised his arms.

'My empire, Gal. Which stretches a lot further than you think.'

'I see. You're giving me the lanes, no strings attached...'

He nodded. 'The lanes, the pubs... the webs I own – webs of favours.'

A very sick feeling was trafficking its way through my lower body. My gut was contracting like an accordion. It couldn't be, could it?

'What pubs?' I asked.

'Oh it's all grown, Gal,' said Steve, 'since you went on your sabbatical. There are a lot of names that you wouldn't even know...'

Despite the fact that my knees were trembling, I was still standing. Have you ever drunk tea that has been made rancid with woebegotten milk? No? Well, it gives you a kick in the rectum like shock does. *Revelatory* shock. But right at that moment, I would have taken the bad tea any day.

'What pubs did you own at the time?' I asked slowly.

He could see where I was going, of course; Steve knew precisely what I wanted. 'Oodles. Including the Pig...'

'The Chardonnay Pig?'

'Yip.'

'And The Shark?'

'Yip,' Steve repeated, reaching for the bottle of Scotch.

'You cunt,' was all that I could find to say.

'Now *there's* respect,' he mumbled offhandedly.

'I should kill you right now. Fifteen fucking *years*, Steve. And you think that I'm gonna come out and whisper sweet nothings for the chance of my life.'

'No. I expected you to do *exactly* what you're doing now?' Steve answered, now pouring. 'Top up?'

I had hardly touched my drink, but Steve's offer made me re-notice the glass that was in my left hand. I lifted it to my lips. I needed it.

Easy on that stuff, my brain warned me. But I wasn't listening. All I could hear were bites of the overall meal that Steve had already fed me... *Toughen you up... your old man...* But there were still more questions than solutions.

'No thank you,' I responded to the invitation for more. Manners maketh the man, as Steve had used to say, at meetings early and late. Had those meetings really been Bitch's equivalent of family breakfasts? He had always celebrated national holidays with the staff...

The shakes got too bad. I had to sit down. It was only at this point that I worked out that *anybody* could have entered the lanes downstairs; and that *anybody* could be strolling around, or be waiting for me outside.

Tears were forming in my eyes. 'Cliff as well?' I asked quietly.

'Of course. He'll be here soon.'

'He knows?'

'Oh yes,' said Steve. 'He took it a lot worse than you did, by the way. Which makes me think that I've made the right decision.'

'Well, you could say that I've got bigger fish to fry, Steve.'

'I suppose so,' Steve said. 'Like what?' he asked dumbly.

I took some comfort from the following sentence and its inversion of the usual power-ratio. 'You don't need to know,' I said.

'For now,' Steve admitted. 'Did you know,' he continued, apropos of nothing. 'I'm now officially regarded as a medical anomaly?'

I couldn't help but bite. 'You're talking cancer,' I told him.

'I'm talking cancer. You got the two kinds,' and immediately the fucker digressed. 'You know what they said when my old boy took the cane? The plums? They said: 'There's not an organ in his body that's not affected.' Fuck *that* for a bedside manner, the ole grumpy cunt. Might as well a said: 'Mate? He be fucked lengthways.' What was *that* trying to achieve?'

'Trying to keep you in the frame,' I said, unsure as to why I'd want to pacify Bitch at this late stage.

'Maybe,' he allowed. 'Still came across as cold as a lizard's cunt.'
'But anyway...'

He sipped. He reached for the box of cigars. 'A la-di-dah for you, Gal?'

'No thanks. Carry on, if you'd be so kind.'

Steve nodded. 'I have to say,' he said, 'I thought that fifteen was a bit on the plump side. Thought you'd make it out in ten. And I was getting worried, Gal. My doctors say it's because I'm so *resilient* that I've hung on this long. As I say, I'm an exception to the rule. *Every* cunt thought I'd be dead by now. But you know what I think I was doing? I think I was waiting for you. I do.'

'That's very sweet of you, Steve,' I deadpanned.

'Less of it. I did my best, mind, to get you released early; but there's only so far that my influence stretches: even an old boy like me.' And he laughed. The noises he made as he tried to get the cigar going were motorboat sounds: *putt-putt-putt...* Eventually, a whale-blow of smoke shivered across the ceiling.

Not amused but crazily incredulous, I said, 'You're not telling me that you have feelers inside Sugville West, are you?'

He sniffed. I also sniffed: the cigar smoke smelt good. 'Nah, not much,' Steve replied. 'A few odds and sods. Noel was mine, for instance.'

'Yours?' I said, appalled.

'The private lessons,' Steve clarified, and then added into my stunned silence: 'Well, who do you think was paying the cunt for the extra work? Don't disappoint me now, Gal: start the dot-to-dot. Join up the *nightmares.*' He smiled. 'You're fond of that fucking word, intcha? Nothing wrong with that, of course.'

I waited for it all to catch up. 'You've read my *book*?

'Selected highlights,' Steve answered coldly. 'Noel read it for me. Gave it to me in précis. You're not bad, mate. Come a long way.'

What I really didn't appreciate was literary criticism from a Neanderthal like Steve Bitch. What would he know about a narrative, after all? Even his dirty jokes had needed recaps, rethinks and radical character swapping at the last minute: *oh yeah, I forgot – the vicar was blind.*

'Your education, I mean. What would a cunt like me know about style?'

'Well, quite.'

'*Well, quite.* Listen to him. The only fucker who goes into nick and comes out at a *higher* social class.' Steve laughed. The whiskey was waving in his glass; I thought that it was going to rise over the barriers again. For the umpteenth time I was ready – fully prepared – to shoot him. 'Defying expectations: that's my boy,' Steve brayed through his drunkenness.

That was when somebody knocked at the door.

VIII.

'Tell me honestly, Steve, if that's possible,' I would say slightly later. 'Was this all connected with Cheryl Abbey? Was it all her fault?'

The scene was the duck pond, near the lanes. The sky was white. There was rain in the air on this early May day: what else?

Drizzle has been my companion, as it has the citizens of the British people, for time immemorial. In its way – for its sublime suitability – it was perfect; it made me smile.

Present were Steve, and Cliff, and me. It had been Cliff at the door. And now we were outside, pretending that we weren't getting cold.

'Oh yeah? Fill me in, genius,' Steve had said, back in the office. I had just repeated my assurance that I knew one more thing than he did. He'd made the challenge in a friendly way: he'd been well drunk, naturally speaking.

'Steve. You want the best for Cheryl, don't you? It's understandable,' I had answered. 'What better way of ensuring that she's protected by the code than setting her up as a victim from day one.'

We had all been sitting down. Of all things, we had all been eating *cake*: the cake that Cliff had brought to the proceedings. Not a joke: the cake that Cliff had proffered – it had had an iron file in it, just like in the comics of old.

'You won, Gal,' Cliff had told me. 'Love you, bruv.'

Minutes later, among the laughter and the brouhaha, Steve had replied to my final accusation. 'Oh Gal,' he had seemed to lament. 'What was it with you? Always so fucking *literalminded*. Throw some timber on the blaze, for fuck's sake, mate; spark it up a bit. *Of course* Cheryl's not my daughter. Did you drink a pint of paraffin before I told you that? Before I offered you my whiskey? My *best* whiskey, I might add. Okay? Cheryl's not my daughter. *Mitzi's* my daughter...' And he had dipped his nose to his plate of cake, defiantly.

Me and Cliff, and Mitzi: the ones that he hadn't declared to his longsuffering wife, Julie. Julie had died six years earlier: I hadn't known about that. Steve had given bribes to Grassy Noel to give to Dean Bolt, among others, not to fuck with my manuscript: I hadn't known that either. But what

bothered me most was: Me and Cliff, and *Mitzi*: the illegiti-
mate, the unwanted...

Yes. It was hot on my head that I had, in the old-fashioned
phrase, shared relations with Mitz. Never had the term rung more
true. I felt sick. There would always be those thoughts to think of,
to consider; to abhor.

'Where's Mitzi?' I asked, at the duck pond, a little later.

'Northumberland. Where else? She lives with her sister,
Wendy?'

I turned to face Cliff. 'So what was it with you and her?'
I asked.

'There *was* no me and her, Gal,' Cliff said, surely. He knew
my secret: the one that had graduated into a guilty one. 'It was all
bullshit and wank. Designed to keep you angry, Gal.'

'Mitzi,' said Steve, unexpectedly, 'is a cunting gold-digger.
I'll love her forever, but let's face facts. Tickety-boo? And nuts. Not
to forget fucking *loony*. No. Mitzi even says *of herself* that she's fucky
bad news. Too right! For all aranda. But sons, she's me daughter,
too. Okay, boys? I want you to treat her with the respect that she
don't deserve...' How much was he ignoring? How much did he
know but was refusing to acknowledge? I honestly couldn't...

'Remember,' said Steve. 'This was a woman who even fucked
Ernie Gurney because she knew that he held all me financial. What
sort of Braveheart is that?' he continued, his feverish disgust all
too evident. What *wouldn't* she do to get her hands on my sixpence, that's what I'd like to know...'

'Start walking, Steve,' I said with perfect diction.

'Is it time?' Steve replied. The fear on his face could have
been decoded and read by a blind man in a hurricane.

'It's time. Start walking.'

'Where, Gal?' was the answer. What he didn't mean was
where, geographically, the damage would be done: Steve was taking short, careful – was taking old-man steps into the duck pond.

The water was making an advance for his shins. Not the expensive footwear: the shins. Steve had meant where would the bullet go?

'Car's ready?' I asked Cliff.

His face had grown heavier, meatier; Cliff's face resembled a dead cow's hindquarters. 'We're ready, Gal,' he told me, but I doubted his conviction.

Too late. Steve had directed it all, from afar. Even Cliff's assertion that he and Mitzi had been an item: all crap. Designed to keep, as it were, my pecker up. Could I trust him to keep my secrets? How many people had read the diary that I would now, before every other priority, need to destroy in a lake of fire?

Steve was waist deep in the water. 'Enough?' he asked.

'A bit further,' I said, thereby answering his question of bullet destination.

Although the tides on the pond were non-existent, it was clearly treacherous underfoot. Steve slipped like a disco dancer. Parenthetically, I suppose, I wondered if the old cunt could swim.

I raised the pistol. The years that I had wasted rained down upon me with sudden storms. To have been such a *pawn*: it was tragic. Unforgivable. Nothing else made much of a lick of sense. It was the time that I'd wasted that burned.

He had done it for the kids that were not his by marriage. And I understood that. I could *dig* that (man). But it didn't make me feel any better. Many facts would need sorting out, of course, but Steve had told me that Ernie, his financial assistance for nearly three decades, would know the truths. Ernie Gurney had drawn up contracts. Disallowed from benefiting directly from a client's demise, Gurney had nevertheless drawn up *sub*-contracts that would see that before I earned a penny of the estate, his own bread would be well buttered... This was why nobody ever left Steve. Greed. Future plans.

And this was why I'd earned the whole caboodle. Because, in Steve's eyes, I had shown the potential for one who could exist without him.

My promotion had been as the result of this decision. God love him. God bless Steve Bitch, Steve Birch... or the other word. I aimed at his chin. 'Goodbye, Dad,' Cliff said, turning his attention from Steve to me.

But I couldn't say it. I simply couldn't.

'Don't smile,' I said with a smile. And then I did it.

Ducks burdened the morning sky. Smoke rose: *foul-smelling* smoke. The noise rattled in an echo against the wall of the swimming baths. Vomit coursed. My eyesight quivered and then focused, unbelievably sharp. The world revolved. There were sprays of blood in the air, on the frogspawn...

Sensing the end – the snapping end – of a payroll string, Cliff said, 'Shall we go?' The loss, it seemed, meant very little whatsoever: as well as Steve had, Cliff had been waiting too. And the truth was that common sense and logic suggested that from hereon in, he would be so much more of a friend than he'd displayed throughout my formative years – my wilderness years. My decades of well-concealed triumph. He would always know his place in the hierarchy.

'No, Cliff,' I replied, turning to my brother with my right hand raised. 'No.'

Acknowledgements

An earlier version of 'Residua' appeared in *The Horror Anthology of Horror Anthologies*, edited by D.F. Lewis (2011). An earlier version of 'Mia and Zoe' appeared in *Pantechnicon* Issue 8 (2008). The remaining six stories are original to this collection.

Interview with *Sick Dice* Author David Mathew by Charlie Franco

Your time working in a Juvenile Hall facility appears to influence much of your writings. Why do you think it is important to tell stories from those places? Do you think the fact that your protagonists are often innocent of the crimes that they are incarcerated for makes their stories more acceptable?

It's certainly true to say that my time working in a maximum security Young Offenders Institute has left a mark on me, psychologically speaking. It was, by some distance, the most inspiring place that I have ever worked in. It was also the most terrifying – and curiously enough, the most *boring*. You might wonder how one place can be both terrifying and boring, but a YOI can! And I think about that place often. There are two stories in *Sick Dice* that owe a bit of a debt to my time there – 'Residua' and 'Strokes' – and although I haven't written about *juvenile* detention in this book, I did in my previous novel with you, *O My Days*. That particular novel was a direct result of my time at Aylesbury YOI; some days it was just like taking down notes. I had a notebook and I would write down some of the things the offenders said and then weave this slang into the novel, enriching it as I went along.

But to answer your question, the reason that I love telling prison tales is partly the obvious one – that these prisoners are trapped together and yet (paradoxically) can hardly get to one another. So, if there's something you need to say to someone on another Wing – or residential block – it might take a fortnight to be able to say, when you're both attending the same Gym session, for example. This alone sets up an internal tension. And this tension lends itself very well to fiction – and to non-fiction too, for that matter. My latest non-fiction book (*The Care Factory*) has a section on incarceration as well, though in that case my offenders are even younger than the ones I actually worked with. In other words, that book has a chapter specifically on children's prisons, exploring the topic with psychoanalytic frameworks.

Why do I think it important to tell stories from prisons? Well, first and foremost, if it wasn't fun to do so, I wouldn't do it. I love writing prison stories; that's at least *one* of the most important things. Your observation that some of my characters are innocent is interesting, though not quite the whole story. Certainly, here in 'Residua', the story even begins with a mob shouting 'Bilty's not guilty!' – Bilty being the protagonist's surname – but he is guilty of other things entirely. In *O My Days* the main character has been imprisoned, but not for the crime he actually *did* commit. So, when we think of innocence and these characters in the same breath, it's a warped kind of innocence; a parody of innocence; or an *ironicisation* of innocence (if I put my academic hat on for a moment).

There is often an undertone of same-sex sexuality in your stories, sometimes more explicitly, sometimes less so, which hovers over the violence perpetrated within. Where does this proximity of same-sex sexuality and violence come from?

There *is* an element of that in *Sick Dice,* isn't there? I hadn't thought of that; it certainly wasn't consciously planned in that way. Definitely in 'Mia and Zoe', the two main characters are women who live together, and one of them has an affair with another woman. That's not exactly what the story is *about*, of course, but I needed a lever to wrench them apart, emotionally speaking, to make the other stuff that happens to both of them more painful and real. The male relationships in 'Residua' are extremely abusive; and in 'Strokes' there's even a character with a horribly comic name who organizes who is going to get attacked in the communal showers, and whose turn it is to have sex. It's extremely sick – and there's a character like Zsa Zsa in many prisons, though of course I take his ability to control his surroundings to satirical heights.

That said, there are male-female relationships too in *Sick Dice*. The important thing about the relationships, and the rare bit of sexual activity that I actually describe, is that it must be about a system of control. Throughout my work, with very very rare exceptions, any sexual content – or even sexual allusion – is a metaphor and means for systems of control. I rarely write about loving relationships and healthy, loving physical activity. Plenty of other writers do that, and good luck to them. It just doesn't interest me to write titillating sex scenes; I much prefer to write something that will be disturbing, disquieting or which will give rise to the notion that the participants may well be psychologically scarred, or at least scar-able.

I suppose the other thing I could add (and this is hardly a profound revelation) is that I write what isn't me and in a way that stretches me a bit. I happen to be heterosexual man in his early forties, so having characters who happen to be (for example) homosexual men in their twenties or eighties is a fun challenge from time to time.

While the violence in your stories often stems from deep passions within the characters, you, as the author, appear to take a deeply dispassionate position on violence, where it instead simply becomes a way that characters communicate with each other. Why do you do this as a writer?

Yes, that's it exactly. Sorry to repeat myself, but violence is another way of my showing systems of control. There are no equal partners in my fiction (and very few in my non-fiction either). I do like your analogy with a language. Just as one can learn a language, one can be more proficient in a language. To do this day, what astonishes some of us about the Nazi atrocities (for example) is not only the sheer numbers but the *creativity* of the cruelty. Imagine a system of control where *people were employed* to think of new and original ways to make other people feel pain. This interests me – not so much the physical descriptions of someone getting beaten up or murdered, but more the work of the psychic apparatus and the synapses that flare at the *thought* of someone getting beaten up or murdered. I was absolutely delighted with Don Webb's comments about *Sick Dice* sounding like William Burroughs in places. I love that! He had the same cynical view of violence as a multiplex system – rather than a binary – that I favour. Which is not to say our voices are similar, because they are not.

Most of your characters are untrustworthy, but your female characters appear to exhibit deep currents of treasonous intentions, why is this? How do you see gender impacting the nature of your characters?

To be honest, the women characters are no better or worse than the men characters in *Sick Dice*! They're all as bad as one another. I wouldn't trust a single character in this book to give me the right time if I asked him or her to! The prostitutes in 'Lapsus' are enterprising and (I hope) funny to listen to, at least in places, but trustworthy? No. They are working women with their eyes on the till. When one of them falls in love with one of her customers, that becomes a disastrous dynamic.

You appear to have a deep distrust, and even an animosity towards time in your stories. What is the problem with time, and why do you force it to slip in and out of the sprockets of even regularity?

Time is endlessly fascinating to me. My wife pointed out to me once that just about everything I wrote contained time being distorted in some way – and at least one body of water, whether it's a sea, a lake, or a duck pond (in 'Strokes') or a swimming pool (in 'Humiliation Days'), to name but a few. I can hardly defend myself from the charge, Your Honour! I love writing about time – and how it changes us. But also how we change time, as well. In another life I might have been a physicist working on time conundrums… assuming I am reborn with more 'smarts' than I currently possess!

Many of your characters spend a significant amount of time negotiating waking states with dream states. Why do they do this? What is your motivation as an author, in analyzing the difference between the two ways of experiencing life?

Most of my characters either live in their heads to the point where the inside takes on a life of its own outside and becomes 'real', or it is already an outside that filters into the character's head and lodges there. Either way, the important thing is movement away from something secure (not necessarily pleasant but something that does not move) and towards confusion. It's the confusion that creates the tension – or some of it. The characters must not know where they are or exhibit too much confidence. A pretty sure way of predicting a character's unpleasant downfall is if he or she is cocky about being able to control the environment in which he or she has found himself or herself. My liminal states don't work that way! My characters come to realize that sometimes they are simply embarrassments or burdens to their destination. My dream worlds are not always welcoming places, to say the least. One of my favourite scenes in *Ventriloquists* is when the tour party is in the dream world, and they are trudging for days; and when they finally reach a village, there's a big crowd gathered around a sports event. When they get close enough to see, the event is a sort of netball game – but the 'ball' is the head of someone they knew who had reached the village first. Well, talk about a friendly welcome!

It appeared to me that Gal and Gal's tutor, Noel Winnett, best represent the two sides of you. Would you agree?

Well, I was certainly a teacher in a prison, so 'Grassy' Noel Winnett has something of a resemblance to my own personal character. The reason I took on the job in the prison was that I honestly believed I might be able to do some good. It did not take me long to realize that I could not do anybody any good, and that my very presence was at best a tolerated inconvenience to many of the offenders, and at worst it was something to rebel against. Noel is in something of this kind of predicament. He wants to do something worthy – as does the Sociology teacher, Clive, in 'Residua', it occurs to me now – but to say the odds are stacked against them would be one way of putting the matter!

I don't know if Gal is me or I'm Gal; but we certainly share a sense of injustice – a lot of Kafka-esque injustices occur in my stories. Things happen to people that they haven't asked for; things they don't want – unpleasant things (usually) that they cannot even learn from, let alone recover from. I don't have Gal's reliance on physical violence as a way of sorting out problems.

Mental health issues surface throughout your stories. What are your thoughts on how mental health is being addressed in your community, and how do your stories reflect those initiatives?

I don't think anything I write is a factual representation of anything political in my immediate environment, or even in the U.K. …Sorry – but I'm not that kind of writer. I do believe that we – as a global community – understand mental health issues better than we ever did, but there remains a long way to go before we understand anything completely.

David Mathew is the author *O My Days* and *Ventriloquists* (Montag Press) and two other novels and two volumes of short stories. A novel, *The Parry and the Lunge,* will be published by Montag in due course. His academic writing has been published as *Fragile Learning* and *The Care Factory* and he has also published two novels and a volume of author interviews under the name of Tom Lockington. A keen traveller and researcher, David Mathew is also active in education and psychoanalysis.

www.ingramcontent.com/pod-product-compliance
Lightning Source LLC
Chambersburg PA
CBHW022243020726
47496CB00004B/1041